PENGUIN BOOKS

SIMEON'S BRIDE

Alison Taylor was born into an Anglo-Welsh family, and brought up in rural Cheshire and Derbyshire. After reading for a degree in architecture, she turned to a career in social work and probation, in which she holds MA qualifications. She has been instrumental in exposing the abuse of children in care, and has written a number of papers on child care and ethics. She remains active in children's rights issues.

Alison Taylor is married with two children, and has been resident in north Wales for many years. Her interests include seventeenth- and eighteenth-century music, literature of the Enlightenment, art and the history of architecture, and riding. She has recently completed a second novel and is researching a biographical study of Beethoven.

To my husband Geoffrey and
my children Aaron and Rachel

This novel is a work of fiction.
Names, characters, places and
incidents are the product of
the author's imagination and
any resemblance to actual
events or persons, living or
dead, is unintended.

'Less of the old woman from you!' Mary Ann snarled. 'Whore's dog!' She spat at him, and slammed the door in his face, leaving him marooned on her polished doorstep. He deliberately scuffed his dirty boots on the purply slate, scarring the sheen with filth, before trailing off down the lane, away from the church, towards the main road. He looked behind again, then sat on the garden wall of somebody's house, making a roll-up, cogitating on his plight, and the fear scouring like poison through his bowels.

Sunshine cut the tattered rags of storm cloud, warming his face, making the sweat rise. He lit his cigarette, pungent smoke curling in the air with the stink of his body, remembering what he had seen in those dark woods. The memory stirred him from the wall, gave his feet a life of their own, to pace the square of weedy grass at the roadside, and to kick their owner for his stupidity. He could have rid himself of his job, thrown the pittance of a wage back in the arrogant face of the castle gentry, abandoned the rancid hovel in which he lived, and the poverty suffocating his smallest dream, trampling it into the dirt before it even took shape. And best of all, he could be rid of his wife, the one ugly enough to frighten the Devil from his den.

He sat again on sun-warmed stone, smelling the scents of late-blooming roses in the garden behind him, watching leaves flutter down from the trees to lie in drifts of gold and copper-brown against walls and tree boles, and looked at the manicured acreage lavished with flowering shrubs and succulent roses in pinks and yellows and ivory white. He stared at the cottage within the garden and felt envy enough to break the stoutest heart, recalling the other cottage, its reek of wealth, the rich fat furniture, deeper and more tempting than the breasts and thighs of any wench. He sighed, shaking his head to nudge the memories out of the darkness where he thrust them long months before. It was not too late even now. John Jones ground his jaw, stumps of teeth crunching together, and called himself worse than a fool. He spat on the ground, a phlegmy globule which lay glistening in the sunshine before sliding off the edge of a dead leaf. In his mind's eye, he saw the man staring at him from the night-dark trees, eyes glittering like black coals, face white as death. He shivered violently, thinking the man might have set a trap in the deepest woods, a gin-trap big enough to snare him, strong enough to hold him until his death throes ceased.

Jumping to his feet, he loped back to the village, sticking up two fingers as he passed Mary Ann's cottage, and on to the path to his own place, head high, fear quenched by resolve and the prospect of a brighter dawn to come. Time for the other one to have some shocks, he said to himself. A taste of their own bitter medicine might sicken enough to stop the flaunting and the sneering, the swaggering in that fancy car. He licked his lips, tasting revenge. Folk said money stank, and it was time the stench in John Jones's house and about his person took on another flavour. He started whistling, a shrill rendering of 'Bread of Heaven', his ugly wife's favourite hymn, and scuffed his way back down the path beside the graveyard.

Spring: Chapter 1

Tall and dark and, in the eyes of most of the women and not a few of the men who saw him about his daily business, more than a little handsome, Dewi Prys, twenty-seven years old come June, when he would have been a policeman for exactly eight years, a detective for almost three, and reared on the big council estate just outside Bangor city, hastily folded up the *Daily Post* and pushed it under a sheaf of files when he heard Jack Tuttle walking up the stairs from the cell block. Dewi had little time for the inspector. Born and bred in gentler territory near the English border, Jack knew nothing of hardship and isolation, of melancholia scavenging a man's soul through long days and nights when rain and wind stalked the mountains, beating against doors and rattling draughty windows, threatening invasion like marauding English, or when God wrapped village and chapel and earth and trees in a pall of mountain mist as stifling as all the guilt in Christendom.

Dewi looked up. 'What did our young friend in the cells want, sir?' he asked. 'Did he confess? Did he say "Yes sir, it was me nicked the video from Dixon's in Caernarfon and took it back a week later to Dixon's in Bangor for a refund?" I'll bet he didn't, did he?'

Jack sat down. 'He wanted to speak to the chief inspector. So he could speak Welsh.'

'Mr McKenna's not on duty 'til Monday, is he?' Dewi said. 'Wouldn't he tell you, then?'

'Well,' Jack said, 'in among a lot of garbage about how it was his right to be able to speak in his own language – the language of the hearth, as he calls it – your mate Ianto told me Jamie Thief has two lady-friends and a fancy car.'

'Very into nationalism, is Ianto,' Dewi said. 'Been known to do his fair share of rabble-rousing with the Welsh Language lot.' He leaned back, and crossed his legs. 'He's not really a mate of mine, sir. I just happen to know him because he lives on the estate; so I can't help it if I hear he's bragging about spraying paint on walls by the new road, can I? Ianto reckons it was him wrote that rude message about the Queen just before she opened Conwy Tunnel.'

'Did you hear me, Prys?' Jack snapped. 'He said Jamie has a new car. What d'you know about it?'

'Nothing,' Dewi said. 'You actually said, sir, that Ianto said Jamie has a fancy car. Or, maybe, a lady-friend with a fancy car.' He paused. 'Or even, two ladyfriends.'

'Well?' Jack snapped; Dewi thought, like an evil-tempered little dog.

'Well, Jamie's never had a problem pulling the women,' Dewi observed.

'What's that got to do with it?'

'Nothing, most probably. He's making hay. He'll be inside again before long.'

'Why? What for?'

'Don't know yet, do we? But Jamie's always done *something*. It's just a matter of waiting to find out what, then dropping on him.'

Jack tapped a pencil tip on the desk. 'I suppose I should've asked your mate for a few details.'

'Wouldn't be much point to that. He'd only tell you a tale . . . in any language. He's probably hoping to set us on Jamie to pay him back for something. Anyway,' Dewi continued, 'Jamie hasn't got a car. I'd know, wouldn't I, seeing how he only lives a few doors from my nain. Somebody wants to see us, by the way. The duty officer called through.'

'Who?'

'John Beti.'

'Who's he?'

'John Jones. Beti Gloff's husband.'

'And who, Prys, is Beti Gloff?'

'Lame Beti, sir. From Salem village,' Dewi said. 'Beti Gloff.'

'Why's she called Beti Gloff and not Beti Jones?'

'She is called Beti Jones, sir.' Dewi sighed. 'Gloff means lame in Welsh.'

'Oh,' Jack said. 'So what does her husband want with us?'

'Don't know, do I? Nobody said.'

'We'd better find out, then, hadn't we? Bring him into my office.'

'Yes, sir.'

'Prys?' Jack stopped by the door. 'What do we know about this John Jones? Does he have a record? Always as well to know your villains, isn't it?'

'I wouldn't call John Beti a villain. Don't reckon he's got the belly for it. He's been done for this and that over the years, mostly thieving . . . we thought he pinched some detonators from Dorabella Quarry a while back, but it wasn't him.'

'Who was it, then?' Jack asked. 'One of the terrorist lot? What's the expression, Prys? The joke about fire-bombing Welsh properties so the English can't buy them?'

Dewi sighed again. 'Something along the lines of "Come home to a nice warm fire in a Welsh cottage", sir,' he said. 'A local farmer nicked the detonators to blow up a tree-stump in the middle of his best arable field.'

'That's bloody typical, isn't it?' Jack said. 'Why on earth didn't he just go out and buy some?'

John Jones sat in the chair beside Jack's desk, making a roll-up. In between spreading shreds of tobacco on grubby paper, licking the edge of the paper with flicks of a thin and pointed tongue, he smirked at Dewi. Dropping a match into the wastebin, after dousing its flame with a calloused thumb, he said, 'Put you in long pants now, have they, Dewi Prys?'

'Why did you want to see us, Mr Jones?' Jack asked.

'Got something for you, haven't I?'

'Have you?' Jack said.

'Yes.' He smirked again. 'Doing your job for you, I am.'

'Are you?' Dewi intervened. 'How's that, then?'

'Found you a body, didn't I?' John Jones looked from Jack to Dewi, looking for a pat on the back, Dewi thought, and thought he would rather send him back to his hovel with a flea in his ear to keep company with those infesting his bed.

'Where is it, then, John Beti?' Dewi asked. 'Where's this body you've so kindly found for us?'

John Jones turned to Jack. 'You should do something with him,' he said, flicking a thumb towards Dewi. 'Got a gob on him like a parish oven.'

Jack fidgeted. 'Where's the body?'

'In the woods, isn't it?'

'We don't know, do we?' Dewi said. 'We're trying to find out. Which woods is it supposed to be in?'

'What d'you mean? "Supposed to be"?' John Jones screeched. 'It's not *supposed* to be anywhere! It's in Castle Woods. I've seen it there, haven't I?'

'If you say so,' Dewi said.

'Who is it?' Jack demanded.

'Who is it?' John Jones repeated, raising meagre eyebrows. 'How the fuck should I know? It's all bones and rags.'

Dewi and John Beti in the car with him, Jack turned off the expressway on to the narrow old road by Salem village, crossed Telford's graceful bridge spanning the river, and stopped outside high blue gates guarding one of the private entrances to Snidey Castle Estate. Glimpsing John Jones's thin face as he suddenly shifted on the seat, Jack thought the man like a fairy-tale character: wizened and strange and not quite real.

'I see the crime-scene lot beat us to it,' he said, pointing towards the white van parked over the road. He turned to John Jones. 'How far into the woods were you when you saw the body?'

'Dunno. Maybe a mile from here. Maybe a bit more. I wasn't taking much notice, just wandering round.'

'Doing what?' Dewi asked. 'Poaching?'

'Minding my own fucking business, Dewi Prys! You should try it sometime.'

Dewi unbuckled his seat belt. '*You* should try minding your mouth!' He climbed out of the car, and looked back up the road. As night drew near, cloud again massed behind the mountains, in the wake of a gale still not spent. Broken twigs littered the verges, drops of rain spattered here and there. The wind, turned during the night, carried a harsh chill from the north-west, and in the distance, drifts of snow left over from earlier storms lay deep and treacherous in mountain hollows and crevices. By morning, Dewi thought, the mountains above Dorabella Quarry would be capped with a fresh fall.

Anxious to be out of a car beginning to smell of something odd and stale and rather unwholesome, Jack followed. Taking wellingtons from the boot, he changed, placing his shoes neatly in their own space, eyeing the nut-brown leather with distaste as a spiteful jibe, mouthed by Ianto in the cells under the police station, returned to taunt him. A brown nose, Ianto called him, and accused him of trying to trample McKenna into the mud to gain promotion. Then, staring long and hard at Jack's shoes, Ianto had said, 'Come to think of it, Mr Inspector, I daresay folk has problems seeing anything but the soles of your fancy shoes at times.'

'Are we to wait for the chief inspector, sir?' Dewi asked.

'I haven't been in touch,' Jack said. 'No need to disturb him until we know what's what. Let's get on with it. It'll be dark before long.'

'We'd better mark the way with this, then,' Dewi said, pulling a roll of Dayglo plastic tape from the van.

'Like Theseus in the maze, going after the Minotaur. Wouldn't want to get lost, would we?'

'Fat chance!' John Jones sneered. 'Could smell you lot under fifty fucking feet of water, never mind in a few trees!'

A short way along a gravelled lane driven through ranks of tall Scotch pine, John Jones stopped to get his bearings before plunging down a muddy slope into the trees. Knotting tape round a tree trunk, Dewi followed the others into the deep woods where pine gave way to slender columns of birch and alder, close-grown elm trees rotten with disease, their branches tangled into crippled distortions, as if the struggle for light had proved beyond their strength. John Jones moved hesitantly forward, standing now and then to look for signs of earlier passage, while dead leaves from a hundred autumn falls lay sodden underfoot, mouldering and dirty, the stench of decay filling the air.

'How often d'you reckon people come down here?' Jack asked him. He shrugged, and ploughed on without a word, down a steep incline towards the river, its slimy banks littered with outcrops of pale marbled rock. Wellingtons skidding, Jack almost tumbled in, and Dewi caught his arm, hauling him upright.

'You could hide a hundred bodies down here and nobody'd ever find them,' Dewi observed. He turned to John Jones. 'Funny how you managed, isn't it?'

By the river, waters creaming in spate over rock debris and glittering gravel on the river-bed, the light was magnificent, filled with steely-blue and grey-white tones, the sun long obscured behind thick winter cloud driven hard and fast by winds off the sea. Branches creaked in the heavy silence, yet the air remained so still it was like, Jack fancied, being submerged. Wherever he looked, he saw trees: sombre, dark trees, some frosted with the sharp livid green of budding foliage, others dying, life choked out by dark tendrils of ivy. Along the riverbanks, lichen-covered rocks tumbled, wrapped in fronds of dead bracken. No birdcall broke the stillness, no small animals scuttered in the undergrowth; nothing relieved the grandeur and symmetry of nature reclaiming its own. His eye caught the drift of a shadow within the phalanx of trees directly ahead, and he stared, trying to make sense of the mass of grey and mouldy green splashed in his line of sight like drab colour running from a painter's careless brush strokes.

John Jones moved forward, boots squelching. 'It's there. I can see it.' Slowly, almost reluctantly, they followed the crabbed figure. On a mound within the woods, amid a convolution of dead trees throttled with ivy, the body, barely more substantial than the shadow of a shadow, swung on the end of frayed rope, clothes which had once been black hanging in grey tatters about its limbs. Little fillets of dried flesh still clung here and there; a few tufts of matted hair sprouted from its head. The eyes were long gone, a feast for the crows and magpies. Jack looked upon their find, and his scalp crawled. How many days and nights had she hung there, drenched by rain, scalded by the summer sun, scoured by the winds, and made brittle by deep mid-winter frost?

The corpse dangled close to the ground, rope and neck and spine and legs stretched by gravity and damp: elongated into some surrealistic form, feet pointing like those of a dancer, motion frozen in mid jump. A ragged skirt swung with a life of its own, giving off heady puffs of some strange scent. Touching nothing, in fear of damaging the frail remains, Jack examined the body. As he moved around, it seemed to swing after him, attracted by a strange magnetism, the head leaning forward to watch his progress. He felt its hip brush his shoulder, and almost screamed with terror.

A suicide, he decided, and a typical way for a woman to kill herself.

He stood behind her, that strange scent drying the back of his throat, and looked at what remained of her hands, crippled and clawed below the thick leather strap which bound her wrists tight together like those of the convict ready for execution.

Chapter 2

'Have you told McKenna yet?' Emma Tuttle asked her husband.

'Couldn't raise him. Been trying all afternoon and evening.' Jack yawned.

'D'you want me to call Denise?'

'No, love. I'll ring again before we go to bed. Nothing to be done tonight, anyway.'

Emma threw another log on the fire. 'Is anyone still down in that awful place? On a night like this?' she asked. 'You haven't left anyone there on his own, have you?'

'No point. We don't know how long the body's been there until Eifion Roberts does the post-mortem . . . if then. From the looks of it, she died at least before winter set in.'

Emma shuddered. 'Poor woman!' she said. 'It's absolutely dreadful, isn't it?'

'I suppose . . .' Jack yawned again. 'Are the twins all right?'

'Of course they are,' Emma said. 'Why shouldn't they be?'

'They're very quiet.'

Emma smiled. 'Typical policeman, aren't you?' she said. 'Just because they're not making a noise, you presume they're up to no good.'

'Well, that's usually the case with them, isn't it?'

Full darkness fell before police and forensic officers left the woods, trailing after stretcher-bearers and the pathologist. Cutting down this anonymous woman was a delicate task, two people needed to hold her as Dewi climbed up to untie the rope. The knots too tight, the rope too sodden to unravel, he was forced to saw it through, while the others steadied the convulsive swinging and jerking of the body below.

'Well, we can be sure it's not suicide,' Eifion Roberts observed. 'Nobody could strap up their own hands like that . . . That belt might tell us something eventually.' He straightened up, pulling off surgical gloves. 'Don't envy you this one. Looks more like an execution than a common or garden murder. You might well find yourselves looking at a terrorist link.'

'What sort of day did you have?' Jack asked his wife.

'Not very enjoyable, to be honest,' Emma admitted. 'Chester was terribly crowded. I don't know why we bother going on a Saturday afternoon, except Denise seemed to need some time to herself . . . she bought a lovely suit from Browns.'

'And how is our elegant Mrs McKenna?'

'I do wish you wouldn't talk about her in that nasty tone,' Emma snapped. 'She's very unhappy.'

'So is her husband,' Jack said.

'Is he?' Emma asked. 'Well, that doesn't give him the right to make her life a misery. She was actually crying today. In public! They'd had another row this morning. And d'you know what about?' Emma demanded. 'Religion, of all things. How can any normal person row about religion?'

Jack sighed. 'He's Catholic, she's Chapel.'

'So?'

'So she keeps harping on about him going to chapel with her even though she knows he won't.'

'I suppose that's his story, is it?'

'What's hers, then?' Jack said.

'Oh, don't be so bloody spiteful!' Emma exclaimed. 'For Denise of all people to sit in a café, crying . . .'

Jack stood up. 'And we've all seen Denise cry when it suits her, haven't we? Tears welling out of those baby-blue eyes . . . how did you describe it, Em? Like glass beads, you said, sliding down porcelain cheeks, then shattering on the ground. Very fanciful. How long d'you think she spent rehearsing that?'

'Why must you be so absolutely horrible about her? What's she done to you?'

'Emma!' Anger put an edge to Jack's voice. 'Denise McKenna is spoilt. Have you ever wondered what she does with herself all day, except spend his hard-earned money? No kids, no pets, every gadget you can think of in that house. And a cleaner! She's bored! And women like her,' he added, 'are bloody dangerous, because they make everybody else as bored and dissatisfied as they are.'

Jack arrived at the police station early on Sunday morning to find house-to-house enquiries in Salem village already organized, and McKenna seated at one of the computers, trawling the missing persons index.

'Roberts is already doing the post-mortem, so he can go sailing this afternoon,' McKenna said.

'Did he tell you his theory?'

McKenna looked up. 'Terrorists? A possibility, I suppose, but unlikely.' He pushed his chair away from the desk. 'Our local outlaws haven't killed anybody yet. They seem quite content with arson and the odd letter bomb.' Reaching for his cigarettes, he added, 'Anyway, you expect a bullet in the back of the neck from proper terrorists. After the knee-capping, of course.'

Jack said, 'You're not supposed to smoke near the computers, sir.'

'Why not?'

'It says so on that notice on the wall.'

'I know that, Jack. Why not?'

'I dunno . . . I suppose the smoke buggers up the works or something.'

McKenna stood up. 'Well, we wouldn't want to do that, would we?'

Expecting one of the mercurial changes of temper which characterized McKenna's personality and made those around him feel they had blundered with shrouded eyes through a minefield, Jack forbore to ask why McKenna preferred to work on a precious weekend off. Some things, he told himself, were best unsaid, for such questions might draw a response no one could ignore.

Demons of folklore and wraiths of legend danced the twisting narrow lanes of Salem village, padded on silent feet in the wake of the living, and wove threads of dark magic through the woods. Its dwellings built within sight of the squat-towered church and graveyard, the village inhabited the dark shadow of Castle

Woods: acres of impenetrable growth along the foreshore of the Menai Straits and beyond the bluff of land on which Snidey Castle stood.

Fashioned by local skills, local labour, more than a century before for an Englishman gorged on the slave trade, fat with riches and cruelty, the castle swallowed the ruins of an ancient manor. The Englishman named his grotesque folly Castell Ebargofiant – the Castle of Oblivion – and the slate quarry gouging a huge wound in the distant mountain, where Welsh slavery further bloated his riches, he named for his wife Dorabella.

Castell Ebargofiant became Snidey Castle almost as soon as the last stone was bedded into place, a small revenge for a huge injustice: Snidey because it hid itself within the shroud of trees, only the top of a battlemented keep in view; Snidey because it was bogus, a fake castle, embellished beyond all reason or sense. Every time he glimpsed those grey battlements, Dewi Prys wished upon that long-dead Englishman and his Dorabella all the torments of imagination, prayed for the ghosts of all the souls, black and Welsh, from which greed had stripped dignity in life, to lie entwined with them in death in their ornate and vulgar tomb in the village graveyard.

His colleagues interviewing people at the castle and in the houses near the main road, Dewi wandered around the easterly side of the village, past the old schoolhouse, the vicarage, and the little row of single-storey dwellings next to the primary school, before making his way down the path beside the graveyard, under dripping trees and branches dragging low and heavy. The path debouched eventually at a small gateway in high stone walls marking the estate's southern boundary, beyond which a little drinking fountain still trickled with brackish water pooling stagnant and spotted with slime.

Smells of rotting leaf mould curled in the air, reminding Dewi of the riverbank and the deep woods and the poor ravaged body dangling from its rope. 'There'll be some story behind that,' his nain had observed. The old ones on the council estate, safe from whatever horrors languished less than a mile up the road, relished long into the early hours of Sunday morning, on ghosts and tragedy and those secret things, just out of sight of this world, lying in ambush for the unwary.

Lame Beti, out on her wanderings, her perambulations around the countryside, yawed from side to side up the path towards Dewi. She was never still, as if her crippled frame could not rest with its deformity, or bear to contemplate its ugliness. She grinned, showing teeth more crooked than the gravestones in the churchyard next to where they stood. 'Hiya, *del*. No need to ask what you're doing here.'

Her voice, mangled by a cleft palate, grated on the ear. No one could look Beti in the eye: one bulbous muddy eye, to quote Nain's picturesque description, looked towards Bethesda, the other to Caernarfon: east and west. She was the most extravagantly ugly person Dewi had ever seen: more grotesque than any gargoyle leering from the church walls, as ugly as a gathering of all the sins in the world.

'Nain and her cronies were up half the night jangling,' he said.

She cackled. 'John Jones given folk something to talk about, has he?'

'You could say that,' Dewi agreed.

'Was you on your way to see me, *del*?' she asked. 'Only I'm not there, like. What did you want to know?'

'Anything you've got to tell me.'

She started off up the path, moving with surprising speed, lame legs swinging out each side of her body. Dewi went with her. 'I'm going to see if Mary Ann wants any messages. You come with me. She's always glad of a bit extra company.'

Chapter 3

At lunchtime, when a spiteful north-easterly wind, the back end of recent storms lashing its tail like an angry cat about to spring, splashed squally rain against the windows of Eifion Roberts's laboratory, he abandoned all notions of an afternoon's sailing on the Straits.

The post-mortem on the unknown woman was undemanding, cause of death apparently throttling at the end of a rope. The rope, grown thin with time, its running noose tightened almost horizontally around the neck by the weight of her body's descent, shed bits of stringy fibre on the bench where it now lay. Dr Roberts photographed and X-rayed the body, giving particular attention to an old and complex fracture he found on the left ankle bone. Too little flesh remained, except for where clothing had protected her from the elements, to show evidence of injury prior to death. The skull, stripped almost clean, by birds and nature and insects, bore no fracture. Putrefaction was long complete; the internal organs shrivelled, almost mummified. He removed, with tremendous care, the major organs and uterus, sealing them in jars ready for dissection.

Emrys, his assistant, carefully unwound the belt which had bound the woman's wrists. Made of dark brown cowhide, without ornamentation of any kind, it was three and a half inches wide, its colour bleached where rain and sun and wind had touched. Someone had cut off the buckle, leaving a jagged end.

Spread on a table, the woman's ragged garments gave off a faint scent. Dr Roberts sniffed at the clothing, trying to place the smell in memory. Redolent of funerals, but not the scent of death, it was a dry mustiness catching in the throat, and would, he thought, make him feel terribly and inexplicably depressed if it became too cloying.

Emrys looked up from a thick manual detailing garment makers and labels. 'The clothes are German in origin, Dr Roberts,' he said. 'Only problem is, they're sold through at least a hundred outlets in Britain. Middling expensive, but nothing special.'

'Bugger!' Eifion Roberts fingered the garments. 'Not much hope of finding out where she bought them, then?'

'I'll fax some photos to Germany, anyway. They should be able to tell us when they were made, where they were sold . . . might narrow it down a bit.'

'Fat chance! When did we last strike gold with that line of enquiry? Women's clothes, they're like I don't know what . . . Like grains of sand, they are, millions and millions of the bloody things. Makes you depressed just thinking about them . . . We'd need Princess Di on the slab before we stood a chance of getting an ID off her clothes.'

Emrys smiled. 'If Princess Di went missing for as long as this lady, somebody might notice.' He fingered the belt. 'I'll send a photo of this as well. It's very good quality leather.'

Dewi's two colleagues returned to Bangor in mid-afternoon, with odds and ends of information, but nothing apparently relevant or of real interest.

'They'll have to go out again tomorrow,' Jack said to McKenna. 'Half the village was off somewhere for the day.'

'Any decent programmes on TV tonight?' McKenna asked. 'Because if not, we'll send a team out from the evening shift. Nothing like entertaining people of a dull Sunday evening.' He lit a cigarette. 'Pity none of the missing women had an injury like the one Dr Roberts found on this lady's ankle.'

'Hard graft time again then, isn't it?' Jack said.

By late afternoon, each police force reporting missing women had received a faxed package of description, X-rays and photographs of teeth, injury and sinuses, and a request for enquiries to be made of hospitals, doctors and dentists in their areas. Dr Roberts tentatively, as he told McKenna, put the dead woman's age at between twenty-five and forty-five, but probably around thirty-five. She had probably, but only probably, he emphasized, been dead some eighteen to forty-eight months, but most likely somewhere in between.

'May as well put the file in pending now, Jack,' McKenna said. 'If it wasn't for the bound wrists, we'd simply have an unfortunate suicide. Where's young Dewi? He should have been back with the others.'

'He called in a while ago. He's talking to some of the old women in the village. Reckons they might know something useful.'

'Doubt it. Still, no harm in trying . . . has anyone talked to Jamie Thief yet?'

'Sorry, no. Slipped my mind with all the excitement.'

'He'll keep. You get off home, Jack. We'll start again in the morning.'

Driving home, Jack wondered how McKenna would avoid Denise when excuses about pressure of work were finally exhausted, and why so many policemen's marriages ended in disaster, with bitterness and drunken violence sadly commonplace. Management maintained a bland public image, fed on the misapprehension that admission of imperfection would damage public confidence. Complaints against the police multiplied, but became muddied and obfuscated, the complainant often victimized, while the media railed about accountability, made allegations of rank-closing and wilful disinformation. Word had travelled about the woman's bound hands, as Jack knew it would: two London journalists simply insulted him when he refused to comment on possible terrorist involvement.

Emma was pleased to see him, last night's anger dissipated. Jack was less than delighted to find Denise McKenna draped elegantly across the sofa, sipping white wine, looking as if she intended to stay, questions about her husband, his whereabouts, hanging unspoken between them.

The inspector was too abrasive, too dismissive of things not neatly fitting his own views, Dewi told himself, relieved to find Jack Tuttle gone. He liked and respected McKenna, even if others said the chief inspector was difficult, too prone to heed his imagination.

'Sorry I'm late back, sir. Been talking to the old ladies in the village.'

'And?'

'They had a lot to say, but then, they always do . . . Beti took me to Mary Ann's. Then Faith and Mair Evans turned up, probably' – Dewi looked up and grinned – 'because they saw me going into Mary Ann's and couldn't wait to nosey-parker. Anyway, they were jangling about this and that, then Faith says did I know about the woman who lived at Gallows Cottage some time back, and Mary Ann says, "I told you! Didn't I tell you last night? Didn't I say she'd gone the same way as the other one?" So I said, "What other one?" and nobody took a blind bit of notice of me for ages 'cos they were going on about what happens to women living at Gallows Cottage. Fair made my flesh crawl with their tales, sir.'

'And where's Gallows Cottage?'

Spreading a large-scale map of the estate on the desk, Dewi traced his finger along the seaward boundary, bringing it to rest on a small spur of land jutting into the Straits. 'The cottage is here, at the edge of the woods, according to the ladies. They reckon you can't see it except from the sea, and if you don't know about it, you'd never find it. It's almost as old as the village church, and it's called Gallows Cottage, they say, because women who live there end up swinging off a gibbet somewhere.'

McKenna pulled a notepad in front of him. 'Who was the woman living there recently?'

'They don't exactly know, which rankles . . . she was definitely a foreigner – er, a foreigner like from England, sir. No idea what she was called. Beti says she saw her the odd time, in a car. No one knows anybody who spoke to her. Beti reckons she was about thirty odd, fair haired.'

Making notes in his loose, rapid handwriting, McKenna asked, 'How long ago?'

'They can't make up their minds. From what they said, three years ago – three years ago last autumn. Beti said the weather was turning cold when she first saw her, and doesn't remember seeing her during the spring or summer.'

'Well,' McKenna observed, 'the time ties in with what Dr Roberts has come up with so far. Did you see the cottage?'

'No, sir. There's a path through the woods from the village, but it's quite a long way and none of the old ladies would come with me because it was getting dark and they reckon it's haunted. There's a track you can get a car down, but that starts on the estate somewhere.'

'What kind of car did this woman have?'

'Beti doesn't know. Modern, she says, then says all modern cars look the same to her. She thinks it was some sort of grey colour, but she can't be sure of that either, on account of the light being poor 'cos of all those trees and the time of year.'

McKenna sat smoking. 'Tell me about Gallows Cottage,' he said.

'To tell the truth, sir, I feel a bit of a divvy going on about ghosts and what-have-you . . .' Dewi sounded uncomfortable. 'I mean, it doesn't seem to have much to do with anything, does it?'

'Don't know yet, do we? Who's to say someone didn't decide to recreate history or whatever it was the old ladies were talking about?'

'Bit far-fetched, sir, if you ask me,' Dewi commented. 'Anyway, centuries past, this man and his wife lived at Gallows Cottage. He was called Simeon the Jew, and his wife was called Rebekah, and they had a baby daughter. Nobody seems to know what he did for a living, but one day, he came back from wherever they went in those days, and found the baby dead. Fallen down the stairs, so the wife reckoned.'

'Nasty. What happened then?'

'Dunno, sir. Not exactly,' Dewi said. 'But next thing anybody knows, Rebekah's up at Caernarfon getting tried for murdering her baby. She's found guilty, so they cart her off to Twt Hill and string her up. Then, legend has it, Simeon comes along and cuts her down. Nobody tries to stop him on account of they're all scared of him 'cos he's foreign, and he takes her body away and disappears. Not a word of what happened to him after. Never seen again. And nobody knows where Rebekah is buried.'

'Probably threw her body in the Menai Straits and himself after it, Dewi,' McKenna said. 'Poor bugger didn't have much to live for, did he?'

'Well, no, sir. I suppose not. Not if you look at it like that. But it's not the end of the story, not quite. Simeon's said to have done a fair bit of cursing when they hung his wife, and also threatened to walk. Like in ghosts walking,' Dewi said. 'Haunting. They say he threatened to walk the earth 'til he found his wife again. That's what the old ladies were getting at, you see. They reckon Simeon lit on this woman living at Gallows Cottage, decided she'd do, and strung her up in the woods so he could have her soul . . . say her hands were tied up because Rebekah's would've been when she was topped at Twt Hill. Mary Ann says any woman living at the cottage is likely to go the same way,' he added. 'She says the place should be burnt down 'cos it's cursed.'

'I daresay our terrorist friends would oblige if they were asked,' McKenna grinned. 'Has anyone ever seen Simeon?'

'Well, a few of them would have you believe he's around, but they're bound to, aren't they? It's a good yarn, sir, especially for a dark night, or some poor sod just moved into the village.' Dewi paused, frowning slightly. 'There's a funny atmosphere in that village. It's a sort of woman's world, if you understand what I mean, and the men don't count for much. I didn't hear a word about John Beti actually finding the body. To listen to Beti and the others, you'd not know he existed.'

'We men don't count for much anywhere, Dewi. It just suits the women to let us think we do.'

Chapter 4

In a mood as foul and dismal as the weather, Jack arrived at the police station on Monday morning to find McKenna haunting his office as Denise haunted his home. Eyeing Jack's sour countenance, McKenna wondered what it was about rain which made people so evil-tempered.

'Dewi Prys heard some interesting gossip yesterday, Jack. We might have a lead on the woman.' McKenna handed over Dewi's report, and disappeared to the canteen.

Jack trailed behind, glancing through the report. Dewi Prys plagued him like a thorn in the side of a dog, yet there was no fault to be had with his work. 'Don't underestimate him,' McKenna was saying. 'He lets people talk, lets them relax, and just points them in the right direction now and then with a question.'

Waiting with ill-concealed impatience for McKenna to drink two mugs of tea and smoke two cigarettes, Jack asked, 'What's on the agenda for today?'

'I want to have a look at Gallows Cottage. And another visit to the old ladies might be useful, while you get someone to talk to Jamie about this car. Nothing's come in on the missing women, but I don't expect it to for some time.' McKenna lit his third cigarette.

'Don't you think you should cut down on the smoking a bit, sir? Bad for you, you know.'

McKenna took off his glasses to rub his eyes, and Jack noticed the smudge of shadow beneath them. 'Kind of you to think of my health, Jack, but are you doing yourself any favours? You know promotion in this force is usually a matter of dead men's shoes.'

A sombre place on the brightest summer day, under a pall of rain and heavy cloud, the wet blue slate of its cottage roofs livid in the dull light, Salem village took upon itself a sinister aura. Densely massed trees, tall and overbearing, surrounded cottages, school and church, suffocating and oppressive. McKenna parked in the lane beside the row of cottages next to the school. The air was still, sodden with rain, and he was struck by an absence of noise, although he could see children at their desks in classrooms bright with fluorescent lighting. The trees were empty of birds, rooks' nests in the high branches abandoned. Only half a mile from the shoreline, no gulls wheeled and screeched in the sky. He pulled his coat around him, and walked quickly to Mary Ann's front door, rapping at its fox-head knocker.

Lame Beti whipped open the door, a brilliant smile lighting her gargoyle face. 'Hiya, *del*,' she greeted him. 'You want to see Mary Ann, do you?'

People made jokes about Beti, the most cruel to be given currency that she had never been quite pretty enough, even when young, to stop the traffic, and that was why she looked as if mown down by a juggernaut. Following, as she weaved her way into Mary Ann's parlour, McKenna wondered on the sins she had committed in a past life to carry with her through this one for all the world to see.

Mary Ann's cottage smelt of old damp in walls and floors, seeped into furniture and fabrics. The walls, once painted in pale emulsion, were stained yellowy brown with nicotine, a huge gas fire burned in the opening of an old range covering half the chimney wall, adding its fumes to an atmosphere drying McKenna's throat more each time he drew breath.

Squashed tight into an old armchair, Mary Ann held court, fluffy white hair as yellowed above her forehead as the walls. A tin ashtray overflowed on the chair arm, and her feet in grubby pink carpet slippers pointed at him from the end of swollen, varicosed legs. Cruel cold daylight filtered into the room through old-fashioned lace curtains, to light on her face, the make-up peeling away from her nose like old varnish.

'Dewi's boss, aren't you?' she asked. 'He had us all in stitches yesterday. Isn't that right, Beti?'

Beti bobbed her head, then went to the kitchen, where McKenna heard the sound of a kettle being filled.

'Didn't you wed Eileen Owen's youngest?' Mary Ann asked. 'Denise, isn't it?'

McKenna nodded, accepting her interrogation as a necessity if he wanted anything from her. 'We went to school with Eileen.' She looked sly, McKenna thought; mischievous. 'Nasty piece of work she was. Always snitching on people.'

McKenna said, 'I didn't know her very well, Mrs Edwards. She died not long after I married Denise.'

'You didn't miss much. You can call me Mary Ann, by the way, then I can call you Michael.' She chuckled.

'I shouldn't tell you this, but that family of your Denise's doesn't half put on the airs and graces, what with Eileen's eldest nearly born the wrong side of the blanket. Seven months gone was our Eileen going to the altar.' She grinned. 'She got religion afterwards, and went respectable. Well, at least, she pretended to. No better than she should be, that one, for all her going off to chapel every Sunday with a posh hat on her head. Don't let me go jangling on, young man. You'll want to be knowing about that woman and the cottage, won't you? We told Dewi all we can remember, though it won't hurt to tell it again, will it?'

The children were out in the schoolyard on their lunch break before McKenna left Mary Ann's cottage, their shrieks and shouts muffled by the weight of trees. The rain had eased a little, to what his mother called a 'mizzle', the old Irish name for mountain rain. His clothes smelt of the damp in Mary Ann's cottage, and he had learnt nothing new, yet the time with the two women was restful with the comfort to be found in old age when it threatened nothing more than quiet decay.

Once out of the village, the day seemed brighter, although heavy-bellied cloud festooned the distant mountains, promising more rain. Cars swished past on the roads, water spurting from under their tyres as McKenna parked outside the entrance to the estate office, beside Jack's car, aware of a sense of depression and futility trying to creep upon him like dark cloud off the mountains.

'Any news?' he asked.

'Nothing much,' Jack said. 'Jamie's away somewhere, his mam reckons. Doesn't know when he'll be back. I had the impression the longer he stays away, the happier she'll be.'

McKenna locked his car. 'Having a child like Jamie must be a burden.'

'I suppose so. But you can't avoid blaming the parents, can you? Somebody must've done something wrong to end up with a villain like him.'

The manager of the estate office sighed. 'We're going back some time, gentlemen. Maybe three years, if not more. Gallows Cottage no longer belongs to the estate: it was sold several months ago as part of a rationalization programme.' He sat at his desk, twiddling paper clips. 'It really will take a while for me to find what you want . . . quite a while.' He smiled brightly. 'Why don't you leave it with me, and I'll get in touch as soon as I locate the documents?'

McKenna crossed his legs and lit a cigarette. 'I would much prefer you to look now, Mr Prosser. And I want to visit the cottage today. You realize we are engaged on a murder investigation?'

Capitulating with ill grace, Prosser pulled a stack of ledgers from the shelves beside his desk and began to leaf through them, glancing up every so often at the two police officers.

'I'm surprised your records aren't computerized, Mr Prosser,' Jack said. 'Makes life so much easier, don't you think?'

'They will be, once the rationalization is complete,' Prosser said, with some acerbity. 'Hardly worth it at the moment.'

McKenna stood up, and began to wander round the

dusty, untidy office. 'What exactly does this rationalization programme entail?' he asked.

Prosser leaned back in his chair, his finger marking the place in the heavy ledger. 'Oh, didn't you know, gentlemen? The trust took over the estate some time ago. Or rather, it was handed over by the family in lieu of death duties after the old lord passed away. Naturally, the trust is anxious to have the estate run on a viable basis, whilst still, of course, retaining it for the nation, preserving it as part of our heritage. That has meant,' he continued pompously, 'cutting away a certain amount of dead wood, so to speak.'

'I see,' McKenna said. 'Don't you remember this woman? You must have dealt with her at the time.'

'This is a very busy office. You've no idea of the amount of business we have to deal with. I can't be expected to remember everything, can I?'

McKenna leaned over and removed one of the ledgers. 'Perhaps we might help? Three pairs of hands, you know . . . What are we looking for? Do you have a separate file for each property?'

'This really is most irregular. These transactions are confidential. And no, the records are simply chronological.'

Jack picked up another ledger, spreading it open on his knee. 'Don't you worry, Mr Prosser. We deal with highly confidential matters every day.'

Handwritten in a variety of scripts ranging from neat copperplate to almost illegible scrawl, ledger entries covered years of business transactions, and Jack was struck by the fundamental inefficiency of such an archaic system. He found the entry as the old clock set into the pediment above the main door struck three, its delicate chime faint and leisurely. An entry dated 29 August, almost four years previously, showed Gallows Cottage leased, for a six-month period, to a Ms R Cheney at a Derbyshire address. An unusual name, he thought. And not one which he could remember seeing on the list of missing persons. He passed the ledger to McKenna.

'Ms R Chainey, or Cheeney, Mr Prosser. C-H-E-N-E-Y. Do you remember her?' McKenna asked. Prosser looked where McKenna pointed. 'Oh, dearie me, gentlemen. This is not my writing, so I'm afraid I can't help you.'

'Whose writing is it, then?' Jack asked.

'It looks like Miss Naylor's.' Prosser held up his hand and smiled. 'I know what you're going to ask me. And the answer is no. She left last year to get married, and I have absolutely no idea where she lives, or even what she's called.' He closed the ledgers, and began to put them back on the shelving.

McKenna stood up. 'I'm afraid we shall have to take the ledgers with us, to have them searched properly. And it may be necessary to examine other documents. We'll give you a receipt, and return them as soon as possible. And now, Mr Prosser, you can do us one final favour for today and escort us to the cottage.'

Following Prosser in Jack's car, McKenna could not rid himself of the mental image of the little office manager flouncing out of the building. 'Right little twerp, isn't he?' Jack said, as they trailed the cumbersome red Volvo along a narrow tarmac lane, then over a graceful little bridge under which a small lock had been built for boats collecting slate from Dorabella

Quarry. Prosser drove through a massive gateway leading out of the estate and took a gravelled lane leading to the left, the ever present trees soon thick around them, darkening the meandering lane.

'I hate this bloody estate!' Jack muttered. 'Turn a corner, and you get lost in the sodding woods! You're lucky you didn't have to go traipsing down to the river on Saturday. What are these trees anyway?' he added, peering through the windscreen. 'They look like great overgrown weeds.'

Chapter 5

Gallows Cottage, at the bottom of a track hedged with tangles of bramble and hawthorn, was surrounded on three sides by the waters of the Menai Straits, its gardens falling to the sea, which suckled and slithered against the rocky boundaries. The building seemed to have grown from the soil on which it stood, walls thick and ponderous, rendered with scabbed and salt-stained plaster. Little sash windows, sixteen tiny panes of glass to each, stared blindly from the walls. Rank grass and scrubby bushes straggled round its footings. An empty bird's nest, torn down by winter gales, tumbled gently in the wind.

Jack drew to a halt on a patch of heathland. Prosser was already waiting for them, one hand brushing a veil of rain from his thinning hair. 'I don't have a key, so I don't know how you think you're going to get in.'

The woods formed a dense semi-circle, a windbreak of sorts, behind the cottage exposed to the elements on its other sides. Across the water, misted by rain, the island of Anglesey lay to the north, the humped shape of Puffin Island off its most easterly point. The sea was grey, choppy, pitted with raindrops, its gentle sucking the only sound apart from the patter of rain on the car roofs. McKenna wondered if the trees had been planted by some erstwhile landscaper, or if their seeds had merely been borne on the winds, come to rest in this desolate place.

A man in stained and dusty overalls emerged from the front of the cottage, through a low door set in the middle of the wall. Above him, a small triangular canopy protected the doorway from the ravages of rain and snow, its projection supported by a carving. 'Can I help you?' he called.

Prosser went to his car. 'You won't need me anymore, will you? I'm sure you can find your own way back. I'll be expecting you to return the ledgers very soon, Chief Inspector.' As McKenna thanked him for his help, Prosser disappeared in a swirl of exhaust fumes.

'Doing up the place for the guy who's bought it off the estate,' the builder said. 'Not,' he continued, leading them into a dark hallway, 'that it needs all that much doing. Somebody's already done the donkey work, and didn't ruin the place by modernizing too much, if you know what I mean.'

McKenna lingered, reaching up to trace his fingers over the worn stone of the carving above the door: a dog with three heads. Cerberus, he remembered, legendary guardian of the entrance to the underworld, the Queen of Poisons distilled from its saliva. He drew his hand away, a little worm of dread slithering and sliding in his mind, some portent of the nastiness of it all which lay in wait.

Treads worn hollow in the middle, the ancient stone staircase climbed the centre of the building. McKenna had a sudden vision of a child's broken body lying at its foot, the stone bloody and daubed with bits of brain and splinters of bone.

Taking Jack and McKenna into the kitchen, the builder gave them seats on upturned crates. 'What can I do for you, then?'

Jack said, 'We're trying to find out about a woman who lived here around three and half years ago. She rented from the estate.'

'Oh, yes? Probably who did the repairs and suchlike,' the builder said. 'The place has been empty at least three years. That's why it's a bit of a mess.'

'Odd for someone to spend money on a place they're only renting,' McKenna said.

'Well,' the builder said, lighting a pipe, 'unless she didn't mind living in a slum, she wouldn't've had much choice. A lot of properties on the estate've gone to rack and ruin over the years. Nobody bothered with them. And you can take my word for it, the estate wouldn't argue with a person willing to spend a bit of their own cash.'

Another man walked into the kitchen, nodded to Jack and McKenna, and put a kettle on a Primus stove. 'This here's my mate, Dave. He's deaf, so don't expect him to talk to you.' The builder looked at the other man, and gestured for him to make tea for all of them. McKenna wondered how it felt to be stuck in this place with only a deaf man for company. 'Who's bought the cottage?' he asked.

'Bloody English!' the builder sneered. 'For letting out to the tourists. That's if,' he smirked, 'it doesn't get torched by the arsonists first!'

'Careful what you say,' Jack warned.

The builder stared at Jack. 'I'll say what I think, whether you like it or not. Not from these parts, are you? Otherwise,' he went on, 'you'd know how folk feel about that bloody great castle up the road and the huge great rooms and the posh curtains and carpets, and furniture you couldn't buy with a million-pound win on the pools. And,' he added, 'you'd know about the dirty little hovels the quarrymen lived in, cottages owned by that lot who had the castle built, cottages a man and his wife and kiddies got thrown out of on to the streets when it suited the lord of the manor, or when a man's lungs'd rotted to pulp from the quarry dust.' He stopped to draw breath, chewing at the pipe. 'So don't be surprised if we don't want the English coming buying houses the locals should be living in, especially if they're just going to use them for holidays. There's too many young families round here can't even afford one roof over their heads, never mind two!'

'What's to stop them getting a mortgage for one of these places?' Jack asked.

The builder said, 'This dump fetched about three times what a normal person could afford.'

'Why?'

'Because it's on the estate, and the estate decides how much the properties get sold for. After all,' he added with some bitterness, 'they wouldn't want any local riff-raff living here now when they've managed to keep them out for so long, would they?'

Dave passed tin mugs of tea around, and took his to sit at the bottom of the stairs. McKenna said to the builder, 'I suppose you wouldn't by any chance know who did the other building work?'

'No, but I'll ask around. Doesn't that little fart from the estate office know? Expect he has trouble finding his backside to give it a wipe when he's had a crap!'

He cackled gleefully, puffing out little belches of smoke. The cottage was cold, a chill of age and time, trapped within its walls, coming at you, McKenna thought, like fingers. The builder said, 'Why d'you want to know, anyway?'

'We're trying to locate the woman who rented the house,' Jack said.

'Why? D'you think it was her you found in the woods the other day?'

'We don't know,' McKenna said. 'Tell me, was anything left behind, in the way of furniture or clothes or whatever?' He watched Dave come back into the kitchen to rinse his mug.

'Nothing. The place was stripped.'

'What work are you doing?' Jack asked.

'There's a bit of damp to be got rid of . . . thorough clean-up, decorating . . . The only big job is building proper sewers. The drains just go straight into the sea, so the council's making the new owner do a decent job with a septic tank. We'd have started today but for the weather.'

Dave stared at McKenna, then tapped the builder on the shoulder, pointed to McKenna, then to somewhere beyond the kitchen walls. He made sounds in his throat, guttural and gulping, about a carpet in the parlour, taken up and put in the outhouse.

Little more than a shed with a sloping roof built on to the side of the cottage, the outhouse was once a scullery. A stone sink mouldered under the single window, the remains of a copper tub beside it. The carpet, rolled up and placed upright in the far corner, stank of must. Dave and Jack heaved it to the dirt floor, unrolling it as best they could. 'Good bit of carpeting,' the builder said, fingering the edge. 'Wool, by the feel of it. Must have cost a fair bit. Somebody must've dropped a fag end and burnt it. There's a big stain as well. Probably why it was left.'

He tugged at the carpet until the burnt part came into view. Nearby, a large dark stain spread through the fibres. McKenna felt a little tingle of excitement. Where discoloured, the wool felt matted and stiff under his fingers. Jack looked at the stain, then at McKenna.

'Look,' McKenna said to the builder, 'leave everything as it is until we can get people here to have a good look round. Can you lock this shed?'

'Think it's blood, do you?' The builder eyed the carpet. 'Could be, I suppose. Mind you, could be anything, couldn't it? Been there a fair while. Could just be some English arsehole spilling a glass of wine.'

'Yes, well we won't know that until we examine it properly.' Jack's irritation was obvious. 'And in the meantime, you keep quiet.'

'Don't bully me!' the builder snapped. 'I'm quite capable of knowing when to keep my mouth shut!'

Sighing, McKenna thanked the builder and Dave, trying to soothe ruffled feathers. Glaring at Jack, the builder said to McKenna, 'Anything we can do to help *you*. I'll ask around in the pub tonight about the other builders. Where can I get hold of you?'

Taking his car slowly up the lane, avoiding as many pot-holes as possible, Jack said, 'You realize we don't even know what the man's called, don't you, sir? He could be anybody.'

'Oh, give it a rest, Jack!' McKenna snapped. 'The

man's a builder. Who d'you think he is? Simeon come back looking for another bride?'

'Who the devil's Simeon?'

'If you'd read Dewi's report properly, you'd know!'

Jack sulked through tea-break, ostentatiously reading Dewi Prys's report. McKenna, with a strong urge to shake his deputy, shut himself in his office instead with other reports and papers, to find no novelty anywhere, even Dr Roberts's report devoid of further interest. Asking Derbyshire police to find and interview Ms Cheney, he suspected the investigation would simply move sluggishly around, for a few weeks or months, to end up where it began. Death wrought violently in these parts was usually fashioned by kith or kin: a farmer run amok with a shot-gun, made crazy by years of servitude to a harsh and barren land; young men settling age-old tribal feuds with a flash of sharp blade or the pounding of studded boots against the face and skull of the enemy. This woman's death had the feel of coldness and deliberation, undignified by the heat of any passion, however aberrant.

Chapter 6

Driving slowly down the main road of the council estate, Dewi Prys thought the weather might at last be improving. Winter, seemingly interminable, followed an autumn cold and damp enough to eat through bone. Vicious storms, driven in off the sea, had raged week after week since New Year, tearing slates from roofs, snapping telephone and power lines like so much rotted string. On Snidey Castle Estate, the huge bulk of castle keep, pale grey in morning sunshine, rose through trees clothed in bright new leaves. High fluffy clouds ran before a wind freshening out at sea, piling up towards the mountains behind him. Jamie Thief, dressed in a brown leather jacket and black jeans, ran across the road in front of Dewi's car, on his way to the local shop.

Dewi drew into the kerb, and followed, waiting outside the shop until Jamie, tall, his fair hair lifting in the wind, emerged with a copy of the *Sun* tucked under his arm.

'Hiya, Jamie,' Dewi greeted him. 'Where's your car?'

Jamie glanced around as if to start running in autonomic reflex. Only four months out of prison after a long stretch for aggravated burglary, Jamie wore an aura of innocence unless you looked, Dewi once told

McKenna, into his eyes; eyes as grey and cold and treacherous as the sea on a stormy day.

'What car, Dewi?'

'Oh, some posh new vehicle you've been seen in,' Dewi said. 'Where is it?'

Jamie grinned, exhaling breath as if in relief. 'Oh, that!' He smiled brilliantly. 'You want to get yourselves some new snitches. Not mine, Dewi, old mate.'

'Whose is it, then?'

Jamie tapped the side of his nose with a forefinger, still grinning. 'That's for me to know and you to find out. A kind person lent it to me. For services rendered, you might say.'

He began to walk away. Dewi caught his arm. 'Don't get too clever, Jamie,' he warned. 'You might find Mr McKenna wanting chapter and verse on this kind person.'

'Why?' The smile disappeared, leaving menace crawling the pale features. God alone knew what evils Jamie might eventually put his hands to, Dewi thought. Time-served already in juvenile custody and prison, Jamie began his criminal career, people said, literally the moment he learned to walk.

'Well,' Dewi said. 'That's for me to know and you to find out, isn't it? See you around, Jamie.'

'Something might turn up from the cottage, sir,' Jack offered. 'And Derbyshire police might have some information.'

'They haven't. They called back last night. The person living at that address bought the house three years ago from a bloke by the name of' – McKenna rummaged under piles of folders and retrieved a notebook – 'Robert Allsopp, and has no idea where Mr Allsopp might be now. Anyway, I've asked them to find him via building societies, solicitors and whatnot. Somebody must have a forwarding address.'

'Could've been living with Ms Cheney.'

'That occurred to me, too,' McKenna said. 'I was also struck by the time factor. Everything seems to have happened around three and a half years ago.'

'Well,' Jack hesitated. 'I – er – daresay a lot of things happened around then. I mean, they don't necessarily have to have anything to do with our body.'

'You can be really pedantic at times.' McKenna scowled. 'Did you know that?' He lit a cigarette, exhaling smoke through his nostrils. 'I want you to go and have a chat with Special Branch this afternoon.'

'Do I have to? I had a bellyful of that lot during the royal visit.'

'They might know something about this woman.'

'Yes,' Jack said. 'And if they do, they won't tell us.'

'You know we have to ask. If we don't, and Eifion Roberts is right about a terrorist connection, we'll be in the shit.'

'Amazing how the smooth progress of a police investigation might depend on the say-so of a bunch of spies, isn't it?' Jack remarked.

McKenna straightened the papers on his desk. 'Looks like it, doesn't it?'

'And what am I supposed to say?'

'Oh, use your brains!' McKenna snapped. 'Just find out if they know anything useful.'

'Oh, I see.' Jack considered. 'Whose brilliant idea was this, then?'

McKenna glared at his deputy. 'Mine,' he said. 'I thought it up all by myself.'

'You surprise me. I thought it might be an order from on high.'

'You should really have gone yourself, Michael.' Superintendent Griffiths lounged in McKenna's office. 'Jack doesn't have the experience to deal with Special Branch.'

'Do him good to get some, then, won't it?' McKenna said. 'Look good on his service record when he comes up for promotion.'

'Don't you like Jack?'

McKenna shrugged. 'He's all right . . . gets on my nerves sometimes.'

'Usually, you either hate somebody, or like them so much you're blind to any faults. Like with young Dewi.'

'Don't exaggerate, Owen,' McKenna said.

The superintendent rubbed his finger along the edge of McKenna's desk. 'How are things at home?' he asked quietly.

'I don't want to discuss Denise.'

'I'm not one to pry into things which aren't my concern, Michael, but I don't want it said your personal life is interfering with your job.'

'It won't.'

'We've got enough on our plate without that sort of thing.'

'Like what?'

'Oh, the usual,' Griffiths said. 'Complaints about this, that and the other . . . Poor performance, poor clear-up rates, and a sodding awful public image. And,' he added bitterly, 'instructions from the top to put it all right.'

'I see.' McKenna lit a cigarette. 'And how d'you propose to do that?'

'I thought you might have some ideas.'

'Me?' McKenna looked amused.

'You're the one with the university degree. Education's supposed to teach you how to deal with problems.'

McKenna grinned. 'Some problems, Owen, are beyond solving.'

The superintendent sighed. 'You might be right,' he said. 'I blame it on the miners' strike. That's when the rot set in. We should never've got involved. That wasn't police business, and somebody should've had the guts to tell the government to get somebody else to do their dirty work. And then, of course,' he went on, 'the bad apples you get in any police force saw what they could get away with at the pit heads, and others've just followed suit. I reckon policing's taken on a different colour since then.'

After lunch, McKenna returned to Gallows Cottage, finding it no less desolate in bright sunshine than under dismal cloud and rain. The builder, knee deep in the beginnings of the drainage trench, waved, and scrambled out.

'Your lot are tearing the cottage apart, so we're making ourselves useful out here.' He looked up at the sky. 'Nice day, for a change, isn't it?'

'It is indeed.' McKenna smiled at him. 'What's your name? I forgot to ask yesterday.'

'Wil Jones. You can call me Wil. You Irish, are you?'

'A long way back,' McKenna said.

'I'm from the noble Jones family of Wales.' Wil grinned. 'I've been asking around, but nobody seems to know who worked here before.'

Inside the cottage, three forensic specialists foraged for information, white overalls rustling and crackling in the still air. 'This is a bit of a waste of time, Mr McKenna,' their senior said. 'If there was anything here to find, dust and damp's got at it.'

'What about the carpet?'

The man scuffed his feet on the tiled floor. 'I've done a patch test on the stain, but it definitely isn't blood. We're taking the carpet away to have a proper look, but it'll probably be a waste of time.'

'You sure?' McKenna asked. 'Yes, of course you are . . . What is it?'

'Dunno . . . could be anything. Probably red wine, by the feel of it.'

McKenna called on Mary Ann before returning to Bangor. Having afternoon tea, she offered him a drink and a wedge of fresh cream cake. 'Beti got me the cake in town this morning. A body needs a little treat now and then.'

'D'you know Jamie Wright?' McKenna asked.

'Jamie Thief?' she frowned. 'Everybody knows him! The little bugger robbed Mair's electric meter when he was barely out of nappies. He used to come to the school here, 'til Social Services put him in care. Didn't stop him thieving, did they?'

'Have you seen him around the village recently?'

'Well, not recent. He's careful where he shows his face these days. Why?'

'Somebody told us he's driving a fancy new car,'

McKenna said, wiping cream off his fingers. 'Jamie reckons someone lent it to him. I just wondered if you might know who.'

'What kind of car is it?'

'Dunno, Mary Ann, and Jamie isn't volunteering any information.'

'I'll ask Beti. I don't get out much except when my son comes of a Sunday with his car. My legs, you know.' She smiled. 'And old age. Beti might know something. Not much gets past her, for all she can't see straight.'

McKenna sent Dewi to search for the buckle missing from the belt around the dead woman's wrists. 'You've got about five hours of daylight left.'

'Couldn't somebody else go, sir?' Dewi ventured. 'I've not finished ringing the builders in *Yellow Pages*.'

'They'll keep. You're to look for a buckle to fit a three and a half inch wide belt. Probably something fancy and expensive. And bring back anything else that looks interesting.'

Already formless, the investigation lacked any focus, and until the woman was identified, much expensive police time would be frittered away. Checking on the search of the estate ledgers, McKenna found only that Ms Cheney had paid six months' rent in advance on Gallows Cottage: £1,820. Seventy pounds a week for what must have been little more than a derelict hovel. He looked at the little notation beside the record for some moments before realizing it indicated a cash payment, unusual for such a large sum.

'No, Chief Inspector.' Mr Prosser was adamant. 'I did not take up references. I didn't ask for any.'

'D'you do all your business that way?'

'Really, Chief Inspector, I don't think you have any call to ask such questions about the estate's business.'

'Do you know, Mr Prosser,' McKenna said, 'I'm beginning to think the estate's business might bear a little scrutiny. All this strikes me as being somewhat irregular, to say the least. How could Ms Cheney, or anyone else come to that, know the cottage was for rent?'

There was a silence at the end of the telephone line. McKenna waited patiently. 'Well,' Prosser volunteered eventually, 'she probably saw an advertisement.'

'Where do you advertise?'

'I don't advertise anywhere.' Smug satisfaction coloured Prosser's voice.

'Mr Prosser, are you aware I could arrest you now for obstruction? How d'you fancy swapping your cosy office for a cell?'

Prosser's laugh tinkled over the line. 'Oh, Chief Inspector, no need to be like that. Indeed, no . . . always willing to help. Why not call the trust headquarters? They deal with all the advertising. A lot of properties are let out during the summer months, and again from autumn until Easter. Quite normal procedure, I do assure you.'

'Why did Ms Cheney pay in cash?'

'Did she?' Prosser asked. 'I really couldn't say, Chief Inspector. Why don't you ask her?' McKenna heard Prosser put down the receiver very gently.

Clearly implying errands for other forces were of minimal importance, Derbyshire police grudgingly promised a response on Robert Allsopp's current whereabouts by the end of the week, by which time, McKenna thought, the investigation would have lost what little impetus remained. Curiosity about the dead woman nudged at him, posing questions to which he had no answers: why had no one missed her, how could she be so solitary that her disappearance had gone totally unremarked. If she was indeed the erstwhile tenant of that haunted cottage, she had spent thousands of pounds on a place she would never own simply to live in comfort for a few months.

Jack returned empty-handed from his visit to Special Branch. 'They weren't exactly helpful.'

'They never are,' McKenna said. 'Unless they want something. What did they say?'

Jack's eyes flashed with anger. 'Well, apart from implying we should go forth and multiply instead of bothering them, nothing! Who the bloody hell,' he added, jaw muscles bunching, 'do they think they are?'

'Special Branch.' McKenna said. 'With the emphasis on the special bit. We're just old PC Plod . . .' He leaned back in his chair. 'Rude, were they?' he asked.

'Rude?' Jack almost shouted. 'Bloody insulting!'

'Oh, well,' McKenna said. 'Our turn will come.' He grinned at Jack. 'I'd like you to fax the package about our body to the police in Ireland. On both sides of the border.'

'Why?'

'She doesn't seem to be missing in Britain, so she might be missing from Ireland, mightn't she?' McKenna said. 'It's but a short hop over the Irish Sea.'

'Oh, I see.' Jack frowned. 'D'you think the body's this woman from Gallows Cottage?'

'I hope so,' McKenna said. 'If she isn't, we may as well stop bothering now.' He eyed Jack speculatively. 'Don't you?'

'Ms Cheney at Gallows Cottage doesn't appear on any missing list, does she?' Jack said. 'Ms Cheney's most probably happily going about her usual business somewhere, in total ignorance anybody's looking for her. She rents that dump for a while, spends pots of money on it 'cos she's not short of a bob or two . . . and who's to say it was her money anyway? She might've rented it for the specific purpose of having a nice little place in the middle of nowhere for her dirty weekends . . . her and a married boyfriend . . . both of them married. Having it off when they got the chance down in the woods and nobody any the wiser. Beats the back seat of a car any day.' Jack grinned. 'Then, back home on a Monday morning, all respectable. That's probably why she paid the rent in cash. No records that way, no cheques to be explained to her husband or his wife.'

Disgust with Jack's graphic analysis of Ms Cheney's weekend sport pulled at McKenna's face. 'We've still got a body,' he said. 'And unless we can put a name to it, we'll never find out who killed her.'

Dr Roberts telephoned, excitement sparkling in his voice. 'I removed various organs, Michael, and tried to reconstitute them for section,' he said. 'With some success, I might add, even though I do say so myself!'

'Oh, yes?' McKenna sounded sour. 'And what have you found?'

'No heart disease, no liver disease, no kidney disease.'

'That's very interesting,' McKenna commented. 'We know she was healthy until somebody decided to string her up. Should aid the identification process no end.'

'God, McKenna, you're a sarcastic bugger! I gave you the bad news first,' Eifion Roberts snapped. 'I actually called to say the woman had had at least one, and possibly more than one, pregnancy.'

'Are you sure?' McKenna asked. 'How could you possibly tell from the state she was in?'

'You don't listen, do you? I reconstituted the organs. You may not know the uterus is the last one to decompose, because it's made as tough as old boots . . . came up almost as good as new . . . So good, in fact, it set me thinking of a way to provide donor organs.'

'Donor organs?'

Eifion Roberts's throaty laugh rumbled in McKenna's ear. 'Hundreds of graveyards choc-a-bloc with bodies, and their innards all going to waste.'

Dewi, too, returned empty-handed, and long before dusk.

'I told you to stay there until dark, Dewi Prys,' McKenna said. 'Why are you back so early? Have you found the buckle?'

'No, sir,' Dewi muttered. 'I don't reckon anyone'd be able to find anything down there.'

'Why not?'

Dewi looked at Jack, who stood feeding sheet after sheet of paper into the fax machine, then back to

McKenna. 'Well, sir, I mean, we don't even know what this buckle looks like, do we?'

'So?'

'So, it makes things a bit difficult . . .' Dewi paused. 'And,' he added, 'the whole place got really trampled about on Saturday, sir. If the buckle was around in the first place, it's probably under a load of mud by now . . .'

McKenna looked at the mud and grass-stains streaking Dewi's jeans. 'How did you get so dirty?' he asked.

'Because it's filthy dirty down there, sir,' Dewi said. 'You haven't seen it, have you? All mud and dead leaves and God knows what.'

Looking up from the fax machine, Jack said, 'Did you fall in the river, Prys?'

'No, sir,' Dewi said.

'Get lost then, did you?' Jack asked.

'Sort of,' Dewi admitted. His face flushed. 'Some stupid bugger's moved all that tape we left at the weekend, haven't they?'

'There's your answer, then,' Jack said to McKenna. 'He's back early because he was scared of getting lost in the woods. And I don't blame him, either.'

Chapter 7

Bored and irritable, convinced the woman in the woods and her death would remain forever a mystery, Jack spent Wednesday morning dealing with the paperwork accumulated since Saturday. Frowning over duty rosters for the coming month, he listened to Dewi Prys, at his most efficient, say over the telephone to Trefor Prosser, 'If you wish to be less than co-operative to an important investigation, sir, we can always obtain a court order to retain the ledgers. We have that power, sir, under the Police and Criminal Evidence Act. Of course, it also gives us the power to obtain any other documents which might be relevant . . . What other documents, sir? Well, we wouldn't know that 'til we had them, would we, sir?'

Returning from the canteen after lunch, Jack met a man walking along the corridor towards McKenna's office, a man of medium build and nondescript appearance, a grey sort of man, almost a ghost of a man.

'Can I help you?'

Grey eyes flicked over Jack's face, and away. 'No, thank you.' He continued on his way, reached McKenna's room, opened the door and walked in without knocking. The door closed quietly behind him.

Jack hesitated, then followed.

McKenna stood by the window, his face striped

with shadows from the venetian blind. The grey man sat on an upright chair in front of the desk. 'Who are you?' he asked Jack.

'This is Inspector Tuttle,' McKenna said. Turning to Jack, he added, 'This gentleman is from Special Branch, Jack. It appears our inquiries in Ireland have caused a little anxiety. Special Branch feel we might be treading on their toes.'

The grey man smiled. A most unwholesome smile, Jack thought. Like the wicked old woman in Hansel and Gretel. 'I said nothing about treading on toes, Mr McKenna. Do you have connections in Ireland, by the way? In the Republic?'

McKenna sat down. 'Why?'

'Why did you send details of this dead woman to the Royal Ulster Constabulary and the Garda in Dublin?'

'Because,' McKenna said, with a warning glance at Jack, 'she doesn't appear to be reported missing in Britain. Quite feasible she's Irish.'

'Oh, come now, Mr McKenna!' the grey man sneered. 'You can do better than that! You know as well as I do this killing has all the hallmarks of an execution. Death by hanging, in a remote spot, and the hands strapped up behind her back? Don't tell me you hadn't made the connection.'

'Then why didn't your mates say as much to Inspector Tuttle yesterday?' McKenna asked. 'He went all the way to Caernarfon to talk to you.'

'Don't play games, McKenna. You know the score, and you damn well know the procedure! You get told what you need to know, and nothing more.'

'Quite,' McKenna agreed. 'I therefore presumed there was nothing to know.'

'You,' the grey man insisted, 'have absolutely no right to contact police in Ireland. Thought you were being clever, did you? Thought you'd stir up the shit for us, did you?'

'I didn't think anything at all, as a matter of fact.' McKenna was smiling slightly. 'All we have done,' he continued, 'is to treat this as we would any other suspicious death. And of course, unlike you, we have not indulged in any paranoid over-reaction. As a matter of interest,' he added, lighting a cigarette, 'how did you know we made inquiries in Ireland?'

'Mind your own business!'

'Oh.' McKenna looked bored. 'I suppose one of your stooges over there rang up in a panic. Pity they've nothing better to do.'

The grey man stood, leaning his fists on the desk. 'You obviously haven't yet learned your place, McKenna. Rogue bloody coppers we can all do without. Particularly Irish ones!'

McKenna opened the door, and stood aside for the man to pass through. 'You know where the chief constable spends most of his time,' he said. 'I'm sure your boss will be getting together with him soon enough. They'll be able to have a nice little chat about it, won't they?'

'I don't know how you keep your temper!' Jack exploded as soon as the man was out of earshot. 'I thought the Gestapo'd been outlawed years ago.'

'He's just a playground bully.'

'What's he called?'

'I believe he's called Jones.' McKenna smiled, although Jack noticed a tremble in the hand holding McKenna's cigarette. 'They're all called Jones. They all look the same as well, so nobody can identify them.'

'His sort gives the security services a bad name,' Jack said. 'God knows where they dig 'em up.'

'D'you know, Jack,' McKenna sighed, 'I wish that bloody John Beti'd minded his own business! But for him, the woman could've stayed happily swinging from that tree until she turned to dust, and nobody any the wiser.'

Walking down to the canteen for coffee, Jack thought about the man from Special Branch, and about the dividing line, at times almost non-existent, between those who made evil, and those whose job it was to fight the wickedness. He was in the canteen queue, standing behind a pretty policewoman with the scent of fresh air on her uniform and in her hair, before he realized McKenna had quite deliberately provoked Special Branch with the Irish inquiries.

Wil Jones the builder, one of those Joneses whom God must have loved because He made so many of them, McKenna thought, paraphrasing Abraham Lincoln on the ordinary people of this world, turned up at the police station at precisely 16.57, according to the report made out by the duty officer. Covered in dust, his shoes gritty with sand, Wil sat on the edge of a chair in McKenna's office.

'You're not going to be too happy about this, Mr McKenna,' Wil offered. 'I reckon we've found you another body. In the ground where we was digging the trench to the septic tank that isn't there yet. You've no idea the trouble we're having digging, which is why I reckon nobody bothered before. We started off in one direction yesterday, got so far, and the bloody sides of the trench kept caving in. All sand, you see, once you get a bit away from the cottage. Anyway, this morning, I said to Dave, we'll go another way, p'raps find better ground. So we did. Been at it all day,' he went on, glancing at the wall clock. 'Then Dave, he jumps out of where he was digging, like he'd been bitten by a snake, and starts yelling fit to wake the dead! I looks, and there it was. A leg, as far as I can make out. And a foot on the end of it.'

'Would you like a cup of tea, Wil?' McKenna asked.

'I'll have a quick one. Don't want to be too long away. I left Dave on his own, and it's not fair on him.' Wil shivered. 'Not in that place, fair play.'

Dr Roberts looked with some pleasure at the foot and lower leg extruding from the right side of the drainage trench. 'Well preserved, Michael,' he said. 'Most interesting. No doubt because of the acid nature of the soil.'

'Well, you might be able to reconstitute some organs for donor use, then, mightn't you?' McKenna snapped. 'Save a bit of grave robbing, won't it? Especially if nobody owns up to this body either!'

The doctor regarded McKenna, a little smile lingering around his mouth. 'D'you know, Michael, people say Jack has a sharp tongue at times,' he observed. 'Could strip paint with yours, you could.'

McKenna stalked off. 'Oh, get on with it! Dig it up, or whatever you intend to do, and tell me when you've finished.' He stopped, then walked back. 'And its hands had better not be bound. I've had enough of executions to last me a long time.'

He disappeared into the cottage, while Jack stood by the trench, watching as the pathologist instructed Dewi, another officer, and two of the forensic team, on ways and means of disinterring the body without causing further damage.

The work was made easier for them by the same factor which frustrated Wil. Peaty, crumbly soil trickled away from the trench side, exposing the other foot, then more of each leg. Patiently and carefully, the soil was brushed away, pushed into heaps well away from the body. Bits of fabric came with it, shreds of some thick cotton, bereft of any colour. Jack stood with Dr Roberts, watching and waiting.

'What's wrong with your boss these days?' Roberts asked. 'He's always been one to speak his mind, but he's really on a short fuse at the moment. Give himself a heart attack if he's not careful. Trouble with that flighty wife of his, is it?'

'Denise? Flighty?' Jack asked. 'Plain bored, more likely.'

'Well, happen you don't know her so well.' Dr Roberts chewed his lower lip. 'Flighty and frivolous, our Denise. Takes after her mother in that way. Not right for McKenna at all. Too shallow. He needs a woman with a bit of bite to her.' He paused. 'A woman with fire in her belly, like him. There's the heat of a lot of passions in that man, Jack.'

'Well, it doesn't give off much warmth for others most of the time,' Jack commented.

Eifion Roberts stared. 'It won't, will it, with only Denise for company,' he said. 'It'll just burn up McKenna to a cinder. I reckon it's the end of the road for those two.' The pathologist peered over the side of the trench. 'Best thing, too, if you want my opinion. That marriage was doomed from the start. Denise only married him because he was a good catch, so she could climb up the social ladder on his back.'

'McKenna's not exactly socially prominent,' Jack said.

'That's the trouble, isn't it? Denise thought she'd be getting something she wanted, and now things aren't going her way, she wants out. You mark my words, Jack,' the doctor went on, walking forward to look properly over the lip of the trench, 'within six months or so, our Denise'll have found herself somebody more to her liking. Golf-club type, with a fancy house and big posh car. I'll put money on it.'

McKenna sent Wil and Dave home, taking the keys to Gallows Cottage. Night cloud gathered in the east, drawing a blanket over the day, as he made his way back to the trench, and stood with Jack and Eifion Roberts as more and more of the body was exhumed from its resting place. A drift of woodsmoke scented the dusky air, gulls screamed, a flock of birds streamed out over the sea to their night's roost on Puffin Island. Save for the slither of soil against shovel, the heavy breathing of the four men in the trench, the gardens of Gallows Cottage lay swaddled in silence. McKenna heard a noise behind him, a crepitation of leaves, and turned. A figure slid from view into the woods, the figure of a man, garbed in a white flowing shirt, long dark hair framing a thin, sallow face. McKenna made as if to call out, but when he looked properly, there was no one there.

'SHIT!'

Dr Roberts plunged forward. 'What is it? What've you done?'

The four men in the trench stood pressed against its far side, watching as earth cascaded, bringing the body with it. She fell out of her grave at their feet, a small pathetic thing, and rolled on to her side, coming to rest with her head against Dewi's boots. Her neck was stretched and thin, the head pulled hard to one side by the remnants of noose and rope. Her hands were behind her back, their fingers clenched and clawed. A thick strap bound her wrists, and began to crack and crumble to powder as they watched.

'Seventeen ninety-three. I'm answering your question, McKenna. She's been here since 1793, or thereabouts.' Dr Roberts knelt by the body, looking up.

'How can you possibly know that?' McKenna demanded. 'If you can't tell us how many months the other one's been hanging around, how can you possibly say how many years this one's been here?'

Dr Roberts stood up, brushing soil from the knees of his trousers. He climbed out of the trench, assisted by Jack. 'It's Rebekah, listed on official documents as "Wife of Simeon the Jew". Close your mouth, Michael!' he said. 'You'll swallow a fly if you're not careful, then you'll be like that old lady who had to swallow a spider to catch the fly.' He surveyed McKenna speculatively. 'Be interesting doing an autopsy on you after you'd swallowed the horse, wouldn't it?'

Jack giggled. McKenna glared at him and the doctor. 'Are you having a bit of fun at my expense?' he demanded.

'No, I'm not. Straight up, this is, in your criminal

parlance.' Dr Roberts removed his surgical gloves. 'After you'd told me that yarn the other day, I went to look in the archives in Caernarfon. It's all there, word for word as you heard it. This is your Rebekah, final resting place finally found. It actually says "Resting place unknown" in the records. What a thing, eh? They'll be able to fill in the gaps and draw a line under that story now. She'll have to have a proper funeral, of course. Wonder who'll arrange that?' he asked. 'Wouldn't be quite right just to throw her into an unmarked grave and toss quicklime on her, would it? She's a bit of history.'

'Will you be cutting her up?' Jack asked.

'Oh, most certainly.' Dr Roberts surveyed the body. 'Very interesting it'll be, as well. I've never had occasion to autopsy an executed criminal before. They'd abolished the death penalty before I started practising, you know. Be able to see how efficient they were in those days, won't I?' he added, sneaking a look at McKenna.

'I think you've got something wrong with you, I really do,' McKenna told him. 'You treat these poor devils like specimens or something!'

'Well, this one at least is a bit academic, so to speak, isn't she?'

'Are you really sure it's Rebekah, Dr Roberts?' Jack asked.

'Look for yourselves,' he invited. 'Come on, McKenna, there's no need to be squeamish. She won't bite.'

'Not all of us share your ghoulish interest in corpses,' McKenna snapped. 'How can you be so sure it's this Rebekah?'

'She's virtually mummified,' the pathologist said. 'Comes from being in ground like this. If she'd been put anywhere else, she'd be nothing but dust by now.' He turned to the four men waiting silently in the trench. 'Let's move her, shall we? And make sure you put all those bits of fabric in with her. I want those.'

Jack and the pathologist walked together to the parked cars and the mortuary van, McKenna in front, but close enough to hear the pathologist's conversation. 'D'you know, Jack, after the riots at Strangeways Prison, they had to dig up the burial ground for the new extensions,' he was saying. 'Took nearly forty bodies out of there, and gave them a proper Christian burial.'

'Who were they?' Jack wanted to know.

'About fifty years' worth of executions, if not more. I've got some details on it at home, if you'd care to have a read. Who they were, why they were topped, when . . .'

McKenna left them gossiping by the vehicles, and walked a little way into the woods. Darkness closed about him and, within a few paces, he was out of sight and earshot of the others, surrounded by whispering silence. Hopeless, of course, to expect to find the man he had seen, or follow the way he had gone. The familiar smell of rotting leaves and damp filled his mouth and nose. He stood for a while, trying to look through the trees, then turned to go back to the others, and knew a moment's panic when he thought he might be lost. Only headlights glimmering at the edge of the wood as one of the cars set off up the track showed him the way out.

*

Rebekah's pitiful remains lay on the autopsy table in the hospital mortuary, denuded now of the scraps of cloth which had hung from her shrivelled flesh. Looking at her, Dr Roberts felt it would be almost sacrilege to cut into her, as if destroying a little of his own history with a few strokes of the scalpel.

Emrys stood beside him. 'D'you really think we ought to, Doctor?' he asked. 'Two hundred years you said she'd been there. Why are we doing this?'

'We're doing it for several reasons, Emrys, one of which is scientific research,' Dr Roberts said. 'Another one is simple curiosity, and the fact, of course, if she'd been left on the gibbet like they usually were instead of being carted off by her hubby, the powers-that-be would've cut her up at the time, so they could certify how she died.'

'Pretty obvious, I'd've thought.'

'Procedure, Emrys . . . You can't say for sure how a body died unless you cut it up, even if you were the one who killed it.' He picked up a scalpel, and fingered its blade thoughtfully. 'Anyway, despite what I told McKenna, we really do need to make sure this body is as old as I think, and therefore who I think.'

'Even if it's as old as that, you can't be sure it's Rebekah.'

'Well, no. But who else is she likely to be? Eh?' He placed the scalpel at the throat, whilst Emrys held the twisted limbs and trunk as straight as possible. The doctor laughed. 'Let's hope it is Rebekah, Emrys. McKenna'll have a blue fit if any more corpses turn up round there, especially one's that've been hung!'

Jack and Emma lay side by side, gazing up at the

bedroom ceiling, watching patterns flow across sculpted plaster as moonlight beyond the uncurtained window fled back and forth behind scudding cloud.

'What d'you think Michael and Denise are doing now, Jack?' Emma asked, her voice soft.

'Not what we've just been doing, that's for sure!' His teeth gleamed wolfishly in the silvery light.

'Don't be so crude!' Emma exclaimed. 'I was being serious.'

'Sorry, love.' Jack was still smiling to himself. 'Why are you bothered, anyway?'

'They're our friends, in a way,' Emma said. 'At least, Denise is my friend.'

Jack sighed. 'McKenna's been in a hellish mood all day. People are beginning to talk.'

'Did you ask him what was wrong?'

'Not my business, really, is it?' Jack said. 'We don't have the sort of relationship where I can go barging in asking personal questions.'

Emma put her arm across his chest, twisting the wiry dark hairs in her fingers. 'People need to have friends to talk to. Denise has got me and her sisters.'

'She's all right then, isn't she?' Jack snapped, and turned over, his back to Emma.

Chapter 8

'Oh, SHIT!'

'Jack, please!' Emma flashed a warning glance in the direction of the twins.

'What's up?' one of the girls asked. 'Who was that on the phone, Mummy?'

'Nobody.'

'Mummy! You've been talking to yourself again!' Both girls erupted in a fit of giggles.

Jack slapped his hand on the table. 'That's enough! Get ready for school. Now!'

The twins rose from the table and went into the hall to gather books and bags and coats. Jack heard them muttering and laughing, lost as usual in their own world.

'Are you taking them to school or should they get the bus?' Emma asked.

'They can go for the bus. They're quite old enough.'

'Don't take it out on them, Jack. It's not their fault.' Emma went after her children, fussing about raincoats and the weather, and money for lunch and bus fares. The front door slammed, footsteps skittered along the garden path. Emma returned to the kitchen and slumped in her chair.

'What do we do now?'

'How the hell should I know?' Jack demanded. 'What exactly did Denise say?'

'She said Michael told her he's leaving her. Just like that, completely out of the blue.' Shock still tarnished Emma's voice. 'She wants me to go round right away.'

'Why? What are you supposed to do about it?' Jack asked. 'Anyway, it's hardly out of the blue, is it? What else did you expect?'

'Oh, I don't know!' Emma was distressed, and it angered Jack that other people's dramas, their selfishness, should intrude on his own family.

'Em, there's nothing to be done.' He touched her hand. 'They've got to sort out their own problems.'

'I know . . . I know,' Emma said. 'But I can't just leave her in the lurch. She'll be relying on me.'

'To hold her hand, I suppose,' Jack observed. 'And agree that her husband's a rotten miserable bastard!'

'Please!' Emma cried. 'Michael's been a bit brutal. You can't deny that.'

He stood up. 'I'm going to work, Em. God knows what state McKenna'll be in,' he said. 'And if you want my opinion, I think Denise is up the wall because it wasn't her decision.'

'What d'you mean?'

'Oh, use your brains, Em. She wanted to leave *him*, have a big drama,' Jack said. 'Be centre stage in the big dramatic role of the wronged wife. He's really taken the wind out of her sails, hasn't he? Cut her right down to size . . .' he added. 'Well, she could still have her starring part; all she needs to do is change the words a bit, become the abandoned wife. Serves her right, if you ask me!'

'I wasn't asking you!' Emma snapped. 'You're getting to be as cruel and nasty as he is!'

Dewi Prys hunched over the computer in the CID office.

'What're you doing?' Jack asked.

Dewi looked up. 'Morning, sir. Mr McKenna had one of his brainwaves. He's like a dog with two tails this morning.' Dewi grinned. 'You remember we had the name of a bloke who lived at the address where this Ms Cheney was supposed to be? Well anyway, Mr McKenna's told me to put that name – it's Allsopp – through all the missing persons on the list to see if it matches.'

'And does it?' Jack wondered how McKenna could possibly be in a good mood.

'Dunno yet, but I haven't been at it long. Keep our fingers crossed, eh, sir?' He punched more keys, and gazed at the screen. Jack decided to leave him to it.

'Sir!' Dewi called out. 'Sir, Mr McKenna said to remind you the Press conference is at half ten.'

'Where is the chief inspector, Prys?'

'Don't know, sir. He was talking to the superintendent last time I saw him.'

'This is sad news, Michael,' Owen Griffiths said. 'Are you sure there's no other way?'

'No point in prolonging the agony, is there?'

'I suppose not . . .' The superintendent sighed. 'I don't know, Michael . . . the number of times I hear of policemen's marriages going down the drain, and often, there's no reason you can lay a finger on.'

'Not much point in looking for reasons,' McKenna

said crisply. 'These things happen. I told Denise I'd move out as soon as possible.'

'Then why not take the day off to look for somewhere? Jack can deal with the Press. Nothing much to tell them, anyway.'

Questions, McKenna realized: Jack would ask questions, would want to know why routines were disrupted, set plans thrown to the winds. There would be intrusions into his privacy, and gossip; others would know of this most private thing, and speculate. Denise would talk to her friends and family and Emma Tuttle; her family would whisper and make judgements and spread their mischief through the chapel grapevine, and Emma would talk to Jack.

'Michael?'

'Yes, Owen?'

'People are bound to talk. But it'll be nothing more than a nine days' wonder . . . What're you going to do about Jack? He's bound to know from your Denise telling his Emma.'

McKenna sat on a wooden bench in the Bible Gardens, under a huge horse-chestnut tree, its candles still green among brilliant emerald leaves tossing in the wind. Gorgeous weather, blustery and warm, promised enough to lift the dourest of spirits. Waiting to meet an estate agent to view a house to let, he felt light-headed, detached, as if making a decision had taken away an intolerable burden. Still anaesthetized, he knew pain and doubt would come later.

The garden, laid out, according to the plaque by its wrought-iron gates, 'For Your Pleasure' by one Tatham Whitehead, nestled below the cathedral yard.

Had Tatham been a man or a woman? McKenna wondered idly, picturing a goodly Puritan fellow, pounding the pulpit in chapels across the land, intent on saving the lawless Welsh from themselves. And where had it got Tatham? Same place as everyone else in the end: mouldering bones, flesh gone to the worms and grubs. Nothing mattered, McKenna decided. His own little tragedy was nothing, a speck of dust on the winds of time, having no memorial, except in his own heart while he still lived. No one would come this way in a hundred years' time and say, 'Oh, yes, Michael McKenna sat under this tree the day after he told his wife he was leaving her.' Neither pleasure nor pain would he leave behind him, no green shoots to delight the eye as Tatham had.

A fat tabby cat crossed the path, stood eyeing McKenna, its pupils tiny slits in the sunshine. He smiled. The cat stared a while longer, then moved on about its mysterious business.

Pleased with himself for his professional touches at the Press conference, Jack could not suppress a smile at the memory of television cameras almost constantly focusing on his own face.

'Stop preening,' Eifion Roberts said. 'Where's Michael? He should've been there.'

'Gone off somewhere.'

'Stop hedging. What's happened?'

'Only what you predicted,' Jack said, relief mingling with the reluctance to talk. 'He's told Denise he's leaving her.'

'Doesn't let any grass grow under his feet, does he?' Dr Roberts said admiringly. 'How d'you know?'

'Denise rang Emma first thing this morning.'

The pathologist fiddled with the paper clips on Jack's desk, shoving aside papers and reports to find enough to make a chain.

'Stop that, will you? You're getting on my nerves,' Jack said.

'Sorry, SIR!' Eifion Roberts saluted. 'Can't have you upset as well, can we? Where's McKenna gone off to?'

'I don't know. He spoke to the superintendent, then disappeared.'

'Oh, well, he'll turn up. Don't expect we'll have any call to go fishing his body out of the Straits,' the pathologist observed. 'He's made of sterner stuff.'

'What are you talking about?'

'Suicide. I'm saying Michael's not likely to do himself in. Won't throw himself off the Menai Bridge, even if things are a bit lousy at the moment.'

'I never for one moment imagined he would!'

'Exactly. I'm agreeing with you,' Dr Roberts smiled. 'When you see him, tell him I found a mummified little foetus in poor Rebekah's tum, will you? Obviously didn't have any qualms about hanging expectant mums in those days.'

Unlike the elusive Ms Cheney, McKenna paid six months' rent by cheque, on a narrow three-storey house set in a terrace on a mountainous street overlooking the city, and bought himself a hiding place, a respite wrapped around with old-fashioned comfort. From his windows, he could look to Puffin Island in the east, to the lego blocks of the new hospital far over to the west. The Menai Straits glittered in noonday sunshine, a huge dredger unloading its cargo of sand far away at the old port. Immediately beyond a tiny back garden, the land fell sharply to the back yards of High Street shops, small patchworks where nature ran amok over ancient outbuildings. Ash and rowan trees grew on the slope, their branches dipping and swaying in the wind. A scruffy cat crouched on the slate wall dividing the house from next door, its black and white coat dusty and unkempt.

Jack wandered back and forth from his office to the general office, badgering Dewi for information the computer could not yield. No one named Allsopp had disappeared anywhere, at any time; nothing was forthcoming about the clothing and belt taken from the dead woman; no one called to claim her as their missing wife or daughter or sister or niece. He fidgeted with files and pieces of paper, and breathed a sigh of relief when McKenna walked through the door.

'You OK, sir?' Jack asked, and regretted the words as soon as they were spoken.

McKenna nodded. 'I wondered if you'd do me a favour?'

'Of course.'

'I've rented a house on Caellepa,' McKenna said. 'I could do with some help moving in. How are you fixed for Saturday?'

'Fine. No problem,' Jack said. 'Emma and the twins are off to this big wedding, and Em'll twist my arm to go with them if I don't have a good excuse.'

'Denise is going,' McKenna said, his eyes opaque behind the spectacles. 'It's the daughter of the revered chairman of our police authority. Councillor Williams, CBE.'

'I know. Big chapel do, all the trimmings.' Jack grimaced. 'Not my idea of a fun day out . . .' He looked up. 'Williams hasn't got a CBE, has he?'

'Yes, he has.' McKenna smiled. 'Chairman of Bloody Everything! You should go and shake the man's hand, get matey with him. Tell him how beautiful his daughter is, even though she's like the side of a house. Could do your career no end of good.'

Jack laughed. 'Brought her down to earth, did it? With an almighty crash, I hope!'

'You're horrible!' Emma had tears in her eyes again. 'Denise was only trying to protect herself. Then the solicitor said she probably wouldn't get a penny maintenance and she'd have to sell the house. It's not fair,' Emma railed. 'It's not right! *He*'s walking out. Not her.'

'What d'you expect him to do?' Jack demanded. 'Stay with the miserable bitch, or spend the rest of his life letting her bleed him dry? Some choice, I don't think.'

'What choice has he given her?' Emma snapped. 'And don't call Denise a miserable bitch! She's my friend.'

'She is a miserable bitch, Emma,' Jack said. 'And a spoilt one, as well.'

'I suppose you're sticking by him now, aren't you?' Emma almost spat at him. 'I suppose he's been slagging her off all day.'

'He's got more about him,' Jack snapped. 'She's

doing enough slagging off for both of them by the sounds of it!'

'What d'you expect?' Emma shouted. 'He's pulled the rug right out from under her. She'll have nowhere to live. How can she possibly afford to buy another house?'

'Then she'll have to rent a house like he's doing,' Jack said grimly. 'And get off her backside and find a job. My goodness!' he exclaimed. 'That'd be a miracle, wouldn't it? Our Denise getting her ladylike hands dirty.'

Emma stared at him. 'He's moving already? Where's he going?'

'I'm not telling you, Emma. It's not your business. He'll tell Denise if and when he wants to.'

'I never thought the day would come when you'd treat me like this. Never!' The tears spilled over, and she scrubbed at her face with the cuff of her cardigan.

'Don't cry, love.' Jack reached out, and she backed away.

'Don't you touch me!' Emma shouted. 'Leave me alone! And don't you dare come crawling to me in bed! You can sleep in the shed for all I care!'

Chapter 9

'What is it, Dewi?' McKenna, morning sunshine highlighting the shadows painted by misery's palette about his eyes, smiled vaguely at the young detective standing rather uncomfortably at the office door.

'I wouldn't bother you, sir, only Mr Tuttle's like a bear with a sore head this morning, snapping at anything moving, so I thought you'd better see these.' He placed a pile of flimsy paper on the desk. 'They're faxes, sir. Come in overnight on the missing women.'

'Anything useful?'

'No, sir. Not a thing,' Dewi said. 'I suppose you can always look at it the other way, and say we know who the woman isn't. Narrowed it down a lot.'

'You should be an alchemist, Dewi. Turn negative into positive,' McKenna said. 'How many are we left with?'

'Forty-one. The Irish police don't reckon there's anyone missing who'd fit the description. Seems not half so many women go missing in Ireland.'

'Which police in Ireland?' McKenna asked. 'North or South?'

'That lot in Dublin.'

McKenna grinned at him. 'Well, don't be surprised if we don't hear from the police in the North . . .

although we might well have a response from Special Branch.'

'Them?' Dewi looked as if he would like to spit. 'Wouldn't give you the dirt from under their fingernails if they could help it. We may as well write off Northern Ireland, then. Sir, d'you mind if I ask you something?'

'Not at all, Dewi.'

'It occurred to me when we were looking through the computer files . . . I just wondered where all these missing people go.'

'I don't really know,' McKenna admitted. 'Maybe some of them just can't stand things any more, and run away . . . escape . . . some are probably on a life insurance fiddle, because the family can have them declared dead after seven years, and collect the money.' He paused, then said, 'I think quite a few may well be murder victims.'

'My nain reckons some of them fall off the edge of the world,' Dewi grinned. 'She still won't have it the earth's not flat. She says you couldn't see the horizon otherwise.'

'Dr Roberts left a message for you yesterday.'

'Did he, Jack?' McKenna asked. 'What is it?'

'Said to tell you Rebekah was pregnant. About three months gone.'

'Oh, I see.' Jack's face was drawn, his eyes red-rimmed. 'What's wrong?'

Jack hesitated for a moment before replying. 'Did you speak to Mrs McKenna last night, sir?'

'She's gone to stay with her sister.'

'Oh.'

'Jack, unless whatever is worrying you is entirely private, perhaps you should tell me.'

'Bloody hell!' Jack exploded. 'It's like telling tales out of school!' He squirmed in his seat. 'Oh, sod it! I had a row with Emma, and ended up sleeping on the sofa, and I can't remember the last time that happened.'

'And I suppose the row was about Denise and myself?'

'Too right,' Jack agreed. 'And whether or not I should say so,' he added, 'I think you're well rid of her. She saw a solicitor yesterday, and dragged Em along to hold her hand, and had a hell of a shock when the solicitor said she couldn't expect you to keep her for the rest of her days. I'm sorry, I really am, because she should have told you herself. Oh, God!' He buried his head in his hands. 'What a mess!'

'I see,' McKenna said slowly. 'Well, no point in fretting, Jack. The mess'll get bigger before it gets smaller.' He lit a cigarette, drawing smoke hungrily into his lungs. 'Don't make things worse by falling out with Emma.'

At lunchtime, Mary Ann telephoned, wanting McKenna to visit. Thinking she had no doubt heard of his split with Denise, he told Dewi to say Jack would go instead.

'Mary Ann says she's got to see you, sir.'

'What does she want, Dewi?'

'I don't know,' Dewi said. 'But she doesn't know Mr Tuttle, does she, and these old ladies can be peculiar about talking to strangers.'

'I've not got you here to talk about yourself, young

man,' Mary Ann said, closing the door behind McKenna. 'If you want to say anything to me, I'll listen, but I'm not one for poking my nails into other people's wounds.'

'How are you?' McKenna asked.

'Middling,' she said, easing her bones into the armchair. 'Fair to middling at best. Can't expect much else at my time of life, can I? I should be grateful I can still get about.'

They sat in silence for a while, shouts from the schoolyard beyond the open windows of her cottage disturbing the quiet.

'Don't you think it's strange the seagulls don't come here?' McKenna commented.

'Too many trees,' Mary Ann said. 'Gulls like open spaces. Plenty of rooks and crows, though,' she added. 'Hundreds in the trees by the church, and more each year . . . sitting up in those high branches cawing and shrieking at each other from morning 'til night . . . it's like that film, sometimes. I half expect to see them swoop down on the kiddies out playing, tearing their hair and pecking their eyes out.'

'Do many children live in the village?'

She thought for a moment. 'D'you know, I doubt there's any nowadays, never were that many . . . My lad was always begging us to move, but his dad worked on the estate, and the cottage went with the job.' She paused, looking down avenues of time. 'Tied cottages. Tied down the folk in them as good as slaves.'

'Weren't you expected to move out when your husband died?'

'In the old days, there'd be no choice,' Mary Ann

said. 'Could've freezed to death in a field for all them at the castle cared . . . By the time Dafydd passed on,' she went on, 'most of these cottages were sold, because there wasn't hardly anybody working the estate any longer. They'd run out of money, see. Frittered it away on high living and fineries. One of the sons gambled away the few coppers left over. A fortune they had, Michael. A fortune . . .' she said grimly. 'Still, I get to stay here as long as I pays the rent every week. Not that I get much for it . . . not even a bathroom, in this day and age. Have to make do with the kitchen sink and the *tŷ bach*.'

'Don't you ever feel bitter?' McKenna asked. 'Hard done by?'

'I've a roof over my head as long as I need it. It's enough. At one time, I'd've liked my own place,' Mary Ann said. She grinned. 'I used to feel so bad with jealousy sometimes I gave myself the bellyache! Seeing the girls I went to school with getting wed and buying a little house somewhere nice in Bangor, getting it ready for the babies . . . Then you see them a bit later on,' she went on, the smile gone, 'when there's another mouth or two to feed, with grey hairs at twenty-five, worrying about paying the house loan, and bitter, hating their husband because he isn't bringing enough money in to pay the bills. More than one marriage I've seen go to the devil that way.' She struggled to her feet, and went to the kitchen to make tea. 'No cake today, Michael,' she called out. 'I've fallen out with Beti Gloff . . . temporarily, you might say.'

'Why?' McKenna followed, leaning against the doorframe, watching the old woman creep from sink to cooker in the dingy little lean-to. 'What's she done?' he asked.

'Well, she does messages for me on account of my legs, and for Mair and Faith as well,' Mary Ann said, putting a match to the gas stove. 'Our Beti likes going off to town, so it's no hardship . . . gets her away from that useless husband of hers, except on pension day when he goes with her.' She leaned on the table, waiting for the kettle to boil. 'She fiddles the cash a bit, you see. Adds fifty pence or so here and there to the bills, shortchanges us, even though we all pay her for going. I know she does it, Mair knows, Faith knows, and Beti knows we all know, but every so often, it doesn't hurt to remind her, if you get my meaning.'

He laughed. 'No flies on you, is there, Mary Ann?'

'I like to think not,' she said. 'Not like that poor little thing you dug up the other day. Rebekah, was it?'

'We think so,' McKenna nodded.

'I told young Dewi,' Mary Ann said, 'they should burn that Gallows Cottage to the ground. It's an evil place.'

'The woman who lived there a few years back had some building work done. Any idea who did it?'

'Did you know she paid for it, as well?' Mary Ann said. 'Paying through the nose in rent, and doing it up into the bargain. Must've wanted her head seeing to! It wasn't anybody local did the work,' she added. 'Saw the vans once or twice. From somewhere Manchester way, but I couldn't say where . . . didn't take any real notice. Now, if I'd known it was important, I could have, but I didn't, did I?'

'How d'you know she paid for the work?'

'How do folk know anything?' She shrugged. 'I seem to recall Prosser told the vicar.'

'The vicar doesn't remember seeing the woman at all. Says she never went to church.'

'He wouldn't, would he?' Mary Ann sneered. 'Pickled any brains he ever had in gin, he has. Has a hard job remembering to go to church himself of a Sunday, by all accounts.'

McKenna took the tray of tea, and carried it into the parlour. She followed, shuffling and snickering. 'Nothing to beat a bit of nasty gossip, is there?' Sitting down again, she added, 'I've a bit more gossip. That's why I asked you here. Beti wanted to tell you herself, because it's her gossip, only I wouldn't let her because she's been a bad girl, diddling us out of our pennies. I don't know if it's any use to you,' she rattled on, 'and I really can't say whether Beti isn't making it up, looking for a slice of the attention John Jones got for finding the body, but she reckons she's seen the car that woman from Gallows Cottage was driving. And very recent. Round Bangor, she said, and going along towards the council estate.' Mary Ann smiled at the expression on McKenna's face. 'Says there was a man driving it, but she couldn't see his face.'

'There must be thousands of cars like that on the roads,' McKenna said. 'How could Beti know it was the right one?'

'I asked her that, didn't I?' Mary Ann said. 'Said she couldn't get you on another wild goose chase. She swears it's the same car because there's some odd-looking ornament dangling in the back window. Sort of thing she'd notice, you know, even if she hasn't a clue otherwise.'

He poured out tea, and offered Mary Ann another cigarette. 'D'you think Beti would come to the police station to look at some photographs of cars?'

'Oh, she'd love a bit of excitement like that. Just so long as you send a police car for her.' Mary Ann's eyes gleamed with amusement.

'If I didn't have my wits about me,' McKenna said quietly, 'you'd lead me astray. If I send a police car for Beti, she might think you'd grassed her up about her little fiddles. Mightn't she? And that would be very exciting. Wouldn't it?'

Mary Ann smacked her hand on her knee. 'Worth a try, Michael! Send Dewi. He's got the patience of a saint, and he'll need it to get any sense from her. D'you know,' she went on, 'I can't help but wonder sometimes if Beti's not one room short of a house. She keeps wittering about that Simeon . . . swears blind she's seen him in the woods.'

'Simeon?' McKenna repeated. The memory of the elusive figure at the edge of the twilit woods on Wednesday swam to the surface. 'What does he look like?'

'I don't know what he looks like, do I?' Mary Ann said. 'I've never seen him. But there's always been talk in the village. Tales handed down . . . Beti says it must be Simeon because she knows everybody round here, and he's a stranger, but I said he could be one of them gipsies off the site down the road, doing a bit of poaching.'

'Does he look gipsyish, then?'

Mary Ann nodded. 'Longish dark hair, according to

Beti. Darkish skin. Thin, she said; sort of hungry-looking.'

'I might've seen him on Wednesday, when we dug up the body. In the woods,' McKenna said. 'He legged it when he saw me.'

'He would if he were up to no good, wouldn't he?' Mary Ann pointed out. 'If he's poaching, coming across a van-load of coppers is the last thing he wants.'

'Why don't we just put Mary Ann and Beti on the payroll?' Jack said tetchily. 'It's a bit galling, you know. Mary Ann mentions gipsies, so we hare off to the site. Beti sees a car, which, you must admit, sir, could be any of the millions of cars in Britain, so we rush up to see her with photographs. Don't you think,' he went on, 'there's a distinct possibility they're making monkeys out of us?'

'Even if they are,' McKenna said, 'there's bugger all we can do about it. What else have we got to investigate? And by the way, Jack, the assistant chief constable wants an interim report. So I thought you can write it up. Stretch your imagination a bit.'

'Oh, thanks very much! Why me? Training for promotion?'

'An exercise in creative thinking.'

'Well,' Jack reflected, 'if nothing else, it'll keep me out of Emma's way until she's calmed down a bit.'

A worm of unease wriggled in McKenna's gut. Not for one moment did he believe Emma would calm down unless she kept well away from Denise, who would be marshalling forces for an onslaught on her husband. Emotional, loyal Emma was ideal cannon fodder . . . He must warn Denise. There was no room in his conscience for another ruined marriage.

'What is it?' Jack asked.

'Eh?'

'What are you thinking about?'

'Oh, this and that . . .' McKenna said vaguely. 'John Beti finding the body when he did, for one thing. Doesn't that strike you as being rather odd?'

'No,' Jack said. 'Why should it?'

McKenna pulled a cigarette from the open packet lying on the desk. 'John Beti's lived in those woods for years. I daresay he knows every inch of them like the back of his hand. And I think Dewi was right about the poaching. Fresh salmon come upriver, not to mention rabbits and whatnot in the woods.'

'So?'

'So it's a bit hard to swallow, isn't it?'

'What is?'

'That John Beti has not,' McKenna said, lighting the cigarette, 'in the past three or four years, ever set foot in that particular part of the woods. And it is, therefore, rather strange he only found the body last week.'

'Maybe he didn't notice it before,' Jack said. 'It wasn't much more than a shadow in the trees, you know.'

'Maybe so,' McKenna said. 'I still think he knows more than he's letting on.'

'We could interview him again. Put the screws on . . .' Jack smiled. 'You never know, he might've topped her himself. Maybe she was his girlfriend, and threatened to tell on him to Beti. They do say,' he added, 'we should go after whoever finds the body.'

McKenna frowned. 'If John Beti's involved, it'll be more devious. That man's got a personality like an onion. You know, the more you peel away, the bigger the stink. I think he's blackmailing somebody.'

'And who would that be?'

'Whoever killed the woman, of course,' McKenna said. 'Who else?'

Chapter 10

Beti Gloff identified fourteen different cars as probably the one driven by the tenant of Gallows Cottage, still maintaining she would know the actual car if she saw it again.

'She did say all modern cars look the same, didn't she?' McKenna pointed out, when Jack told him.

'She's romancing,' Jack said. 'Or just plain batty. And by the way,' he added, 'rumour has it, according to Dewi Prys, that Jamie's up to some big-time thieving.'

'That so?' McKenna asked. 'Well, you might say thievery is Jamie's way of expressing his individuality, being somebody in the world and having his few minutes of fame. Don't let it bother you overmuch, Jack.'

Derbyshire police, fulfilling their promise, sent a fax late on Friday, providing Robert Allsopp's new address, and the information that Ms R. Cheney, his erstwhile mistress, had decamped some years previously, without a word of warning or farewell. Mr Allsopp expressed no surprise, no regret, as if the liaison was nothing more than a casual arrangement, enjoyable only while it lasted, and of no consequence at any time.

By late Sunday afternoon, McKenna was driving

eastwards towards Derbyshire, raincloud in the west following apace, Saturday a day he intended to forget, to thrust into the Stygian darkness of the subconscious. Nothing dramatic had taken place. He quietly packed up his belongings and moved, out of the marital home and Denise's life, out of the stagnant pool of his marriage, into uncharted waters, there to sink or swim, knowing as he did so it would be easier simply to walk back, to say he was sorry, to suffer whatever punishments and humiliations Denise might invent to garnish the rest of his days. She, pushed into waters equally stormy, would doubtless fare better, rescued by some full-rigged vessel, while he floundered, clinging to that bit of flotsam he labelled integrity.

Jack unpacked clothes and books and records, wired up the stereo system, made the bed, and went shopping for groceries and cigarettes and a bottle of whisky. He cooked a pan of spaghetti for supper, and after he left, midnight long gone, McKenna sat by the fire in the downstairs parlour, drinking, listening to music and a soft breeze whispering in the trees below the garden. He heard a cat sing outside the door. The black and white lady he had seen before crouched on the slate flags in the yard, staring with fluorescent eyes, backing away when he held out his hand. He put a dish of milk on the doorstep, and shut the door. When he looked again, the dish was licked clean, the yard empty. He went to bed, taking a sleeping tablet and a mug of hot chocolate, hoping for a little of the oblivion found by the woman in the woods.

Beyond Macclesfield, he began the long climb into the Pennines, stopping for dinner at the Cat and Fiddle Inn on the crest of a high moor, before the last leg of his journey through Buxton, and into a town distinguished by street after street of Victorian terraced houses, by tall old mills standing foursquare and turreted behind high walls, and by its inhabitants, remnants of invading Saxon hordes, their voices grating, words befouled by flat 'a's and mysterious dialect. He booked into a small hotel at the foot of Snake Pass, then walked along lanes and stony tracks until night fell swift and sudden, its silence punctuated only by his own soft footfalls and a keening wind off the moors.

Robert Allsopp occupied an elegant apartment, one of several in a large Edwardian mansion called Howard's End, the last of a group of large Edwardian mansions in the matured and manicured grounds of Howard Park on the outskirts of the town. And very literary, thought McKenna, parking outside the front entrance. The circular drive embraced smooth lawns around a great flowering tree, its icing of pink-white blossoms melting at its foot. A small row of bells, a name card inscribed in copperplate under each, hid within the front porch. McKenna put his finger to the bell of Flat 4 and waited. He rang again, and waited again, and watched as a shadowy figure grew larger and larger behind the ornate leaded glass of the inner door.

Invited into a spacious, luxurious room, he found Allsopp at breakfast, his table, set under the bay window, overlooking well-tended fields, and a red-brick farm with a little tower, its outlines blurred by rain gusting off the hills.

'I hardly expected you to come all this way to see me,' Allsopp remarked. 'Can I offer you some coffee?'

Around McKenna's age, Allsopp was shorter, more sturdily built, with quite piercing blue eyes. His appearance, the contents of his flat, suggested no dearth of money, no impact of recession on his well-ordered life.

'I don't wish to take up too much of your time, but there are some questions I must put to you.'

'Fire away.' Allsopp continued with his breakfast. He poured milk from a squat little jug laced with posies on to a heap of muesli in a matching bowl. Two croissants lay on a flower-decked plate. He pushed sugar and the milk jug towards McKenna. 'Help yourself.'

McKenna looked surreptitiously for an ashtray, in a room bearing that unsullied look peculiar to the homes of non-smokers. Allsopp bore the same look.

'You lived with a Ms Cheney for a while,' McKenna began. 'At your old address.'

'That's right.' Allsopp munched on his muesli.

'She rented a cottage in North Wales some three and half years ago,' McKenna went on.

'Did she?' Allsopp took a gulp of coffee, pushed aside the empty cereal bowl, and reached for the croissants.

'She didn't tell you?'

'No.' The croissants were torn apart, soft yeasty insides spread with low-fat margarine, and apricot jam from a tiny pot embellished with a picture of Chatsworth House and a coat of arms.

'Wasn't that a little strange? You were living together.'

'Yes.' Allsopp took a large bite of croissant, licking jam-sticky fingers: thick, sturdy fingers, more than capable of tying an efficient noose. 'She walked out on me.' What better way to explain her disappearance, McKenna thought?

'Did she say anything before she left?'

'No.' The second croissant went the way of its companion, washed down with more black coffee.

'Weren't you worried?'

'Why should I be? Up to her what she did with herself.'

'Mr Allsopp.' McKenna's temper began to make knots in his stomach. 'I have come a long way to see you. It really is most important you tell me everything you can about Ms Cheney.'

'Why?' The blue eyes turned full on him, strong and uncompromising. 'What she does is her own business.'

'We need to eliminate her from an investigation.'

'What investigation?'

'A murder investigation.'

'I see.' Allsopp finished his coffee, and stacked his plates on top of each other. 'Who's been murdered?'

'We don't know. That is why I must speak to Ms Cheney.'

Allsopp stood up, gathering the dirty dishes. 'Best of luck, then. If you find her, tell her to let me have my books back, will you? She took a set of Dickens' novels, in matching leather bindings, and I rather miss them.' He walked out of the room, and McKenna heard the sound of running water and clattering pots. Allsopp returned to find his visitor standing by the fireplace, smoking a cigarette. The two men stared at each other. Allsopp sighed. 'Look, I don't know what you're waiting for, but feel free to hang on until the rain lets up a bit.'

'Mr Allsopp, you have a choice.' McKenna tapped ash into the grate. 'You can talk to me here or you can talk to me at the police station.'

The man's face flushed. 'I'm beginning to feel just a little under pressure,' he said. 'Exactly what are you suggesting I might have done?'

'I don't know if you've done anything,' McKenna said quietly. 'You won't co-operate. At the very least, you are a material witness.'

'To what?'

'I've already told you: to a murder investigation.'

He stared at McKenna. McKenna stared back, until Allsopp sat down rather suddenly at the table. 'This is no joke, you know.'

'No one's joking,' McKenna said. 'I want to know every single thing you can tell me about Ms Cheney. And you can start by telling me her name.'

Allsopp looked not so much defeated as resigned; defeat a concept allowed no hold in his scheme of life. 'Give me a cigarette, will you? I'm trying to give up, stopped buying the things . . . Cheney was her maiden name.' He drew on the cigarette. 'She was called Margaret . . . Madge for short. She didn't think it suited her, so she called herself Romy. After some character in a Virginia Woolf novel.'

'And what was her married name? Come on!' McKenna snapped. 'Stop making me drag out every single word. It's your time we're wasting.'

'Bailey. Her husband was a Tom Bailey.'

'And where will I find him?'

'No idea,' Allsopp said. 'She'd left him before she met me . . . Bit of a bolter, if you ask me, but I didn't know that at the time. I met her at a party about five years ago, and we sort of clicked . . .' Jumped into bed together, McKenna interpreted sourly.

'Then what?'

'We decided to live together, see how it all panned out.'

'Where did she live with her husband?'

'Somewhere in Yorkshire. I'm not being difficult,' Allsopp said. 'She wouldn't talk about him, said it was all too painful . . . Wasn't up to me to intrude, was it?'

'Did she ever talk about children?'

'Children? Her children, you mean? Oh, no, she never had any children.'

'Are you sure about that?' McKenna frowned.

'Well, I can't be sure, can I? But she never talked about children, and women normally do, don't they?'

Allsopp poured coffee from a freshly brewed pot, found an ashtray, and begged another cigarette from McKenna. 'It never really occurred to me before,' he said, 'how secretive she was.'

'Why, d'you think?'

'I don't know. We had an odd sort of relationship . . . we weren't really close, and that suited me, I suppose. I don't like being wrapped up in other people. She went her way, and I went mine, most of the time.'

'Did you have other women friends? Other lovers?'

'Not while we were together. Nor, as far as I know, did she. But I could be right off the mark about that. It's not likely she'd have told me if she did.' He sipped his coffee, and smoked McKenna's cigarette. 'She gave me no warning, you know.' He looked at McKenna, the blue eyes cloudy. 'She just upped and left.'

'Did she leave much behind?'

'Some clothes, a few odds and ends . . . I gave them to Oxfam when I moved. There was no sign of her wanting them.'

'She must have taken some things. You mentioned some books.'

'Yes, I did, didn't I? I suppose I should've seen it coming . . . for some time before she left, she was going away weekends, and odd days during the week. And before you jump down my throat, I don't know where to. I'm away a lot on business, and I just assumed she was bored, going off to see friends. And no!' He held up his hand. 'If you offered me money, I couldn't give you the name of one single friend of hers. I never took that much notice.'

'You seem to have been remarkably uninvolved,' McKenna observed.

'People do what suits, don't they? I've already said: it suited me, and it suited her. Both of us grown up, nobody to answer to.'

'Did you miss her when she left?'

He scratched his head. 'Can you spare another cigarette? Thanks . . . To tell the truth, I was bloody seething! Here was I, gone to all the trouble of buying a house, buying furniture, setting it up, and for what?' Allsopp asked. 'Nothing, in the end. That's what I meant about her being a bolter. She'd probably done the same thing with her husband, and maybe other men, for all I know. Staying until the novelty wore thin, then off to trample the grass on the other side of the fence.'

'An opportunist.'

'No, just self-centred, I guess. Like me.'

'And you believe she left of her own free will?' McKenna asked.

'Oh, yes.'

'So you didn't think of reporting her as a missing person?'

'Would you have done? Suppose I had, and the police arrived in some little love nest . . . I simply wasn't worried about her. Just angry, as I said.'

McKenna read through his notes, filling in bits here and there in the very sketchy drawing defined by Allsopp's words, which might be nothing more than a web of lies, rehearsed over and again, in the event anyone ever came looking for his erstwhile paramour.

'How long is it since she left?'

'Four years ago October coming . . . late October, nearly November. I put the house on the market the following spring and it went almost right away. I was lucky. Got out before the market slumped.'

'What did she look like? How old was she?' McKenna asked.

'Thinnish, quite lanky, a bit shorter than me . . . about five foot eight or nine. Short brown hair, bleached somewhat. Her birthday's in January, around the seventh or eighth. She'd have been thirty-eight the next year.'

'Any scars? Any signs of old injuries? Any talk about having an accident when she was younger?'

'Not that I recall,' Allsop said. 'She was very healthy . . . surprising, really, because she drank red wine like most people drink water . . . addicted to the stuff, and never any the worse for it.'

'Did she ever talk of connections in North Wales?'

'No. I'm sure about that. Nothing at all.'

'And where did she work?'

'Work?' Allsopp raised his eyebrows. 'She didn't. I paid most of the household expenses. Romy had her own money. I presumed it was alimony.'

'She was divorced, then?'

Allsopp rubbed his hands over his face. 'I don't know! I've told you, she wouldn't talk about it. I assumed she was.'

'I've nearly finished,' McKenna said. 'Although you'll be expected to make a formal statement. What kind of car did she drive?'

'A metallic grey Ford Scorpio. She bought it during the summer . . . traded in a Mercedes, which, I presumed, was spoils of the marriage.'

'Any chance you remember the licence number?'

'Sorry.' Allsopp shook his head. 'It was local . . . Manchester area. That's really all I know.' In the dull white light breaching the large window, his face looked grey, eyes bleak as the distant moorlands. 'D'you think she's dead?' he asked. 'Is that why you're asking all these questions?'

'I don't know,' McKenna admitted. 'Some days ago, a woman's body was found in dense woodland near Bangor. Been there for some considerable time, apparently. At present, we've no idea who she is. We know Romy Cheney rented a cottage near the woods about the time she left you. So,' he added, 'until we locate her, we won't be much further forward.'

'I see,' Allsopp said tonelessly. 'I wouldn't like to think of that happening to her. I was fond of her.'

McKenna sat in his car outside the big house, wondering whether he should trust his own judgement and believe Robert Allsopp, whose tale told more of wanton selfishness than of the moral default likely to make a murderer. He climbed out of the car and rang Allsopp's bell again.

'What is it now?' Allsopp sounded quite weary, the puffing and stuffing blown out.

'A couple more things.' McKenna consulted his notebook. 'The names of her doctor and dentist. Where she banked, and in what name. And how long did she actually live with you?'

'That's three things. You said two.' A ghost of a smile touched Allsopp's mouth. 'The dentist I don't know. The doctor was Dr Kerr on Norfolk Street. The bank I don't know. And she was with me just over eleven months.' He began to close the door.

'Mr Allsopp,' McKenna said.

Lines of worry, or perhaps even grief, were being drawn over Allsopp's face, changing its texture and expression, blurring the contours. 'What is it?' he asked.

'We found a belt on the body . . .' McKenna said.

'What about it?'

'It appears to be an expensive belt,' McKenna said. 'Any ideas?'

'Romy had lots of belts. Went with all the clothes she had . . .' Allsopp said. 'And all expensive.'

'Just a thought,' McKenna said. 'This belt's made from thick brown leather. Very plain. The buckle's missing, so it isn't much use to us.'

'How wide is it?'

'How wide is what?'

'The belt, of course!' Allsopp snapped. 'That's what you're asking about, isn't it?'

McKenna glanced at him sharply, then riffled

through his notebook, looking for the notes culled from Eifion Roberts's report. 'Three and half inches,' he said.

'Thick leather? Like hide?'

McKenna nodded.

'It could be one I bought for her in Switzerland. I mean,' Allsopp hesitated, 'it could be . . . I can't be sure.'

'What about the buckle?'

'If it's the same belt – *if* – I bought it because of the buckle. It caught my eye. The belt was just plain brown . . . sort of chocolaty colour.'

'And the buckle?' McKenna found he was holding his breath.

'Silver,' Allsopp said, looking beyond McKenna into his memory. 'Solid silver, if the price was anything to go by.'

'And?' McKenna said. 'The design? The shape?'

'Round . . . a wreath of leaves of some description round the edge . . . very finely carved, or whatever you do with silver.'

'Yes?' McKenna wanted to shake the man.

'I'm trying to think,' Allsopp said. He scratched his head. 'It looked like a Greek or Roman carving . . . anyway, it was a man with two faces, one pointing left, one right.'

'Thank you!' McKenna closed the notebook with a snap. He crunched over the gravel to his car. 'We'll be in touch. And by the way, the two-faced man is Janus, the Roman god of doorways.' Lingering under the grand porchway of the house, Allsopp watched until McKenna's car turned out of the drive and into the road.

*

In a café in the town centre, McKenna absently watched the waitress, a chit of a girl in short tight skirt and stiletto heels so high she could barely stand upright. Tottering past, she bestowed an arch smile, and asked, in that dreadful local accent, if there was anything else he would like her to do for him. He thought of the other woman, selfish and wayward, caring nothing for the havoc she caused in passing, to whom the doctor's records, dusty and untidy in a filing cabinet, and a brittle foggy X-ray of a smashed ankle bone, had given a name at last.

Romy Cheney had indeed had two pregnancies, both aborted: inconvenient accidents of Nature, remedied by Man. Without sympathy for Allsopp, a man of little insight or sense, governed by the expediency of desire, McKenna saved his opprobrium for Romy Cheney, a woman without shame or conscience, a woman whose most significant contribution to life appeared to be her conspicuous failure as a keeper of morality.

He telephoned Jack. 'We have a name for the woman.'

'About time too,' Jack said. 'What d'you want me to do?'

'Start the paperwork,' McKenna said. 'I want an order for the GP to release her medical records, arrangements made for a full statement from Allsopp, and inquiries to Yorkshire Police about her ex-husband and family. I've got a few addresses from the GP to begin with. The first thing you can do, Jack,' he added, 'is put all the names she used through the DVLC computer. We need the number of the car.'

He could hear Jack's pen scratching. 'Any likely suspects?'

'Allsopp, perhaps?' McKenna suggested. 'Can't say I'm struck with him. But I suppose the ex-husband's a better bet.'

'I probably won't be able to get into the computer before morning,' Jack said. 'Things here seem to have come to a full stop. Forensic reported a red wine stain on the carpet.'

'Allsopp said she drank a lot of the stuff,' McKenna said. 'You could try Beti with a picture of a Scorpio. And ask her to describe this ornament she saw in the car . . . try to see Beti tonight, Jack,' McKenna added. 'Pumping her about John Beti wouldn't be a bad idea, either . . . there's no love lost between those two. See if she's anything to say about him knowing there's a body in the woods and keeping quiet about it.'

'I'll send Dewi Prys.'

'Did you do the report for the assistant chief?'

'I did.' Jack paused. 'There's a memo from HQ about contacting them before making inquiries about anything relating to Ireland, North or South.'

'Is that all?' McKenna laughed. 'Mr Jones from Special Branch can't be too pleased. By the way, what did the gipsies have to say?'

'They threatened to report us for harassment to their tame councillor,' Jack told him.

Night fell from a clear starlit sky as McKenna drew again into the car-park of the Cat and Fiddle Inn. A chill wind blew off the moors, bringing cold scents of peat and heathers. He stayed in the pub for an hour, washing down sandwiches with a pot of coffee, wanting to stretch out on one of the benches in front of the huge fire, and go to sleep.

The last thirty miles of the journey to Bangor seemed the longest, as if travelling into another culture, another time. Even in darkness, he noticed the encroachment of decay with each passing mile, saw the true nature of the beast of poverty which dwelt within the mountains and lakes and forests of North Wales, for all the disguises of the beautiful setting. Arriving in the city at midnight, he found himself taking, from force of long habit, the road out to his marital home, and drew into a layby beyond St David's church, to sit weary with despondency and regrets. A few yards up the road, the lights of a Chinese takeaway made a puddle of yellow on the empty pavement.

The cat waited for him, staring through the parlour window. He opened a tin of sardines and scooped the fish on to a plate. Drawn by the smell, she ventured into the kitchen, sniffed the dish, crouched on her haunches, and began to eat ravenously, scraping up every last morsel of fish, every last drop of milk, before sloping off into the night. She lingered for a while in the back yard, grooming herself meticulously while McKenna watched. He left the door ajar, hoping she would come back in, and reluctantly closed it, long after she had disappeared over the garden wall.

Chapter 11

'The DVLC reckon it'll take all day at least to put the various names through the computer,' Dewi told McKenna.

'Can't be helped. We'll have to wait.'

'Mr Tuttle's in your office, getting together the things you want doing.'

'Did you see Beti again?'

'Yes,' Dewi groaned. 'Drives you potty trying to talk to her, sir, because with the way she talks, it's bloody hard to follow what she's saying. Apart from the fact she rambles as well . . . I showed her a picture of a Ford Scorpio, only we've only got a photo of a black one, so all I got from her was a maybe. Or, then again, a maybe not, I suppose.' He grimaced. 'She was a bit more help with the ornament. It's a gonk, she reckons. Have you any idea what one of those looks like? Because I haven't, and neither has Mr Tuttle.'

'A gonk.' McKenna racked his memory. 'I think it's one of those hideous toys with an ugly face.'

'Sounds like Beti Gloff,' Jack said, walking into the room with a pile of folders in his hands. 'Probably why she remembered.'

Closing the door of his own office, McKenna regarded the ill-tempered features and unkempt appearance of his deputy. 'How are things with you?' he asked.

'You really want to know? Sodding awful!'

'Why?'

'I don't know why!' Jack snapped. 'Emma's had a right cob on her since the weekend, and takes every opportunity to drag up every little thing I might've done wrong in the past sixteen years!'

'What happened at the weekend?' McKenna asked.

'For a start,' Jack began, 'I wouldn't go to that bloody wedding. I didn't want to, I didn't get a special invite, so I don't know why the hell she's making a fuss . . . but she says I should've gone to see the twins being bridesmaids.'

'Maybe you should.'

'Why?' Jack frowned. 'The twins didn't want me there.'

'You know mothers have different ideas.'

'She should've said, then, instead of letting me think it didn't matter one way or the other. Why are women so bloody unreasonable?'

McKenna lit a cigarette, and leaned against the window ledge. 'I suppose she saw Denise there, Jack.'

'And that's another thing. Emma's mad as hell because I won't tell her where you are so she can tell Denise.'

Standing on Emma Tuttle's front doorstep, McKenna thought that death could never be as bleak and empty as life. The last time he stood here, he and Denise were together, and if not happy, with no real or urgent thought of separation. He had torn apart the remaining fabric of their marriage, wilfully and with no thought to the outcome, perhaps unable to believe that some miracle would not stitch up the holes, pull the tattered bits back together into some form wearable for a few more years without too much discomfort. And he had been so sadly wrong. The marriage lay behind him, a few rags trodden into the mud.

Emma, never at ease with him in the past, did not know what to do with this new McKenna, the one who suddenly walked out on his wife, had bared his teeth and bitten Denise where it would hurt her most.

'I want to talk to you, Emma,' he said. 'I'm not sure it's either the best thing to do, or the right one, but I think it's necessary.'

'Does Jack know you're here?' she asked.

'No.'

'Oh, well, I won't tell him, then.' She smiled slightly. 'What he doesn't know won't hurt. Have you had lunch? It's getting quite late.'

'Is it? No, I haven't.'

She made sandwiches and a pan of coffee, and buttered scones still hot from the oven, their sweet yeasty smell filling the kitchen. He ate absently, silently. She waited.

'I've been to see Denise,' he told her, 'because she and I seem to be causing trouble for you and Jack.'

'What's Jack said?'

'Only that you've had a disagreement. I virtually had to drag that out of him,' McKenna said. He sipped the scalding coffee. 'He's upset. He can't understand why you and he should be fighting over other people's problems.'

Emma stirred her coffee. 'We haven't before, even though we knew things were getting worse by the day with you and Denise . . . But since last week, Jack seems to have taken sides.'

'He mustn't.' He ate a scone, wiping buttery fingers on one of Emma's napkins. 'And neither must you.'

'I know,' Emma said. 'But these things happen, don't they? Before you know it.'

'Only when other people make them, Emma,' McKenna said. 'Don't let Denise use you and Jack to get at me.' He reached out to squeeze her hand, his warm and fine-boned over hers.

She felt the treachery of desire thump her body, and rose. 'Have some more coffee.' Standing at the cooker with her back to him, she said, 'Will you tell Denise where you're living?'

'When she needs to know. It's not urgent.'

'I'll tell you what is urgent.' Emma turned. 'You should get yourself a solicitor. Denise has.'

'How can nobody know anything at all about this woman?' Jack demanded. 'No trace of her husband, no sign of parents or family, nothing on the car.'

'There's no record at DVLC of any car belonging to our body under any of the names,' Dewi offered. 'They've double-checked, tried the husband's name and Allsopp's. He's got just the one car registered, bought a couple of years back . . . Our body must've sold the car to somebody. And,' he added gloomily, 'unless we find out the registration number, there's not a cat in hell's chance of finding out who's driving it around now.'

Romy Cheney remained an enigma, even her name unreal, stolen from the pages of a novel to promote some treasured private image. What brought her to the foreign territory where only death awaited her? Why did she leave her husband? Why had she twice aborted children? No one missed her, except perhaps Robert Allsopp, after his own casual fashion.

Inquiries met with apathy, almost indifference, for there were no tearful children or gaunt-faced husband to make plaintive appeals on television, no gruff-voiced father or harrowed mother to care if the killer died a free person in their own bed, if Romy's body busied a niche in the mortuary until Judgement Day. Her file was already hidden under new files, under reports of burglaries and assaults and suspected fraud. Life went on, and simply forgot about the woman who had called herself Romy Cheney, if it had cared very much in the first place.

McKenna requested authority from police headquarters to have a head cast from her skull, convinced the request would meet only exasperation, then asked DVLC to search under all the names she had used for the past ten years. On the desk, he found a cutting from the local paper, and read that the vicar of Salem village was anxious to lay Rebekah to rest at the expense of the church. McKenna smiled a little, wondering what vengeance Simeon might devise for those who gave his wife a Christian burial, then put the cutting in the file, glancing at his watch. Time dragged its feet, only moving when he engaged in some burst of activity, and McKenna could not bear to think that such spasmodic and fitful behaviour might characterize his time for the rest of his days.

On a whim, he telephoned Prosser.

'Oh, it's you, is it?' Trefor Prosser greeted him.

'Yes, Mr Prosser.' McKenna tried to put a smile in his voice. 'You can probably help tie up a few loose ends. Who cleared out Gallows Cottage when Ms Cheney's tenancy came to an end?'

'Who cleared it out?' Prosser snapped. 'How the devil should I know?'

'Well, who handed in her keys?'

'Nobody. Nobody handed them in, that's who!' Prosser said sharply. 'I had a spare set in the office, so it didn't matter.'

'When you checked the cottage after she'd left, what was in there?' McKenna asked.

'Nothing.'

'Well, how long after she'd left did you go there?'

'I don't know!' Prosser exclaimed impatiently. 'I don't know when she left, do I? According to you, she was dead and gone long before the tenancy lapsed. I don't got spying on people. She'd paid her rent so it was her business what she did.'

'D'you know, Mr Prosser, I find you singularly unhelpful.'

'Do you indeed!' McKenna could almost see him bridling. 'Well, let me tell you what I think about you!' Prosser squealed. 'I'm sick to death with all the trouble you're causing! Not to mention harassing me morning noon and night! Anybody'd think I murdered the woman myself! You've caused no end of trouble!' he raged. 'Did you know that? First you find that silly mare's body in the woods, then you have to go and dig up some two-hundred-year-old corpse! I've had reporters and nosy parkers trampling all over the bloody place for days!'

'Did you, Mr Prosser?' McKenna asked.

'Did I what?'

'Murder Ms Cheney?'

McKenna heard Prosser gasp, then the telephone went down with a slam which made his own receiver whine.

Tears glittered in Mary Ann's eyes as she buried her face in the sheaf of daffodils and freesias McKenna handed to her. 'First signs of spring,' he said. 'I thought they'd brighten up your parlour.'

'I can't remember when a man last brought me flowers.' She smiled a watery smile. 'You've taken me back years.' Mischief glinted behind the tears. 'My Dafydd was never a one for flowers . . . if I remember right, the last time I had flowers off a man was before we married, when Dafydd was away in the war, and I walked out for a bit with his friend. That shows you how long it's been.'

McKenna stretched out his legs, feeling the heat of her gas fire singe his skin through the cloth of his trousers.

'How's Beti?'

'Pah!' Mary Ann choked on the cigarette she was lighting. 'That one wants her backside kicking! She's got a gob on her bigger than the hole that quarry makes in the mountain!'

'I hear she's seen Simeon,' McKenna said. 'Dewi tells me the local paper's doing an article about her.'

'I've told her it's one of them gippos, but will she listen?' Mary Ann seethed. 'Making a fool of herself, she is, coming out with any old tale just to get noticed! Well,' she added, with grim satisfaction, 'I've told her.

Things always come home to roost, one way or another. You see if I'm not right.'

The cat arrived, mewling at the back door, while McKenna was listening to a late news bulletin on the radio. A freshly slain mouse, her gift to him, lay on the doorstep at his feet. He watched happily while she ate the food he put out for her, imagining the dusty coat bathed and brushed and gleaming. Instead of leaving as usual, she explored the parlour, rubbing the back of her ears on furniture and walls, laying a scent. He followed her outside, watched her nosing through the plants in the little garden, and decided he would spend time at the weekend weeding and tidying up, cutting back the overgrown bushes straggling along the fence. She followed him back into the house, and went to sleep in front of the fire after proudly grooming every part of her scruffy little body.

Chapter 12

On Sunday morning, anxious to test whether the calm surface beguiling his eye since Friday hid any treacherous currents in his marriage, Jack told Emma he intended to visit McKenna.

'Why don't you ask him over for a meal this evening?' Emma suggested. 'He's probably fed up with cooking for himself.'

'What?'

'I said invite him for a meal tonight.'

'Right.' Jack watched her face, her eyes, and found nothing save a bland smile.

Emma watched him back the car from the garage and turn into the road. As soon as he put his feet back under the table from where she had kicked them last week, Jack would want an explanation for her unexpected kindness towards McKenna, for Jack and anything approaching tact or subtlety were uneasy bedfellows. She would simply put forward a change of heart, Emma decided, an access of common sense. He might not believe her, but the best of marriages had a few white lies billowing somewhere in the passageways of their history. It was strange, she reflected, clearing the breakfast table, how some little thing, some tiny thing, could force a person so violently into your thoughts you couldn't prise them out again, and you spent your days engaged in normal trivial activity while the mind engaged itself with an excess of fantasy.

The twins began fighting in their bedroom. Emma went upstairs, summoned by rising voices, and screams of 'Mummy!' from both, and stood in the bedroom doorway, wishing it was McKenna who stared back at her, waiting and wanting.

Jack followed McKenna, still in pyjamas, puffy-eyed and dishevelled, down the stairs. The cat, curled up in front of the unlit fire, head tucked under paws, opened her eyes, yawned hugely, stretched, and returned to sleep.

'Looks like she's moved in,' Jack commented. 'Denise won't like that.'

'Denise won't have to live with her. How are things at home?'

Jack sat at the kitchen table, watching McKenna make toast and scrambled egg and put the kettle on to boil. 'Emma's back to her old self. Or nearly. She wants to know if you'd like to come for a meal tonight.'

'That's very kind of her.' McKenna made tea, lit the small burner on the gas stove, and put the teapot back to brew. 'Tell her I'd like that. Very much.'

McKenna let the cat out, washed up, vacuumed the house, and spent the afternoon happily uprooting weeds, trimming back the few shrubs, stopping every so often to gaze at the beguiling view of a city studded with burgeoning trees, sunlight glittering on the waters of the Straits where yachts tacked slowly back and forth, their sails slack. The cat went backwards and forwards, climbing trees, basking on the wall. A large and beautiful tabby leapt over the wall into the garden, to rub itself around McKenna's legs, and to flee screeching as the piebald stray came after her.

After a poor Sunday dinner of sausage and mashed potatoes, coloured with a dribble of thin gravy, Beti Gloff went out on her afternoon walk: three hours to herself before she must make tea for John Jones then leave dutifully for chapel. Some days, she roamed the city streets; on others, she would crab along the pathways of the mountain, staring down upon the little back streets, envy biting into her heart. She dwelt on the estate because John Jones odd-jobbed for the owners, his meanness too huge to pay rent on another house when one came free with his wages. That the house was little better than a hovel worried him not at all. Mary Ann and her cronies said among themselves that John Jones was too mean in every way, and that was the reason why no child added riches to Beti's impoverished existence. He gave no thought to Beti's comfort, to the pain her crippled body thrust upon her night and day, year in and year out. He sluiced himself down at the stone sink in the kitchen once a week in winter, twice each summer week, stood upright in the ramshackle privy hidden in blackthorn and bramble bushes at the bottom of their overgrown garden, and strung torn-up newspapers on a hook behind the privy door. Never once in the long dreariness of their marriage had John Jones thought his wife might like an indoor toilet, might need a warm bath to ease her poor body and its pain.

This fine Sunday, when the first real sunshine of

the year warmed her twisted bones and caressed her ugly features as no man's hand had ever done, Beti took a turn around the cemetery before making her way into Bangor. Happy to see those whose memory was bedecked with fresh flowers, she fretted for the others forgotten, graves untended, sour with weed and mossy gravel. She read again the inscription on the elegant marble gravestone guarding the mortal remains of Councillor Hogan: fine verse, she thought, without understanding of its meaning, but taking comfort from the instruction that 'All Shall Be Well'. In her chapel prayers, she tried not to ask God too often when exactly that perfection might manifest itself.

She made her way up the High Street to the Town Clock, and sat to rest her aching legs on a bench outside Woolworth's, watching pigeons scavenge in Saturday's litter, staring at the overhanging escarpments of Bangor Mountain, butter-yellow with gorse. There would be bluebells under the trees, she thought, enough to pick a bunch to set on her window ledge. The sweet scent of gorse and fresh green leaves drifted on the breeze, and Beti wondered absently why no bluebells grew in the woods around the village, why her cottage stayed dusky dark even on the most brilliant summer's day.

Sighing with pain and the misery of it all, she rose, and began limping back the way she had come, into the little lanes behind the High Street, where she and Mary Ann and countless other girls had dreamed and played long summers past. The rows of two-up, two-down terraces were gone, bulldozed to make way for new brick dwellings, lining each side of the lanes, filling every available space: houses without gardens, merely concrete yards just large enough to turn a car. The builders had cut deep into the lower slopes of the mountain, leaving raw wounds in the soil, exposing tree roots to frost and rains; and looking upon this little Eden of the twentieth century, Beti felt a grief so deep and harsh she wanted to weep.

At the lower end of High Street she turned on to the long road leading down to the distant sparkling sea, a road once called Margarine Street, Beti remembered, laughing a little amid her tears, because the folk trying to better themselves in the fancy terraces beggared themselves simply to pay the fancier rents. She roamed further, criss-crossing the warren of old streets higgledy-piggledy behind Margarine Street, past cars parked bumper to bonnet where once a bicycle would be a luxury. Her legs hurt, more than usual, although the warmth of spring always burnt deep in her bones, as if this gentle heat swelled badness deep within, drew it out and cast it behind her in the long shadow that, in the dark days of winter, moved back inside her body, hiding itself and its pain and ugliness, running with the thin marrow in her bones. She rested briefly, leaning on someone's garden wall, an unkempt garden behind, where an unpruned rosebush, spiky and sickly and feeble, yielded all its strength to vicious green thorns. Grass straggled around the bush, dandelions blossomed in the grass, weeds forced their glory through cracks in the front path, and Beti eyed the sleek smart car at the kerbside, its grey paintwork glittering like the distant sea.

Under the heat of a brilliant sun, the car reeked of heavy enamel and chemicals, resembled some nasty dangerous animal, come to rest for a while, but sleeping with one eye open, ready to pounce and kill. Beti peered inside, slumping a little further down on the wall to do so, and saw upholstery like smooth grey suede. In the rear window, an ugly furry object of many colours hung on a length of black and yellow elastic, and she felt the blood run from her face so fast she expected to see it gush from the toes of her twisted shoes and pool on the pavement. All thoughts of tea and chapel driven from her mind, she yawed back up the road, stopping at the top to catch rasping breaths, glancing with terror over her hunched shoulder in case the owner of the car knew, by some mystical process, what had taken place on the sunlit street, and should even now be coming to shut her mouth for ever, to do to her what had been done to the woman in the woods.

Listening to a late concert on Classic FM, McKenna thought about the family whose evening he had shared, where the tensions beneath the surface ran like heavy currents in water, pushing the flow towards its destination, unlike the taut and vicious stresses which flowed between Denise and himself. The cat jumped on his knee, pushing her nose into his hand, and burrowed into his lap, her bones fragile and limp.

Chapter 13

'Talk about having your hopes dashed!' Jack stalked McKenna's office. 'The first decent lead we get, and what happens? Turns out to be a dud. Just like all the rest!'

'Maybe we can't see the wood for the trees,' McKenna said. 'Like John Beti never noticed her body before . . . that is, of course,' he added, 'if John Beti and his wife are to be believed.'

'D'you think we'll get the cash to have a mock-up of the head made?'

'No, but if nothing else, it looks as if we're trying.'

Jack riffled the papers in Romy Cheney's file. 'We'd best keep quiet about the old women. Beti made us look a bunch of fools.'

'I hear she'll be in the local paper this week.'

'Let's pray she says nothing about that bloody car, then.'

'D'you think she really believes it's the same one?' McKenna asked. 'Still?'

'Swears on all the graves in all the graveyards this side of Chester, as well as her mother's,' Jack announced. 'She's got to be wrong! The man in Turf Square bought the car from a neighbour some months back.'

'And where did the ornament come from?'

'He can't remember,' Jack said. 'He thinks his wife bought it for the kids from a service station . . . says he never really noticed it until I asked.'

Mary Ann was utterly scathing. 'I told her!' she said. 'Over and over, and now she's done what I told her not to. Led you right up the garden path, hasn't she, Michael?'

'You heard, did you?'

'Heard?' Mary Ann exclaimed. 'Couldn't do anything else, could I? Comes screeching in here last night after she'd rooted young Dewi out to look at this car, and sits where you are now, huffing and puffing, and telling how she was scared out of her wits – not that she's got that many – afeared the man would come and get her because she'd seen the car that woman had. I tell you, all this attention she's been getting from reporters and such like has turned her brain, and that wouldn't take much doing. After all,' she continued, handing McKenna a mug of tea, 'she's never had any attention off anyone before, any pleasure, so you can't blame her. I told young Dewi you'd all be fools to take notice of her. She's rabbiting on day and night about this Simeon, reckons she's scared to walk home on her own after dark because he's everywhere in the woods, and staring at her, if you believe a word she says.'

'Have you seen him?' McKenna asked. 'Has anyone?'

'Of course not.' Mary Ann puffed on her cigarette. 'It's one of them gippos. I've told Beti, but will she have it? And now she's even got the vicar believing her. That silly devil's talking about doing an exorcism round the cottage and in the woods. He's as bad for the attention as Beti, only he's got no excuse, 'cos he's got a permanent audience every Sunday.' She frowned. 'Beti's more to be pitied than condemned, I suppose, but that doesn't excuse her making a nuisance of herself. Now then, Michael, how are you settling in to your new house? I hear a stray cat's moved in with you.'

Leaning on the stone wall by the lych gate of the village church, looking into the graveyard, McKenna thought of death, that of others as well as his own. Less than a mile down the road lay the big council cemetery, the smoke-blackened chimney-stack of its crematorium poking up into the sky. Sometimes, driving past, he imagined the grey smoke curling from the chimney was the detritus of his own bones and flesh, a burden disposed of furtively by Denise. He wanted to be buried on a bleak hill overlooking the Irish Sea, but there was no one but her to know of that wish, no one to care if his spirit joined the other restless souls thwarted in death as they were in life.

High in the sky, the sun burned warm and bright, yet the church crouched in deep tree shadows, its yard awash with a thin sheet of dewy mist billowing gently between broken and crooked gravestones, exuding chill and dampness. Buried here, McKenna thought, he would perforce rise and walk, this patch no bed for a Christian soul. Before him, an angel spread wide wings over the grave of some forgotten worthy, marble drapery rising from a tangle of bushy overgrown shrubs, pitted and lichen-stained and livid against the backdrop of dark moss-stained trees, its eyes staring vacantly and coldly into his.

Rooks cawed and chattered in high branches, dead leaves rotted underfoot, small things scurried about him unseen as he walked down the stony path hugging the graveyard wall towards Beti's cottage. He walked with his head lowered, watching the few yards of earth before his feet, afraid that if he raised his eyes, he might look into those of Simeon the Jew.

The cottage huddled in the woods, no smoke rising from its single chimney, no light of life behind either of its mean little windows. McKenna struggled up the overgrown path, long brambles reaching out to snag his trousers, for all the world like Rebekah's skeleton fingers clawing through time. He rapped on the door, and waited. No one came to answer him, and he left, almost running, taking the path to its other end only some few yards further. He stood on the pavement by the gateway panting, some ordeal survived, and walked back the half-mile to where he had left the car.

Wil Jones, as frustrated in his own way with the comings and goings around Gallows Cottage as was Trefor Prosser, had a contract to fulfil, a time limit, written in, which would cost him money if breached, and this morbid interest in a two-hundred-year-old body interfered with his work. The trench dug out, Wil agreed not to lay the drains until historians from the university completed their survey of Rebekah's grave.

Standing at a bedroom window, he watched the people scratting round, as he called it, in the trench. Forced indoors, he and Dave began decorating, although Wil wanted to put that finishing touch last of all, and could not settle while other work remained undone. He wondered about the thin, dark-haired man, standing just inside the trees, watching, as he was himself, the activity at the trench.

Dewi tried to read the fax as it came off the machine, rolling too fast for him to catch more than one line out of three or four. He waited patiently, then glancing at the cover sheet, sat down to read. Apart from himself, the office was empty.

'The chief inspector's in Caernarfon,' Jack said.

'P'raps you should see this then, sir.'

Jack took the fax from Dewi, read through its two pages, and said, 'Oh, bloody hell!'

McKenna, arriving back well after five o'clock, found Jack waiting in his office, where he had waited for over an hour, thinking of nothing in particular, noticing how the once white venetian blind and the once magnolia walls had all assumed an ochreish hue. The room was always chilly, because McKenna opened the windows summer and winter, claiming the smell of stale cigarette smoke unbearable.

'I thought you'd have left by now, Jack.'

'I thought I'd wait for you,' Jack said.

McKenna sat on the corner of the desk and lit a cigarette. 'Crime continues apace in Caernarfon. A spate of car thefts last weekend . . .' he said. 'You wouldn't think anyone in Caernarfon could afford a car worth nicking, would you . . .? Anything turn up here?'

'Fax from Yorkshire Police.' Jack handed over the paper.

McKenna read the terse paragraphs and put the

paper back on the desk. He wandered over to the window, looking at the sliced-up view of road and bus shelters and the side wall of the telephone exchange. 'Well, that's that, then.'

'Why?'

'Because,' McKenna said, 'I was relying on something turning up to point us in the right direction . . . but it's not going to happen, is it? Parents dead of old age. Ex-husband dead in a car crash, only he wasn't quite her ex, only separated . . . no brothers or sisters.' He picked up the fax again, and read the last page. 'Yorkshire say no known relatives . . . So what's left? Nothing.'

'I thought you were keen on fingering Allsopp?'

'I can't, can I?' McKenna sat down. 'Nobody saw hide nor hair of him round here, and we can't start demanding to know where he was every minute of every day between three and four years ago.'

'Maybe her husband finished her off, then got his comeuppance.'

'He was dead before she moved in with Allsopp,' McKenna said. 'Must be where she got her money from. Insurance and whatnot.'

'We've only got Allsopp's word for when she moved in.'

'We know when she rented the cottage. She was alive then, and for a while after . . . No, Jack, this isn't going to be one of our successes.'

'I think you're being defeatist,' Jack said. 'And who's going to bury her?'

'The council,' McKenna said. 'A pauper's funeral, like Mozart. Open-ended coffin and a bag of quicklime.'

'Surely not!' Jack was horrified.

'No, Jack,' McKenna sighed. 'We're a tad more civilized these days. She'll have a nice discreet hygienic cremation. You can contact the coroner's office tomorrow and arrange for the inquest to go ahead. I don't expect Eifion Roberts needs her any longer.'

Chapter 14

John Jones, when reporters came knocking on their door to talk to his wife, refused to be included in the photograph, and churlishly said nobody would be done any good from putting a face to the name of the man who found the body in the woods. Functioning by instinct rather than reason, an instinct which nourished the delusion that if his face remained unseen, his body would remain safe, John Jones imagined himself as a child playing hide and seek will imagine himself: invisible prey so long as he cannot see the predator. But John Jones's instincts were too primitive, honed only by opportunism, for too little danger had come his way in the past.

He hoped the picture of Beti showed her ugliness in all its terrible glory, prayed her shame would make her hide for the rest of her days. The paper went to press soon, and there remained only a few more hours for him to wait before he could crow in her face, as raucous and nasty as the rooks in the churchyard trees.

Wil Jones eyed the sky to the east, then to the west, where the wind had changed course during the night, rising off the Irish Sea. He lifted his nose like an animal, scenting rain in the air. Leaves, still limp, newly dropped from their buds, trembled on the wind, turning up their pale backs.

Dave worked in the trench, laying and sealing drains ready for delivery of the septic tank. Wil roamed the cottage, from room to room, trying to decide whether to finish painting upstairs, or begin downstairs. He sat on an upturned crate in the kitchen to read his check-list, always systematic, knowing without ever being told if things were done arse-about, as he said, they usually had to be done again.

The staircase was finished, treads scrubbed clean of a thick patina of dirt and grease. Close-fitting oak planks formed the stairwell, their heavy grain, rendered almost black with age, burnished and glowing with life after 400 years. Standing at the foot of the staircase, Wil realized, with a funny little jolt in the pit of his stomach, that the cottage was already two centuries old when that poor creature they found in the trench had dropped, or perhaps thrown, her little baby down those stairs, to see it die in a welter of blood and brains on the hard flagstones at the bottom. Then Wil thought of other deaths, whose memory might be steeped into the heavy walls of Gallows Cottage.

The decorating finished, he would rub the stone treads with paraffin, to put a sheen on their surfaces, the way housewives in the mountain villages polished slate doorsteps and window ledges, those folk too poor to spare precious paraffin using soured milk instead, so their remnants of pride were not dirtied by the poverty.

He smoked a pipe, put the kettle on for morning break, and decided to finish painting the bedrooms. He took his toolbox up, ready to nail down a couple of loose floorboards in the back bedroom. Glancing through the window, he saw Dave bent over in the trench, his backside sticking up in the air, and the hungry-looking man, watching again from the trees. Losing all patience, he went carefully down the stairs and out of the front door but, by the time he reached the garden, the man had disappeared.

Late on Tuesday afternoon, McKenna took a call from a solicitor in Yorkshire.

'I would have contacted you days ago, Chief Inspector,' the solicitor said, 'if I'd realized it was Mrs Bailey's body found in those woods of yours. Where on earth did you come up with the name I saw in the newspapers?'

'It was the name she was using,' McKenna said. 'What can you tell us about her?'

'Not much, I'm afraid. I was sorting out her divorce when Tom was killed. Nasty business all round.'

'Oh, yes?' Jack saw McKenna's eyebrows twitch. 'Why was that, then?'

'Oh, you know . . . accusations of this and that.' The solicitor sounded as if he regretted broaching the subject.

'Accusations of what? Why was she divorcing him?'

'I didn't say she was divorcing him, did I?' the solicitor said. 'As a matter of fact, he was giving her the heave-ho.'

'Why?'

The man's sigh whispered down the line, like the sorrow of an earthbound spirit. 'Can't do her any harm to tell you now, I suppose. They do say the dead are out of reach, don't they?'

'Out of reach of what?' McKenna asked.

'Everything, I suppose. Envy them sometimes, don't you?'

'Are you asking me?' McKenna said.

'I don't quite know, to tell you the truth. Has anybody been able to tell you about her?'

'Tell me what?'

'Tell you what she was like. As a person.'

'No.' McKenna was beginning to grind his teeth, Jack noticed. 'No, they haven't. It would be very helpful – very helpful indeed – if you could flesh out the skeleton a little, so to speak.'

'Well, I don't know that I can help you over much, because I never knew her well. I knew them both socially, up to a point, but only as acquaintances. Not what you might call friends.'

'And was there any particular reason for that?'

'For what? Oh, I see! No, not really. We just didn't mix with the same people. Tom Bailey was a dentist, with a decent private practice. Mad keen on driving. Rallies, racing . . . he was the most reckless and stupid driver I've ever seen in my whole life. We all knew he'd either kill himself or somebody else one day.' The solicitor coughed. 'Well, he got himself first, didn't he?'

'What about Margaret?'

'Margaret. Yes . . . a strange woman, Chief Inspector. Unusual. Different, if you know what I mean.' He paused. 'Actually, not the sort of wife to suit Tom Bailey when you come to think. She had something about her, I suppose, though for the life of me, I couldn't say what it was. He was one of those people who go through life taking everything they can lay their greedy hands on, and giving nothing back.'

'How was she different?'

'I can't really say, because I don't really know.' McKenna waited patiently for the man to continue.

'You always tended to notice Margaret, even though you could hardly ever say why . . . I mean, she didn't look special, she didn't look any different from anybody else, really, from any of the people you pass a thousand times in the street . . . all those faceless sorts of people you see all around you everywhere . . .' His voice tailed away.

'Even they,' McKenna said, trying to prompt the man's memory, touch his imagination, 'even they are individuals, aren't they? They have passions and fears and hopes and their own despair.'

'I suppose so, yes. Margaret certainly had her despair. She looked sometimes, Chief Inspector, as if it was eating her up, like some cancer. Eating her up from the inside out, and one day it would consume her completely. She was so terribly painfully thin, as if she couldn't stomach solid food. I used to be afraid her bones would come poking out through her skin when she moved. And her eyes looked as if they were falling right out of her head sometimes . . . I expect that's the reason she drank so much. That and other things.'

'Was she an alcoholic?'

'Not quite. I daresay she would've been, given a little longer in this vale of tears.'

'Why was her husband divorcing her?'

'Margaret said he used to beat her.'

Jack watched McKenna flinch. 'Then why wasn't she divorcing him?'

'Because he beat her when he found out she was having affairs with other women.'

McKenna filled in circles and ellipses on his doodles. 'The architect of her own destruction, Jack.'

'Is that all you've got to say?'

'What else am I supposed to say? None of this gets us any nearer to finding out who topped the poor bitch.' McKenna opened desk drawers, threw in files and papers, slammed the drawers shut, and stood up. 'I'm off.'

'And what am I supposed to do?'

'Go home to that pretty wife of yours if you've any sense.'

'Don't you think we should be looking for another woman, after what that solicitor said? Or a disgruntled husband?' Jack stared at McKenna, unable to fathom the absence of interest. 'There's any number of motives there.' He held up his hand, ticking off items as he listed them. 'First, her husband was divorcing her. Second, her husband beat her . . . and maybe that accounts for the abortions . . .'

'Well, we're never likely to know,' McKenna said wearily. 'She's dead and her husband's dead.'

'We could ask around the hospitals,' Jack said. 'Thirdly, this solicitor reckons she was a lesbian, of all things. God alone knows what that might've provoked!'

McKenna sat on the edge of his desk. 'Jack, because someone says someone else is something or other, it doesn't necessarily mean it's true.'

'Then why say it?'

'Margaret Bailey may have said it to dramatize herself. Or perhaps she didn't. Someone else could have said it . . . A snippet of gossip, sly whispers in the right ear, and before you can draw breath, Margaret Bailey's a fully paid-up, card-carrying member of the great sisterhood of Sappho.' He pulled a cigarette from the packet. 'And Margaret Bailey doesn't have the slightest clue why people start giving her a wide berth and the cold shoulder.'

'Why are you so negative?' Jack demanded. 'As soon as we might be getting anywhere, you go and put the mockers on it.'

'Because I don't think any of this is relevant.'

'Not relevant?' Jack stared. 'Of course it is. It must be.'

'Why must it?' McKenna argued. 'Even if she was a lesbian, what's that to do with her being killed?'

Jack considered the question. Eventually he said, 'I don't know.'

'Quite.' McKenna put the unlit cigarette in its packet. 'You don't know . . . and unless you invent a scenario with a jealous lover, or a *ménage à trois*, or something bizarre like that, you're not likely to find out.' He regarded Jack, smiling a little. 'The English aren't very passionate, Jack. They don't usually kill, or get killed, for love. They kill for greed, for envy, for hatred, for revenge, for fear, or simply to save face.'

'So you're saying she wasn't killed by somebody local?'

'I'm saying she wasn't killed because she provoked passion. But she may well have provoked fear or greed or envy, and therefore more than enough hatred to fuel the will to kill,' McKenna said. 'Think about it.'

Jack rubbed his hands over his jaw. 'I can't think straight about anything much at the moment.' He stared at McKenna. 'This is a real human tragedy, isn't it? Big enough to kill Margaret Bailey, big enough to ruin the life of whoever murdered her . . .' After a moment's thought, he added, 'And ruin the killer's family.'

'You think so, do you?' McKenna asked. 'You think it's a terrible human tragedy?'

'Don't you?'

McKenna eased himself off the desk, turning to pick up his briefcase. 'Depends, doesn't it? You could argue all human tragedy is trivial in the extreme. After all,' he added, checking the briefcase lock, 'what difference does one tragedy or ten million make to the turning of the earth and the flow of the seasons and the moon and stars in the sky?'

Profoundly shocked, Jack said, 'How can you say such things?'

'How can I?' McKenna asked. 'I'm simply putting words to a thought.' He looked at Jack. 'If it bothers you, just forget I said anything.'

Low-voiced, Jack said, 'I can't, can I? You can't unthink a thought once it's come, and no more can you get rid of a thought once somebody else puts it into your head.' After a long pause, he added, staring hard at the silent McKenna, 'And you can't ever wash away the effect of the thought, can you? Any more than we can unlearn how to split the atom.'

Jack heard the sough of the fire door at the head of the stairs closing behind McKenna before he began to think about the veiled warning not to neglect Emma.

'I am not staying in, Denise,' Emma said to the distraught woman on her doorstep. 'This is the first time we've had an evening out as a family for ages.' Upon Denise's ashen face, Emma thought, surely lay the scars of tears as hot as molten glass. 'Look, why not come with us?' she suggested. 'Take your mind off things. We're only going to see a film suitable for fourteen-year-olds, and you can come back for supper.' Emma took her arm, pulling Denise into the house. 'And I don't know where Michael is, so stop fretting, and relax for a few hours. You never know, Denise, you might have a new perspective on things afterwards.'

They were already seated in the car when one of the twins said to Denise, 'Your husband's very sweet, isn't he, Mrs McKenna? He came round for supper the other evening, and we enjoyed it so much!'

Chapter 15

At work for 7.30 in the morning, Wil fidgeted for almost an hour before the lorry bringing the septic tank made its way down the track to Gallows Cottage. Rain had fallen overnight, the light sandy soil in the trench blotted with dark patches of water. Wet grass in the garden squelched under his boots, little beads of water garlanded the low eaves of the roof. All being well, Wil said to himself, he would finish on schedule, provided no more bodies emerged from ancient resting places, nothing happened to encourage the police to tear the place apart.

Leaving Dave to supervise unloading the tank, he went upstairs into the back bedroom, where the floorboards were loose, and kneeling, began to prise the boards from their moorings. The planks came up with a small flurry of gritty dust and a crackling of splintered wood. He put them to one side and stuck the hose end of the vacuum cleaner into the cavity. The whine of the motor drowned out the throbbing of the lorry's engine pulsing stinking diesel fumes into the clear morning air as the tank was slowly unloaded and positioned. He could hear the dust and debris of centuries rattling up the hose, then that strange plopping sound of something too big blocking its inlet. Cursing under his breath, he found a bundle of dirty cloths stuck to the end. He yanked it away, and threw the bundle to one side, then pushed the hose back again.

The planks fitted beautifully into the clean space. He had nailed them back to the joist, vacuumed the floor, coiled up the cleaner and put away his tools in the right places in his box before he looked at the bundle again, and then only to glance casually, picking it up to take downstairs to the rubbish bin. The pattern caught his eye when he dropped it on the kitchen floor, and the rags scattered a little. The cloth on the outside of the bundle was dirty and faded, that on the inside quite clean, except for grubby marks here and there where the vacuum cleaner had caught.

Wil put the kettle on, adding extra water for the lorry driver, lit his pipe, and sat on a crate. He picked up the bundle and untangled it, spreading out on the kitchen floor a woman's skirt, in pale silvery-grey wool, and a jacket, the fabric woven with dusky faded flowers on a background to match the skirt. The jacket was fastened with tarnished buttons, once bright and gilded.

Seated at the table of an empty kitchen, listening to the silence of his house, Jack wondered how much fall-out was yet to come from the firestorm of McKenna's marital disaster. Never had he seen a person turn as Denise had last night, like a woman possessed by demons, screeching, clawing at the air, calling Emma foul names. Bundled off to their room in total mystification, the twins' bewilderment became a screaming adolescent rage to add to Denise's banshee wailing. Emma screeched too, at Jack, blaming him for the fiasco because he refused to let her tell the twins about the McKenna marriage, maintaining it was none of their business.

Last night dragged eventually to some horrible conclusion, time almost stultified, as after a bereavement. Denise left – he could not remember when – her skirt hanging out from the door of the car, the car veering on to the lawn before plunging through the gate. Emma simply refused even to look at him, and locked herself in with the twins, their voices cadences of sound, ebbing and breaking like the sea on shingle, until they were stilled. Emma slept in their room, coming out surreptitiously, like an animal venturing from the safety of its den, to go to the bathroom, where Jack heard the shower splash briefly and the lavatory flush. He lay awake, anger pushing adrenalin through his body, until rosy light began to colour the eastern sky, then dozed restlessly, wide awake long before the alarm clock summoned him at 7.30.

On the afternoon shift, Dewi Prys slept soundly until past eleven, when his mother's voice eventually broke up his dreams. He ate his breakfast-cum-lunch, drank two mugs of tea, read the local paper, smiling at the tale of Beti and her ghost, marvelling that she looked much less hideous in the photograph than in real life, and walked down to the shop to buy groceries for his mother.

The main road through the council estate was busy, with cars and buses and vans, young girls with babies making their way from the morning mother and child clinic, where local doctors kept an eye on the youngsters, most of whom came into the world without benefit of a father's name to their birth certificates. It was beyond Dewi's understanding why girls barely out of childhood themselves could not wait before clamping the shackles of motherhood around their future, chaining hope to the railings of tedium. He walked slowly home, passing pushchairs and prams and girls in jeans and padded coloured jackets, their hair tangled by the wind, their faces bright with lipstick and eye colour. The babies, anonymous little lumps in quilted suits, some clean and rosy faced, others whey-faced, dirty and thin, already scavenging off the state for every crumb, every drop of milk, which passed their lips, were, he realized, the next generation of Jamies and his ilk, misery-makers of the future. The baby boys would grow up to spawn fear into the hearts of the law-abiding and more babies on to the girls; the lowest social classes overbreeding, overweighing the fragile balance of a society teetering like a seesaw with too great a burden at one end; too many in need and not enough to make the wealth to keep them.

He passed a pretty, fair-haired girl, tall on her black high-heeled shoes, slender legs clad in denim, and looked briefly at the child in the pushchair she guarded. The baby, large and aggressive, looked as if aware the world owed it a living, and was already learning how best to call in the debt. But for the child, the girl might have taken Dewi's fancy, and he wondered about the men who gave not a second thought to taking on another's offspring, those he met almost every day at work: vicious, stupid, bestial humanity wearing its customary familiar face.

Jamie Thief lived but four doors down from Dewi's nain. Dewi called on the old woman on his way to work, to take a meat pie his mother had baked. Jamie was on the pavement as he came out of his grandmother's house, closing the door of a shiny grey Ford Scorpio.

Dewi sat with Jamie in the squad room, empty save for the two of them. As whey-faced as any baby from the estate, eyes red-rimmed and watery, Jamie pulled hard on a thin cigarette.

'When's your birthday, Jamie?' Dewi asked. 'Soon, isn't it?'

'None of your sodding business!' Jamie snarled. Dewi watched the shaking hands.

'What're you on? Dope? Speed?' Dewi asked. 'You look a mess. Did you know that? From where I'm sitting, you look like you might be six feet under long before you get to your next birthday.'

Jamie made no response. He sat stony-faced, staring at the small patch of floor between the toes of his Nike baseball boots. Dewi remembered sitting in this same room countless times, watching Jamie stare at the floor and Doc Marten boots on his feet. Times changed, and fashions changed, but the likes of Jamie stayed the same, new ones growing up to join the mob each day. McKenna once told Dewi that the world must be balanced between good and bad, neither able to exist without the other, the social function of criminals so crucial that their absence would force society to pass laws to bring them into existence. Staring at Jamie, Dewi wondered where that process might begin, and realized the greater importance of knowing where it would end.

'Why've you brought me here?' Jamie demanded. 'I haven't done anything.'

Dewi grinned. 'Jamie, you've always done something. There'll be a whole string of things you've done waiting for us to find out about sooner or later.'

'You always did talk a load of crap, Dewi Prys.'

'We want to know about the car. That's all.'

'I've told you! How many more times do I have to tell you? I borrow it now and then. No crime in that, so hard bloody luck!'

Dewi wrote 'borrows the car now and then' in his notebook, while Jamie tried to read the words upside down. 'Who d'you borrow it from?' he persisted.

'A mate.'

Dewi added 'from a mate' to his notes.

'Why're you writing it down?' Jamie demanded.

'We write everything down, you know that, Jamie. So you can't come back at us and say you never said whatever it is. And so you can't make out in court we beat a confession out of you.'

'I'm not confessing anything!'

'Did I say you were?' Dewi smiled. 'Shall I get us a *panad*?'

'I don't bloody want a drink! I want to get out of here!'

'All in good time. Mr McKenna'll want to talk to you about the car.'

'Why?'

'Well, you'll have to ask him that yourself. Not for me to tell you, is it?'

Jamie jumped to his feet. 'I'm going!'

'Sit down, unless you want to be arrested,' Dewi ordered. Jamie sank on to the chair, once again locked into the ghastly ritual, neither he nor Dewi Prys able to escape the consequences of their role in life.

Jack walked into the squad room, and saw the pair seated at the table. 'What's he doing here?'

'I brought him in to talk to Mr McKenna, sir.'

'Well, Mr McKenna's not here, so you may as well send him away.'

'Perhaps you'd better talk to Jamie, then,' Dewi said. 'I found him with the Ford Scorpio, so I thought we'd better do something about it.'

'You what? Not that bloody car again!'

'It's the same car, sir. We should sort out why Jamie gets to borrow it. And who he borrows it from, if you get my drift.'

Jack looked from Jamie to the young police officer, and wondered which of the two was the bigger thorn in his flesh. 'All right, Prys.' He sat on the edge of the table, sharp creases in his trousers pulled taut over his thighs. 'Who d'you borrow the car from, Jamie?'

'I've already told him.' Jamie gestured towards Dewi. 'He's too bloody thick to understand. Typical copper, isn't he?'

'Jamie says he borrows the car from a mate. I was just about to ask him again who the mate might be.'

'Give me a name, Jamie. Stop farting about!'

Bravado returned to Jamie. 'I don't have to tell you anything. I want my brief.'

'Oh, yes?' Jack's eyes narrowed. 'And why should you want some piddling bloody solicitor to hold your hand? What've you done you don't want us knowing about?'

'Nothing!' Jamie spat the word.

Dewi's voice was silky. 'If you've done nothing,

Jamie, you've no reason to have a brief. We're not saying you have done anything. We're almost agreeing with you that you haven't done anything. Isn't that right, Inspector?' he said. 'We just want you to tell us about the car, then you can walk right out of here, all legit, and not have to come back again.'

Jamie stared at Dewi, his eyes cold. Dewi wondered irrelevantly how many of those babies seen today might be the fruit of Jamie's loins. Rotten fruit, so to speak. 'What's so important about the car anyway?' Jamie asked.

'That's our business.' Jack was losing patience. 'Who lends it to you? Why is this *mate* of yours quite happy to hand over fifteen thousand quid's worth of car whenever you want it?'

The silence lengthened. Jamie felt like a cornered animal, the feeling engendered by the sight of any policeman. 'What happens if I don't want to tell you?' he asked. 'If I decide it's none of your fucking business?'

Jack hissed, 'You'll find out in the next thirty seconds.'

Dewi intervened. 'You're making life hard for yourself, Jamie. Beats me why you should want to do that. The inspector'll have to arrest you unless you tell him.'

'Why?'

Dewi said to Jack, 'The trouble is, sir, Jamie's conditioned to not telling us anything, even when there's no reason for him not to . . . I don't reckon he thinks the car's important, to be honest. Aren't I right, Jamie?'

'Maybe. Maybe not.'

Jack banged the table with his fist. 'I've had enough of this! Take him down to the cells!'

'What for?' Jamie leapt to his feet, Adam's apple bobbing up and down as he gulped air.

'Wilful bloody obstruction. To a murder investigation!' Jack stalked off.

'What the fuck is he talking about?'

'What he said, Jamie,' Dewi sighed. 'That's the bottom line. So don't you think it might be a good idea to stop playing silly buggers?'

Chapter 16

I have known Christopher Stott for some time. I can't remember where I met him. He is married and has a child, and works at Snidey Castle as a guide or something like that. He has never taken part in any criminal offences with me. He got the Ford Scorpio car about three years ago. It was second-hand. I do not know where he got it. He said I could borrow it sometimes. I think he said this because he did not drive it very often himself. He told me his wife does not know how to drive. He sold it to somebody last summer. The new owner agreed I could still borrow the car sometimes. I think Chris Stott made this arrangement. Chris Stott used to live in Turf Square. I have not seen him since some time last year. That is all I know. I have never used the car to commit any criminal offences. This statement is made of my own free will.

Signed: James Wright

Jack re-read the statement, trying to unravel the implications of its terse sentences, and failed. Jamie had been sent home. Dewi fretted and nagged, wanting to chase after the philanthropic Christopher Stott. Jack decided nothing would be done until he had spoken to McKenna, and thought about the fact that Mr Stott worked at the castle.

'Blackmail, Jack. That's what this is all about,' McKenna decided. 'Jamie's got something on this bloke Stott. Why else would the car loan arrangement continue after it was sold? We'll go and talk to him.'

'And probably get led up another garden path,' Jack said bitterly.

'What's bugging you?' McKenna demanded.

Haltingly, reluctantly, Jack reported the events of the night before, Denise's hysteria and Emma's rage. 'And it was my fault,' he admitted. 'If we'd told the twins, none of it would've happened.'

'Never mind,' McKenna said. 'Water under the bridge now . . . I'll talk to Denise.' Shame for her behaviour scorched him, disgust that she should let her emotions flap around outside her body like dirty rags blown on the wind of circumstance, and anger that she had made a puddle of her problems for Jack and his family to fall into unwittingly.

'Mr McKenna,' Wil said, 'I've got a deadline to meet. I don't care overmuch if the Dead Sea Scrolls are under the floors. I want to be done with that bloody place and out of there!'

McKenna fingered the jacket and skirt Wil had brought to the police station, smudges of dust staining his fingers. 'Where exactly did you find these?'

'Under a couple of loose boards in the back bedroom. And it's only because I always clean out the hole before putting boards back that I found them at all. They'd have lain there 'til the place fell down otherwise.' Wil puffed hard on the pipe. 'And before you ask, there aren't any more loose boards anywhere. I've made sure of that, so there's no need for your lot to go tearing the cottage apart, looking for things which aren't there.'

'What d'you think?' Jack asked, after Wil had left. 'Should we get forensic back?'

'If we do, the owner will send us an almighty bill,' McKenna said. 'Pulling up floors'll do no end of damage, and it'll be our responsibility to put it right. Let's have a think about things, shall we? Ring Eifion Roberts and tell him to bring that file with clothing labels.'

'And what about Jamie's boyfriend?'

'Jamie's boyfriend?'

'Mr Stott.'

McKenna laughed. 'Come on, Jack! Jamie's not interested in other men.'

'Jamie would be interested in anything and anybody which might be useful to him,' Jack said. 'Man, woman, child or beast. He's got no conscience; he's the most evil bastard I've ever come across, and he makes my flesh crawl.'

'Dewi says he'll kill somebody one day.'

'Well,' Jack said, straightening out the jacket, 'for once, I agree with him.'

Jack, Dewi and McKenna sat in McKenna's office, sandwiches and a pot of coffee on a tray on the desk, the suit folded over the back of a chair. McKenna pushed the tray aside, and spread out the skirt, turning it inside out, then back again, rubbing the fabric between finger and thumb, feeling the harshness of synthetic fibre woven into the wool. Half-lined with matching satin, both lining and outer fabric bore creases where they had been stretched tight around hips and belly. The back of the skirt bulged, its side seams pulled so taut stitches were exposed. A grubby label was sewn into the inside waistband, along with two tape loops for hanging the garment.

'One thing's for sure,' Jack observed. 'There's no way our lady in the woods wore that. It's so short her backside would've shown.'

'It's too wide as well. Size 16 according to the label. 16S. What does that mean?' McKenna looked from Jack to Dewi.

'I think it means "short", as in short fitting,' Dewi offered. 'For short women, sir.'

Jack looked at him. 'All right, Prys, you've made your point. It belongs – it belonged – to a short woman. *Ergo*, not Romy Cheney, or whatever her name was.'

'What does *ergo* mean?' Dewi asked.

'*Ergo* means "therefore", Dewi,' McKenna said, before Jack could snap at the boy. 'It's Latin.'

The jacket had fared better from its wearing than the skirt, although the fabric was heavily creased across the front of the elbow area. A shapely little garment, with curved rever collar, curved hem, and a slightly shaped waist, its fabric appeared to be the same blend of wool and synthetic as the skirt, and its lining matched. It bore the same brand name as the skirt, on a silky label sewn into the front left-hand facing. 'This is just a size 16,' McKenna said. 'A pretty fabric, rather unusual.' A picture of Denise came unbidden to his mind. She would look well in this suit, the skirt smooth over her hips, not tortured by surplus flesh, the slender length of thigh below its hem, the pale bones of her knees beneath.

Eifion Roberts pushed open the office door, marched in and dropped a heavy black file on top of the skirt. 'You look like a bunch of perverts sitting there with those clothes,' he grinned. 'Washing-line thieves. Got the undies as well?'

'No, Eifion,' McKenna smiled. 'Sorry to disappoint you.'

Dr Roberts fingered the clothes. 'Not much to show for all this intensive police work, is it? Anything new cropped up since we last spoke?'

'I told you about the solicitor, didn't I?' McKenna said. 'Wil the builder found the suit stuffed under the floorboards in one of the bedrooms at Gallows Cottage.'

Dewi coughed. 'Er – what about Jamie and the car, sir?'

'Shut up about bloody Jamie!' Jack roared. 'And shut up about that sodding car!'

Dr Roberts favoured Jack with an oblique look. 'You want to get your blood pressure seen to. You've gone quite purple in the face.' He turned to McKenna. 'What's this about the car, then?'

McKenna sighed. 'Dewi found Jamie with the car today, and brought him in. Here's the statement.'

'Has the car still got that silly toy in the back window?' Dr Roberts asked.

'I don't know,' McKenna admitted. 'Has it, Dewi?'

'No, it hasn't, as a matter of fact. I recognized the number plate.'

'There you are, then.' Dr Roberts dropped Jamie's statement back on the desk. 'That's very significant.'

'What is?' Jack demanded.

'Moving that toy,' the pathologist said. 'Somebody's obviously got the wind up. That's how Beti Gloff fingered the car in the first place, isn't it?'

'Yes, but the toy was bought after the guy in Turf Square got the car,' Jack said. 'Jamie's been borrowing the car all along.'

'How d'you know it was? You've only got this man's word for it.' Dr Roberts opened the file, turning over pages. 'You lot strike me as being remarkably slow, considering what we pay you. Beti's seen the same car being driven by our body as she's seen somebody else driving since,' he went on. 'Beti recognized the car in Turf Square, not because of its colour or shape or make or any of the usual reasons, but because of that silly toy in the back window. *Ergo*, that toy must have been there when Beti saw it the first time. When our Romy was driving it, in other words. QED.'

Jack glared at Dewi. 'Don't you dare ask what "QED" means!'

'I know, as a matter of fact,' Dewi said. 'We learnt it at school: "That which has been proved".'

Dr Roberts grinned. 'Precisely! You'd better talk to Beti again. Where would you be without her, eh?'

'Not quite so far up shit creek as we are at the moment,' McKenna responded. 'What can you tell us about the clothes?'

'Wouldn't fit Romy Cheney, for starters.'

'We already deduced that.'

'Doubt if they'd fit Rebekah either . . . There's a right old to-do going on about her, you know.' Dr Roberts made himself more comfortable. 'This rabbi'd read about her in the *Daily Post*, so he comes to see me, does a bit of tutting and says she should have a Jewish burial, and the nearest cemetery's in Liverpool. I told him there was no way of knowing if the lass was Jewish or not. I mean,' he added, 'if I'd had her hubby on the table, I'd've been able to tell from the bits lopped off his parts, wouldn't I?'

Jack squirmed. McKenna said, 'Not after two hundred years you wouldn't.'

'Don't you be so cocky, McKenna,' Dr Roberts said. 'Put our Romy's parts in some sort of order, didn't I? Anyway, I sent the rabbi to see the vicar in Salem village, and they're at it hammer and tongs, because the vicar reckons she's a bit of local history, and they'll ship her off to Liverpool over his dead body.'

'Does it really matter, Eifion?' McKenna asked. 'She's long dead, and her soul will've gone to the right place.'

Dr Roberts shrugged. 'I don't know if it matters, do I? These holy souls of one persuasion or another seem to think so, and while they're arguing, she's taking up space in my chill cabinet, and I'm not at all sure what might happen. She'll probably disintegrate, turn to dust, then we can sweep her up and put her in an urn, and she can be awarded like an Oscar. A year to the Jews, a year to the Church. To and fro 'til Kingdom come.'

'How come you don't know if she'll fall apart?' Dewi asked.

'Mummified bodies don't come my way very often, Dewi,' Dr Roberts said. 'We either get nice and fresh ones or nice and maggoty ones. Both types keep well enough, if you look after them. Like what your mam does when she puts the Sunday joint in the freezer. Now,' he added, 'let's have a look at these clothes. They've only been worn two or three times, I'd say. No sweat stains . . . and traces of a very unusual perfume on this jacket. Smell it.' He thrust the jacket under McKenna's nose, then Jack's, then Dewi's. 'Remind you of anything?' he asked.

'Carnations,' Dewi said. 'Sort of dry and musky.'

'And there's only one perfume in the world which smells like real carnations, and keeps on smelling the same.' Dr Roberts paused, staring into space. 'There was an odd dry scent on the skeleton's clothes. Reminded me of death, it did.'

'How long does it keep on smelling that way?' Jack asked.

'Indefinitely. It's called "Incarnat", which is old French for carnation . . . means flesh-coloured, as well, if you're interested in that sort of thing. The perfume's made by Corday in Grasse, and I doubt you'd be able to buy it this side of Chester. The clothes came from Debenhams, by the way, their own label . . .' Dr Roberts looked at the suit, a slight frown creasing his forehead and the skin around his eyes. 'It's a bit odd, come to think of it, because with all due respect to Debenhams, I wouldn't expect a woman who buys her clothes there to wear this perfume. A small bottle of it would cost ten times the price of this suit.'

McKenna touched the jacket. 'I don't know. It matches the jacket, in a way. Matches the pattern . . . faded and flowery.'

'They don't go together,' Dr Roberts argued. 'Price-wise or personality-wise. I see the woman in this suit as a middle-aged sort, mentally if not physically. Maybe a bit vain. And no sense of style, because the skirt was obviously far too tight round the bum. Perhaps a bit frumpish as well.'

'Even supposing you're right, although for the life of me, I can't see how you can deduce all that from a jacket and a skirt,' McKenna countered, 'what's to say she didn't splash out on a new perfume to go with her new outfit?'

'It's the wrong perfume,' Dr Roberts said. 'Apart from the difficulty of buying it, a woman will only wear that scent if she really loves it. It's very exotic, very individualistic. Not in the least fashionable, not the sort of perfume advertised in women's magazines, not the sort many women know about.'

Dewi stood up. 'Shall I get to Debenhams before they shut up shop for the day, sir?' he asked McKenna. 'Find out when the suit was on sale?'

'Ask about the perfume as well. What's it called, Eifion?'

Dr Roberts wrote the name of the perfume in Dewi's notebook, tucking the book into his pocket. 'Just a thought, sir,' Dewi said to McKenna. 'Lots of women use their friends' scent, don't they? Spray on a bit to see if they like it. This lady could've done that, couldn't she? Maybe Romy liked carnations.'

Chapter 17

McKenna dialled Robert Allsopp's home number. The telephone rang twenty-three times before Allsopp responded.

'How much longer is all this going to go on?' he demanded.

'All what, Mr Allsopp?'

'Being hounded! I'm sick to death of it!'

'We're not hounding you. I did say we'd need a formal statement.'

'How many formal bloody statements d'you need to do your job?' Allsopp shouted. 'Eh? First her, then the car, then her husband, then the bloody car again! What next?'

'Hopefully, not much, provided you're willing to answer a few more questions now.'

Allsopp sighed. 'What d'you want to know?'

'What kind of perfume did Madge – Romy use?'

'What kind? How d'you expect me to know that? The kind that smells!'

'Yes, Mr Allsopp,' McKenna said. 'Perfume usually does smell, otherwise there'd be little point in using it. What did her perfume smell of?'

'Jesus Christ! Flowery sorts of things.'

'Which flowers? Any in particular?'

'Oh, God! You're like a bloody terrier with a bone! I can't remember.'

Jack could hear the rise and fall in Allsopp's voice, the whine of despair. 'Think,' McKenna was saying. 'Just cast your mind back. Try to picture the scent bottles, where she kept them, how many. Then try to recall their actual smell. Did you prefer one or the other? Did you dislike any of them? Take your time. Did you associate a particular scent with clothes she wore, or places you went together . . . little things like that?' He lit a cigarette from the stub of the last, and swivelled his chair back and forth.

'You still there?'

'I'm still here, Mr Allsopp.'

'There was one I remember, because I hated it, and she would insist on using it because she said she liked it. Actually, she said she loved it because it made her feel special.'

'Why did you hate it?'

'It got right up my nose. Literally! Gave me sneezing fits, and runny eyes.'

'D'you know what it was called?'

'Some French name . . . they've all got French names, haven't they?'

'Well, then, what sort of smell was it?'

'Really pungent. Like anaesthetic with flowers, if you know what I mean. Romy used too much of it, sprayed it on all over, even though I told her it was very strong. You couldn't sit in the car with her.'

'Any chance of picking out the flower?'

'I'm not very good at that kind of thing . . . I can't say . . . not really.'

'Shit!' McKenna exclaimed.

'I beg your pardon? You say something?'

'Mr Allsopp, this is very, very important. I know you're sick of the sight of policemen, but I wonder if you'd do us a favour?'

'I suppose so. Anything to get you off my back.'

'As soon as possible, I'll send someone round to see you with a particular perfume for you to test. All I want from you is yea or nay as to whether it's the one you didn't like.'

Allsopp laughed. 'So I'm to expect some bloody great flatfoot with a bottle of scent, am I?'

Dewi returned well after six o'clock, having left the suit with Dr Roberts. 'I hate those women's shops,' he announced, sinking into a chair opposite McKenna's desk. 'They reek of perfume. You can smell it out in the street. Enough to choke a body.'

'Mr Allsopp said one of Romy's perfumes made him sneeze. But, of course, he couldn't remember which one. Derbyshire police are getting a bottle of this Incarnat for him to smell.'

'Have to find it first, won't they? The girls in Debenhams had never heard of it, tried to sell me Estee Lauder instead. I tried Boots and the other chemists, but nobody stocks it in Bangor. Anyway, the suit.' He flipped open his notebook. 'This book's nearly full, sir. Mostly with old women's gossip.' He pulled his tie loose. 'Quite a bit warmer tonight than it's been so far. P'raps there's some proper sunshine on the way . . . Debenhams were eventually very helpful. The buyer said they'd stocked that particular outfit around three and a half years ago, just one consignment, and some of it sold off in a sale. Twenty jackets: three size 10, seven size 12, six size 14 – 12 and 14 being the most popular sizes – and four size 16. Before you get too hopeful, sir, the buyer said there's nothing to say the jacket was bought in Bangor. She thinks it was probably available nationally, but she's going to ask the head office where the jacket was sold, when, and how many.'

'And a lot of use that'll be!'

'It could narrow down the field, sir.'

'We haven't got a field!' McKenna snapped. 'We haven't got anything, except a lot of gossip, a woman's suit, two dead bodies, and sodding Jamie Thief and his borrowed car!'

'D'you want me to see that Mr Stott?'

'I haven't decided what to do with him yet. You're on lates today, aren't you?'

'Yes, sir. Off duty at ten.'

'You'd better have your tea break now. I'm going home to feed the cat.'

The cat ate in the kitchen, placidly crouched over a plate of fresh cod, while McKenna waited for a frozen lasagne to cook through, thinking he ought to buy a recipe book. He should telephone Denise, but decided if he did so now, the lasagne might burn, and if he waited until he had eaten, he would be delayed from returning to work. He needed time to think, to decide what to do, what to say, and sat forking food into his mouth, tasting little, thinking about women in general, that mysterious race, and Denise and Romy Cheney in particular. The cat sat at his feet, grooming herself fastidiously. Her eyes were brighter already, her coat developing a gloss.

*

'Mary Ann wants you to go and see her, sir,' Dewi greeted him.

'Why?'

'She says there'll be another murder in the village if you don't,' Dewi grinned. 'It's about Beti Gloff, but I only got half the story because Mary Ann was whispering into the telephone on account of Beti being in the next room.'

'Oh, Lord above!' McKenna ran his hands through his hair. 'What next, Dewi? What next?'

'Beti's said to be mad with rage, sir, talking about knifing her old man. And it's all to do with that article about her in the local paper today, although what I don't know.'

'We'd better go and see her, then. And on the way back, we'll call in on Jamie's buddy.'

The telephone rang as McKenna was shutting the office door. Allsopp sounded weary. 'No, I haven't had a visit from any perfume-bearing PC Plod, Mr McKenna. I remembered all by myself without any help from anybody, because I haven't been able to stop thinking about it since you rang, and that bloody smell's been wafting under my nose like Romy's bloody ghost was walking around beside me. And shall I tell you why, Mr McKenna? I'm sure you want to know. I've got a vase of flowers in my sitting-room, on the mantelpiece, and I've got the fire lit because Derbyshire's a bloody cold place in April, and the heat from the fire's bringing the scent out of the flowers, even though they're greenhouse grown and don't have all that much scent to them. They're pink and white flowers, very pretty, and the heat's making their petals go a bit brown already. And they're carnations, Mr

McKenna. That's what the perfume smelt of. Carnations.'

McKenna, almost jubilant, telephoned Jack, disturbing him from a nap in front of the television. 'D'you realize what this means? Not only do we have the suit, an actual physical clue, but we can now connect it directly with Romy Cheney. What d'you think of that? Good, or what?'

'I suppose so . . . not much use unless we find a woman to fit into the suit, is it? And why she stuffed it under the floorboards.' Jack sounded gloomy. 'I've just had a thought.'

'What?'

'Suppose it wasn't the woman who wore the suit who hid it.'

'What's that bit of garbled syntax supposed to mean?'

'Well, suppose she witnessed what happened to Romy, so she had to be got rid of as well, and the murderer stuffed her clothes under the floorboards. This other woman could've been hung as well. She might be dangling from another tree in the woods, or a tree in some other woods. She might even be buried under the earth floor in that outhouse.'

'I see,' McKenna said slowly. 'Why don't you just come round and throw a bucket of cold water in my face? What am I supposed to do, eh? Search every sodding wood from here to Chester? Pull down Gallows Cottage stone by stone, then dig up Snidey Castle Estate looking for bodies which might or might not be there?'

'There's no need to take on like that!' Jack whined. 'It was only an idea!'

*

'Mr Tuttle could have a point, sir,' Dewi offered, as they drove out to Salem village.

'I know he might have a point.' McKenna had taken to grinding his teeth, Dewi noticed. 'That is why Wil Jones is going to find Gallows Cottage being dug up in the morning, and why you and several other people will be spending the day bashing your way through the woods looking for bodies which probably don't exist.'

'I don't mind, sir. I like being out in the fresh air.'

McKenna drew to a halt by the school gates, now closed for the night, and turned to look at the young officer beside him. 'I sometimes wonder if you're not a bit puddled, Dewi Prys. That's why you drive Jack Tuttle to screaming point at times. Well, it's going to rain tomorrow. I could hear the trains clearly when I was having tea, and I can only do that when there's rain on the way. So I hope you enjoy a bit of water with your fresh air.'

'Funny you noticing that, sir. I thought it was only the old ones like my nain knew you hear further when there's rain around. She reckons she can hear the cathedral clock if it's going to pour down, and that's at least a mile as the crow flies.'

'Talking about crows,' McKenna said as he locked the car, 'look at that lot up there.' Black shapes hunched along the spreading limbs of the tall trees, looking down on the cottages, the church, the graveyard, and the two men, darkening an already sombre sky.

'And on the electric wires. Wonder what they're waiting for?'

McKenna shivered. 'I don't like this place. I came

here the other day in brilliant sunshine, and it was no nicer than it is now.'

'Nain says it's evil ground. Folk reckon the church was built here to keep the badness under control.

'Doesn't seem to be working too well, does it?'

Beti and Mary Ann sat in Mary Ann's uncurtained window, one each side of a small gateleg table, like two geraniums in pots, McKenna thought, looking at them. 'Pull up chairs for you and Mr McKenna, Dewi,' Mary Ann said. 'This is talk to make around the table.' A pot of tea under a stained knitted cosy sat on a trivet in the centre of the table, a plate of custard creams and arrowroot biscuits and jammy dodgers beside.

'There's been trouble,' Mary Ann told them, 'between Beti and him, because Beti had her picture in the paper and people thought enough about what she was saying to put it in print. Bitter jealous, he is, because the newspaper people thought Beti and Simeon more interesting than him finding a poor body everybody knew was there for any fool to find.'

'What's he done, then?' Dewi asked, taking the last of the jammy dodgers.

Beti opened her mouth to speak. Mary Ann held up her hand. 'You let me tell this, so we get it right. Now then. About Beti's husband.'

'Hasn't John Jones got a name any longer?' McKenna asked.

'Of course he has! But he doesn't deserve we use it for what he's done today. The local paper came this morning while Beti was doing her early errands. That no-good was still indoors, and Beti says he hadn't even sided the breakfast pots, never mind washed up.'

'Yes?' Dewi said. 'So why's Beti wanting to stick the breadknife in his guts?'

McKenna watched Beti. She sat as stiff as one of the marble angels in the graveyard, only her eyes showing life, glittering with unshed tears in the light from Mary Ann's parlour lamps.

'He started on her, didn't he?' Mary Ann said. 'In that horrible, sour, vicious way of his. Calling her wicked bad names and saying she was no fit wife for any God-fearing soul.' Mary Ann took the cigarette McKenna offered. 'When Beti tells him what she thinks of him, he hit her. Smacked her in the mouth.' She sipped her tea, little finger crooked. 'I know he's not done anything wrong in your books, but he's done something to offend God, and any decent-thinking person.'

'Did he hurt you, Beti?' McKenna asked the old woman.

She turned towards him, looking with the one eye she could focus. Tears oozed out and slithered unchecked down the wrinkled cheeks, running into the deep creases at each side of her mouth, dripping off her little pointed chin. McKenna saw the darkness of bruising under age-grimed skin, seeping into a faint weal above the frayed collar of her blouse. Dewi squeezed her hands, rubbing the thin papery flesh, murmuring comforts. Mary Ann puffed smoke towards the ceiling. 'She's not going back there tonight. But I'm worried he'll come looking for her, because he's bound to know she'll like as not be here, and I don't know what might happen if he turns up. I'm fretted out of my mind over it.'

'And what's Beti going to do in the long run, Mary

Ann?' McKenna asked, asking himself why they spoke of and around Beti as if she were an incompetent.

'I don't know,' Mary Ann admitted. 'This isn't the first time he's done cruel things to her . . . but it's the first time Beti's got off her backside, if you get my meaning, and not just taken whatever he dishes out.'

'Better late than never, eh, Beti?' Dewi pulled a folded handkerchief from his pocket, shook it open, and handed it to her. 'Wipe your eyes, love. Mr McKenna and me'll go and talk to John Jones.'

McKenna stood up. 'We'll tell him to keep right away until you decide what you want to do. If anything crops up, ring the station. I'll arrange for someone to come right away.'

Beti's mouth trembled with the vestige of a smile.

In the car, McKenna picked up the telephone and punched out a number, 'Who're you ringing, sir?' Dewi asked. 'Social Services?'

'No, I'm bloody not!' McKenna snapped. 'What d'you think they'd do with her, eh? They'd cart her off to Gwynfryn Ward, and lock her up because she's threatening to harm that no-good!'

While McKenna spoke into the telephone, Dewi sat quietly, gazing through the windscreen at the darkening sky above the church tower; half-listening, half-not-listening.

'Can you do that, sir?' he asked. 'Isn't it against regulations? We can't very well get John Beti arrested over that body just because he's clouted his missis.'

Both men walked down the path towards Beti's cottage, Dewi shining the torch, scanning the beam against tree trunks gleaming silver in the twilight, frightening small animals in the undergrowth.

'John Beti won't get arrested if he keeps his hands to himself and his nasty mouth shut,' McKenna said. 'And as nobody but you and me and the bodies in the graveyard is going to be knowing about it in any other way, it doesn't matter if it's laid down in the Holy Bible that you can't do it, does it?'

John Jones lolled in the room which served himself and Beti as kitchen and parlour, a can of beer in his hand, the debris of breakfast, lunch and tea littering the table. Dirty dishes overflowed the sink. The room smelt, of nothing in particular except dirty humankind, the smell of unbathed flesh and unwashed clothes, of sweaty hair and rancid armpits.

'What do you want, Dewi fucking Prys?' he demanded, as Dewi and McKenna walked in.

'We've come to tell you to keep away from Beti,' McKenna said politely.

Beti's husband smirked. 'Setting coppers on me now, is she? Makes a change from that old witch up the road. And what am I supposed to've done to her?'

'You insulted her,' McKenna said, leaning over the man. 'And you hit her.'

'So what?' John Jones said. 'That a crime now, then, is it? Can't a man keep his woman in order these days?'

Dewi leaned against the door jamb. 'Depends what comes of it. Depends what he does to her, John Jones.'

'Why don't you go fuck yourself?'

'Why don't you shut your mouth and give your arse

a chance, old man?' Dewi asked. 'Listen to the chief inspector here. He's telling you to leave Beti alone.'

'So why don't you both fuck off back where you came from? So I don't have to complain to Councillor Williams about how I'm getting grief from the fucking coppers for doing nothing except find a body they're too fucking slow to find themselves. Councillor Williams wouldn't like to hear that. Not at all.'

Dewi advanced into the room. 'Well, old man, if you're going to complain to Councillor Williams, you may as well have something to complain about.'

'Dewi!' McKenna warned.

'Oh, come on, sir! He makes me want to vomit! Got the bloody cheek to make snide remarks about Beti, and look at him! No oil painting, is he? And the stink on him!' Dewi looked John Jones up and down. 'I pity Beti, I really do! Fancy finding that lying next to you of a night!'

The old man leapt to his feet, lunging for Dewi. '*Hwrgi!*' he spat.

Dewi grabbed him by the throat. 'No man calls me a whore's dog!' He shook John Jones, making his head snap back and forth on its skinny neck.

McKenna pulled them apart, pushing Beti's husband, furious as a fighting turkeycock, back into his chair, and holding Dewi at arm's length. 'Stop it! Both of you!' He dragged Dewi towards the door. 'Wait outside!' To the old man, McKenna snarled, 'You go within a hundred yards of Beti, and I'll lock you up. D'you understand? And I won't care how much trouble you or your fancy bloody friends cause!'

He slammed the door behind him, and pushed Dewi down the path. 'You bloody fool, Dewi Prys! Don't ever behave like that again! D'you understand? My officers do not act like pit bull sodding terriers!'

Dewi stood in the darkness of the path beside the graveyard, his face mutinous in the light from his torch. 'I don't care!' he stormed. 'The bloody bastard asked for it! He should be swinging from some tree with a rope round his ugly neck! How could anyone be so horrible to Beti?'

'Dewi, Dewi!' McKenna sighed. 'They're married to each other, aren't they? You can't know what goes on between them. Nobody knows what goes on in people's marriages.' They walked slowly up the path. 'You've taken sides, and it's not our job to do that.'

Dewi stopped in his tracks and glared. 'I always had you down for being a straight copper, Mr McKenna. If it's not our job to take sides, what're we doing here tonight?'

'Crime prevention.'

'Well, then!' Dewi strode off. 'It would count as crime prevention if I'd smashed his shitty head into the wall, wouldn't it? Sir!'

McKenna leaned on the wall, delving into his jacket pocket for cigarettes and lighter. Blowing smoke into the musty night air, where it lingered just above his head like ectoplasm seeping from a nearby grave, he thought about the nature of the Celt, a subject on which Jack was given to rhetoric from time to time, of the opinion he dwelt among lawless feuding tribes. He could not grasp the ambivalence sleeping in the Welsh heart, could not understand the legacy of bitterness and sheer distrust left by centuries of oppression and injustice, and could not see why the thin crust of civilized behaviour might be shattered by that older legacy, the lessons of gangster politics and swift reprisal, learned from native forefathers. Jack never suffered the torments which might afflict McKenna or Dewi, could see nothing amiss in the fact that their role was to uphold and impose the law of a foreign government. And least of all would Jack ever understand the fear that rotted the Celtic soul, the fear that oppression only came to those who deserved it, to whom some defect of their deepest being rendered them fit for nothing else. McKenna finished the cigarette, and ground its glowing butt into a pile of leaf mould. Walking slowly up the night-shrouded path, glimpsing only a few faint stars between the overhanging trees, he wondered how long it might be before the afflictions of Ulster found root in the fertile soul of Wales.

Trees rustled about him; he saw the ghostly shape of an owl flitting through the woods, felt the pulse of its huge wings on the air. Beyond the wall, will o'the wisp danced in the graveyard. Fool's fire, McKenna thought, or perhaps the earthbound souls of stillborn children, hovering through eternity between Heaven and Hell. His shadow dogged his footsteps, as if come to life and whispering in his wake. His flesh crawled, waiting for the cold breath on the back of his neck, the icy fingers touching his face. He walked with a measured tread, refusing to look behind him, refusing to run. The round beam from Dewi's torch danced in front of his feet. 'Thought you'd got lost, sir,' the boy said, leading the way back to McKenna's car. As they strapped themselves in, he apologized. 'I'm sorry I gabbed off back there, sir. That horrible old man made me mad.' Peering through the back window of the car as McKenna drove out of the village, he added, 'D'you know, sir, I could've sworn there was somebody behind you just now on the path.'

Chapter 18

'*Cui bono?*' Eifion Roberts lounged in McKenna's office, brilliant morning sunshine behind the venetian blind casting stripes on walls and floors and furniture.

'What did you say?' McKenna asked.

'*Cui bono?* It means –'

'I know what it means!' McKenna said irritably. 'Will you stop rocking backwards and forwards on that chair? You're too fat. What am I to tell HQ if you break the legs?'

'We are in a mood this morning, aren't we? Got out of bed the wrong side, did you?'

'Mind your own business.'

Dr Roberts picked up his mug of tea. 'Woman trouble, McKenna.'

'I bloody know that!'

'What I meant was, you're not getting any,' the pathologist tittered. 'Nothing to get your leg over.'

'Must you be so disgustingly crude?' McKenna snapped.

'Sex is sex is sex, Michael, whatever fancy language you dress it up with. Anyway,' Eifion Roberts smirked, 'it's a well-known medical fact that excess of unshed seed sends a body barking mad in next to no time. That's why Onan in the Bible wasn't as far off the mark as God made him out to be. Better out than in, as they say.' He selected another biscuit from the plate on McKenna's desk. 'There was a case round Llanrwst or Ruthin when Queen Vic ruled our pleasant land. This lad murdered this girl because he was mad with love for her and she was going to marry somebody else. Slashed her throat this way and that 'til her head almost fell off, then trotted off and gave himself up to the local flatfoot.'

'So what?'

'So they didn't hang him, did they?' Dr Roberts said. 'All these eminent medicos testified at the trial how he was suffering from what you're suffering from, and they sent him to Broadmoor.'

'I see.' McKenna shuffled papers on his desk. 'And what am I suffering from?' he asked. 'What pearls of medical wisdom are about to dribble and plop from your fat little lips? Why don't you just say? Then you can sod off and leave me in peace to get on with some work.'

Roberts laughed. 'You can be so nasty, Michael, it's almost a pleasure to listen to you! Jest if you will. Mock if you will. But go and get your end away, and see how much better you feel afterwards. That is, of course,' he looked at McKenna with a sly leer, 'if you can find anyone willing to accommodate you. How about that buxom little policewoman you transferred from Holyhead? She's got a nice bum on her. It'd do you the world of good to unlace your moral stays, so to speak. You waft around like a Victorian virgin getting an attack of the vapours if anyone mentions sex.' He grinned. 'S-E-X, Michael McKenna. Like all things in moderation, it can be good for you.' Suddenly serious, he added, 'Tell me to mind my own business, but is that what's gone wrong between you and Denise? I can't help but see you as riddled with the Papist guilt about matters of the flesh.'

McKenna squirmed. 'I don't want to talk about Denise. She's coming to the house tonight, and I haven't a clue what to say to her.'

'Let her do the talking, then. Always the best way with women, I've found . . . You haven't answered my question.'

'As a matter of fact, Eifion,' McKenna said, 'I'm already unchained from that particular lunatic.'

'What lunatic?'

'Socrates is supposed to have said the human sexual drive is like being chained to a lunatic.'

'Did he?' Dr Roberts stared at McKenna. 'He's got a lot to answer for, hasn't he? Almost as much as that old fraud of a psychoanalyst from Vienna. Must be where all the holy folk got the idea of using guilt as a cudgel to keep the fornicating hordes and their lunatics in order. And why the likes of little Betty Prout got thrown out of her village because she was expecting, and no ring on her finger . . . She threw her baby down a well in the end, to get shut of the guilt and shame, and if that's the best God can do for people, He should be ashamed of Himself.'

'Not so long ago, you'd've been burnt as a heretic.'

'Gone down in history,' the pathologist agreed. 'Hung, drawn and quartered, like that Catholic priest William Davies. Bet you didn't learn about him in church, did you? He was only a Welsh martyr. Not quite the same as an English one.'

'What did he do?'

'Offended Her Almighty Majesty Elizabeth the First

of England by being RC and proud of it. They strung him up at Beaumaris Castle in 1593, and the locals wouldn't supply the hangman, or the wood for the scaffold, so they brought them in from Chester. Then they cut the poor bugger down, carved him up into four neat joints, and put quarters on display at Caernarfon, Ludlow, Conwy and Beaumaris. Needless to say,' he added with a wry grin, 'William Davies doesn't have a grave! And talking of folk rotting in full view, what about the corpses hanging at crossroads, and crows flying over your head with somebody's eyes squashed in their beak . . . our Romy would've felt in good company, wouldn't she?' He drank the last of his tea, dabbing his lips with a paper tissue from the box on McKenna's desk. 'Actually, it was Romy I came to talk about.'

'What about her?' McKenna asked. 'Something about the suit?'

'No, you've had your bit of luck with that. Now you'll have to find somebody with a penchant for nicking other people's perfume to fit into it,' the pathologist said. 'And of course, if you do, you might find the lady's got fatter or thinner in the past few years . . . Bear up, Michael. It'll all be over one day.'

'What's that supposed to mean? I'm to look forward to dying, am I, because there's damn all else to look forward to?'

'All in the same boat, aren't we? Waiting to cross the River Styx as soon as Charon gives the nod . . . How d'you plan to find out who pushed that boat out for Romy?'

'I'm waiting for Owen Griffiths to decide whether or not we start digging up floors at Gallows Cottage and combing those bloody woods. Jack Tuttle has some hare-brained idea the owner of the suit may be mouldering somewhere like her mate Romy.'

'Why?'

'Because she might have seen whoever topped Romy and therefore had to be done away with herself.'

'Doesn't fit, somehow, and don't ask me why, 'cos I don't know. I think this is women's work,' Dr Roberts said. 'There's a feeling of women being at the root of it, and men being nowt a pound . . . Allsopp's a fly-by-night, in the sense Romy flew by and left after dropping a bit of shit on his head. Her husband's killed off in a car smash, and just deserts maybe. Simeon, if you can swallow the rumours, blunders through the centuries like a besotted teenager looking for his missis, who like as not chucked that kiddie of theirs down the stairs. Then there's those old crones in the village with their tales . . . men are getting too hard done by to be perpetrating anything.'

'Revenge?' McKenna suggested.

'What I said before. *Cui bono?* The oldest motive of all.'

'I don't know,' McKenna admitted. 'Who benefits from Romy's death . . .? The solicitor made no mention of a will.'

'Then I daresay it'll be whoever can get their greedy paws on whatever she had. Pity her solicitor couldn't tell you where she kept her bank account, isn't it? Did she pay him in cash, like she did with the rent?' Dr Roberts stood up. 'I'd better be going.' He brushed biscuit crumbs off the lapels of his jacket. 'Expecting the bishop himself, no less, to tell me what's to be done with Rebekah.'

'She's not turned to dust then?'

'No.' The pathologist grinned. 'I could quarter her, couldn't I? Give 'em a piece or two each . . . they'd still squabble, wouldn't they?' He sighed. 'Like as not, they'd be rowing over this one 'til Kingdom come.'

Jack affected disappointment that his suggestion had been dismissed. 'We've got no grounds to think this other woman's dead, Jack,' McKenna said. 'HQ will not sanction the expense and manpower for any more digging or searching unless we can show good reason. And we can't.'

'It's the most likely explanation.'

'It isn't really, sir,' Dewi offered. 'It's more than likely this woman bumped off Romy and hid the suit because somebody'd seen her wearing it when she was with Romy, and it's quite distinctive, because we know Debenhams only had twenty jackets like that for the whole of North Wales from Pwllheli to Chester.'

'Shut UP!' Jack roared. 'Just SHUT UP!'

'Dewi could be right, Jack.'

'In a pig's eye!' Jack exploded. 'I don't know how you put up with him. He gets on my bloody nerves!'

McKenna drummed his fingers on the steering wheel, waiting for a huge articulated truck to manoeuvre into Glynne Road, and up to Kwik Save supermarket. 'That much is obvious, but you really needn't be quite so abrasive with the lad. He has some good ideas.' He looked at Jack. 'Change your face, Jack! That expression is enough, as my old gran would say, to turn the milk in the cows' bellies from here to Donegal.'

'Dewi Prys might be clever, but he's as mouthy and cocky with it as Jamie Thief. They're like some kind of bloody twins, one each side of the law . . . why doesn't Jamie speak Welsh? He only lives a few doors away from Dewi Prys.'

McKenna shrugged. 'Same reason half the Welsh people in North Wales don't speak Welsh, I suppose. Are you going to start learning?'

Jack grimaced. 'Looks like I won't have much choice if I want to stay around here. We've enough to do keeping the locals in order without having to learn Welsh.'

'Policy, Jack,' McKenna said. 'The powers that be daren't upset the Welsh Language Society, and they want everybody in Wales speaking Welsh. And, those who don't like the idea are welcome to bugger off over the border.'

'It's all become very hardline political, hasn't it? Near enough fascist, if you ask me . . . I wouldn't mind if Welsh wasn't so bloody hard. I don't know how you get your mouth round some of the words. Owen Griffiths doesn't speak Welsh, does he? I haven't heard of anybody trying to make him.'

'Yes, Jack, but he's a superintendent.' The road ahead finally cleared, and McKenna accelerated past the swimming baths. 'Anyway, it's not as hard as English. Did you know, there are bilingual mongols and subnormals? Makes you think, eh?'

'You're not supposed to say mongols or subnormals. It's very politically incorrect.'

'What else are you supposed to call them?'

'I dunno,' Jack admitted. 'People with learning difficulties?' he suggested. 'Where're we going?'

'To see Mr Stott.'

'Well, you've gone right past the entrance to Turf Square.'

'He'll be at work, won't he? Showing visitors the glories of Snidey Castle.'

The huge bulk of Castle Keep soared into a bright blue sky, grey stone and neo-Norman arcades and mouldings in deep morning shadow. McKenna rested his arms on the car door, sunshine striking gold lights in his hair. 'This place, Jack, is built on blood. I wouldn't shed any tears if our terrorist countrymen reduced it to a heap of burnt-out ruins.'

'That's anarchist talk. What else were the locals supposed to do except work for the lord of the manor? Starve?'

'The Welsh starved anyway. But without any dignity.'

'I don't think,' Jack observed, 'there is ever dignity in poverty and starvation. Do you? Come on. I want to have a shufti at Jamie's boyfriend.'

Waiting upon Christopher Stott in a large vaulted room overlooking the back of the castle grounds, where lambs and ewes grazed in meadows undulating towards a distant seascape, Jack stared at dingy oil paintings in tarnished gilded frames hung against bare stone walls, wiped his fingers across the surfaces of heavy oak furniture, timbers dark with age and wax, made scuff marks with his shoes on the golden velvet pile of wall to wall carpeting. 'How the other half lives, eh?' he said. 'Bet this place is colder than Eifion Roberts's mortuary in the winter.'

'Not so warm now, is it?' McKenna, gazing

from the window, shivered a little. 'Gorgeous view from here, Jack. You can see the rhododendron woods.'

A tall thin man with a small beard slithered into the room. 'You wanted to see me?' he asked, looking from Jack to McKenna.

'You're Christopher Stott?' McKenna asked.

The man nodded, his body waving from side to side with the motion of his head, like a sapling bending to the wind. He wore an etiolated look, as if kept in a dark cupboard for many years, his body stretching itself: a plant stem searching for a chink of light. The sickly look of one living under constant stresses dulled his eyes and stripped colour from his skin.

'What d'you want?' he asked. 'My boss doesn't like staff having visitors.' He placed himself carefully on the edge of one of the fat chairs, knees tight together, and his hands balled into fists in his lap. McKenna stared, while Jack spoke of cars and queries, wondering if Jack were not right about Christopher Stott's being someone's boyfriend, if not Jamie's.

'Mr Stott,' McKenna said, 'we understand you recently sold your car to a neighbour. We further understand you regularly allowed someone to borrow the car, a practice which appears to have continued to the present.' McKenna heard himself becoming pedantic. 'Perhaps you would care to tell us why?'

'Why what?' Stott looked again from one to the other, a frown cutting into the dry-looking skin of his forehead.

'Why you lent the car to Jamie Thief!' Jack snapped. 'What d'you owe him for?'

'Jamie Thief?' Stott raised his eyebrows. 'D'you

mean Jamie Wright? That's not a very nice way to talk about him, is it?'

The man was prissy: McKenna could think of no other word to describe him. 'Jamie IS a bloody thief!' Jack shouted. 'That's how he got his name.'

McKenna intervened. 'Mr Stott, the matter of the car has occurred in the course of another investigation. And we must clear up any queries about this vehicle.'

'Oh.' Stott took his time to absorb the words. 'What queries do you have?'

'I've just told you, haven't I?' Jack sounded exasperated. 'Why did you lend it to Jamie?'

'Why not? I wasn't aware it was a crime to lend a car to a friend.' A smirk settled on Stott's lips, thin behind the scraggy little beard, as he answered.

McKenna coughed. 'What we'd really like to know, Mr Stott, is why Jamie should be a friend of yours.'

'Really!' The thin mouth made a moue of distaste. 'What a question! And what, I may add, a waste of expensive police time, not to say mine, to come here asking such a question.' Christopher Stott bridled with indignation. Watching him, McKenna saw fear beneath the bluster. He sat down, and leaned forwards.

'It rather bothers me, Mr Stott,' he said, 'that a person whom we have no reason to believe is other than law-abiding should be on such friendly terms with someone of Jamie's background and inclinations as to lend them a very expensive car. And,' he added, watching Stott's eyes, 'it bothers me even more when the loan of this vehicle continues even after the car has acquired a new owner.'

Stott relaxed. 'If Jamie is still borrowing the car, it's nothing to do with me. Why don't you ask the new owner?'

'Oh, we will,' McKenna said. 'But right at this moment, we're asking you.'

'I've already said I can't help you. I merely let the boy borrow the car once or twice, several years ago.'

'How many years ago?' Jack demanded. 'And why?'

'Two, three years ago . . .' Stott said. 'I sold it last year, as you no doubt know. And,' he sighed, 'if you really must know, Jamie borrowed it because he helped out doing odd jobs round the garden . . . in lieu of payment.'

'Can't you do your own gardening?'

'I can. If I choose. And if I'm not too busy.'

'Where did you meet Jamie?' McKenna asked.

'Where did I meet him? How on earth do you expect me to remember? I've known him for years, off and on.'

'Funny,' Jack observed. 'I wouldn't've thought your path would cross with his all that easily.'

'Well, you're obviously not local, are you? One knows almost everybody by sight, and most people to speak to. It's a small place . . . Or hadn't you noticed?' The smirk returned. McKenna, convinced the wrong questions had been asked, had not the most remote idea what might be the right ones. He regarded Stott, wishing he could simply walk from the room, drive from the castle, and expunge all thoughts of Romy Cheney and her past from his mind. Instinct insisted there was treasure here, if he found the right place to strike with his spade.

'When did you get the car?' he asked.

'I can't quite remember. Around four years ago. Why?'

'Trade in, was it?' Jack took the ball into his court.

'No.'

'Why d'you sell it?'

'For a number of reasons.'

'Name a few.'

'Why should I?'

'Because I'm a policeman, and I expect people to answer my questions.'

'You may well be a policeman, but I'm beginning to think you're a bully as well.'

Jack grinned wolfishly. 'You're too sensitive, Mr Stott. I'm asking you a perfectly reasonable question, and here you are getting all hoity-toity on me.'

'Just tell us,' McKenna sighed, 'why you sold the car.'

'It really is none of your business!' Stott announced. 'If you must know, it cost too much to run; I didn't use it very often, and I thought it might end up stolen or vandalized if it was left sitting in the road. Does that satisfy you?'

'Pity you didn't think of all that before you bought it,' Jack remarked.

Stott rose to his feet, anger shaking his wand-like frame. 'You really are a bully!' He stamped his foot on the carpet. 'I've a good mind to complain about you!'

'Councillor Williams will be more than happy to hear from you,' Jack grinned. Stott turned on his heel, and flounced towards the door.

'Mr Stott,' McKenna called.

'What is it now?'

'Did the car have a gonk in it when you had it?'

There was a sharp intake of breath. McKenna could not tell if the greyness in Stott's face was shock, or merely shadows in the deep recess of the doorway.

'A what?'

Jack gave McKenna an odd look. 'A gonk, Mr Stott,' McKenna went on. 'It's a coloured furry toy you hang in the back window of a car.'

Laughter, almost hysterical, brayed from Stott's open mouth, as he faded into the darker shadow of the hallway. 'I have no idea what you're talking about!'

'A fat lot of use that was,' Jack said. McKenna hunched over the wheel of the car, staring through the windscreen at early visitors wandering around the castle courtyard, furiously drawing on the second cigarette since leaving Stott. Jack opened the door to let out smoke. 'I told you, he's Jamie's boyfriend. The neighbour's probably another boyfriend . . . a bit of rough.'

'Jamie's not queer,' McKenna said. 'Stott's another kettle of fish, though.'

'Queer is another politically incorrect term. You're supposed to say gay.' Jack saw a scowl crease up the skin above McKenna's long nose.

'And what have homosexuals got to be happy about?' McKenna snapped. 'Shut up and think!'

'What about?'

'Stott . . . Jamie . . . the car. Blackmail.'

'Jamie knows Stott's got a boyfriend, so puts the heavy on him.'

'It's not illegal.' McKenna's eyes narrowed against the glitter of noonday sunshine bouncing off the car bonnet. 'Stott could have thousands of boyfriends, and not be breaking the law.'

'Well, I don't know, do I?' Jack said irritably. 'Maybe he does it for money. That job can't pay very well, and he's a wife and kid to support. His clothes aren't very good quality.'

'If he does, we'll never find out,' McKenna said. 'You're right about his clothes, but most people don't dress up for work. We'd look pretty scruffy if we didn't get an allowance. Look at the mess on some of the drugs squad.'

'They're supposed to blend in with the background . . . Maybe Stott likes little boys.'

'Maybe,' McKenna agreed. 'And how're we supposed to find out if he does? Stop all the lads in Bangor and say, "Hey, kid, is Mr Stott giving you one every so often?"'

'You're quite vulgar sometimes, sir. Anyway,' Jack laughed, 'nobody does that sort of thing for love, do they? They want a big fat reward for their pains, as well as hush money.'

McKenna thumped the wheel. 'That's it, isn't it? Money! Where did Stott get the money to buy that car?'

'Never-never, like the rest of us, I imagine. And I'll bet he sold it 'cos he couldn't keep up the payments. Then again, it could've been a present from an admirer.'

McKenna started the engine. 'Are we going to talk to Jamie again?' Jack asked.

'Not yet awhile.' McKenna swerved violently to avoid a coach, laden with trippers, making its way up the winding narrow driveway. 'Don't want to give folk grounds to accuse us of harassment, do we? There's too many beating a path to Councillor Williams's door as it is. Anyway, I can't see Jamie dropping himself in the shit.'

Jack leaned towards the open window, enjoying the warmth of the sun and the wind in his face. 'Perhaps we could get them to grass each other up . . .' He jerked his head back as a cloud of diesel fumes from the exhaust of a bus befouled the air. 'Eifion Roberts reckons it's all to do with money, doesn't he? Who gets Romy's millions? *Cherchez la cache.*'

'I didn't know you spoke French.'

'Just a bit left over in my head from school. I was thinking of *cherchez la femme*. You know, find the lady.'

'We've already found her,' McKenna said. 'And another to be on the safe side in case we mislay the first. Is it *le cache* or *la cache*?'

'I don't know, do I? Doesn't matter anyway, because with our track record, we're not going to find it, are we? We don't know who took all her furniture and clothes and personal bits and pieces from Gallows Cottage; we don't know where it all is; we don't know where her money is, even though every bank and building society in the country's been circulated.'

McKenna turned into the yard at the rear of the police station and parked. 'Swiss bank account?' he suggested. 'Liechtenstein? The Bahamas? We don't even know if she had a solicitor, because she paid off the other one in cash and went to earth.' He slammed the car door. 'Come on. Let's do something!'

'What?' Jack trotted behind.

'I don't know, do I?' McKenna snapped. 'Get off our backsides and *cherchez la femme* in the suit for starters.'

Chapter 19

'Are you sure you've looked in the right places?' Owen Griffiths asked. 'Have you explored every likelihood? We get too much flak as it is, and I don't want to hear accusations of negligence about this woman.'

'Press on your back?' McKenna asked.

'And the deputy chief. All wanting to know when we're going to make an arrest.' The superintendent rubbed his chin. 'Never, probably, is the answer to that, only I can't very well say so, can I?' He tapped his pen on the desk. 'You sure she wasn't connected with the terrorists?'

'Don't see how. There's a huge gulf between torching the odd holiday cottage and killing in cold blood.'

'It happens in Ireland all the time.'

'Yes, I know. And it'll happen here sooner or later . . . Anyway, Special Branch would've hijacked the investigation if they even smelt a terrorist link.'

'They would, wouldn't they?' Griffiths agreed. 'Especially after you rattled their cage sending faxes over the Irish Sea. Have we ruled out that man who found the body?'

'John Jones?' McKenna asked. 'Not necessarily.'

'How's that?'

'No particular reason, except he's a vicious little bugger and I don't like his face or his mouth.'

McKenna stubbed out his cigarette, grinding the butt as if it were John Jones's face.

'That's no basis for detection, Michael, is it?'

Dewi said to McKenna, rather gleefully, 'Headquarters'll weep when they see our phone bill. We've sent off hundreds of faxes, and been on the telephones for hours.'

'And what've we got for all that trouble and money?'

'Bugger all, sir. Which, to my mind,' Dewi said, 'means nobody official moved anything from Gallows Cottage, and Romy Cheney's money isn't lying idle in any bank. Whoever bumped her off shifted the gear themselves, and enjoyed themselves with her money. The woman in the suit would've needed help moving furniture. And a van. We checked all the hirings within six months either side of when Dr Roberts said Romy was killed. Another big fat zero.'

'Whoever's getting at the money would need to forge her signature. Whatever name Romy was using.'

'That's not too hard. The banks don't check half the time.'

McKenna stubbed out a cigarette. 'We'll press on, for the time being. You can take those ledgers back to Prosser tomorrow, and make sure he signs for them.'

'Dr Roberts called. Said to tell you Rebekah's to be put in the village churchyard, with an inscription in Hebrew on her gravestone. He reckons there'll be a media circus at the funeral. And he wants to know how much longer Romy's going to be left in his mortuary "wrapped in a white sheet", as he put it, and "cold and unwanted".'

*

The buyer from Debenhams telephoned the police station shortly before the shop closed, leaving a message at the switchboard for someone to call her back as soon as possible.

McKenna sat on his back doorstep until full night shrouded the earth, watching over the cat at play in the little garden, feeling the heat of the day seep from the slate beneath him. Pulling his shirts and underclothes off the line, he buried his face in the fresh sharp scent on the cloth, and looked out into the distance at Puffin Island, a dark humped whale-shape in a sea the colour of ink, the light of Penmon Lighthouse flashing every sixty seconds to warn of jagged teeth of rock beneath water still as a pond. He wondered if he would be here in the winter, to see the city below through a tracery of bare branches, perhaps under snows come riding the back of the east wind.

He lay sleepless into the small hours, that time before dawn when the blood ebbs its slowest, when life is held by the thinnest thread, and thought of Denise, in whose company he had spent two hours of his life that evening, and for whom not a vestige of desire lingered in his heart, making him want to weep again for the loss of it. Wondering if he might be permitted to laugh in equal measure tomorrow for the tears shed tonight, he fell asleep at last, as a lone seagull took to the sky, calling its fellows to wakefulness.

Morning brought more clear skies, and sunshine gilding the last snows on the flanks of Tryfan and the Black Ladders. Dewi arrived early at work, finding

McKenna in his office, sifting aimlessly through a printout of calls, trying to match them to the handwritten records kept in a battered lever-arch file.

'Why don't these two lots of paper bear any relation to each other, Constable?' McKenna scowled.

'They're not necessarily supposed to, sir.'

'Then what is the point of them?'

Standing obediently before the desk, Dewi wondered if they would all suffer the rough edge of McKenna's tongue before the day were out. 'The printout is an automatic record of all calls through the computer from HQ. That,' he added, gesturing to the file, 'is the log of calls answered where there might be a complaint arising. Sir.'

McKenna riffled the papers. 'Is it complete?' he demanded. 'Is it accurate?'

'I wouldn't know, sir.'

'Well, you should know! How on earth can we solve crimes if we don't even know what crimes have been committed?' McKenna slammed the file shut, and tossed it on to the floor. 'What are you waiting for, Constable?'

Dewi vaguely recalled a wisdom about discretion and valour, saluted and marched from the room. Walking along the corridor to the squad room, he met Eifion Roberts. 'You looking for Mr McKenna?' he asked.

'I am indeed. Is he in?'

'Well, he's in, but he's not in the best of moods from what I could see.'

'Never is, is he, Dewi?'

'It's bad form to bring your home troubles to work,

Michael.' Dr Roberts sat in his favourite chair, and raised its front legs from the floor.

'Shut up and mind your own business!'

'You're a sour bugger, McKenna. When I come to cut you up, I daresay I'll find vinegar in your veins instead of blood. Young Dewi was quite upset from your nastiness.'

'I haven't been nasty to him.'

'You've not been nice to him, have you? You can't blow hot and cold with people the way you do. You've got to be consistent. I take it you saw Denise last night?'

McKenna said nothing. He lit a cigarette from the stub of one only half-smoked, and hid behind the veil of smoke.

'Ah, well. It'll all come out in the wash, as they say.'

'Is that another version of your little homily about everything being over one day?'

'Maybe.' Dr Roberts shrugged. 'Maybe not. We're all as fed up as each other, you know. Life is there to be fed up with.'

'Why don't you write a philosophical treatise, and give everybody the benefit of your great wisdom?'

'You mean like your friend Socrates?'

'If you like.'

'I've been looking up Socrates, haven't I? Trying to find out what he wrote about sex drives and lunatics. And do you know what I found?'

'I'm sure you'll tell me.'

'Socrates never wrote a word.'

'So? He said it, didn't he? A lot of these things are word of mouth.'

'You never admit you could be wrong, do you? How

d'you know it wasn't Aristotle or Plato or some other wop?'

'It doesn't matter who said it. It's the idea that matters.'

'I suppose.' Dr Roberts regarded McKenna, noticing the stain of dark shadows under the fine eyes, the sunken look around socket and cheekbones. He said, his voice more gentle, 'You know, Michael, the trouble could be that Denise isn't unchained from her particular lunatic. Women and sex is a potent evil, if they let it get the better of them one way or another.'

Dewi found the message from Debenhams under an untidy heap of telephone messages sent to the CID office for filing by the switchboard, and decided to tell McKenna, whatever the reaction, that incompetence such as this sent crime astray. He dialled the store's number, and asked for the buyer, who told him, her voice twanging with the accents of Liverpool, 'Head Office accounts have got records of three sales of the jacket in size 16 on credit or store cards, but you'll have to ask officially for the names. Ask for the senior accountant.' From that man, Dewi suffered a lecture about confidentiality, about customer privacy, about the necessity of observing such rules, and waited patiently for the chance to request the information he wanted. He imagined him a little man, fat inside a pinstripe suit and stiff collar, perched on a high stool before a sloping desk covered in leather-bound ledgers, then realized the accountant would be, like himself, a slave to a bleeping electronic console. About to open his mouth, he found himself adrift in the sea of names on which this woman had made her voyage.

'Perhaps you could give me the names of whoever bought the jackets, sir, then I can say if we're interested in any of them.'

'I can't give out our customers' names willy-nilly, even if it is to the police. Don't you know who you're looking for?'

'We have to be most careful never to suggest anything to people. Not leading people where we want them to go.'

'You know the ropes better than I do, I suppose . . . These are the ladies who bought design number H766453291 in UK size 16, Euro size 42.' Dewi scribbled frantically with his pen. 'Number one.' He supposed a senior accountant ate and slept by numbers, made love to his wife by numbers. 'E-L-E-R-I M. Jones. How d'you pronounce that? She used a store card. Number two: Margaret S. Jones.' Dewi's heart leapt and plummeted back to earth. 'She used Visa. Lot of Joneses round your way, aren't there? Number three: M. Bailey. He or she used a Visa card as well.'

Dewi stared at the name he had written. 'How is that last name spelt, sir?'

'B-A-I-L-E-Y.'

Dewi drew in his breath. 'Sir, could you give me the details for M. Bailey, please? Date of purchase, card number, and bank.'

'She bought a skirt as well in the same size. On the 26 October three years – no, four years ago this October. Oh, and she bought three pairs of tights, and a scarf . . .'

'We'll need a court order,' Jack said. 'It's a live account.'

'How can it be live when its owner's dead?' McKenna snapped.

'Well, it's being used by somebody,' Jack retorted. 'Didn't the bank just say so? Anyway, who's to say we've got the right woman and the right bank? And even if it is her, what's she doing buying clothes in all the wrong sizes?'

'She bought them for somebody else, didn't she? A present or something.' McKenna took off his glasses and rubbed his eyes. 'And it's the right Margaret Bailey. The bank last wrote to her at the end of February. They sent the letter to Gallows Cottage.'

'Wil Jones would've said if there were any letters for her.'

'So the post is redirected, although it's a long time for the sorting office to redirect without asking questions, though I suppose if somebody keeps paying for redirection notices . . .'

'Where d'you think it's being redirected to?'

'Bloody Timbuktu, knowing our luck. We'll definitely need a court order to get information from the sorting office, because all their business is governed by the Official Secrets Act. While I take a trip to see Wil Jones, somebody can take Prosser's precious ledgers back. I've photocopied anything we need for now.'

McKenna left the car at the top of the track, and walked down to the cottage, passing through bands of bright light and deep shade where the sun broke through densely massed trees. As always, the woods were quiet, save for a bevy of crows clattering into flight as his presence disturbed their perch in one of the tall weedy trees. No other sound but the pad of his footfalls on mossy earth disturbed a silence almost strident in its intensity. Finding the cottage empty, he stood, hands in pockets, at the edge of the garden where it met the sea, watching tidal waters suck at the low spur of rock, smelling scents of seaweed and heady sea air, feeling on his cheeks the warmth of a west wind off the Straits. He saw them then, two heads poking above the top of the newly installed septic tank over to the right. He walked to the lip of the tank, and looked down on Wil and Dave, sweating in the warm sunshine.

Wil glanced up. 'Hello. Didn't expect to see you today.' He frowned. 'No trouble, is there? You're not coming to tear the place apart, are you?'

'No, Wil. Just something I want to ask you about.'

'Right then. I'll come out.' He climbed up the small ladder resting against the side of the tank.

'What are you doing in there?' McKenna asked.

'Sealing the joints so's we can put the lid on. In the old days, we'd've had to build the thing, brick by brick. There's something to be said for progress.' Wil clumped towards the cottage, his wellingtons sucking into the dewy grass. Looking down, McKenna could see a ring of moisture round the bottom of his own trouser legs.

'How would you know when it's full?' McKenna was curious.

Wil laughed. 'Your lavvy backs up! Mind you, I can see why the council insisted on the tank. If your drains just went straight out to sea, they'd back up every time the tide comes in.'

'And what d'you do when it is full?'

Wil regarded McKenna assessingly. 'Don't know

much, do you?' he commented. 'You call the council or the water board, and they send a truck round to suck it all out so's you can start filling it again.'

Removing his wellingtons at the back door, Wil padded in his socks to the Primus stove, to put on the kettle. 'What d'you want to ask me?'

'We've just found out some letters might have come here, addressed to a Margaret Bailey, or just an M. Bailey.'

'Oh.' Wil sat on his crate and lit his pipe. 'That her real name, was it? Always thought the other one was a bit far-fetched, even for the English.' He puffed smoke rings. McKenna watched them float slowly upwards towards the smoke-blackened beams of the ceiling, pierced by a shaft of sunlight through the dusty window.

'No,' Wil continued. 'Not seen any letters at all. Not even that junk mail folks are so fond of. Why don't you ask his highness at the estate office?'

'I shall . . . all in good time. Have you nearly finished here?'

'All but, provided folk leave us alone, and I don't only mean yourself,' Wil said. 'Word's got out about Rebekah . . . bloody tourists, wanting to be shown where we found her. Mostly Americans, I might add, rabbiting on about history.' He tamped his pipe on the tiled floor. 'Bloody obsessed with history, the Yanks.'

'Can't blame them, Wil. They haven't any of their own to speak of . . . I'd better be making tracks.'

'Stay for a *panad.* The kettle's nearly boiling.' Wil put coffee in three mugs, and stood looking through the window, his back to McKenna, waiting for the kettle to whistle. 'Tell you something you can't quite put your finger on,' he said. 'I keep seeing this bloke hanging round on the edge of the woods, and I'm beginning to wonder if there isn't something in all these tales after all. Dave's seen him too. Dark-haired guy in a white shirt, with a dead pale face and cold eyes.'

McKenna remembered the shadow that dogged his footsteps on Wednesday night. 'Mary Ann in the village says he's a gipsy.'

'Oh, does she? Not what Wednesday's paper reckoned, was it?' Wil took the kettle off the stove and poured steaming water into the mugs. 'He must be the first gippo in history able to vanish into thin air while you're staring him in the face.'

Dewi pulled up outside the estate office, humped the heavy ledgers into his arms, slammed the car door shut with his foot, and walked into the office. A small woman in rimless spectacles sat behind Prosser's desk.

'Can I help you?' she asked.

'I'm from the police,' Dewi explained. 'I've brought these back.' He put the ledgers on a filing cabinet. 'Er – where's Mr Prosser, then?'

'Oh, he's always off sick at this time of the year. He gets the most dreadful hayfever. You didn't need to see him, did you?'

'Well, my boss might. How long is he usually away?'

'A week. Ten days, perhaps. His doctor fills him up with drugs, and he can't drive or do anything while he's on them. I usually take over.'

'D'you deal with everything when Mr P.'s away, then? Mail and whatnot?'

'Oh, yes. I have authority to deal with everything.'

'It must be very interesting. I'll bet these bodies have caused a bit of a kerfuffle.'

'I'll say! Are you going to be arresting anybody soon?'

Dewi tapped his nose with his forefinger. 'Can't say, can I? But make sure you keep watching the news. It's been nice talking to you, Mrs –?'

'Miss Hughes. And you, too. Do call again.'

Dewi was at the door when he said, as if in afterthought, 'By the way, do you ever get mail for Gallows Cottage? In this office, I mean.'

'Mail for Gallows Cottage? Well, not very often. It's empty, isn't it?'

'Just a thought. I wondered what happened to letters if they arrived after the people'd left. You know, who sent them on?'

'Actually, there were one or two letters for somebody called – Bradley, was it? Quite some time ago, but I remember seeing them . . . It wasn't Bradley, though . . . some other English name beginning with B.'

'Oh, yes?' Dewi crossed his fingers behind his back. 'Did somebody collect the mail from the cottage?'

'Collect the mail? No, the post brought them here. Mr Prosser took them. He must've had the forwarding address, but you'd expect him to, wouldn't you?'

'Are you absolutely sure?' McKenna asked. 'We can't go chasing Prosser on a rumour.'

'It's not a rumour, sir,' Dewi insisted. 'That's what she said, clear as day. Mr Prosser took the mail for Gallows Cottage.'

'Yes, but,' Jack intervened, 'it wasn't post for Bailey,

was it? There's no reason why Prosser shouldn't send on mail. It's no crime.'

'Whereas,' McKenna took up the conversation, 'if we say to Prosser: "Why didn't you tell us you were sending on mail for a dead woman?" we'll be accusing him of something he might not have done. D'you see my point, Dewi?'

'No, I don't. With all due respect, sir, if Prosser's just been sending post on for some bod who stayed in the cottage some time, he's not going to mind us asking, is he? And if it's post for Romy he's been handling, then we've got the right to drop on him like a ton of bricks.'

'The boy's right, really,' Jack said.

'We'll give Mr Prosser a visit, then,' McKenna decided. 'A friendly visit. No heavy-handed stuff. Is that clear?'

Chapter 20

Trefor Prosser lived in an ancient and beautiful cottage near the top end of Rating Row in Beaumaris. His sleek Volvo stood at the kerb, gleaming in the sunshine. McKenna drew in behind the car, and peered at the cottage, its small windows shrouded in snow-white netting. 'These places are worth a bundle,' he observed. 'Highly sought-after residences in the most highly sought-after place in North Wales.'

'People want their heads seeing to in my opinion,' Dewi said. 'The houses were only built for fishermen and the like.'

'Yes, Dewi,' McKenna agreed. 'That was then, and this is now. Let's go and beard the lion, and no roaring.'

The front doors of the houses led straight on to a narrow pavement, just as they did in McKenna's street, but by comparison, McKenna dwelt in a slum. The door to Prosser's house, painted a deep glossy blue, was furnished with a brass knocker in the shape of a lion's head. McKenna ran his hand over the paint. 'Nice colour. What would you call it, Jack?'

'Poncy blue,' Jack sneered.

'Actually, sir,' Dewi volunteered. 'It's called French navy. Our neighbour used it on his house last year. You can buy it at B&Q.'

'I don't think the chief inspector wants to know, Prys,' Jack growled.

'I was only trying to help,' Dewi protested. 'For all we know, Mr McKenna might be planning a spot of home decorating now the weather's picking up.'

'Will you two shut up? Knock on the door, Jack. Let's do what we came for.'

The first snapping of the lion's teeth against wood yielded silence. Jack rapped harder, bringing a faint whisper of slippers on carpet. The door swung slowly open, and Prosser squinted around its edge, looking first at Jack, then at McKenna and Dewi. His eyes were bloodshot and red-rimmed, his cheeks pale, the end of his nose cherry bright.

'I'm ill. Can't you see?' he grumbled.

'Just a few words, Mr Prosser. We wouldn't bother you if it wasn't necessary. You know that.'

'What about?' Prosser hung on to the edge of the door, his body shivering gently.

'Let us in for a few minutes, will you, please?' McKenna asked. 'It's not a good idea to stand out in the street, is it?'

The door glided open far enough to admit them in single file. McKenna trod on a carpet so thick he could have slept on it in comfort, along a narrow hallway sweet with the scents of beeswax and pot-pourri, Prosser shuffling in front and into a back room which looked out on to a long, lawned garden. Cherry trees in full glorious bloom tossed in the wind, their petals showering to the ground.

Easing himself into an armchair upholstered in olive-green hide, Prosser waved his hand at the three police officers. 'Find yourselves a seat,' he invited, his voice muffled, catarrh blocking the sinuses. McKenna sat opposite on a matching sofa, Jack beside him, Dewi leaning against the wall by the door. Padded silk brocade draped the windows, thick velvety carpet lay underfoot, antique china was displayed on window ledge and mantelpiece. The chimney alcove held an ancient chest in aged and mellow oak. On illuminated glass shelves above stood the figure of an ox led by a young boy, life breathing from every line of the exquisitely carved ivory. The room was spotlessly clean, sweetly scented like the hallway. Prosser dragged a handkerchief from his trouser pocket, and wiped his watering eyes.

'What's so bloody urgent it can't wait?' he demanded. 'Why do three of you need to come? Scared I might attack you?' Clad in carpet slippers, grey flannel trousers, and a silk roll-neck sweater, he ran his fingers inside the collar, loosening it from his throat, wiped his eyes again, and held the handkerchief balled up in his left hand.

'We haven't progressed very far with the investigation into Ms Cheney's death,' McKenna began. 'However, we are pursuing several leads.'

'I should bloody hope so! That's what you get paid for, isn't it?'

'One of the things we're looking into,' McKenna went on, 'is the matter of some post which arrived at Gallows Cottage quite recently.'

'Post?' Prosser wiped his eyes again, hiding his expression behind the handkerchief. 'What post?'

'Post addressed to someone whose name begins with B. We understand it was sent on to the estate office.'

'Well, it would be, wouldn't it, if they weren't there any longer?' Prosser's tone was acid.

'Miss Hughes seems to think you might have taken it to send on. To a forwarding address.'

'Miss Hughes is probably right then, isn't she? Part of the job.' Prosser sniffed loudly.

'Would you perhaps remember the letters, Mr Prosser?' McKenna asked. 'Could you recall who they were addressed to? After all, you must know who's been in Gallows Cottage.'

'Of course I can't remember!' Prosser raged. 'Why d'you ask such a bloody stupid question? Is that what you've come here pestering me about? Is it? Why the bloody hell couldn't you use your common sense and look in those ledgers of mine you were so keen to take?' He was standing, shaking with rage. 'Go on! Get out! And don't think you've heard the last of this, because you haven't!'

Jack and McKenna stood up. Prosser stamped to the door, and waited. McKenna sighed. 'You've made your point, Mr Prosser. But I must warn you, if we find you've been withholding information, all the complaints in the world won't make any difference.'

Prosser's small plump frame stood in the shadow of the doorway, as, McKenna recalled, Christopher Stott's willowy body had been darkened by the massive embrasure of the Snidey Castle door. He stared at Prosser. 'You see, Mr Prosser, we can't exclude the possibility that you know more about Ms Cheney than you've told us ... Like her real name, for instance.'

'I don't know what you're talking about.'

'Maybe you don't,' McKenna said thoughtfully. 'We

know that post addressed in her real name of Bailey was sent to Gallows Cottage in February . . . and redirected somewhere. We haven't found out where as yet, but we will. You can be quite sure of that.'

Prosser turned on his heel and walked down the hall. They heard the front door open. McKenna went after him, Jack and Dewi trailing behind, and expected to see Prosser waiting to show them out. Instead, he saw him, small as a child, behind the wheel of the Volvo, its motor running. He rushed out on to the street as the car roared away up the hill.

Dewi erupted from the front door. 'Prosser's full of drugs!' he shouted. 'That's why he's not in work. He's not supposed to drive!'

Jack, the better driver, took the wheel of McKenna's car, and went after Prosser, up the hill and under the old railway bridge to the first junction on the road criss-crossing the uplands. 'Where now?' he asked, skidding to a halt by a signpost. 'Llanddona or Pentraeth or Menai Bridge?'

'How the hell do I know where the bloody fool's gone?' McKenna snarled. 'The man's crazy!'

'Guilty, more like,' Jack muttered, turning into the pot-holed lane to Llanddona, racing through the village, past the twin television relay masts crowning a hill apiece, and on until the road petered out at a sweep of sandy heathland overlooking Red Wharf Bay. 'Well, he's not here, is he?' he commented. 'Unless he's driven into the sea.'

'That's what I'm afraid of,' McKenna fretted. 'Why did he do it? What did I say?'

'I dunno.' Jack turned the car, driving on to an unfenced field dotted with pale brown cows and bright yellow gorse bushes. Salty sand crunched under the wheels. 'We'd better try the other road.'

'Which one?'

'Pentraeth. He might've gone that way.'

'What's the use? Wherever he went, he's miles ahead of us.' McKenna picked up the telephone to call the police station in Llangefni. Jack drove back to the crossroads, and turned up the Pentraeth road.

'I want to go back to the house,' McKenna said, holding the telephone. 'The local police can sort him out, and tell us when he turns up.'

'Yeah, well suppose he doesn't?' Jack asked, as the car slewed on a blind bend. 'Turn up, I mean.'

'Oh, for heaven's sake! Just leave it be, will you? I don't know how, but we've made some almighty blunder!'

'You have, you mean!' Jack's face flushed. 'You were the one did all the talking.' He accelerated along a road winding through folds of hilly pasture, crowned here and there with little thickets of trees in bright new leaf. McKenna fell silent, anxiety gnawing his innards, that dreadful Celtic prescience which knew when disaster stalked a person's own small patch of earth.

They found Prosser fifteen minutes later, on the narrow walled road outside Llansadwrn village, the Volvo rammed hard against the left-hand wall, heavy grey stones pushed out of the centre and tumbled on to the bonnet by the impact. A red, green and white Crosville minibus, a red dragon emblazoned on its sides, slewed across the hummocky verge opposite, its few passengers and the driver milling around in the road like so many sheep, moving this way and that, towards the Volvo then away from it. The bus driver sat down suddenly in the middle of the road, and wiped his hand over his head. When he saw the blood running down between his fingers, he fell backwards in a faint. McKenna, out of the car before it stopped, rushed to the Volvo. Jack summoned ambulances and fire engines before following him.

Trefor Prosser might never again enjoy the comfort of his luxurious home, Jack thought, or any other earthly pleasure, for he had ignored all advice, and neglected to fasten his seat belt. He hung over the steering wheel, fat little buttocks in their grey flannel clothing reared in the air, arms outstretched, his head rammed hard against the shattered windscreen. McKenna put his hand to the artery in Prosser's neck, holding his breath. 'He's still alive.'

'I've called in. They should be here soon. We'd better look at the others. The bus driver's head looks stove in.'

'Shit! Shit! SHIT!' McKenna seethed. 'Why did this have to happen?' He wrenched at the door of the Volvo. 'We must get him out! The car might go on fire!'

'Leave him!' Jack ordered. 'Don't you know you can do more harm that way?' He moved around, sniffing for petrol fumes. 'Anyway, when did you last hear of a Volvo going on fire? There's not a whiff of petrol. They build these things like tanks.' He surveyed Prosser. 'And if that daft bugger'd fastened his seat belt, he'd be legging it across the fields by now.'

Prosser had lain in the ambulance on the gurney opposite the bus driver, his vital signs monitored by paramedics, one of whom kept searching ears and nostrils for signs of blood and fluid leaking from a fractured skull. Watching Prosser's waxen face and still body, McKenna had felt a great guilt fall upon his shoulders, with all the weight of God behind it.

In between retching agonizingly into an oval container made of what looked like old egg boxes, the bus driver told McKenna how Prosser came storming along the narrow road in the big red car, how he and Prosser each swerved to avoid the other, how Prosser's car rammed the wall with a crunch the driver said he would remember on the day he died.

Jack and Dewi drove McKenna's car to Bangor, Prosser's home secured, the crashed Volvo towed away to be examined for mechanical faults in the event of Prosser's dying.

Owen Griffiths awaited them. 'This is a bad show,' he commented. 'What on earth happened?'

'Something must've put the wind up Prosser, and he took off,' Jack replied.

'He wasn't supposed to drive, sir,' Dewi added. 'Mr Prosser knew that. It was the reason he was off work.'

'But what did you say?' the superintendent asked. 'Oh, my God!' His face blanched. 'You were chasing him when he crashed, weren't you?'

'No, sir,' Jack said. 'We didn't see hide nor hair of him until we found him outside Llansadwrn, and he'd already crashed by then.'

'I suppose we should be thankful for small mercies, then.' Griffiths looked weary. 'Go and do your reports, then bring them to me.'

*

'There really is little point in your staying here, Chief Inspector,' the registrar said. 'Your friend has a depressed fracture of the skull, and a number of broken ribs. He's still unconscious, and could remain that way for days.'

'Will he live?' McKenna's face was gaunt.

'Oh, he'll live. Well, God willing, as we always say, although I've seen a lot worse than him get up and walk out of here.'

'Can I see him? Just for a few minutes?'

'Not at the moment. We're getting him ready for theatre. Ring us back later. Leave it for a few hours, eh? Give us chance to patch him up.'

McKenna scratched away with his pen, filling sheets of paper with looping untidy script, and lit another cigarette, the fifth by the superintendent's counting since he had begun writing his report of the accident.

'There shouldn't be any comeback,' Owen Griffiths commented. 'Prosser's clearly guilty and we're being put to a lot of trouble over him. It's his own stupid fault he's lying in that hospital.'

McKenna put down his pen. 'Guilty of what? You can't make assumptions because he ran off. He was scared. And' – McKenna picked up his pen and began writing again – 'all those hayfever drugs probably screwed up his thinking.'

'He's guilty of something, Michael,' Griffiths said. 'As we've lost so much time already on this investigation, I called the sorting office instead of waiting for a court order. Margaret Bailey's post has been redirected to the estate office for over three years.'

'Well then, as soon as Mr Prosser can string two

words together, we'll ask him what he does with it,' McKenna said. 'Who's sending in the redirection notices?'

'Margaret Bailey, of course.'

'Who else?' McKenna said. 'Who else?'

Chapter 21

'The insurance company won't pay out a penny,' Jack said.

'What insurance company?' McKenna asked.

'Your wits addled or something?' Jack's voice was tetchy. 'Prosser's, of course. Serve the fool right! He'll have to fork out himself to get his fancy car back on the road. Are we going to charge him?'

'With what?'

'Dangerous driving, of course. Driving under the influence of drugs. And not fastening his seat belt.'

'No, Jack, we are not.' McKenna sounded depressed. 'Don't you think we've done him enough harm?'

'Us? Done him harm? If you think I'm taking the rap for that little crook getting his head bashed in, you've another think coming!'

'We don't know he is a crook. I wish you'd stop jumping to conclusions.'

'Somebody's got to, haven't they?' Jack said acidly. 'While you're wallowing in guilt, he's getting off scot free. He's in this up to his fat little neck. He might even have murdered Romy Cheney himself.'

'Why should he want to do away with her?'

Jack paced the office. 'I don't know, do I? I don't know why anyone should want to bump her off, but somebody did.' He threw himself into a chair. 'God, am I fed up!'

'Prosser's accident made everything worse. I blame myself because I should've seen it coming.'

'How? Suddenly acquired psychic powers, have you?'

'Oh, don't be facetious! I should know enough about people to know what they're likely to do.' McKenna stared at Jack without, Jack thought, seeing anything but the accident scene in his mind's eye.

'What do we do next?' Jack interrupted the reverie.

'Nothing much we can do until Prosser comes round, which, according to the hospital, might not be for days . . . Weeks, knowing our luck.'

'Why can't we get a search warrant to go through his house?'

'On what grounds?'

'What grounds? The letters, of course.'

'Can't you stop repeating everything I say? It's very irritating!' McKenna looked savagely at his deputy. 'Anyway, why are you here? It's supposed to be your day off.'

'If you must know,' Jack said sulkily, 'it's the twins' birthday, and I'd rather keep out of the way as long as I can. I take it that's all right with you?'

'How old are they? Fifteen? What presents are they having?'

'Whatever teenage girls want these days. CDs, clothes, more CDs . . .'

'Are they having a party?'

'They're too old for parties. Girls of fifteen don't have parties. Or, at least, not the sort parents don't mind them having. We're taking them out for a meal instead.'

'That'll be nice for you all,' McKenna observed.

'Are you being sarcastic?' Jack bridled. 'Because if you are, it's uncalled for. They had a party last year, and there was nothing but trouble from start to finish. They were still bloody fighting at midnight!'

'I was not being sarcastic! Why must you be so bloody sensitive? Eifion Roberts told me yesterday not to bring home problems to work.'

'All right for him to talk, isn't it? Kids flown the nest, and a wife still thinking the sun shines out of his backside!' Jack glared at McKenna. 'Where else am I supposed to take my home problems, then?'

'I'm only telling you what he said. I don't mind if you have a grouse now and then.'

'That's decent of you.'

'Now you're being sarcastic.' McKenna ground out a half-smoked cigarette. 'Where's Dewi Prys?'

'Hijacked by uniform for the football match. Bangor versus Caernarfon.'

'Then if you've any sense, you'll go home before the cells start filling up.' McKenna grinned. 'Even the twins can't be as bad as footie fans on the rampage.'

'Want to bet?' Jack said gloomily. 'Tell me why we can't get a warrant on Prosser.'

'There's no evidence he's taking letters addressed to Gallows Cottage for Margaret Bailey. We only know the letters are going to the estate office.'

'I suppose you're right. What about a court order to view her bank account?'

'It wouldn't tell us anything we don't already know, and it may alert whoever's using it. Can't trust everybody in a bank to keep quiet . . .' McKenna twisted a paper clip into a ravaged shape. 'At this present moment in time, as they say, we're going to wait and see what happens.'

'What happens when?'

'When we get those ledgers back from the estate office, and have another chat with that gossipy lady there. Dewi can talk to her. He's good at extracting information from women . . . Would you and Emma mind if I bought something for the girls?'

'Er – no. Of course not.'

'Good. I'll see you all later.'

'Can't do right for doing wrong, can I?' Jack fumed.

'Oh, stop moaning!' Emma snapped, kicking his outstretched legs to make her way past. 'Maybe you should've thought of asking him to dinner.'

'And how was I to know the twins would want him there?' Jack demanded.

'You could've asked, couldn't you?' Emma pointed out. 'Used your imagination for once. You know they like him.'

'Well, hard luck! They'll have to be content with having presents from him.'

'And he might have enjoyed the company. He doesn't look at all well, and he's lost an awful lot of weight lately. Not,' she added caustically, 'that I expect you've noticed . . . I think he's depressed.'

'He's always depressed or something. He's the moodiest person I've ever come across.'

Emma stared at her husband, eyes glittering with anger. 'You can be so stupid! Don't you realize what I'm saying? I think he might try to kill himself! And you wouldn't know a thing, would you, until you found his body somewhere?'

'Eifion Roberts doesn't think so. He said as much not long ago, and he should know.'

'Oh, I see.' Emma sat down, shoulders drooping. 'I see . . . Eifion Roberts must've thought about it, mustn't he? Why else should he say anything?'

McKenna fidgeted sleepless in his bed, the cat by his feet, her new fluorescent collar shining now and then as she too fidgeted herself into a comfortable position. He smiled a little as he recalled the twins' lavish greeting, the warm scented kisses placed gently on his cheeks as he handed bouquets of flowers to each. Emma watched, face alight with some emotion, her eyes sparkly, and his own smile died into the night at the memory of the *frisson* cutting through his body as he looked into those eyes. He turned on his side, drawing a mewling protest from the cat, and heard the rising wind flute through the broken downspout on the wall outside his bedroom and pluck with idle repetitive malice at the open sash of the window.

A civilian typist brought the letter to McKenna's office early on Monday morning. Slitting open the envelope, he took out a sheet of paper and a photograph.

I know I said I didn't have a photo of Madge, the letter related, and went on: *but I found this the other day when I was sorting a few things and thought you might be interested. Don't bother sending it back.* Robert Allsopp's signature was an extravagant scrawl across the bottom of thick expensive paper.

There was no date or inscription on the back of the photograph. Margaret Bailey regarded McKenna as if she still lived and breathed and loved and sorrowed, a rueful half smile to her lips, her short fair hair ruffled by winds coursing the moorlands behind her. He could not see the colour of her eyes, only fitful sunlight highlighting angular planes of cheek and jawbone. She had not been a pretty woman, but striking and tall, with shadows in her face, traces of sadness and harsh lessons learned. She looked older in the photograph than when she met her death, and tired, as if vitality had been beaten out of her. Where light caught the fullness of her cheek, fine translucent skin seemed veined with a thousand tiny wrinkles, like crazed glaze on old china. Just visible in the bottom left-hand corner of the photograph was the front end of a car, colour darkened by its own shadow. McKenna stared at woman and car, thoughts miles away on that bleak moorland. Walking in after receiving no response to his knock, Jack found him with hands spread on the desk top, eyes mesmerized.

'What's that?' he asked.

'Romy Cheney.' McKenna turned the photograph so that she now looked up at Jack. 'Aka Margaret Bailey. Allsopp sent it.' His voice was flat, expressionless.

Jack eyed McKenna surreptitiously, Emma's concerns refusing to relinquish their hold. 'What shall I do with it?'

'Get colour copies and send people out asking questions.'

'Right. What else d'you want us to do?' he asked into the lengthening silence.

'I haven't decided.'

'Well, maybe Beti Gloff'll be able to say this was the woman she saw in the car.'

'Maybe.' McKenna's tone was listless. 'Even if she can, I can't see any court taking much notice of her.'

'Why not? She saw the driver, she identified the car.'

'And how does Dewi's nain describe her? One eye pointing to Bethesda, one to Caernarfon! D'you think a judge and jury are likely to believe she can see anything properly?'

'Oh, I see what you mean.' Ill at ease, Jack took a deep breath and plunged into the deep and murky waters of McKenna's personal life, out of obligation to Emma, and because he could see for himself how turbulent those waters had become. 'Is everything all right, sir? With you, I mean?'

McKenna sat very still, arms on the desk. 'Everything is all wrong, Jack, and I have neither the will nor the knowledge to right it.'

'Oh, I see.'

'Do you? You're cleverer than me, then.'

'Emma says,' Jack ventured, 'it's normal for people to get despondent after a personal crisis . . . then you get better, like getting your strength together again when you've been ill. That is, I suppose, unless you've put yourself in it, so to speak . . . D'you think you might've made a mistake leaving Denise?'

'I don't know.' McKenna rummaged in his pockets for cigarettes and lighter. 'I wasn't happy with her, and I'm no happier without her. And what makes it worse,' he went on, drawing hungrily on the cigarette, 'is the selfishness of it. It's all what I want and don't want, isn't it? Never a thought for Denise.'

'But you could say –' Jack struggled to find words to express the vagrant thought. 'You could say if your marriage was OK, you'd never have needed to think about it. And if you hadn't needed to think about you and Denise, you wouldn't need to make any decisions about staying or leaving . . . if you understand what I mean.' He fell silent, then added, 'I mean, there's no call to ask myself if I'm happy with Em. It's all sort of there . . . ever since you left Denise I've been thinking about marriages and Emma and me, and I can't imagine life without her.'

McKenna felt an envy so powerful he expected Jack to smell its stink on the air, foul and greedy and suffocating. Despair flowed in its wake, telling him he would never know such simple contentment, because he lacked the sense to recognize its worth.

Trefor Prosser lay inert in his hospital bed, bandages swathing his skull, tubes taped into his nostrils and the back of his hand. McKenna was permitted to look at him, and told he would be called as soon as consciousness returned, however fleetingly.

'Should we put a constable to sit by him?' Jack asked, as they drove away from the hospital complex. 'In case he comes round suddenly?'

'Couldn't justify the man-hours,' McKenna said. 'Prosser won't be going anywhere, even when he is conscious.' He waited by the pedestrian crossing on Beach Road for an old woman with a shopping trolley to trundle her way from one side to the other. 'There's no forwarding address for Margaret Bailey in the estate ledgers. Did Dewi tell you?'

'Yes.' Jack watched a dredger anchored in the old port unloading more sand on to a huge sand pyramid at the end of the dock, its motor thumping, conveyor chains rattling. 'That's why I asked about Prosser, because there's nobody else likely to tell us anything, is there?'

'Won't know until we ask, will we? Did you bring the photo to show Stott's neighbour?'

'I did. What about Jamie?'

'All in good time, Jack. Shut the window, will you? That stink off the sea's turning my stomach.'

Christopher Stott's neighbour was home for lunch, at table in a dingy unaired kitchen, eating fish and chips, swilling lager from a can, expressing only truculence. He was alone in the house, wife out, any children they might have spawned elsewhere. 'I told that Dewi Prys all there was to tell.' He pushed chips into his mouth. 'So why don't you two bugger off?'

McKenna breathed in smells of greasy chips, a dirty kitchen, and the drink, nausea welling in his throat. 'I want to know why you lend the car to Jamie Thief.' He opened the back door. The man took a huge bite from the fish, and crammed more chips into his mouth. 'Jamie helps out,' he said, words slopping out through the food. 'He borrows the car instead of being paid.'

Staring out at an unkempt garden, the debris of bicycles and sheets of corrugated plastic from some long-collapsed shed or greenhouse, McKenna said, 'He doesn't do much gardening. What does he do?'

'This and that.' The man wiped his fingers on chip wrapping, and drank more lager.

'Jamie can't do anything except cause trouble,' Jack said. 'He can't do plumbing or building or anything useful. There's nothing he could do you'd need to pay him for.'

'Know it all, do you?'

McKenna leaned against the back door frame, wanting to light a cigarette to kill the smells pushing themselves into his face, sure he would vomit if he put flame to tobacco. 'We know Jamie is involved with drugs. Might he be helping you out that way?'

The man leapt from his chair. 'Don't try pulling a stunt like that!' Looking from Jack to McKenna, he backed towards the door into the hall, and McKenna wondered if he would run to the front door, leap into that big shiny car, the object of so much mystery, drive into a wall and smash in his head. He thought he should move to stop him, but had no strength, legs heavy and torpid as if he waded in water, or tried to flee danger in a dream.

Glancing at McKenna, seeing the yellowish pallor on his skin, Jack went for the owner of the Scorpio, grabbing his arm. 'I reckon a night in the cells might loosen your tongue.'

The man slumped against the wall. 'Leave me be!' he whined. 'I was doing Stott a favour, that's all. Keeping him out of the shit.' He sniggered. 'Queered his own pitch, Stott has, without any help from anybody!'

Jack drove McKenna home and listened to sounds of retching from the bathroom while he telephoned the surgery. When the doctor arrived, McKenna was crouched on the sofa, clutching his stomach and gasping with pain. Stripped to his undershorts, he suffered the prodding fingers of the doctor, palpating his gut.

'He's in pain,' Jack said defensively, staring with ill-concealed curiosity at McKenna's near-emaciated frame, ribs pale and bony protuberances, belly muscles clenched tight.

'Pain is the body's way of telling us all is not right,' the doctor observed.

'What's wrong with him?' Jack demanded.

'Don't know yet, do I?' The doctor pulled down McKenna's lower eyelid, staring at the red-veined inner flesh. He picked up each hand, pressed the nails, and examined the thin skin. 'D'you drink?' he asked McKenna.

'Not much.'

'What's "not much"?'

'What he says!' Jack insisted. 'He hardly ever drinks.'

'Just wondered. Could be cirrhosis of the liver. There's a lot of it about.' He turned to McKenna. 'Been passing any blood or mucus?'

'Where from?'

'Either end.'

McKenna flushed. 'I don't know. Not when I was sick.'

The doctor sighed. 'And I suppose you're too polite to look in the lavvy. Animal droppings are great barometers of health, you know.' He returned his stethoscope to his bag. 'I think we'd better be on the safe side and have you in hospital. Got to observe Nature's etiquette, you know.'

McKenna struggled upright. 'No!'

The doctor sat down beside him. 'You haven't been near the surgery since you had 'flu a couple of years back. I don't know what's wrong with you, and there's nothing in your medical history to give me any clues.'

Jack asked, 'What might it be?'

'Jaundice. Meningitis. Onset of some bowel trouble . . . It's not appendicitis because he's got no appendix. It might be food poisoning. Or maybe too many sleeping pills. People sometimes take more than they should at times, hoping for a decent night's sleep, a bit of peace . . .'

An ambulance took McKenna away, his pyjamas and odds and ends hurriedly stashed in a holdall. Jack packed cat food from the kitchen cupboards, clean bowls and the brush, put them in the car, and went back into the house to switch off central heating and stop tap and lock up. Finally, he gathered up the cat, she suspicious and watchful, and carried her up the stairs and outside. She crouched on the back seat throughout the journey, bewildered and forlorn.

'I'm going to the hospital,' Emma announced. 'You try Denise again, and keep trying until you get her.'

'Will he want to see her?'

'Probably not. I just want her to know, that's all. Might make her sorry.'

'What's Denise got to be sorry for? He left her.'

'And why? If I'm not back by teatime, you can all have fish and chips.'

Chapter 22

'Is that what all the fuss was about, sir?' Dewi asked.

'It seems so,' Jack told him. 'Mr Stott is Mr Prosser's boyfriend. Jamie borrows the car in consideration for not grassing up either of them to their mates, employers, spouses or the chapel.' He grimaced with distaste. 'Nauseating, isn't it? The thought of those two together.'

'Actually, sir, I reckon Jamie and his blackmail is a lot more sickening than a couple of blokes fancying each other. What're we going to do to him?'

'I wouldn't've thought you'd have any time for the likes of Prosser and Stott.'

'I've got less time for the likes of Jamie, because I don't expect either Stott or Prosser thought much about anything 'til Jamie brought it to their attention, as you might say, and persuaded them it was worth forking out cash to hush up. How did he know, anyway?'

'Dunno. Our informant didn't know the ins and outs.'

'What are we going to do with Jamie?'

'Stop badgering! You're like a bloody sheepdog. Until we know how long Mr McKenna's likely to be off, I'm not starting anything. You'll have to curb your enthusiasm.'

'I don't see the point. Jamie'll know, won't he?'

'Not if our friend in Turf Square has any sense.' Jack twiddled McKenna's pen. 'Bit odd, you know. Stott's got a wife and child.'

'You don't know much, do you, sir? Fancying other blokes never stopped anyone going with women and having children. He'll be what they call bi-sexual. Being married is a good cover, anyway.'

'Have you shown that photo round the village?'

'They're burying that Rebekah today, so we didn't get to speak to a soul. Half Bangor hanging round the church, sticking their noses in and getting on TV. May as well leave it until tomorrow.'

'Tomorrow! Everything gets left for some reason or another! Tomorrow never comes, or don't you know that in this neck of the woods?'

'Oh, I don't know, sir. More like God putting the mockers on things, isn't it? Having Mr McKenna ill is the last thing we need. What's wrong with him? Does anybody know yet? I hope he's not very poorly. Don't you?'

At one moment Emma hoped Denise would rush in, flushed, anxious, dishevelled, and the next, she prayed for her continuing ignorance of McKenna's condition. Perched on the edge of a plastic-covered chair in the ante-room to one of the medical wards, Emma asked herself what she intended to say to McKenna when allowed to see him, knowing she could say the house was locked up, the heating and water switched off, and the cat safe in her care. She could sit by his bedside and smile and prattle and soothe, and if he looked at her again with that light in his eyes which shone so briefly the other day, she could excuse herself if she stroked the russet hair from his forehead, and warmed his cold thin hand with her own. She thought of physical contact with him, and a fearful longing shafted her body, leaving her shaken, weaker than the man upon whom she waited.

'Silly bugger's got gastro-enteritis.' Eifion Roberts perched on the corner of McKenna's desk.

'I'm not surprised,' Dewi said. 'Some of the places we've been lately . . . he probably caught it from John Beti breathing in his face.'

'Oh, shut up, Prys!' Jack snarled. To the pathologist, he said, 'How long will he be in hospital?'

'Oh, no time at all, so long as he doesn't get dehydrated from all that vomiting and the runs. They won't let him take up a bed unless he's dying, and not always then these days.' Dr Roberts dismissed McKenna as of no further interest. 'What's the latest?'

Told the tale of Prosser and Stott, Dr Roberts said, 'You're being very naive thinking that's all there is to it.'

'What else could there be?'

'I don't know, do I? It might've started out that way, but I can't see it going on. When it comes to the crunch, Jamie could say what he likes, but I doubt he could prove it. And even if he could, they've not been doing anything either illegal or that half the male population isn't doing some time or another.'

'I don't do that sort of thing,' Jack pointed out.

'Don't you? Not even when you were a teenager? My goodness! According to some folk's reckoning, you're not normal.'

'Don't start winding me up because McKenna's out of your clutches for a while!'

'There's a body of legitimate and respectable research which argues most men go through a homosexual phase during adolescence, and that it's quite normal. There's other research which suggests those who don't grow out of it have a chromosome disorder or abnormality. I rather favour that myself. You know, the third sex syndrome. Poor buggers can't help themselves, imprisoned by their own genes.' He sighed. 'Might get to the root of it one day, when I've cut up a few more homosexuals. God knows, there's enough of them round here for any amount of research.'

'Stott and Prosser are prisoners of the chapel mentality,' Dewi said. 'All that Sunday respectability's got to be kept up, no matter what.'

The doctor's words wrought devastation to Emma's dream of nursing McKenna through near mortal sickness, willing him back to life and health, and reaping the rewards. Gastro-enteritis was such a menial sickness, unlovely and not in the least heroic. And probably self-inflicted, she thought sourly, following the doctor's billowing white coat into the ward where McKenna had been admitted for the night.

He looked yellow and ill and pallid and utterly lost, smiling the lopsided smile that cut her to the quick. He held out his hand.

'I can't tell you how sorry I am, Emma. I keep putting you and Jack to the most awful trouble.'

She stood over him, his hand resting lightly in her own. 'You mustn't worry. Have they any idea what made you ill?'

'Something I've eaten, they say . . .'

'You should be home soon.' Emma smiled. His hand still rested in hers, quiet, acquiescent. Wishful thinking intruded itself, putting something into the relationship which had no right to be there. She felt embarrassment, shame for her own imagination. He squeezed her hand and let it go.

'Does Denise know I'm here?'

'Not unless Jack's managed to contact her. I'll make sure she knows as soon as possible.'

'I'd rather you didn't, Emma.'

'Why not?'

'I don't want her here, that's all.' His eyes were bleak. 'Anyway, it's not really worth bothering her.'

'I suppose sick visiting isn't quite her forte, is it? Won't you be lonely?'

He sank back on the pillows, and gazed at her, an expression in his eyes she could not read. 'Would you come again? If it's not too much trouble I'd like to see you.'

She left without asking if he wanted to see Jack as well. She thought she might allow herself a few more hours with the dream like spun gold in her heart, before she had to let the deathly chill of common sense prevail upon its promise, tear its diaphanous fabric to shreds.

Jamie slouched in an armchair in the unheated front room of his mother's council house, his feet thrust out in front of him.

'How much did those boots cost?' Jack asked.

'What's it to you?'

'Jamie wouldn't know how much they cost because they'll be nicked,' Dewi offered. 'The sports' shop on the High Street lost a few pairs like that a while back.' All three stared at Jamie's feet, encased in black nubuck flashed with red, silver and green.

'D'you think they could identify these if we took them in?' Jack mused.

'Sure to be able to, sir.' Dewi smiled at Jamie. Jamie stared back, his face bland.

'Well, Jamie?' Jack turned to the youth.

'Well what?'

'What've you got to tell us?'

Jamie lit a cigarette, blowing smoke into the chilly air, where it settled in ragged bands.

'All I've got to say is if you don't stop giving me grief, I'm going to complain.' He took a long pull, and let smoke dribble from his nostrils and mouth. 'I went to see Councillor Williams the other day. He's not very happy with you lot, is he?'

'Councillor Williams can go stuff himself,' Jack said quietly.

'Tut tut!' Jamie said. 'I hear he's dead matey with that posh wife of your boss. She went to his daughter's wedding. Did you know that?'

'I don't think Mr Tuttle or Mr McKenna give a toss about Councillor Williams's mates, Jamie,' Dewi said. 'They're not overkeen on the likes of Councillor Williams interfering and stopping us from doing our job properly. You know, we all take an oath to do our work without malice or favour. That's right, isn't it, Mr Tuttle?'

'Indeed it is.' Jack smirked at Jamie. 'Got something on the councillor or his cronies, have you?'

Jamie stared at the ceiling. 'I don't know what you're talking about.'

'Maybe, sir,' Dewi said, 'Councillor Williams or some of his friends belong to the fifty per cent Dr Roberts was talking about.'

Mystified for a few seconds, Jack laughed when realization dawned. 'You could well be right, Dewi. How about it, Jamie?'

'How about what?' Jamie fidgeted. 'You two're getting on my fucking nerves! You're like Laurel and sodding Hardy!'

Jack watched the sweat begin to bead Jamie's forehead, noticed fingers yellowed with nicotine, the bloodshot eyes and trembling hands. 'What muck are you putting in yourself now?' he asked. 'Apart from fags and booze.'

'I don't know what you're talking about,' Jamie repeated.

'We'll find out. When we're ready ...' Jack responded. 'Right now, we're more interested in something else. Would you like to know what that is?'

Jamie sighed. 'Not particularly, but I'm sure you'll tell me.'

Dewi flipped open his notebook. 'It's this car, Jamie. The Scorpio. We can't get to grips with it.'

'How many more times!'

'Well, as many as it takes to get to the bottom of things. We had another chat with the new owner. Well, at least, Mr Tuttle and Mr McKenna did.'

'So what?' Jamie lit another cigarette from the stub of the old one. 'Haven't you got anything better to do with yourselves? You're supposed to be looking for a murderer, aren't you? Taking you long enough, isn't it? Did you know people are talking? Saying they're not safe in their beds, and you lot couldn't organize a piss-up in a brewery, never mind catch a killer.'

'That's a long speech coming from you, Jamie,' Dewi observed. 'People aren't safe in their beds with you around, are they? Don't I remember you being arrested in the early hours with your pockets so full of fifty pence pieces from all the meters you'd robbed you could hardly move?' He turned to Jack. 'Jamie can get places water can't reach, sir.'

'I've done my time for that. Twelve sodding months banged up. You don't let folk forget a thing, do you?'

'Not some folk we don't. Because some folk go from bad to worse, don't they? From robbing meters in the middle of the night to blackmail, and maybe even worse than that.'

'Blackmail?' Jamie sniggered. 'You're off your trolley, Dewi Prys.'

Jack intervened. 'We have it from a very reliable source you get to borrow that fancy car because a certain Christopher Stott has been made afraid of what you might say about him.'

Jamie said nothing.

'Ever get to drive a big red Volvo, Jamie?' Dewi asked casually.

Jamie uncoiled his body from the chair, walked to the window and peered out through dingy net curtains. Empty crisp packets and bits of cardboard skittered along the street, fretted by the wind. A child with feverish cheeks and runny nose dragged a tricycle with only two wheels over the pavement, bumped it into the road, and tried to pedal away. Jamie turned to face the room, his face shadowed. 'Why don't you say what you're hoping to fit me up for, then you can sod off, can't you?'

'Nobody's trying to fit you up,' Dewi said. 'It's

what other people are telling us, you see. They're the ones putting all these thoughts in our heads. You don't do gardening or anything else for Mr Stott, and you never did. You get the car instead of money, 'cos he probably can't afford to pay you to shut up.'

'Shut up about what?'

'Stop acting innocent!' Dewi snapped. 'It doesn't suit you.'

'Give him the benefit of the doubt, Dewi,' Jack said. 'We are obliged to say why we're arresting somebody.' He stared at Jamie. 'You've been blackmailing Mr Stott. Forcing him to lend you that car, even after he sold it, so you'd keep quiet about his rather squalid little liaison with a certain Trefor Prosser. Blackmail isn't very nice, Jamie, and the courts take a very dim view. They're likely to send you down for at least five years.'

Jamie spent a moment absorbing Jack's words, then burst out laughing. 'Is that all you've got to say?'

'It's enough, isn't it?'

'Got a statement from Chris Stott, have you? Made a complaint, has he?' Jamie sat down again, stretching languidly. 'Thought not. Let me give you a bit of advice, eh? Both of you go out through that front door and get into your little cop car and go and see Chris Stott. And then,' he added, with rage and malice glittering in eyes as cold as a mountain mist in winter, 'see if you dare show your stupid bloody faces again!'

Dewi drove. 'Where are we going now, sir?'

'Perdition, probably. One-way ticket.'

'I reckon we made a cock-up somehow. Jamie wasn't at all scared.'

Jack stared through the windscreen. 'You know him. Would he be afraid? Does he care? He's been in prison often enough for another spell not to hurt. Anyway, prison's an occupational hazard to Jamie and his ilk.'

'Jamie wouldn't relish the idea of going down again. Dents his pride and clips his wings. Five years would do his head in.'

'I only said five years. I've no idea how long he'd get. Sob into your hankie in front of a senile judge these days, and you get community service for smashing somebody's head in. What's putting the black on a couple of queers worth? A smack on the hand?'

'Jamie was afraid at one point, all the same.' Dewi turned into the yard behind the police station. 'Until he cottoned on to what we were talking about.' He cut the engine and unbuckled his seat belt. 'Perhaps we asked the wrong questions.'

Jack climbed out of the car. 'Know what the right bloody questions are, do you? Because I don't!'

Chapter 23

Hospitals and prisons were, thought McKenna, the noisiest of places, each with its own special noise, each with its own smell, which lingered on skin and clothing and taste buds long after departure. Here, the clang and screech of metal on prison doors and keys and floors gave way to the shuffle of feet and squeal of rubber wheels on linoleum; the smells of metal and sweat and despair to those of disinfectant and blood and faeces and sickness.

He awoke in the dead hours of morning, roused by hushed urgent voices, the squeak of unoiled wheels as a trolley rolled down the ward; his dream, of walking on a black shore where thousands upon thousands of human skulls crunched underfoot seared into memory, the taste of his own death sweet and heavy in the back of his throat, its dust dry on lips and tongue. He raised himself on one elbow, feeling the pull of a drip taped into the back of his left hand. Screens were drawn around a bed at the far end of the ward, and within a few minutes of arriving, an Asian doctor departed, followed by the trolley, its cargo hidden under a sheet whose hem billowed gently in a draught from the open doors. The screens were opened to a bed bare and empty, and a young nurse about to lift a large plastic sack with 'Contaminated Materials' written bold on its side.

McKenna lay back, wondering if the soul of his departed companion hovered still somewhere above his head, seeking exit and flight, released from a husk of a body collapsed with old age and mortal frailty. Eyes squeezed shut against wavering and fragmenting images of lights and windows, he felt a cool hand brushing away tears come of their own free will.

'Did we wake you?' a voice whispered. 'I'm ever so sorry.'

A sweet-faced girl, too young to have sickness and ugly death soil her youth with its dirty paws, stood by the bed.

'Can I get you anything?' she asked. 'We're making a pot of tea, if you'd like some.'

He crawled slowly from the bed, finding his legs wobbling and weak. The nurse unfastened the drip, closed its tap, and told him to put his arm around her shoulders. He shuffled like an ancient to the ward kitchen, and slumped into a chair.

'I expect you'll be glad to get home, won't you?' said his ministering angel, pouring boiling water into a teapot. 'I'm sure your wife will be glad, as well. She's very smart, isn't she?'

Summoned by Jack, Denise had arrived in the early evening, shortly before Emma returned. She and Denise chatted over him, around him, past him, of odds and ends of gossip, a flurry of women's talk, whatever hostilities might linger between them suspended for the sake of propriety in the face of sickness. Denise brought flowers, a bunch of blossoms like every other bunch bedecking lockers along each side of the ward, flowers grown especially for hospital patients, with no regard to season.

Emma left first, as was only right, he thought, with a few words about the cat, and the best wishes of the family. Denise lingered and fidgeted, glancing at the clock on the wall, then at her watch, watching for other visitors preparing to leave.

'You don't have to stay,' he had said to her.

She smiled, rather patronizingly, and he wondered if she believed him weakened, vulnerable to whatever persuasion she chose to impress. His innards began their churning, and he vomited again, sparsely now, for his stomach was vacant. Saying she would return in the morning, Denise left. He stared after her, asking himself why there could be no catharsis of spirit as rapid and cleansing as that which his body had undergone.

The nurse placed a mug of tea at his side. She leaned against the worktop, sipping her own, content with silence or talk, whichever he chose, content, he thought, to continue giving in the full knowledge of little or nothing in return.

'What happened earlier?' he asked her, taking a sip of tea, and feeling scalding heat course down his throat and into his stomach.

'Mr Jones finally went, poor soul. We've been expecting it for days. He was seventy-eight! Can you imagine being so old?' She shook her head at the sadness and wonder of it all.

'What was wrong with him?' McKenna drank more tea, waiting for his insides to warn of imminent rejection.

'Old age?' She smiled her sweet smile. 'He was diabetic, actually, and both his legs had to be amputated because of gangrene. Too much of a shock for his system.'

McKenna shuddered violently, mortality screaming through every fibre. 'Oh, you're cold!' She rushed to place a blanket around his shoulders. 'Perhaps I shouldn't have let you get out of bed.' She frowned, as if at her own stupidity.

'I'm all right, really . . . The old man . . .'

She stood over him, still frowning. 'I shouldn't have told you, should I? We don't think sometimes. Drink your tea,' she instructed. 'There was nothing to be done for him, you know.'

Escorted back to bed, told to press his buzzer if he needed anything, McKenna drifted into fitful sleep as dawn broke over the mountains in the east, feeling hunger grope in his belly.

Dewi missed McKenna, the empty office down the corridor underscoring the absence of its occupant, the loose end on a chain of command Dewi saw running clear between himself and McKenna. Jack was merely a kink in the chain, hopefully soon to be straightened out. He had rushed through the office earlier, snapping instructions to show the photograph in the village, before leaving for the Magistrates Court, where Dewi prayed he would be detained all day.

Calling the hospital to ask after McKenna, Dewi was told simply that the chief inspector was 'comfortable'. The call transferred to Prosser's ward, he was told there was no change. Dewi too felt guilt, not as strongly as McKenna, but enough to niggle his conscience into unease. He pulled Romy Cheney's photograph from the file, stared into her eyes, then put the photograph into a clear plastic envelope.

Rain squalled against the car windscreen, blown in from the sea, leaving a faint crusting of salt against window trims, as Dewi turned on to the track to Gallows Cottage, and drove slowly down, mud spattering up the sides of the car. The cottage crouched low in misty air, and he had a fancy it was hungry, wanting another woman to send to her death with a rope around her neck. He sat in the car, and sounded the horn. No one came, nothing stirred, no shadow pushed its way through the drizzle. He sounded the horn again, before turning in a slow circle, leaving deep wounds in the sodden grass.

Parking near the lych gate of the village church, he donned an oilskin coat bought from Dickie's Chandlery, and began the house to house, knocking on doors, showing warrant card and photograph, asking questions, receiving nothing in response. Mary Ann and Beti shuffled the photograph this way and that, held it to the dingy daylight, indulged in muttering and pursing lips and sorrowful head-shaking. Dewi drank his tea, hope draining as the tea drained to its dregs. Beti could not say if the woman might be the one she had seen in the car, nor the car the one she found in Turf Square. Mary Ann was more interested in McKenna. 'And is that Prosser still out for the count?'

Looking from one to the other, thinking of reprisal for talking out of school, he said, 'We've been hearing gossip about Mr Prosser, Mary Ann.'

'Oh, yes?' Her eyes were sharp. 'What sort of gossip?'

'Well, there's talk he's friendly in the wrong sort of way with another man.'

Beti snickered. 'D'you mean that big girl's blouse what works up at the castle? Everybody knows about them two.'

Dewi stared at her. 'Why didn't you tell us before? We've been running round like blue-arsed flies chasing this and that!'

'Didn't know you was interested, did we?' Beti scowled frighteningly, a gargoyle slithered off its perch and come to life.

'What's Prosser and the other one got to do with this killing, anyway?' Mary Ann asked.

'Well, nothing, as far as we know.'

'There you are, then,' Beti announced. 'Didn't need to tell you, did we?'

Dewi eyed her, watching a little smug grin twist her mouth. 'Prosser might have something to do with it, though.'

'What?' Mary Ann asked.

'He just might know something we need to know, and we can't ask him now, can we?'

Mary Ann smoked her cigarette. Beti put the mugs on a tray and hobbled into the kitchen, servant masquerading as house-guest, Dewi tempted to ask if she knew she was no better off here than with her husband. He stood up to leave, sensing undercurrents and atmosphere, mischief and not a little spite beneath the wide-mouthed amiability of the old women.

'Why don't you ask whatever his name is at the castle what you can't ask Prosser, then?' Mary Ann suggested.

*

McKenna looked ghastly, grey parched skin masking a death's head on the shoulders of the living.

'How are you, sir?' Dewi asked.

McKenna smiled weakly. 'Surviving. Any news?'

'Nothing exciting, except I get the idea sometimes Mary Ann and her mates are taking us for a ride.' Dewi hesitated. 'Any idea when you'll be back in work, sir?'

'I'm being let out of hospital today, I'm told.'

'Where will you be going, sir?'

With a sharp glance at the young constable, McKenna said, 'Home, of course. Where else?'

'Is Mrs McKenna coming for you then?'

'Mrs McKenna? No, she's not. I'm going to my own home, Dewi.'

Dewi flushed bright pink with embarrassment. He stood up. 'I'll be off then, sir. Hope you're better soon.'

'Dewi?' McKenna called after the fast retreating back. 'D'you think you could come around five to drive me? My car's not here.'

'No problem, sir. You won't be up to driving anyway, and it wouldn't do to risk ending up like Mr Prosser, would it?'

Trefor Prosser stirred in his hospital bed, eyelids fluttering like the wings of a butterfly too weak to depart its chrysalis. Behind the quivering membrane, memory stirred, great draughts of despair and fear breaking the calm surface of unconsciousness into heaving peaks. He moaned, and turned slightly to one side. The nurse in charge of ICU watched the monitor, saw brain waves suddenly leap into frantic rhythm, before subsiding to a steady flow of mountains and troughs, and wondered what disturbed the poor little man, what terrors might lurk in the night of the brain, knowing Trefor Prosser would not be the first human soul willingly to exchange the bright hard world for the comforting arms of unconsciousness. She walked quietly down the small ward to where he lay again on his back, tears glistening on the pallid flesh of his cheeks.

'I don't see how we can avoid talking to Stott, sir.' Jack was adamant.

'You're on dodgy ground.' Owen Griffiths was equally sure. 'We can't just ask him if he's being blackmailed, can we?'

'What about that bloody car?'

'There's no evidence the car's connected with this woman's death, is there?'

'No, but it's connected with Jamie, and whatever he puts his oar into is usually very bad news for somebody.'

Griffiths looked ill at ease. 'We've not got very far, have we? And I doubt McKenna's got any more ideas than you have.' He rested his elbows on the desk and his chin on his hands. 'I think we should call it a day, Jack. There's pressure coming from on high, and a deal of it because a certain councillor reckons we're harassing innocent citizens, to say nothing of wasting expensive police time.'

'And we all know who that is, don't we?'

'We can't afford any more bad press. I don't like politicking any better than you, but it's a fact of life. There's flak right left and centre about costs and efficiency.'

'I suppose that's why we get sent to the sorting office to collect suspect packages, is it?' Jack asked.

Griffiths sighed. 'We'd already had the bomb squad out three times, and it costs more than you and I take home in a year every time they show their faces.'

'So as long as we save a bit of money, it's all right for some poor copper to drive through Bangor with a bomb in his car, and it's all right for us to sit here with any number of bombs in the building, so long as we don't try to open the envelopes.'

'Looks that way,' Griffiths agreed. 'You see my point? I know all this goes against the grain, but we're no nearer putting a name to whoever killed this woman, and quite frankly, no one seems particularly bothered about her anyway. All we've done so far is upset a lot of probably innocent people. And we shouldn't forget what happened to Prosser, either.'

'Is that an order, sir? Mr McKenna won't be too happy.'

'There'll be plenty to keep him occupied when he comes back. And yes, it is an order, so get a disposal certificate from the coroner's office, and find out if her man-friend is willing to foot the bill for the funeral. If not, the council can pay. I daresay there's enough in her bank account to cover it.'

'And how can the council get at the bank account to pay for its rightful owner's funeral when it's still being used, apparently by its rightful owner?'

'I don't know, do I? McKenna can sort that out! And you can take that mulish look off your face! You should've learned by now that when certain people tell you to jump, all you do is ask "How high?"'

*

Alone in the CID office, Dewi chewed a sandwich and riffled through the papers accumulated around the death of a woman who had used names, he thought, not as a statement of identity, but as devices behind which to hide. He thought of her simply as Simeon's Bride, a name most descriptive of her fate, of the loneliness and despair and horror she must have known in those dark woods for the last few seconds of her life, and wondered how she had offended God or man to warrant such a punishment.

The last piece of paper to go into the file was a copy fax to the council, confirming the release of her body. Driven by some need he did not understand, Dewi telephoned Dr Roberts at home.

'Don't tell me,' Roberts groaned. 'You've found another woman hanging in the woods.'

'No, sir, nothing like that. We've been told to release the body. The disposal certificate's already here.'

'Hallelujah! You've found who killed her, then?'

'Afraid not, sir. We've been ordered to stop looking.'

'Can't say I'm surprised. Politics, lad. And money, of course. Interfere with bloody everything these days. Still, you never know what might turn up out of the blue. How's the boss?'

'He's out of hospital, sir. We took him home this afternoon.'

'Where to? That hovel he's renting? Was he well enough to be left on his own?'

'I think so. Mr Tuttle said he could stay with them for a while, but the chief inspector said no. Anyway, Mrs Tuttle arrived soon after with the cat, because she's been fretting for Mr McKenna. Then Mrs

McKenna turned up, and started nagging because he wouldn't go back with her.'

Dr Roberts chuckled. 'Got the women fighting over him, has he?'

'They weren't fighting, sir.'

'Not while you were there, I daresay, but I wouldn't lay any bets on what happened after.' Dr Roberts chuckled again. 'Anyway, lad, what did you ring me about?'

'I – er – sort of wondered what'll happen to Mrs Bailey.'

'Who's doing the funeral?'

'The council.' Dewi's voice expressed the melancholy he felt. 'Her ex-boyfriend came up with a lot of lame excuses, but what it boils down to is he doesn't want the bother or the expense, not knowing if he'll get the money back, so I suppose you can't blame him too much.'

'It's a poor do, isn't it? They'll cremate her. It's cheaper, and it saves on precious land. Let me know when the funeral is, Dewi.' Dr Roberts fell silent, then said, 'People make you sick sometimes. There's all that to-do with the other one, and nobody gives a tinker's cuss about this poor soul.'

The photograph sent by Robert Allsopp lay atop the fax copy to the council. Romy Cheney, as she then called herself, stood alone on the bleak moorlands of northern England, dark cloud sweeping the sky behind her. She looked cold, hunched inside a thick brown-hued jacket, a gaily coloured scarf around her neck, its long ends streaming in the wind. Dewi studied her, wondering if, even then, Death combed the moorlands for her, knowing her to be as unloved and unwanted by Life as her body was now. He picked up the photograph, let his eyes wander back and forth, from the woman to the car, only its front half caught by the camera's eye, parked at an angle, front nearside wheel deep in peaty black soil.

Waiting for McKenna to answer the front door-bell, he looked up and down the miserable street, watching a dog rummage in black plastic bags left out for the dustmen. It came sniffing round his ankles, thin wormy body scabrous looking in the moonlight, and disappeared when McKenna opened the door.

'Sorry to bother you, sir.' McKenna wore a dressing-gown, pyjama bottoms showing under its hem. 'I didn't mean to get you out of bed.'

'You didn't. Come in.'

'You all right, sir?' Dewi asked, sitting on the edge of the chesterfield while McKenna slouched in an armchair.

'I keep getting terribly hungry, so I must be, mustn't I? Want some coffee?'

Dewi sipped his drink, gazing into the sputtering flames of the gas fire, and looked up to see McKenna's eyes, dark and probing, on his face.

'What's the matter, Dewi?'

'The photo Allsopp sent showed part of a car. I know you can't tell what sort. It's too small, too much in shadow . . . But you can see the bonnet and radiator and the front wheel. I showed Beti, but she's worse than useless. Couldn't say yes and couldn't say no.'

'And?'

'And I was wondering if we couldn't get the photo enlarged, see if we can bring up the numberplate.'

'It's probably Allsopp's car. Even though he can't, of course, remember if it is or it isn't.'

'I know. But that bloody Scorpio's getting on my nerves! I even dream about it. Wasn't one of those kids Brady and Hindley murdered found by examining photos of people and cars and moorland?'

'Yes, it was. Get Mr Tuttle to send the photo to the lab tomorrow, and tell him to keep quiet about it.'

Chapter 24

Trefor Prosser stirred again during the early hours, exciting his guardians' notice before retreating into coma. The medical registrar on night duty studied the monitors around the cot, took pulse and temperature, spent some moments looking thoughtfully down at the inert figure beneath the sheets, before moving on to check the other occupants of the unit, puzzling still on the man in thrall to relentless unconsciousness. Prosser's head injury was not severe, his vital signs were energetic, and given return to wakefulness, full recovery should proceed unhindered. The registrar entered on file the need for an early referral to the neurological registrar.

Wil Jones went early to work, reluctant and fearful, planning the finishing touches to Gallows Cottage and his escape from a place which had, in yielding bits of its history, disturbed his equilibrium, and led him to think of other worlds just beyond the safe boundaries he recognized as those of his own. Dave taking an early holiday to visit family in England, Wil too had taken a day of rest. And another, unable to return alone to Gallows Cottage after finding the man, white-faced and hungry-looking, quiet and still as the dead, at the foot of the staircase as Wil came down from painting the back bedroom to make his morning brew. He stopped halfway down the stairs, and spoke some words. He could not remember what he said, only how the sounds somehow stuck in his throat, jammed in there with a heart that leapt from its moorings at the sight of the man in his antique dress. The man faded from sight as he watched, evaporated like a wisp of sea fog in winds off the Straits, leaving the same damp chill to creep up the stairs and lick around his ankles.

Christopher Stott, as he had twice each day since the previous week, telephoned the hospital to enquire about Prosser, and received the same bland response as on every other occasion. Fear and anxiety ground their teeth together, his flesh caught between: fear for himself, anxiety for Prosser. He knew he was trapped, had seen the jaws draw closer together, until he now had no escape apart from that so tempting, so gloriously liberating, he viewed its dark shadow with something approaching welcome.

Jamie Thief, brashness beset by the same gnawing anxiety which devoured Christopher Stott, tried to assess if he really had anything to fear from the police, and knew he need only fear Dewi Prys, whose intuitions and leaps of imagination had coloured their childish play with magic, when they larked together in the streets, down in the woods, along the railway lines and under the viaduct at the far end of the council estate; the closest of friends until Jamie was caught out in his first adventure on the far side of the law. Imprisoned then by his nain in the cage of respectability, Dewi could only stare from the windows of his council house as Jamie mooched the streets alone, a hardness growing in his eyes as it made a stone of his heart. Jamie sometimes wondered how his own life might be had he not craved the excitement of thievery, had not learned at such an early age that something could indeed be culled from nothing. He sat in his mother's kitchen, and decided a little absence might be prudent. Packing a holdall with jeans and sweatshirts and trainers and underclothes, he pulled up the floorboard in his bedroom, and extracted what remained of the proceeds from his last trip to Manchester in the Scorpio car delivering a package collected from the pilot of a small boat anchored in Benllech Bay. He left the house, with no note for his mother, no intimation whether he might return this week or next year or never, and walked to the main road, to catch a bus to the small caravan lodged behind old railway cottages dismal in the lee of Dorabella Quarry, where he knew he could safely hide, from Dewi Prys at least, for as long as necessary.

The postman brought one letter for McKenna, which he dropped unopened on to the kitchen table. He felt rather better, having slept well and eaten a good breakfast. He made coffee, and sat in the parlour, the letter on his lap, thinking about Denise, who became more distanced with each passing day, too remote even for nostalgia to reach. He wondered how she might spend the rest of her life, and saw her only as two-dimensional, a cutout pasted on the board of recollection, with no force to her presence to make an impact in his own surroundings. He thought too of Emma Tuttle, and felt a tug of some emotion less than agreeable beneath the warmth his thoughts evoked, as if he stood at the edge of a pool of water, its surface luminescent, reflecting the heat of some sun, hiding treacherous, fathomless depths into which he would plunge if he so much as touched one finger to the mirrored calm to let its heat warm the cold blood running in his veins.

He opened the back door for the cat, watched her stalk the little patch of soil before leaping the wall and disappearing. He went upstairs to dress, thinking a walk would be pleasant, despite low cloud heavy with rain behind the university building. His reflection in the full-length mirror on the wardrobe door showed colour returning to his pale cheeks, life to the eyes, and he dared to hope that bodily health might bring with it a wholeness, an individuality rubbed away by the friction of living as half of an ill-matched pair. Unused to seeing himself thus, he stared at the man in the mirror, behind which, or within, lay still a sense of something lacking, of some deficiency, as if he too might be merely two-dimensional; and wondered, if he looked long enough, whether the orphan child still dwelling within the man would emerge, take hold of his hand, and lead him bravely into that light the man was too afraid to let into his life. But then, he thought, the child he had once been was dead, slain by time, no more than a ghost in the darkness, and no help to the living.

Trefor Prosser's pale and motionless form was wheeled away for a brain scan and skull X-rays, although in the experience of the neurological registrar, coma victims returned to the world when and if they wished to do so. He suspected this man preferred the cushioned peace of unconsciousness, would elude as long as possible whatever terror had forced him into his car and into a wall at sixty miles an hour. Having seen the police report on the accident, and read with particular interest the statement of the bus driver, the registrar was convinced Prosser had tried to kill himself. Not only would memory return with consciousness, but the risk of another suicide attempt hard on its heels, Trefor Prosser yet another lost soul who wished to relinquish all control over his life in an act which was no statement of defiance, but the final act of subjugation, of the worthless, and the last and most abject apology for having dared to live.

Jack thought he might fill the hiatus in his work by taking leave, and wondered if Emma would object too much if he applied for a transfer, for there was a vague feeling deep inside his head that it might be wise to move her as far away from McKenna as possible. Working carefully through the log of outstanding offences, coding them for urgency and the likelihood of successful solution, he found his attention overtaken by other matters, by nagging thoughts of Emma and Michael McKenna, the way she had looked at McKenna yesterday, the expression on Denise's face when she noticed, the spasm of rage which had twisted Emma's mouth when Dewi Prys escorted Denise down the staircase into McKenna's parlour.

McKenna took his walk, returning to find both the cat and Denise waiting on his front doorstep. He hoped the air of disarray about Denise had no cause other than the ravages of weather, of wind and rain in her hair and on her face. He offered her coffee and lunch, and felt a great lightness when she left, having said very little at all and nothing of consequence, spending most of the visit staring blankly through the parlour window at the university building on the hill opposite, its contours misted and twisted by rain sweeping down the valley. As she stood at the front door, putting up her umbrella, he noticed nicotine stains on her fingers, chipped nail varnish, a patchiness to her complexion where make-up was carelessly applied. Daylight that day was cruel to her, marking the lines and shadows of age, signs of disintegration and impending chaos. He told her to take care of herself, and she turned, surprised from her apathy, to see the door closing behind her, and McKenna's form behind its glass panes, walking away.

Sitting on a wall beside the main road, spiky fair hair darkened by rain blowing in from the west, Jamie watched a Purple Motors bus, bound for the mountain villages, take the sharp bend by the entrance to Port Penrhyn, and career past, water spurting from tyres making a swishing noise on the tarmac. The driver never so much as glanced at him; would not, if asked by anyone trying to piece together Jamie's movements that day, even be able to recall the drab anonymous figure by the roadside.

Jamie wondered why he should put himself to the trouble of catching a rickety bus, then walking almost a mile in the pouring rain to the caravan, when there were people down the road who owed him, and whose debt had no completion date. His conscience, perhaps aborted like an unwanted foetus in his early years, did not trouble him with questions about debts of his own. He snatched whatever he could from wherever he could, on a presumption never disproved that the world had no scruples about stripping him of the most primitive rights, the most humble dreams.

Picking up the holdall, he began walking towards the city, down Beach Road, past the haunted Nelson Inn, the bistro which was once a funeral parlour, and then turned right into a small warren of narrow streets. Two-up-and-two-down cottages, once home to seafarers and dockers whose industry kept afloat huge vessels carting slate from the quarry to ports the world over, faced each other across cobbled strips dribbled with a slurry of black asphalt. There were sea-scents in the air, salty and slightly fishy, and on the wind sneaking around corners, slapping bits of litter up and down the street and against the huge blocks of undressed stone which formed the cottage walls. Jamie turned into Turf Square, and walked up a little flight of concrete steps under the front porch of one of the new houses, small poor-looking houses, as mean as the old cottages but without any of their charm. Rendered walls stained and scabby, paintwork salt-scarred, the houses bore already the miserable faces of slum dwellings.

The front door opened. 'He's not in. He's at work,' the woman said, and began to close the door in Jamie's face.

'I know.' Jamie's face showed no emotion. 'That's why I'm here.'

The woman stared at him. 'You'd better come in, then,' was all she said, before opening the door a little wider.

*

'Why has all our leave been cancelled for tomorrow, sir?' Dewi asked.

Jack looked up from the police federation circular he was reading. 'What's that, Prys?'

'Why has all our leave been cancelled?'

'It's that wedding, that's why.'

'What wedding?'

'I'm trying to read!' Jack snapped. 'If you'd listen to what's being said at briefings, you wouldn't need to ask damn fool questions! Haven't you got anything to do?'

'Yes, sir.'

'Then bloody do it!' Jack snatched the circular from the desk in the squad room and stalked out.

A two-page memorandum in the briefings' file from Divisional Headquarters gave notice of the double wedding of couples from the 'itinerant peoples of Britain', with some 600 similar guests expected. Dewi wondered what politically correct diminutive might be gleaned from 'itinerant peoples' which would have the universal appeal of 'gippo', the same pejorative ring. The double wedding at the city's Roman Catholic church would be celebrated later at the Octagon Nightclub, and he hoped the rain would blow out to sea before morning, for no normal person wanted to be wed on a dismal day, and there was nothing to say such feelings were denied to the gipsies. He wondered too if the man who roamed Salem village and the woods around Snidey Castle would be one among the 600.

Donning his waterproof, he went a-wandering in the High Street, tramping in and out of shops, looking for Devil's work abroad on streets awash and near-deserted.

McKenna dozed in front of the fire, the cat draped

across his lap, to wake late in the afternoon, the parlour dim and scented with dampness. Carefully moving the limp animal, he switched on lights, and went into the kitchen to make a pot of tea and cut a sandwich, carrying plate and mug back to the fireside. Lethargic in body and restless in mind, his thoughts were those which disturb, become uncomfortable by trespassing beyond the safe boundaries of thoughts and ideas necessary for survival and enjoyment, into realms of the imponderable and impenetrable. In childhood, he would spend hours staring through his bedroom window on a starlit night, imagining the sky a velvet cloth stitched with jewels, then a gauzy wisp through which those same jewels glittered softly, before seeing the sky as the beginning of infinity, beyond which lay nothing the human brain could conceptualize.

Age dulled the excitement of abstracts, bringing in its place a pernicious notion that all life was futile, all its activities merely the filling in of Time before Death came calling. What lay beyond that event he envisaged akin to the nothingness beyond infinity, where the state of grace his religion told him to seek without telling where to look mattered less than nothing. McKenna sighed, as he did much too often, about no one thing in particular but most things in general, and decided to acquire a television, to acquire one opiate even if the other was of no assistance.

Dewi walked the High Street between the Plaza cinema and Jewson's Yard, a mile each way, overshadowed by dark cloud behind Bangor Mountain. Kicking at litter on the pavement, irritable and bored, he wanted to be part of that great war raging between good and bad which the newspapers reported daily, yet twice in and out of Woolworth's, he failed to apprehend a single shoplifter, found not a single vehicle along those miles illegally parked or untaxed. No urchins scavenged the street picking pockets, no vandals smashed windows, no elderly citizens sat dazed and panting, beaten and robbed. He saw only Jamie's distant cousin, a little the worse for drink, staggering half on and half off the pavement at the bottom end of the High Street. Sheltering by Jewson's gate, he watched until the man turned up Penybryn and disappeared from view, wondering if it was true, as the old-timers said, that bad weather was the best policeman of all, and hoping again for sunshine and a stirring of blood on the morrow.

Chiding herself for being untruthful as well as spiteful, Emma told the twins that another serving of fish and chips would worsen their spots, and that her casserole was their only choice, boring though it might be. As each girl examined the other's face for eruptions of acne, Emma said millions of people all over the world starved every day, and would be grateful for such a meal. One of the twins, meeting fire with fire, said, 'Why don't you put your horrible stew in a parcel and send it to the Red Cross, then?' Sulking in the kitchen, Emma stirred the thickening mess in her big copper stew pan: rightly a stew, she admitted, but less so than it might have been without the benefit of a bottle of red wine.

Tea was a quiet meal, not pleasantly so, but sullenly, with explosive potential. Jack paused every so often in the act of spooning food into his mouth to give her puzzled looks brimming with questions to which he could not give shape.

'Done anything interesting today, Em?' he asked at one point.

'No. Have you?'

'Not much.' He finished his casserole, wiping the plate with a hunk of bread. 'You must have done something.'

'Depends what you call interesting.' Emma countered. 'I changed the beds and cleaned upstairs this morning. Then I went to Safeways for the groceries. Then I came back and peeled the vegetables and cut up the meat and put it all on to cook. Then I did some of the ironing. Oh, and I've had a sandwich and a few cups of tea.'

'Mummy could've saved herself all that trouble if she'd let us have fish and chips like we wanted.'

'Mummy's in a bad mood,' the other twin told Jack. 'She said we've got spotty faces, and it's not true.'

Jack surveyed his daughters' peachy luminous skin. 'Why say that to the girls, Em? It's not fair to upset them.'

'I didn't say they've got spots.'

'Yes you did, Mummy.'

'Well,' Jack said, looking from his wife to the children, 'maybe you got hold of the wrong end of the stick. You haven't got spots, so it doesn't matter.'

'Mummy's pre-menstrual again,' one of the girls said with authority. 'You know how she always gets crabby and spiteful.'

'Maybe she's menopausal,' the other observed. 'Are you, Mummy? Are you having hot flushes?'

Face reddened with anger, Emma lurched to her

feet, snatched plates from the table, and stormed into the kitchen, slamming the door behind her.

'Oh, God!' Jack moaned. 'Now look what you've done.'

'Mummy started it when we came home from school.'

'Well, there's no need for you two to keep it going, is there? Clear the table, and go and offer to wash up. Both of you.'

'We haven't had our pudding yet.'

'And she'll only shout if we go in there. We don't see why we should be nice to her when she's horrible to us!' The other twin folded her arms, her sister following suit. Both stared at their father, mutiny blossoming in pretty brown eyes.

Jack followed his wife. He found her leaning against the kitchen sink, staring on to the misty rain-soaked garden. 'What's the matter, Em?' he asked.

She kept her back to him. 'Nothing.'

'Oh, come on, Em. This isn't like you.'

As he approached, she swerved away towards the counter, and began moving plates around. 'Leave me be. And stop calling me Em. My name is Emma.'

Jack left the room, once again at the mercy of the female psyche and its climatic changes, once again with no alternative than to weather the tempest as best he could. As he sat alone in front of the television, sound turned down and people cavorting through a game show, the worm of doubt began to wriggle towards the heart of the rose he believed his marriage to be, carrying decay and destruction.

Jamie tossed and turned in his narrow bunk, kept from

sleep by the strident silence of the countryside at night eating into his nerves. The inside of the thin caravan shell was stale and unaired, the musty scent of sodden earth beneath seeping upwards and into the back of his throat.

Prosser remained unconscious, for which Jamie would have thanked God if he thought God remotely interested in his gratitude or otherwise. Prosser was the weak link, which might snap and send the taut chain leaping and writhing into a stranglehold around their throats. Christopher Stott was weak too, a weakness of spirit as well as of flesh recognized and held in check by his wife. She and Jamie were the temper in the steel, without which it became brittle and useless, each with their own reasons for staying true to bargains struck and obligations accepted. Chilled and restless, Jamie crawled from the bunk and opened one of the precious packets taped to its underside. He rolled a cigarette, opened a can of lager, and lay back on the pillow, sipping his drink until the can was drained, watching the glowing end of the cigarette spark and fade and spark and fade in the blackness around him until the cigarette was a small mound of scented ash. His body drifted into a languor, his mind into a haze, and thence to sleep.

Chapter 25

Emma placed a mug of black coffee on the table beside Denise, wrinkling her nose at the acrid smell of cigarette smoke despoiling the clean air of her front room. Denise panted slightly, in short little puffs tainted with the heady scents of spicy food and cheap wine.

'I've no sympathy for you,' Emma announced. 'So don't bother whining to me. People choke to death on their own vomit when they get as drunk as that. You should count yourself lucky you've only got a hangover. Even if you've no respect for yourself, you should have more consideration for Michael. He's a reputation to consider, and I'm sure he won't take kindly to having a drunk for a wife.'

Denise picked up the coffee, her hands shaky. Watery sunshine flowed through the window, washing her face and figure with clear cruel light.

'And don't spill anything,' Emma instructed. 'God! You're like a spoilt brat! You didn't know when you were well off, did you?' Emma surveyed the woman crouched on the edge of the sofa in dishevelment and despair. All her gloss stained and dull with tarnish, Denise was like a piece of jewellery, cast from base metal and gilded to fool the eye. The roots of her sweat-stained hair showed dark, her skin blotched and goose-bumped, her expensive clothes like rags about a scarecrow, the fine wool of her skirt embroidered with a mosaic of creases and rucks. 'You know, Denise,' she said thoughtfully, 'Skid Row is just around the corner from Easy Street. But you've never realized that before, have you? You thought it was all right to sneer and make bitchy remarks about other women when their husbands walked out, didn't you? All right to blame them for it, all right to say they deserved it. I mean,' she added mercilessly, 'you've been quite eloquent about women getting thrown back on the muck-heap of dirt and desperation where they belong, dying from the incurable diseases of poverty and loneliness. Haven't you? I've seen you cross the street rather than say hello to women who used to be your friends until their husbands legged it. Well,' she went on, 'you must've caught whatever it was they had, because it looks to me as if you're going the same way. You'll end up dragging from day to day on Valium and sleeping pills and dragging yourself from man to man for a bit of company or a free drink. And each man you take up with will be more of a slob than the last, and they'll all toss you back on that muck-heap, and nobody'll want to soil their hands on you in the end. I shouldn't think Michael will come charging to the rescue, because he's got his own life to lead, hasn't he? It's up to you what you do with yours, like it is for all of us. You can swim or you can sink, and right now, I'd say you're not far off drowning in self-pity.'

McKenna came to consciousness with late morning sunshine glowing through the uncurtained bedroom window, urging him to get out of bed, to pinion the hope of a new day before it fled, as such feeling, hatched in the warmth of night, was wont to do in the light of wakefulness. He reached down to stroke the cat, and had his hand bitten lazily for his trouble. As soon as he rose, she stretched, jumped off the bed, and padded downstairs after him, clawing the bottom of his pyjama trousers at each step he took. Waiting for the kettle to boil and his toast to brown, he read the newspaper and opened the post, while the cat ate her own breakfast. She shouted to be let out as the tinny chimes of the town clock struck eleven. McKenna felt much recovered, rather whole and clean and empty inside, as if his sickness had indeed purged him of more than bodily poisons. Standing by the back door, savouring the first real warmth of the year and the pleasure it brought, he wondered if hope and its twin were simply forms of energy, finite in quantity, his optimism another's despair.

Jack and Dewi stood among their colleagues on the pavement outside the Bible Gardens, watching the men of this great congregation of gipsies make their own assessment of the lines and groups of police officers surrounding them like so many dogs herding a flock of sheep. Hard black eyes, small within sockets perpetually narrowed to read the distances, threatened with no more than a glance. Rough-looking people, Dewi thought, their straight black hair chopped rather than trimmed, brown hands large and calloused with labour, their women no more refined and no less intimidating.

Brilliant sunshine of an April afternoon left Jack unwarmed, his spirit overshadowed by stormclouds gathered in great swags and swathes about his family, as if they waited like some mighty tree for a shard of lightning to split asunder its rotted trunk. He sighed, drawing a questioning look from Dewi, who said, 'I'm glad it stopped raining. Aren't you, sir? Nobody wants their wedding rained off.'

'They got married in church,' Jack said. 'Not likely to get rained off there unless the priest can't afford to get his roof fixed, are they?'

'I don't see the man from Salem village. Do you, sir?'

'How could I if I don't know what he looks like?' Jack snapped. 'You don't either, so I don't know why you come out with such stupid remarks!'

'Just trying to be civil, sir.'

'You shouldn't need to "try" to be civil with senior officers, Prys. It should come naturally.' Jack glared. 'What are you grinning at?'

'I wasn't grinning as such,' Dewi said equably. 'Just smiling, sir. It's a lovely day, and gippos or not, they make a good show, don't they?'

Sunlight gilded the great ranks of horse chestnut trees, filtering through fresh green leaves and pink and cream candles blossoming into light, stippling faces and finery and the bright white bustled gowns of the two brides. A huge white Rolls Royce was parked at the kerb by the gates of the Gardens, a bouquet of creamy silk roses tossed on to the back seat. Two young bridesmaids broke away from the crowd, rushing past Dewi towards the car, their faces garishly enamelled, eyes too shadowed, lips too bloodied, dressed in snow-white satin, with roses of blood-red silk stitched into the folds of skirt and around fichu neck; colours symbolic of the fate in ambush for a virgin bride. He stared after them, entranced by their foreignness, the alien tongue in which they chattered. Jack's elbow dug hard into his ribs.

'Look over there,' he said. 'By the Town Hall. That's Christopher Stott.'

Tall and frail as a sapling, his face pasty-white behind the little beard, Stott leaned against a wall, watching the crowd. Beside him stood a woman, much shorter than he, much more real, dumpy and solid, as if her flesh was constrained from some rampage only by the tightness of the clothes it wore. Dewi walked slowly towards the couple, stopping when he had a clear view of her. Body half-turned, left hand resting on the rough tweed of Stott's jacket, as if to keep him constrained from a different rampage of the flesh, she seemed of that indeterminate age which afflicts those women whose looks are unremarkable, whose hair is neither grey nor brown, whose eyes neither blue nor green, whose form neither grossly fat nor frighteningly thin. She wore a suit of some fawn-coloured fabric, the skirt exposing the back of lumpy knees, the jacket so tight he saw the bunchiness of blouse and flesh and underclothing beneath. In her right hand she held a white plastic carrier bag, Debenhams' pastel-coloured logo on its side, and he suddenly pictured her clad in grey, skirt plain, jacket pretty with leafy strands amid roses faded and soft, not bloody crimson like those bedecking the bridesmaids' gowns. He wondered if the rich heavy scent of carnation would come to him if he moved closer.

'Have you forgotten?' Jack demanded. 'The investigation's closed.'

'That's not what the superintendent actually said,' Dewi countered, noting the peevish set to Jack's mouth. 'We're supposed to follow up anything that comes along.'

'You wittering on about how that suit Wil Jones found would look a treat on a woman who may or may not be shacked up with Stott is not something coming along. It's your imagination running away with you again.'

'I still say there's no harm in asking. And something might come back on the car in the photograph.'

'Asking who? Who d'you propose to ask? And you can shut up about the photograph. We shouldn't've done that.'

'Mrs Stott, sir.'

'Oh, yes? You intend to go knocking on her door, do you, with the suit all nicely folded up in a carrier bag? Then I suppose you drag it out, like a rabbit out of a bloody hat, and say: "we have reason to believe Romy Cheney bought you this suit, and you stuffed it under the floorboards at Gallows Cottage because somebody saw you wearing it when you bumped her off." You're going to say that to her, are you, Prys?'

'Well, you never know, sir. What her reaction might be, I mean.'

'Shall I tell you what her reaction would be? She'll invite you in, then she'll pick up the phone, and she'll call Councillor bloody Williams, then he'll call the chief constable, then you'll be sailing nice and fast up shit creek, and I'll be in the boat with you! No, Prys, you are not going anywhere. Do you understand?'

Dewi shrugged. 'If you say so, sir.'

'I do say so. And let that be the end of it!'

*

Under the warm and careful ministrations of doctors and nurses, Trefor Prosser's unconsciousness began to evaporate, as a morning mist over the Menai Straits burnt away by the heat of the sun. Light broke through the clouds in his brain, poking prying fingers into dark corners, teasing out, from the shadows where he had hidden them, fearful secrets and secret fears. He fought to remain in darkness, to huddle beneath its safe canopy, the bleeps and blips and lines on the monitors telling of that monumental struggle. His eyes fluttered open, and he saw the face of the neurological registrar smiling gravely and assessingly down at him. He closed his eyes again, but found himself unable to close his ears to the voices and sounds which had teased like wind at the canopy of cloud long before light made the final breach.

'About time,' the registrar said, watching quivering eyelids betray the glint of iris beneath. 'Never known anyone so anxious to stay asleep!'

He walked away, deep in conversation with a nurse. 'Keep him hooked up to the monitors for tonight. There's really no need, but I don't want him thinking he's well enough to get out of bed. You never know what his sort is likely to do.'

'The police want to talk to him. We're supposed to call the minute he comes round.'

'They can wait. I want the psychiatrist to see him first. Prosser's a suicide risk, and I don't intend to put my job on the line by letting the police put the frighteners on him so much he takes off and finishes what he started.'

Jack telephoned Emma, testing the waters.

'What time are you coming home?' she asked.

'Not too late. I don't expect any problems. The gipsies seem very well behaved.'

Emma laughed. 'They might not be with a few drinks inside them.'

Laughter could not precede a storm warning, he thought. 'What are you cooking for tea?'

'Nothing! I'm sick of cooking.' Her voice was sharp.

'Shall I get a takeaway, then?'

'Do what you want. The girls are having fish and chips.'

'What about us?'

'I'm going out.'

'Out? Where to?'

'Out! Eating out. You'll have to see to yourself.'

'Who with?'

'Somebody who wants to talk about things other than teenagers and police work and cooking.' Jack heard the receiver placed on its cradle, then the buzzing of an empty line, and felt great cold draughts of terror sweeping over him.

The young constable newly transferred to Traffic Division put the last file away, having managed to find the right place for nearly all the pieces of paper the inspector dropped on the sergeant's desk, and he on the constable's lap. A few odd sheets drifted in the breeze from an open window, homeless and unwanted, all but one apparently circulars of some description or another. For want of anything better, the constable pinned them in a bunch to the bottom right-hand corner of the notice board. The other, a sheet of flimsy off the fax machine with serrated edges top and bottom, was covered in names and dates, all listed under a car registration. The paper had travelled the office for days, passed from one to another, seeking the person who wanted the information. Apparently, no one did, but loth to destroy a piece of paper, no matter how derelict it might seem, the constable carried it along the corridor to the empty CID office, and abandoned it on a desk under an unwashed coffee mug.

McKenna did not answer the doorbell to Jack's persistent summons. Jack searched along the terrace front for a way around its rear, so that he might sneak a view through McKenna's parlour window, to see if McKenna was the thief of his imagination, stealing Emma from the intellectual tedium of her marriage and robbing her husband of the love of his life.

Standing once more on the slate doorstep, finger again on the bell, he heard the front door of the house opposite drag open. 'You looking for Mr M?' an old voice quavered.

'D'you know where he is?' Jack asked of the crone framed in the rotting doorway.

'He went out a while back.' The woman smiled a toothless smile, lips stretched over withered gums. 'That lady came in her car.'

'What lady?'

'The one what's always coming,' she said. The door was returned to its frame, he left to pace the silence of the street, his footsteps echoing from the house walls. He took one last look through McKenna's front door and saw the cat, rakish face distorted by reeded glass, staring back at him.

Chapter 26

Rising early, Emma prepared a cooked breakfast for her husband and children before they awoke. Her head ached slightly, a relic of the night before and reminder of pleasant and invigorating hours away from her family. True to form, the twins stayed abed as long as possible, then clattered downstairs, snatched toast from the table before leaving for school. Saying nothing to either wife or daughters, Jack doggedly ate cereal and egg and bacon and sausage and toast and marmalade, whilst Emma watched confusion pursue anxiety across his face, that barometer of his temper.

'Were you called out last night?' she asked, refilling his teacup.

'No.'

'You had a quiet evening, I take it?'

'Yes.'

'That's good. No problems with the girls?'

'No.' He chewed another piece of toast, swallowing so hard the Adam's apple bobbed high in his throat.

'You could manage them on your own without any trouble, then?'

'Yes.' His reply preceded understanding. Head jerking up, he asked, 'What d'you mean?'

Naked fear shone in his eyes, pulled his mouth into

a rictus. Emma sat down. 'Denise and I are thinking of going on holiday together.'

'Denise?'

'Yes. Denise.'

'When did you speak to her?'

'Last night, of course. We spent the evening together. Who did you think I was with?'

Embarrassment coursing into his face, he stared back.

'I don't know what you thought I was doing, but you were obviously wrong, weren't you?'

Unwilling to let go, the terrier intent on unearthing the last splinter of bone without appreciating that its sharpness might rip blood from flesh, Jack said, 'I thought Denise was out with her soon-to-be ex-husband.'

'She was out with me. We went for a pub meal, then a drive round Anglesey.'

'Where to?'

'Where to what?'

'Where did you have a meal?'

'Is this how you interrogate so-called suspects, Jack? What am I suspected of doing?'

He buttered another slice of toast, and slopped marmalade on top of the butter. 'You're being silly.'

'I am not being silly!' Emma snapped. 'You've been moody and downright suspicious lately. What d'you think I'm doing? More pertinently, who d'you think I might be doing it with?'

'I don't know, do I?' Jack slammed his knife on to the plate. It clattered off, smearing butter and marmalade on the tablecloth. 'And you're a fine one to talk about moods!'

'I see. Well, we all know what sort of mischief wives

get into, don't we? Especially wives who have to put up with a miserable moody sod of a husband and a couple of bloody-minded teenagers day in and day out. Not to mention wives with nothing else to look forward to except more of the same and the sodding housework as well!'

Her eyes glittering with rage and not a trace of tears, Jack thought she looked magnificent, as if she should adorn the prow of a galleon, proud breasts breaking mountainous seas, the light in her eyes brighter than any mariner's lantern. But, he thought, Emma might steer her ship into the whirlpool of Charybdis and laugh as it foundered with all hands off the rocks of Scylla.

'Well?' she demanded. 'Say something!'

'What am I supposed to say? Denise is making you discontented. She's a bad influence on people.'

'Don't be ridiculous! Can't you see I'm in a rut?'

'We're all in a rut. It's what life's about most of the time.'

'Oh, is it? Everybody quietly ploughing their own little furrow until they die? It might suit you, but it certainly doesn't satisfy me!'

'Oh, for God's sake! That's the sort of remark McKenna makes, and the attitude that's wrecked his marriage. Hankering after some ideal which doesn't exist in real life.'

'Maybe Denise is beginning to see his point of view. Maybe she understands where she went wrong as well. What d'you think of that?'

'I think,' Jack said, weary and afraid and overwhelmed with a need to seek the comfort of her body, 'we should stop fighting. I don't understand why this is happening.'

Emma sighed. 'That's half the trouble, isn't it? There's not much to understand. I'm fed up, the way everybody gets from time to time.' She began clearing the table. 'The holiday was Denise's idea. She needs a break. She's been through the mill in the last few weeks, and it's not over yet by any means. It'll be ages before she's back to anything like normal, but at least she's made a start, so I can stop worrying so much. When women stop caring about themselves, they go downhill faster than a runaway truck.'

'Stop worrying? I thought you'd fallen out with her.'

'We're back on an even keel, even if other things have changed. But that's how it goes, isn't it?'

'Where were you thinking of going on holiday?'

'Somewhere warm and sunny. Greece or Rhodes, perhaps. It won't be too busy at this time of the year.'

'Then what?'

'Denise will be moving. She's rented a flat on the marina in Port Dinorwic. She and Michael went to see it last night.'

'I meant, what about you?'

'Me? What about me?'

'Will you come home? Or will you be like that Shirley Valentine character, running away from your boring life and your boring husband and family? Isn't that what women dream about, Em? Romance and excitement under a sunny sky?'

She dropped plates and mugs and cutlery in the washing-up bowl, squirted Fairy Liquid and ran hot water. Jack stared at her plump back and beautiful rounded buttocks. 'Do you have to be in work soon?' she asked.

'Not particularly. Why?'

Emma pulled off the pink rubber gloves she had just donned. 'Let's leave the dishes to soak for a while, then.'

Waiting for the kettle to boil for morning coffee, Dewi absently read the dog-eared fax paper, more interested in the possible reason for Jack's rare unpunctuality than the contents of the message. Scanning the sheet from halfway down the page, as was his custom, he failed to understand its significance until, he told Jack, he looked at the heading.

'Where the hell has it been?' Jack demanded. 'It's dated over a week ago.'

'Dunno, sir. I expect we'll find out eventually. Somebody'll be for the high jump, won't they? What are we going to do about it?'

'I'm going to see the superintendent.'

Dewi dialled McKenna's number. 'Are you coming back to work today, sir?'

'Would it be worth my while, Dewi? Or might I be better occupied doing the garden?'

'Well, sir, you'll likely turn over a lot more worms here.'

'How's that?'

'You could say we've had a bit of a break. And it's not the sort of break one particular person will be able to mend without God's help.'

Not only against outsiders did the police close ranks, Owen Griffiths reflected, for senior officers fared ill when it was their task to apportion blame and discipline. None of his colleagues at any rank, either uniform or plainclothes, would admit even to seeing the fax from DVLC. He returned to his office, knowing further harangue to be futile, only likely to accrue resentments ready to boomerang when he had least defence. His damage limitation exercise would stand or fail on McKenna's reaction, the measure of his righteousness. Owen Griffiths prayed for clemency from McKenna, for an acknowledgement that human error need not cause collapse of the edifice of law and order, and appreciated, perhaps for the first time, how a conscience on the loose, as McKenna's frequently was permitted to be, caused trouble to rival outright corruption.

Slumped at the bar of the Douglas Arms in Bethesda, Wil Jones nursed guilty feelings about his absence from work, along with a large measure of whisky and craven fear. Yesterday brought, with its respite from the vicious Arctic storms so usual in the spring, a different coldness, enough to repel any peace or rest he might seek, enough to force him sweating and shivering from the sleep of exhaustion which eventually overtook him in the dead hours of morning.

The man waited in the cottage, behind a door which Wil unlocked, and did not disappear, did not evaporate, but leaned against the kitchen wall simply watching. Not exactly leaned against the wall, Wil decided, whisky running warm in his belly, but sort of leaned. And only that, he thought, for he saw the scabby plaster of the unpainted wall through the figure of the man, and it was that which sent him stumbling from kitchen and cottage, in fear for his mortal soul. Not stopping to lock the cottage door, he fell into his van and careered up the track at top speed, axles grinding and slipping over stones and tussocks of rank grass.

He wanted to speak his terror, but feared being called a fool and worse. He drank more whisky, and slumped further against the bar, and at closing time, was laid out by the landlord on a bench in the snug to snore away his drunkenness.

Mary Ann relished her power, as if those upon whom it was exerted were marionettes, to be kept in the wings of her little theatre until she wished to jerk a string or two, wanted to watch the figures clacking and jumping to her tune. Michael McKenna had danced down the path to frighten the puppet Beti Gloff could not work for herself, for Beti Gloff could only hop this way or that on her lame bandy legs, too disarrayed to conduct, too much in awe of Mary Ann to choreograph her own affairs.

For John Jones, Mary Ann was not a puppet-mistress, but high priestess of the great coven of womanhood, to which the woman in the woods and the other both had title, and for all his scorn and loathing, his fear triumphed. Blame Mary Ann he might for the terms under which Beti returned to him, terms hammered out, he was sure, by Mary Ann and her coven over pots of tea and sticky fattening cakes in the fuggy parlour of her cottage. But the hex upon him was the work of another, who had every step he took, even down the overgrown garden path to the privy, dogged by the gipsy with staring eyes and ashen face, a face luminous even on the darkest night when God locked moon below horizon, too mean even to light the stars. And that other one might, if John Jones let slip his guard for the tiniest fraction of time, make him reap what he had tried to sow.

'What's she doing here?' Jack asked, returning to the CID office. Nell glared at him from dark piggy eyes punched like holes in the curdles of flesh slopped around the bones of her skull.

'She's been arrested, sir,' Dewi said quietly.

'What for? Shoplifting again?'

'Er – no. Soliciting.'

'Soliciting? You've got to be joking!'

'In the Quarrymen's Rest. The landlord got fed up and called us. We're waiting for a WPC to sit with her.'

Jack stared blatantly at the blowsy, frowsty old woman, her clothes taut around belly and thighs, exposing flabbed knees and varicosed legs. She had the thick ugly feet of a streetwalker, and he wondered if she was born that way, her fate predestined by the configurations of body. 'Christ Almighty! How could anyone go with her?'

Dewi shrugged. 'They do say dirty water puts out fire just as well. What did the superintendent say about the car?'

'Eh?'

'The car, sir.'

'Oh, yes. The car. We're to follow it up. I thought I'd ring the chief inspector before we do anything.'

'He's coming in.'

'Is he? How d'you know that, Prys?'

'He was on the telephone, sir. And he says Mr Prosser's come round, so somebody'll have to see him.'

The psychiatrist frowned and leaned back in his chair,

bringing gentle squeaks and sighs from its upholstery. 'You cannot talk to my patient today, Inspector.'

'Why not, Dr Rankilor?'

Dr Rankilor tapped his fingers quietly on the edge of the desk. 'Mr Prosser,' he intoned, 'is not a well man. In fact, he is a very unwell man.'

'I thought the head injury was healing.'

'The physical injury, perhaps. My interest, however, is with the injuries of the ego, of the conscious mind and its subconscious, not with those of the mere flesh.'

'In my experience, injuries of the mere flesh are far more likely to prove fatal than the other kind.'

'You are a layman. You do not understand how a serious injury to the mind can cause a person to inflict mortal injury on the flesh.'

'You think Trefor Prosser is suicidal?'

'Why do you need to ask? He deliberately drove his car into a wall.'

'He drove into a wall to avoid crashing into a bus.'

'It is the implications of his action with which I must concern myself.'

'What's he said to you?'

'Very little. He wishes neither to communicate nor think. But his psychic distress flaunts itself from every fibre of his being.'

'Don't you think you're exaggerating this out of all proportion?' Jack said irritably. 'I want to ask him one thing.'

'And maybe that one thing will lead to another and another, and then to a homicidal act against his own person, for that is the nature of suicide, after all.'

'Trefor Prosser is a key witness in a murder investigation. I insist on speaking to him.'

'In that case, we must consider an application to the courts for the protection of my patient. Mr Prosser does not wish to see you, and has nothing to say to you.'

Rage blossomed in Jack's cheeks. 'I'll bet he doesn't want to see me! Did he tell you he only crashed his bloody car because he was running away from us?' He looked with disgust at the psychiatrist. 'You're letting him hide behind your white coat and your blasted Freudian fairy-tales!'

'If you approached him with the same attitude you are demonstrating to me, I am not surprised he fled from you, Inspector. You British have a little adage, do you not, about having the grace to see yourselves as others see you? You should consider that whilst you are fulminating against my opposition.'

The house in Turf Square lay empty, silent and dingy in late morning sunshine. Pushing through a narrow wooden gate which reeked of creosote, and down the little alleyway between this house and the one next door, Dewi stood on tiptoe to peer into the room at the rear of the house. Curtains obscured his view, grey-tinged nets looped into swags at the centre and edged with frills, like, he thought, a tart lifting up her skirts to show her tatty undergarments.

'There's nobody home, sir,' he told McKenna, slipping back into the car. 'What shall we do now? Go to the castle and wave that fax under Stott's nose?'

'Dunno, Dewi. It's not quite as straightforward as it seems.' McKenna lit a cigarette. 'We know the Scorpio belonged to Romy Cheney, or Margaret Bailey as she's named here, but there's not a mention of Stott. The next listed owner is our smelly friend down the road.' He turned to look for the sleek grey vehicle, and found its parking space occupied only by a ginger cat crouched upon its haunches.

'But Stott admitted selling him the car,' Dewi pointed out. 'How's he going to worm his way out of that?' He fidgeted with the door handle. 'We won't know unless we ask him, will we, sir?'

Christopher Stott leaned against the wall of the labyrinthine corridor of Snidey Castle, his wilting form wraith-like in the half-darkness. 'Haven't you caused enough trouble?' he asked McKenna. 'Trefor Prosser's in hospital because of you.'

'He's in hospital because he went racketing round in his car doped up to the eyeballs!' Dewi snapped.

McKenna intervened. 'Mr Stott, we have reason to believe you deliberately withheld information central to a murder investigation. We want to talk to you.'

'You are talking to me. You've talked to me before. You're interfering with my work, and my boss wants to know why the police are after me.'

'In that case, it would be better if you don't make a fuss about coming to the police station, then no one need be any the wiser.'

'And what if I don't want to?' Stott jerked his head, as if the muscles in neck and throat were taut and knotted.

'Then I shall arrest you, Mr Stott.'

Red light pulsing, the tape recorder in the interview

room emitted a high-pitched whine. Screwed-up plastic film from the tape cases crackled and unfurled in a grey metal waste bin. Stott's laboured breathing overwhelmed the soft intrusive noise of machinery. 'What do you want to know?' he asked McKenna, eyes frantic, like those of a cornered animal. Sweat beaded his pasty face, trickled in front of his ears.

'You are not obliged to say anything, Mr Stott,' the solicitor advised.

'It would be better if he did,' McKenna said. 'Until recently, Mr Stott was in possession of a car which belonged to Margaret Bailey, the woman found dead some weeks ago on Snidey Castle Estate. Mr Stott sold the car to a neighbour.' He handed the fax to the solicitor.

'I don't see my client's name here.'

'Mr Stott has already confirmed selling that particular car, and we have a full statement from the buyer.'

The solicitor turned to Stott. 'As I said, you don't have to say anything.'

'What will happen if I don't?'

'Well,' the solicitor said, covering a yawn, 'I'd say the police have enough to detain you whether you talk or not.'

Jack paced back and forth in McKenna's office. 'I'm not surprised the government stopped the bloody Irish having the right to silence!'

'Mr McKenna's Irish really, sir, so you shouldn't be so rude,' Dewi said.

'Shut up!' Jack turned to McKenna. 'Can't you find something for him to do?'

'Can't you two act like adults?' McKenna snapped.

'Why don't you exercise your minds instead of your mouths? Then you can tell me what we do next. We can't talk to Prosser because that bloody psychiatrist won't let us, and we can't talk to Stott because he's hiding behind the kind provisions of the Police and Criminal Evidence Act.' He lit a cigarette. 'Not forgetting Jamie, of course, who seems to have done a bunk. Any word round town about where he might be, Dewi?'

'No, sir. Nobody's talking.'

Jack said sulkily, 'Maybe Stott'll change his mind.'

'Fat chance!' Dewi said.

'You got any better ideas, Prys?'

'I might have, but I wouldn't be telling you if I did!'

McKenna jumped up, his chair crashing against the wall. 'Be quiet! I will not tolerate such behaviour!'

Jack looked from McKenna to Dewi and walked out of the room, slamming the door so hard he rattled the walls.

'Sorry, sir,' Dewi offered. 'Mr Tuttle gets my back up at times.' He sat quietly, legs crossed, hands folded in his lap, waiting for the storm to pass. 'Somebody ought to tell Mrs Stott about her husband,' he said into the lengthening silence. 'Did Mr Tuttle tell you we saw her yesterday? Watching the gipsy wedding along with everybody else, she was. I told Mr Tuttle that suit Wil Jones found would fit her like a glove.'

Chapter 27

Gwendolen Stott stared without expression at McKenna and the uniformed policewoman sitting on a fat sofa, the twin of her own seat, furniture crowding this too narrow, too low room. Her feet, clad in scuffed black court shoes with turned-up toes, barely touched the carpet. Beside her lounged a girl in her early teens, dressed in a lilac and pink shell suit, shod in expensive white baseball boots. She drew her feet underneath her body, drawing a frown from her mother. 'Take your feet off the furniture, Jennifer.' The girl scowled, tossed her head, whipping the pony-tail of blonded hair across her face. She shifted into obedience, and ground the toes of her boots into the carpet.

Plain white walls, an ugly shabby carpet garish with whorls and swirls of orange and red and dirty brown, embraced rich furniture dressed in William Morris linens, windows of mean proportions dressed with matching curtains which hung too long. McKenna noticed a rickety shelf unit stacked with antique figures, elegant slipware jugs, leather-bound books tumbled amid the paperbacks and telephone directories and mail-order catalogues. Above an electric fire in a fake hearth, a small mirror reflected the top of Gwen Stott's head, a foreshortened view of her shoulders, the empty vase on the window sill behind her. The room wore an air of fustiness, shut off from fresh sea breezes and spring sunshine.

The woman wore a similar air, untouched by the warmth of any passion, unstirred by any living wind in the dark abyss of her soul. McKenna wondered what nourishment the girl's burgeoning womanhood might scavenge from the barren landscape of her mother's house. Neither mother nor daughter offered the smallest smile to their visitors: he had seen the mother frown and the daughter scowl, and thought that would mark the limit of their offerings.

'I have to tell you, Mrs Stott, that your husband has been arrested, and is being kept in custody,' McKenna said.

The girl stared at her feet, still trying to scrub holes in the ugly carpet. The woman made no response.

'Would you like to know why?' McKenna asked.

'I suppose you'll tell me anyway.' Ungraciousness honed to such finesse provoked McKenna.

'Most women would be only too anxious to know.'

'Most women,' she snarled, 'don't have the likes of him for a husband!'

The girl raised her head. 'You're always saying nasty things about Daddy,' she said. 'I don't know why and he doesn't either.'

'Doesn't he?' Gwen Stott demanded.

Speculating on the nature of those sins of which Stott had caused her to suffer the consequences, McKenna said, 'Mr Stott has been arrested over the sale of the car.'

'Is that all? Be more to the point if you arrested him over Trefor Prosser, wouldn't it?'

'Would it?' McKenna asked. 'We are not aware that Mr Prosser and your husband are involved in anything illegal.'

'More's the pity, isn't it? More's the pity it isn't illegal.'

'I can't comment upon that.' McKenna stood up, the policewoman following suit. 'Your husband will come before the magistrates in a few days. Whether or not we will oppose bail, I am unable to say. That depends on what information arises.'

The girl stared at her mother, tears glistening in her eyes. 'Mummy!' She clutched her mother's sleeve, and the woman jerked away. 'Mummy! Daddy's in prison! What are we going to do?'

'Nothing!' The word bit the air, eating up the soft sounds from the girl's throat. The woman stood against the light, a short and heavy shape casting a pall of shadow. McKenna tried to imagine her dressed in the pretty suit exhumed from Gallows Cottage and, unlike Dewi, failed.

'If you need support or assistance,' he said, 'we can contact the Social Services Department. Or anyone else you care to suggest.'

'I can manage perfectly well.'

'Your daughter?' McKenna asked, looking at the child whose face was ugly and old with misery.

'What about her?'

'She's rather distressed.'

'She'll get over it, won't she? She's her father's daughter, after all.'

'What's he done?' the girl wailed. 'Why won't anybody tell me?'

'I knew that damned car would cause trouble. I've

said so often enough, but nobody listens to me, do they?'

'How did you know it would cause trouble?'

'Ask him.' She walked to the door and pulled it open. 'I'd like you to leave.'

'Mr Stott will be at the police station until he goes to court,' McKenna said. 'You may visit him if you wish. And your daughter, too, of course. If you need financial help, you must contact the DSS.'

'You don't listen either, do you? I can manage.'

The girl tugged again at her mother's sleeve. 'Can we go and see him? Please!'

'No!' Gwen Stott rounded on her daughter. 'No, no, NO!'

Temper cooled, Jack lounged in McKenna's office.

'I feel sorry for that man,' McKenna observed. 'Whatever he is, he doesn't deserve her. She's a cold woman, Jack. Hard as nails.'

'Maybe living with him made her that way. If he's been courting Trefor Prosser, it can't've done her self-esteem much good.'

'Well, if he has, I can't say I blame him. I'd rather cuddle up to Trefor Prosser than Gwen Stott any day.'

'Are we going to interview her? Sounds like she'd be a mine of information.'

'No she wouldn't. She'd just carp and whine and sneer and bad-mouth her husband and daughter. She showed her true colours where the girl's concerned. That woman has a swinging brick where other folk have a heart, Jack. Just imagine how your girls would feel if we turned up out of the blue and said you were in the nick and likely staying there. I really don't know if we shouldn't tell Social Services to poke their noses in.'

'Why?'

'In case she starts taking it out on the girl now the husband isn't around to be a whipping boy.'

Dewi Prys stood at the door of one of the detention cells in the basement, breathing in the cold metallic scent, like that of blood, of every cell in the world. Stott, the only detainee, resembled every prisoner: shocked and cold and desperate and diminished. Dewi wondered fleetingly if the act of taking another's liberty, however briefly, however much warranted, was not the most diminishing act one human being could perpetrate against another, apart from taking life itself.

'Have you had tea, Mr Stott?'

'I don't want anything.'

'Perhaps you'll have something later, then.'

'Perhaps.' Haunted eyes, red-rimmed in darkly shadowed sockets, stared at him. 'Has –?' Stott caught his breath, as if he would choke. 'Has my wife been told?'

Dewi sat on the one chair, opposite the bunk where Stott hunched. 'The chief inspector went to see her a while back.'

Stott was silent for long moments. 'I don't expect she'll come to see me, will she?' he asked eventually.

'I don't know, sir. You can have visitors any time. Well, any reasonable time. Not midnight, for instance.'

Stott smiled weakly. 'I won't hold my breath, Constable. Could my daughter come?'

'We'd need a policewoman sitting in on account of the girl being so young. How old is she?'

'Nearly fifteen.' The man stared unseeingly. 'Thank God she's not a baby . . . I don't know how she'll cope as it is . . . And I don't expect her mother will be any help.' Bitterness twisted at his mouth, sparkled in his eyes. He focused his gaze on Dewi, and said, 'What am I to be charged with?'

'I don't really know, sir. You see, not saying anything at the interview screwed things up a bit in that direction.'

'The solicitor told me not to.'

'I'm not criticizing, sir. It just makes things more difficult. I mean, we know some things about that car, but as you won't tell us the rest, we have to find out what we need to know from other places.'

'I see.'

Dewi waited, but nothing was volunteered. 'I'd better be off. Is there anything you want to be going on with?'

Stott looked down at his hands. 'Can I have a wash? I've no soap or towel or anything. Or pyjamas.' He looked up, eyes wet with unshed tears. 'Shall I have to sleep in my clothes?'

'No.' Dewi suddenly loathed himself and the job he did. 'I'll sort things out now. Would you like something to read?'

'Thank you, yes.' The words were almost whispered. 'Constable? Could you do something else for me, if you're allowed? I've got a sister in Rhyl. Could you see if Jenny – my daughter – can go and stay with her?'

'What are you doing, Prys?' Jack accosted Dewi, temper heating beyond his control, fuelled simply by the sight of this *bête noire* of a youth, reading numbers off the back of his hand as he punched them on to the telephone.

'Making a telephone call. Sir.'

'I can see that! Stop being clever, Prys. Who're you calling?'

'Stott's sister.'

'Why?'

'Because he asked me to.'

'Because he asked you to? What are you, a bloody nursemaid?'

'He's worried about his daughter.'

'Worried about his little girl, is he? He should've thought of that before he got himself mixed up with killing and blackmail and thieving.'

Dewi put the receiver in its cradle. 'We don't actually know he's mixed up with anything. People are supposed to be innocent until proved otherwise.'

'Jesus! Not you as well!'

'Not me as well as who else, then?'

'Don't you dare speak to me like that or I'll have you on a disciplinary charge! Whether or not you're McKenna's blue-eyed boy.'

Smiling to himself, Dewi picked up the telephone again. 'I don't think I'm anybody's blue-eyed boy, sir. Maybe it's just on account Mr McKenna and me see eye to eye on a lot of things.'

'You're an arrogant little sod!'

'Yes, sir,' Dewi agreed. 'If you say so, sir,' he added, then turned away, to speak to the woman who answered his summons.

Christopher Stott dozed fitfully in his cell, strange

noises intruding upon him, the smell about the bedding, the floor, the walls and himself noxious in his throat and nostrils. Occasional sounds came from the building: the slam of a door, a voice raised in anger or mirth, quenched by distance and thickness of wall and the door behind which he lay. A truck or late bus roaring down the main road rumbled through these subterranean corridors and cubicles like earth tremors, shaking the very air, leaving acrid diesel fumes to eddy with the other smells. He stared up at the ceiling, the light dim in its wire cage, the sweating walls scarred with names and dates and words and wounds of abuse, his body cramped and chilled in its little cot. He thought of his wife and his daughter and Trefor Prosser, thoughts surveyed so often their landscape and its limits held no novelty, no promise but perpetual imprisonment, then saw the strangers who had found their way in, through a gate he had never noticed, and wondered if they might have the strength and power he so dreadfully lacked to rid the landscape of its monsters.

McKenna went downstairs as the town clock struck two, and as the bell of the cathedral clock added its more sonorous tone. He sat in the kitchen, a mug of tea on the table, a cigarette in his hand, surveying his own repetitive thoughts, so trapped within their little cage they brought nothing but a leaden tedium, creeping into his bones like a fatal disease. Denise, calling upon him earlier, bubbled with a brew of tales: of the holiday she would take the following week, of her plans to move, to sell at a garage sale what neither she nor he wished to keep, and of Jack Tuttle, jumping hither and thither as his wife, poised on the edge of a small liberation, tweaked at the strong ropes binding her marriage together.

He lit a new cigarette from the stub of the old, wondering if he would be engaged in similar activity, disengaged still from all but futility, in twenty years time, or thirty, or forty. He returned to bed well after dawn reddened the eastern sky, falling asleep to the screech of gulls, the clacking of the duo of nesting jays in the trees below his window. He dreamed he was become an old man, crabbed and skinny and wrapped in papery flesh, as rickety as the chair in which he crouched before a mean fire, chewing upon thoughts of Denise, the old flame guttering in the corridors of time whilst he waited for Death, the only visitor likely to call.

Walking back from Safeways late on Sunday morning, a plastic carrier bag of groceries and cat food in each hand, McKenna saw storm clouds advancing from the east, moved sluggishly along by a chill little wind to build castles in the sky behind Bangor Mountain. Yellow gorse on its crest glowed livid, newly blossomed trees began to bend and thresh as the wind poked at their limbs with mean thin fingers. Large raindrops splashed on the pavement before his feet, turning to a downpour, to sheets of water billowing down the valley, long before he toiled up the hill to his house. As thunder growled and rumbled behind the mountain, McKenna thought of God, irreverently; of God and Mrs God in the throes of marital disharmony, tearing apart their mansion in the skies, dividing up the loot of vanquished love. Lightning flashed and crackled over the rooftops as he hurried homewards panting for breath, sensing electricity in the air enter his body and pull its balance awry.

Dewi telephoned late in the afternoon, when the day had fallen to twilight, the power lines to Nature, leaving McKenna and those areas of the city visible from his windows drowned in sombre purple-grey, drenched with rain, and lit by dancing forks and shards of brilliance as the storm surged back and forth from land to sea like a tide.

'You got a power cut as well, sir?' Dewi asked.

'I do hope you didn't call simply to ask me that.'

'No, sir. I just wondered, that's all. Somebody wants to see you.'

'Who?'

'Mrs Kimberley. She's Mrs Stott's sister-in-law.'

'What's her involvement?'

'She's Mr Stott's sister, sir. I just said.'

'You said she was Mrs Stott's sister-in-law.'

'Same difference, sir. Are you coming?'

'Can't it wait?' McKenna looked out at the storm, gathering itself behind the easterly tip of Anglesey for another onslaught, Puffin Island almost obliterated in an eerie darkness where sea and sky and land merged. 'Can't you deal with her?'

'I could, I suppose. She's been to see her brother. She brought the girl with her. Poor little thing looks like she's not stopped crying since we arrested Stott. Mrs Kimberley actually asked for the most senior officer available.'

'Isn't Superintendent Griffiths there?'

'Yes, but he doesn't know the ins and outs of things like you, does he, sir?'

'I don't seem to have much choice, do I?' The power returned as he went upstairs to look for the cat, who had hidden from the storm beneath his bed, from where she refused to be coaxed.

'The worst thing about my brother is that he can be weak. He's easily influenced, easily intimidated, and God knows that wife of his could scare the Devil!' Serena Kimberley, except in height, resembled her brother only remotely, her build strong and muscular, the oak to his sapling whippiness, her personality more defined, her attitude infinitely more assertive. 'You've no idea what that woman has made him suffer, and now she's doing the same with Jenny.'

Jenny was out of sight and earshot, in the canteen with a policewoman and Dewi Prys.

'My brother hasn't done anything, you know,' Serena added, and McKenna thought Christopher Stott might have spent his whole life both protected and ruled by women; by his mother, his sister, his wife, and possibly by Romy Cheney: willingly ruled, the price of protection from the world. And now the Devil had sent in the bailiffs.

'Mrs Kimberley, I appreciate your position,' he said. 'But Mr Stott has doubtless said why he was arrested.'

'You haven't charged him with anything yet.'

'Not yet, but we shall.'

'The car?'

'Probably. And other things.'

'The other things being to do with that woman's death.'

'Mr Stott was in possession of her car for some

considerable time after she died. Possibly before she died. He's not telling us.'

'D'you mind if I smoke?' Serena pulled cigarettes and lighter from the pocket of her jacket. 'Look, Chief Inspector, I'd be lying if I said I knew what's been going on. I don't see much of Chris, because I will not visit the house, and he doesn't get much chance to visit me. Gwen objects. She objects to Jenny staying with me, but it's the only time the girl gets a holiday. Gwen objects to most things that give people a bit of pleasure because she's a miserable bitch. She's like Death, the great leveller, cutting everything and everybody down to the meanest size.'

'What's she done to you?'

'To me? Nothing. I wouldn't give her the chance. Or the satisfaction.' She smoked, enjoying the tobacco in her lungs. 'I've seen her do enough harm to Chris, and now Jenny . . . Gwen has no joy in her heart, you know. If she ever had a soul to start with, it withered long ago, and she drags other people into her misery.'

'Did you know anything about Mrs Cheney?'

'Not until this weekend.' She stubbed out her cigarette, and immediately lit another. 'That nice young man with Jenny now called me on Friday, and I came over right away, and had one almighty row with Gwen. She said the most horrible things you could imagine, and Jenny was near frantic, so I bundled the child's things into a bag and took her home with me.'

'Didn't her mother mind?'

'Yes.' Serena looked McKenna squarely in the eye. 'She minded very much indeed. She threatened to report me to the police for kidnapping her child, so I told her she should be arrested for cruelty. She'd been slapping Jenny around, because Jenny wouldn't stop asking about Chris.'

Self-disgust overwhelmed McKenna, because he had left the child alone with the mother when all the signs were there for any fool to read. Trefor Prosser was acquiring companions on his conscience, whilst he learned nothing.

'Jenny's a little more settled,' Serena continued. 'Our doctor gave her a sedative on Friday night. She insisted on visiting Chris, even though I don't think it's a good idea for a girl to see her father in a police cell.'

'It's better than not seeing him at all.'

'How long are you planning to keep him locked up?' Serena tapped ash from her cigarette into an over-full ashtray on the desk. 'He's terribly worried about Jenny, you know. She's the only reason he's stayed in that ghastly mockery of a marriage.'

'I know you said Mrs Stott slapped her daughter on Friday, but I would imagine they were both under considerable stress at the time.'

'Who are you making excuses for, Chief Inspector? I think Gwen is so deranged, in the true sense of the word, that she comes over as boringly and utterly sane, as if madness is sort of circular. I think she's bloody dangerous, and I think her husband and child are terrified of her.'

'But you don't know why?'

'I was hoping you might be able to find out.' She lit another cigarette, looked at its glowing tip, then stubbed it out. 'I smoke too much most of the time, let alone when I'm under stress. Chris and Jenny had a long talk, and Chris said Jenny wanted to talk to you because you'd understand. Don't fail her, Mr McKenna. Both her parents have, in their own way, and that's what's eating into Chris like acid. I can't pat myself on the back either. You're the only hope left to the child.'

Chapter 28

Jennifer Stott perched tensely on the edge of a chair in McKenna's office, anticipating one final ordeal before relief from whatever torment she had endured. McKenna saw his office become a confessional, and prayed he might offer the girl more of use than the platitudes of vicarious absolution. She wore jeans and a white sweatshirt, her hair hanging loose and pretty around a face where youth might still expunge sadness.

'My mother knew Mrs Cheney,' Jenny said. 'She used to visit Gallows Cottage. I went with her once, because Mrs Cheney invited me, and Mummy said I had to go even though I didn't want to.' She paused, rubbing a smut from the toe of her white boots. 'I didn't like the cottage. It's a shivery sort of place.'

Serena prompted her. 'Don't leave it there, Jenny. Tell Mr McKenna everything you can remember.'

'Mummy and Daddy used to have terrible rows about Mrs Cheney.'

'Yes?' McKenna coaxed. 'Why?'

'Daddy didn't like her. He said she was a bad influence, making Mummy dissatisfied with everything.'

'Where did your mother meet Mrs Cheney?'

'At the castle. She went to a party with Daddy, and Mrs Cheney was there. And afterwards, Mrs Cheney kept telephoning Mummy and inviting her out and things like that . . . She said I should call her Romy, but I wouldn't because she was grown up and nearly as old as Mummy. Mummy said it was wrong to call her Auntie Romy, because she wasn't my aunt.'

'You must remember, Chief Inspector,' Serena said, 'Jenny was only ten or eleven at the time.'

'Yes,' McKenna said. His hands fidgeted with the papers on the desk.

'I don't mind if you smoke,' Jenny told him. McKenna looked at the eyes gazing gravely into his, eyes which, unlike those of her mother, held the light of life and the darkness of pain.

'Tell me, Jenny,' he said, 'do you remember anything about the car? The grey Scorpio car?'

'It's Mrs Cheney's. She used to drive it very fast.'

'Did your mother ever drive it?'

'She can't drive.'

'Your father?'

'He wouldn't go near it. They had awful rows about that, as well.'

'Do you remember anything in particular about the inside of the car?'

She looked towards the window, at the rain-stained wall of the telephone exchange. McKenna had pulled up the venetian blind to let in as much natural light as possible. 'It smelt a bit. Cigarettes and garlic. Mrs Cheney was always eating things with garlic in them.'

'Didn't keep Gwen away, did it?' Serena muttered.

Jenny's voice droned on, as if her aunt had not spoken. 'It was very untidy inside. Mummy was always saying Mrs Cheney was a sloven. I had to look it up in my dictionary. There were a lot of mucky fingermarks, and Mummy said it was because Mrs Cheney was always reading those big newspapers that the print comes off, and never washed her hands afterwards . . . Mrs Cheney put my present in the car. Mummy said I ought to give her something for inviting me to the cottage, so I bought her a furry toy, and she hung it up in the back window. Mummy was very rude and said it looked bloody silly.'

'What did the toy look like?'

'Red and green and round and not really like anything real. I could do a drawing if you want.'

'Jenny's very good at drawing,' Serena said. 'Aren't you, dear?'

A fleeting smile crossed the girl's face. She stared at McKenna, her eyes dark.

'Do you know Mr Prosser?' he asked.

'Uncle Trefor from the estate office?' She nodded. 'Yes.'

'Does he ever come to your house?'

Her face creased with distress. 'Mummy and Daddy have worse rows about him than they ever did about Mrs Cheney, and I don't know why. He's sweet.'

McKenna fidgeted with his lighter and an unlit cigarette.

'You were talking about the car,' Jenny reminded him.

'Do you remember anything else about it?'

'I think Mummy stole it from Mrs Cheney.'

'Do you?' McKenna was nonplussed. 'Why should she do that? Your mother can't drive.'

'Well, she stole everything else, didn't she?' The girl looked at him as if he were a fool. 'Most of the furniture and stuff in our house belonged to Mrs Cheney.' She paused. 'There was another row about that as well. Oh, there's been such horrible rows!' She covered her face with her hands, and her shoulders shook. 'It's all that Mrs Cheney's fault.' Her voice, muffled by the hands, was broken and childish and wailing. 'I wish Mummy'd never met her.'

Serena hugged her niece, rocking her gently back and forth. Watching the woman and the girl, McKenna felt outside his body, outside this room, watching the drama as might a minor god presiding over the destruction of a family and a childhood.

Jenny rubbed at her face with a fist, and clutched her aunt's hand. 'I'm all right.' Her voice was weary. 'What else do you want to know?'

'About your mother stealing Mrs Cheney's things?'

'She told me Mrs Cheney'd gone away. She was always going away, anyway. She only stayed at the cottage for a few weekends, and Mummy said it was criminal to leave all that expensive furniture and carpets and books and ornaments to get stolen or ruined with damp.' Jenny raised her eyes to McKenna. 'I didn't know she was dead, Mr McKenna. Honestly I didn't! I didn't know 'til I saw the newspaper the other week.'

Serena stroked her hair. 'Of course you didn't know. Mr McKenna knows that.'

'But I knew Mummy must've stolen Mrs Cheney's things. What will you do to me?' she whispered.

McKenna wondered if this child would live the rest of her days beset with fears and dread triggered by the smallest word or incident, the most innocent memory. 'No one will do anything to you. You've done nothing wrong. Do you understand that, Jenny?'

'I've kept Mummy's secret,' she told him, and there

was no answer to be made. 'Mrs Cheney's car was outside the house one day when I came back from school, and it was odd because she only ever came at weekends, and never before a Friday evening. Only it wasn't her, it was that horrible Jamie Thief from the council estate, and Mummy went off with him in the car and I had to get my own tea. And the next day, when I got back from school, there was all this furniture in the house, and Mummy'd put the things Daddy'd bought out in the back yard for rubbish. There were carpets as well, and Mummy cut them up to fit. She went on and on about a carpet she said would've fitted in the sitting-room if Mrs Cheney hadn't been her usual slovenly self and spilt a lot of wine and even ground out cigarettes on it and it was brand new. Daddy was so upset he cried, and it was horrible, and Mummy laughed in his face, and sat on the sofas, bouncing up and down shrieking about how they made such a change from the broken springs of a future which was all he could give her . . . I didn't understand what she was talking about, but I knew it was awful. Mummy made me have things from Gallows Cottage in my bedroom. I don't like them, even though they're very pretty, because they don't belong to me.'

McKenna sat in his office, lights switched off, thunder still growling intermittently in the distance, battle-weary and heartsick. He waited until twilight deepened almost to night before asking for Christopher Stott to be brought from the cells.

'Tell me the rest of it,' he said to the man who sat where the girl had poured out her tale of secrets and greed and spite and human frailty. 'There's no point keeping quiet any longer.'

'What did Jenny say?' Stott asked. After two days, the beard was growing straggly about a face become almost cadaverous.

'Enough.'

'Where is she?' Fear sharpened Stott's tone.

'Dewi Prys is taking her back to Rhyl with your sister,' McKenna said, watching the man slump in relief. 'I want to know about the car. I want to know about Mrs Cheney and your wife. And most of all, I want to know about Jamie.'

Stott spread his hands, palm upwards. 'Where shall I begin?'

'Try the beginning.' Tired, McKenna was becoming irritable. 'When did your wife meet Mrs Cheney?'

'Not long after Mrs Cheney rented that dump of a cottage and started spending money like it grew on trees. She latched on to Gwen, and to this day, I don't know why.' He stared at nothing. 'I was pleased Gwen had a friend, because she'd never had a proper woman friend before, but I couldn't take to Romy Cheney. I thought she was a fake, with a fake name pinched from that book by Vita Sackville-West . . . She drank too much as well. I often wondered if she was trying to drink herself into an early grave.'

'She found an early grave one way or another, didn't she? Maybe she was just looking for oblivion.'

'I don't know what she was looking for.' Lost in thought, Stott's features relaxed. 'Whatever it was, I doubt she found it with my wife.' He laughed, a bitter harsh sound. 'Romy Cheney fared no better than the rest of us where Gwen's concerned. I used to hear her weeping on the phone, begging Gwen to visit, and Gwen would look at me and smirk, and tell Romy she didn't know if I'd let her go, which wasn't true because I was glad to see the back of her.' Stott paused. 'And, of course, she couldn't go because it wasn't safe to leave Jenny alone with me.'

'Why not?'

Like his daughter, Christopher Stott rubbed his eyes with his fist. 'I was supposed to be abusing the child, Mr McKenna. Sexually abusing her. And letting Trefor Prosser do the same. Gwen used to bring Romy to the house, you know, and they'd sit on the sofa, the pair of them, and Gwen would bounce up and down, and say "Oops!", and Romy would laugh and say "Broken springs!", then they'd both start screeching and tittering. Gwen told me Romy spent more on one of her sofas than I earned in a month.' He laughed himself. 'Well, she's got both of Romy's posh sofas now, hasn't she? You might have noticed.'

'What did they say about your daughter?'

'They used to quiz Jenny about Trefor Prosser and how often he visited, and what he did, and what I did . . . then they'd have a bit more sport with me. They were a very strange pair together,' Stott added. 'I could never work out who was leading who. There was something unhealthy about it all, though I don't know why or what . . . Why aren't you taking notes?'

'We have to record statements, and I'm not sure what I want to record yet. I must ask,' McKenna said, 'about your relationship with Trefor Prosser, and the accusations made by your wife.'

'You must ask Jenny yourself, Mr McKenna.'

'And Trefor Prosser?'

'He's a friend. A close friend. He got me the job at the castle, and I'll forever be grateful to him for that. I'm not qualified for anything.'

'There have been suggestions that your relationship with him is sexual.'

'I'm sure there have, but it isn't. I doubt either of us would have the guts, even if we wanted to.'

'Then why did Prosser keep the mail for Gallows Cottage? What did he do with it? And why did he run away and crash his car when we asked him?'

'Keeping the post was Trefor's side of the bargain. Keeping quiet about Jenny was Gwen's.' Stott smiled gently. 'D'you know, I'm telling you things I thought I'd have to keep to myself 'til the day I die.'

'It makes you feel better, does it?'

'Better? No, not really. Even if you know you're weak and stupid, it's not very pleasant when your sins of omission find you out, is it? I've done nothing and said nothing and thought I could make things go away by pretending they weren't there. It doesn't work, does it? Once Gwen acquired the taste for power, she had to have more and more.'

'Why did you marry her?'

Stott laughed then, a bellow of genuine amusement. 'Why d'you think? She was pregnant, and I've often wondered how much that moment of wayward passion actually cost me. Being married to Gwen is rather like catching an incurable disease, an AIDS of the spirit . . . but then, I suppose you might say we deserve each other.'

'Tell me about Mrs Cheney.'

'I've told you. I thought she was a fake, so I never took much notice of her.' He fell silent, trawling again those dark alleyways of his past. 'She was unstable and neurotic. Maybe impulsive . . . what the psychologists call prone to inconsequential behaviour. Women like her are silly, selfish creatures. She and Gwen fed off each other in a way, like parasites, copying each other so you could never tell where one ended and the other began . . . bringing out the worst in each other. She copied Gwen's thinking and behaving; Gwen copied her clothes and drinking and smoking. Romy even bought clothes for her.'

'What sort of clothes?'

'Fancy silk scarves, underwear. She bought her a suit, as well, a grey one with a patterned jacket. It was too tight, but Gwen always has her clothes tight because she thinks she looks thinner that way.'

'Has she still got the suit?'

'Probably.'

'What happened to the money from the sale of the Scorpio?'

'Gwen had it. She has all the money. I keep about twenty pounds a week for fares and odds and ends.'

'What did she do with it?'

'She said she was putting it by for a rainy day, as there were sure to be plenty as long as she was married to me.'

'You astound me, Mr Stott. Why on earth have you stayed married to each other?'

'Now there's a question.' Stott smiled a little. 'I suppose we stay together because we know no one else would want us, and anything's better than being alone. Perhaps we simply became a habit for each other, a very bad habit like smoking or heroin addiction.'

'Let's talk about when Mrs Cheney died, shall we?'

'I don't know when she died. I didn't know she was dead until you found her body.'

'You expect me to believe that?'

Stott shrugged. 'Gwen said Romy had gone back to England when the lease on the cottage ran out. She couldn't be bothered moving out the furniture, and gave it to Gwen.'

'And the car?'

'Gwen said it was a present.'

'Why should she give your wife a car when your wife can't drive? And a very expensive car into the bargain. Are you really so naive? Do you really think I am?'

'Mr McKenna, I'm telling you what my wife said, and it doesn't in the least matter whether you or I believe her. If Gwen says a thing is so, then it is so, as far as she or anyone else is concerned. And you must bear in mind there was nothing unusual about Romy Cheney disappearing for weeks on end. I doubt if she spent more than a month in that cottage all told.' Stott paused. 'What would you have done in my position, Mr McKenna? How would you have set about proving Gwen a liar and a thief? And why? What purpose would it serve?'

'What did she do with the mail?'

'I don't know. Why don't you ask her?'

'Did you really not know Mrs Cheney was dead?'

'No, I didn't, and Gwen still talks as if she expects her to turn up sooner or later. Says she misses her, says Romy wanted her to leave me and shack up with her . . .'

'And Jamie?'

'Jamie knew Romy. He used to borrow the car, and

Gwen said Romy wanted him to go on using it. It wouldn't surprise me if Jamie was having an affair with her.'

Chapter 29

'I've never heard such a brew of a tale. He's trying to pull the wool over your eyes.' Jack lounged on McKenna's own ancient sofa, a glass of whisky in his hand. 'I'm surprised you sat listening to him for so long. And you've only heard his side of the story. Wait 'til his missis gets her oar in.'

McKenna ignored the jibe. 'What about the tale the girl told?'

'Something and nothing, isn't it?'

'She knew about the furniture.'

'So?'

'And she knew about Jamie.'

'Yes, but she doesn't know anything worth knowing, does she?' Jack pointed out. 'Nothing that's any use to us.'

McKenna downed his own whisky. 'It will be when we get our hands on Jamie.'

'Did you get a warrant for him?'

'Yes, and a search warrant for Stott's house.'

'Are you going to impound the car?'

'Yes.'

'We'll have a busy day tomorrow then, won't we?'

'Stop sniping,' McKenna snapped. 'I'm tired.'

'What are we doing with Stott?'

'Holding him without charge for a further forty-eight hours.'

'That should please him and his brief.' Jack finished his drink and made ready to leave. 'I'll be off. I'm trying to relax as much as possible before Emma goes off jaunting with your Denise.' He lingered at the foot of the staircase. 'I'm not very struck with the idea, you know.'

'Why not?'

'I don't think it's a good idea for them to go off alone like that. Why couldn't they have few days in London, or at least somewhere nearer than Rhodes?'

'Because London isn't warm and sunny with blue sea and golden beaches.'

'Well I won't rest 'til they're back safe and sound.'

'Why? Are you afraid Emma might run off with a handsome young Greek?'

Returning from Rhyl, Dewi turned into Salem village and parked in the lane by Mary Ann's house. Dim light glowed behind the closed curtains of her parlour window, its reflection dull on wet tarmac. Raindrops dripped on to his head as he waited at the front door.

'Who is it?' Her voice was muffled.

'Dewi Police, Mary Ann.'

In the musty, overheated little parlour, Beti Gloff perched on the edge of the sofa, her stiff leg poking out on to the hearthrug.

'How's it going with you?' Mary Ann asked.

'So-so,' Dewi said. 'And you?'

'The weather's making my leg play up something chronic. I could hardly get out of bed this morning.'

'It'll perk up soon. We'll be in May before long.'

'I've seen snow on the mountains above Bethesda in

July before now,' Mary Ann said. 'You don't expect any miracles from the weather when you're as old as me.'

'How's John Jones, Beti? Giving you any more grief?'

'He's minding his p's and q's for the present.' Mary Ann spoke for her. 'We'll tell you when he stops. And what brings you calling at this hour, Dewi Prys?'

'Keeping an eye on you two. And looking for Jamie.'

'Jamie Thief?' Beti gobbled. 'He's at home.'

'No, he's not,' Dewi said. 'He did a flit a few days ago, and he's not been seen since.'

'He'll be in the caravan, then,' Beti offered.

'What caravan?'

'The caravan in the woods behind the old railway houses near the quarry,' Mary Ann said. 'Am't I right, Beti?'

'How d'you know?'

'He always goes there when you coppers're after him, doesn't he?'

The last vestiges of day lit the sky in the far west, full night already folded into the crevices and over the steep cliffs of the Black Ladders, as Dewi turned the car towards Bangor and McKenna's house.

'D'you know what time is?' McKenna asked. 'Can't whatever it is wait?'

'Don't know, sir. I thought I'd better ask you that.'

'D'you want a drink?'

'A brew wouldn't go amiss.' He trailed into the kitchen, sat biting his thumbnail while McKenna made tea and put it to stew on the cooker.

'Any problems with Jenny and her aunt?'

'No, sir. Jenny was asleep most of the time.'

'I'm not surprised. The aunt didn't say anything?'

'This and that about the family. Her son's at university in Liverpool. I got the impression she's had a bellyful of her brother and his wife. Weird pair, by the sounds of it.' Dewi poured milk into two mugs, took the teapot off the cooker, swirled its contents and poured.

'Gwen Stott's been keeping Prosser in line by threatening to grass him up for allegedly molesting her daughter. She also allegedly told Romy Cheney that Stott was doing the same.' McKenna picked up his tea.

'Stott told you that, did he?' Dewi sipped his tea, blowing across its surface to cool the boiling liquid. 'Assuming he's telling the truth, it doesn't say much for her, does it? Letting it go on and doing nothing to stop them. She'd have to be pretty stupid not to realize she was dropping herself in it along with them, and I don't think she is – stupid, I mean. Mind you, Stott and Prosser must be really thick to let her get away with it.'

'Perhaps they were simply scared. Once mud like that's been thrown at you, it sticks. Better to dodge it.'

'Will you tell Social Services?' Dewi asked.

'Only if I must. Jenny would be taken into care, and I don't think being in a children's home would do her much good.'

Dewi drained his tea. 'She's safe for the time being, anyway. I came to see you about Jamie, sir, because I might know where he is.'

'And how might you know?'

'I went to Mary Ann's on the way back. She and Beti reckon he's in a caravan near Dorabella Quarry. They say he's been using it as a bolt hole for ages.'

'Why don't they tell us these things? They could've saved us no end of trouble.'

'Same reason most folk keep quiet.' Dewi grinned. 'Shall we go and get him?'

'It's late, Dewi. And I'm tired.'

'Yes, but he might not be there in the morning.'

Dewi drove, McKenna beside him in the front seat fighting the desire to fall asleep.

'Not much traffic around, sir,' Dewi observed.

'Probably because most people have the sense to be indoors on a wet Sunday night, if not tucked up in bed fast asleep.'

The car swished along the wet road, engine running smoothly. 'I'll bet you,' Dewi said, 'a good few folk'd change places with us right now.'

'And why should they want to?'

'For the excitement.'

'You reckon this is exciting, do you?'

Dewi laughed. 'It will be when we land on Jamie! It'll be the biggest excitement he's had in a long while.'

Once a viaduct carrying the railway line from Dorabella Quarry to the port, the bridge fell to industrial decay, leaving only a few feet of its span balanced on either end of slate-faced ramparts. Ugly and ill-proportioned, the red-brick cottages fronted the road beneath the old bridge, windows dark and shrouded. Dewi drew the car on to the verge. 'I'm not sure where the caravan is, and I don't know how we get to it, but we shouldn't need to wake people.'

'We might not,' McKenna said. 'There's no telling what Jamie might do. If he's there, that is.'

Dewi shut the car door with a quiet click. 'Soon find out, won't we?' He swung the torch beam on the ground, on beads of rain clinging to grass stems, a huge black slug glistening by his foot. 'Ugh! I hate slugs. Never get that slime off your shoe when you tread on them.'

'Got your handcuffs, Dewi?' McKenna asked, watching a snail with its house on its back trailing in the wake of the slug.

'Yes, sir.'

McKenna leaned against the car, pulling up his coat collar against chilly tendrils of mist and damp. 'I'll tell you what we haven't got, and that's the warrant.'

'So? That's for us to know and him to find out, isn't it? I shan't tell him.'

Walking fast and quiet along the grass verge, Dewi searched for a gate or gap in the thorny hedge. 'The caravan must be in those trees.' He pointed to a darker mass against the night black sky.

'Into the field, then,' McKenna said. 'You can go first. I'm not dressed for adventuring.'

Dewi pushed into the hedge, parting branches to make way for McKenna, who stopped to disentangle his coat from a thorn, and heard a whistling and rustling surging towards him. 'There're rats on the move, Dewi,' he warned. 'Keep still.'

The tide of rats washed down the road, coats gleaming dully like oily water, then flooded into the blackness on the opposite side. 'The council must be dumping rubbish tomorrow,' McKenna said, watching the last of the tide ripple out of sight.

Climbing the steepening rise of the field towards the copse, Dewi said, slightly out of breath, 'How do they know? The rats, I mean. How do they know where to scavenge?'

'Same way the rat we're after knows where to look,' McKenna observed. 'Jamie always knows where to scavenge profitably, where there's a bit of human misery to benefit him. It wouldn't surprise me,' he added, stumbling on a tussock of grass, 'if he killed Romy.'

'Why would he?'

'For profit. The car, money, whatever she had he wanted.'

'But he didn't get the car. There's no sign of Jamie getting anything, and I've never known him be satisfied with nothing.'

McKenna was tetchy. 'We don't know what he got. Maybe he'll tell us when we find him.'

'He's never told us before. He's not likely to change the habits of a lifetime now, is he?'

The copse came upon them unexpectedly, its shadows overwhelming the two men. They stood by an oak tree, its knobbled trunk slimy with moss, rain dripping cold down McKenna's collar. Whispering night sounds and the pitter patter of droplets falling from trees to earth punctured the silence, the air in the copse heavy and still, almost viscous. The torch beam fanned tree shadows over the ground, catching a glint of metal beyond. The caravan, once painted white and blue, now scabrous and rusting, listed on small pillars of bricks. In total darkness, one uncurtained window grimy and smeared, McKenna thought it bore the look of abandonment, of being vacant of life. He tried the door, and almost fell as it swung outwards, askew on its hinges. A stale odour wafted out, shot through and rippling with other scents.

'Sir?' Dewi's voice, a harsh whisper, cut across the stillness.

'Don't touch anything.' McKenna stepped into the body of the caravan, rocking as it teetered slightly with his weight. He took the torch from Dewi and lit the narrow space with powerful light. Dewi came up close behind, his rapid heavy breathing booming in McKenna's ear.

McKenna saw nothing save the pictures in his head, the models in an exhibition of human tragedy. Romy Cheney, swung from a branch, long and thin and sinuous in the wind, black clothes draped around the Modigliani figure. Lame Beti, brutally ugly, escaped from a Breughel canvas and alive through the centuries. Jamie elegant and silent, marbled flesh and eyes milky in the torchlight, one long-fingered hand resting on a dirty mat at the side of the bunk, the other splayed over his chest, like the poet Chatterton, but dead in a filthy caravan in North Wales instead of a dirty garret in Gray's Inn; captured at the moment of death, bodily degradation still invisible, only the squalor of his circumstances pointing the way forward.

Eifion Roberts, subdued by night and weariness, sat beside McKenna in the car. Arc lights glared blue-white inside the copse, lantern lights flickering in and out of the trees, shadows flitting behind them and through them. Rain came down hard, drumming on the roof of the car, washed in rivulets down the windscreen.

'He's not been dead long, Michael,' the pathologist said. 'Not more than twelve hours or so. He's not even cold.' He smiled slightly. 'The first half-decent corpse I've had off you for some time.'

'What was it? Suicide?'

'Doubt it. Carelessness, perhaps . . . won't know 'til I cut him up, but there's all the signs of a drug overdose.' The pathologist rubbed his hands together. 'Bloody miserable night, isn't it? There might be some bruising round the face and neck, but it's hard to tell with those lights. They make too many shadows. If there is bruising, it wouldn't be all that unusual in an OD.'

'He's been on drugs for years.' McKenna lit a cigarette. The pathologist coughed. 'Odd, though. As far as we know, he only peddled the hard stuff. Preferred to take something safer.'

'You amaze me,' Dr Roberts said, with a touch of his usual asperity. 'For someone in your position, you talk a load of crap at times. There aren't any *safe* drugs! Not marijuana, not speed, not ecstasy, not alcohol, and certainly not that muck you fill your own lungs with. You're a fool to yourself, McKenna. You'll go to an early grave.' He climbed out of the car, easing his bulk upright. 'I'm going to my bed. I'll see to young Jamie in the morning.'

'He'll never be anything but now, will he?' McKenna said.

'Anything but what?'

'Young . . . He won't grow old.'

'You're very maudlin. I daresay the world might be

a better place for the likes of Jamie not growing old in it. It's not true what they say about the good dying young, because he certainly wasn't. Born bad, that one, corrupted in the womb . . . I'll call you tomorrow.' He took a few paces towards his own car, then turned back, leaning in to speak to McKenna.

'If you take my advice, as one who knows about these things, you'll go to your bed as well. You look about ready for the knacker's yard. That lad in the caravan's got more colour in his cheeks than you have.'

McKenna shrugged.

'If you hadn't been at such a low ebb with one thing and another, you wouldn't've been ill in the first place.' He slid back into the car. 'You shouldn't be at work. Barely out of hospital, and here you are, out on a night like this.'

'I'm OK.'

'Are you? What was it that psychiatrist said about Prosser? Something about "psychic distress", wasn't it?'

'So?'

'So it's perhaps as well he can't see you now, isn't it? I'll tell you something.' Dr Roberts eased his bulk, shifting to find comfort. 'Folk've been very worried about you in recent weeks.'

'Why? Who?'

'I'm not saying who. Just say people close to you. They've been fretting you might, as the saying goes, do something daft. More than one person's been worried you might end up face down in the shit at the bottom of the Straits.'

'I see.'

'You don't see at all,' Eifion Roberts said. 'You think people should mind their own business, you think they've no right to say anything. But some people actually care about you, even if you don't give a toss for anyone except yourself and that stray cat warming your bed where a real woman should be. And,' he continued relentlessly, 'if you weren't half eaten up with all this maundering and self-centred navel-gazing you love so much, maybe you'd be doing your job properly, and maybe we wouldn't be traipsing round tonight in the pouring bloody rain dragging that lad's body out of the rathole he died in.'

McKenna waited in the car, shivering from damp and cold and sheer fatigue, the heater turned full on, engine humming gently and blowing streams of fumes from the exhaust to spread like a layer of dewy mist over the greasy road. He fell asleep, and woke to see Dewi's face pressed against the window. Opening the door, Dewi brought the scents of rainwashed night with him, and the musky odour of death.

'Look at these, sir.' He pulled a handful of sealed transparent evidence bags from the pockets of his waterproof. 'Four packets of drugs, probably heroin or cocaine, three hundred and seventy quid in tenners, and a cheque book, and Jamie never had a bank account in his life. Only problem is, there aren't any cheques left and the stubs aren't filled in.'

McKenna stifled a yawn. 'You'll have to ask the bank in the morning. What else did you find?'

'Bugger all really. A few clothes that could do with a wash, bits of food, about a ton of empty lager cans, fags . . . Jamie travelled light, you might say.'

'I should imagine his sins weighed more than enough to carry around.'

'I know we all bad mouth him, and he's only had himself to blame, but it's a bit pathetic in there. Dirty and damp, his few bits and pieces . . . a nasty place to die, sort of poverty-stricken and demeaning, if you know what I mean.'

'Some would say it's as much as he deserves.'

'You wouldn't, would you, sir?'

'No, and I hope you never come to feel like that about people.' McKenna took a cigarette from the packet, then pushed it back unlit. 'I think we should leave the others to it and get some sleep. There's a lot to do tomorrow.'

'What about Jamie's mam?'

'We should tell her, shouldn't we?' McKenna said. 'And what good will it do to go upsetting her in the middle of the night, Dewi? Jamie's dead. He'll still be dead in the morning, no less and no more so than he is now . . . Leave her in ignorance a while longer, eh?'

'But what if she hears about us being here in the night? You can't have a crap round here without the whole world knowing how long you sat on the pan.'

'I'll send someone to see her as early as possible. There's nothing to tell her yet, except he's dead.'

'D'you think he killed himself?'

'Dr Roberts thinks he may have overdosed by accident. Jamie's never struck me as suicidal. Murderous, yes, but not suicidal.'

Dewi stared unseeing through the windscreen. 'I've known him all my life,' he said. 'We played together when we were so high. Now he's gone, snuffed out just like that. I've only known old people die before, except little Barry John, and he was a mongol kiddie, so we all knew he'd never make old bones . . . I feel as if part of me's gone with Jamie. His mam won't care, you know, sir. She never did. My nain reckons that's why he turned out bad. She probably won't even bury him properly.'

McKenna put his hand on Dewi's arm. 'She might not be able to afford a decent funeral. You can't blame people for things they can't help. You can only judge people by what they can or can't do, not what they simply do or don't do.'

Dewi turned, and McKenna thought there were tears in his eyes. 'No? Who do you blame, then? Why should some get off taking the rap, and not the others? It's not fair. Where's the justice in that?'

Chapter 30

By 8.30 on Monday morning, McKenna had briefed a team of officers to execute the search warrant on Stott's house in Turf Square. The Scorpio car, removed from an abusive owner shortly after first light, lodged at the garage of divisional headquarters until required as evidence.

'Evidence of what?' Jack grumbled. 'Our incompetence? And why wasn't I called out last night? I get the feeling you don't want me to know what's going on.'

'I've already told you why. You said you wanted to relax as much as you could.' McKenna regarded the surly angry face of his deputy. 'Not much point in both of us being too tired to stand up, is there? I want you to take charge of the search. You know what to look for.'

'Why?'

'Because I say so!'

'I'm surprised you're not sending wonderboy.'

'Dewi Prys has other things to do.'

'Oh, so you know who I mean, do you?'

'Your attitude is bordering on insubordination.'

'So what? You don't give a toss for discipline! You let that little fart get away with murder at my expense.'

'If you have problems in your relationship with colleagues, I suggest you ask yourself why.'

Fury mottled Jack's face. 'Oh, it's my fault, is it? What about you favouring him? How d'you think that looks? Eh? I'll tell you how. It makes me look a bloody fool!'

'Dewi Prys has the makings of a very good detective, but he's young. I can put up with a bit of cheek now and then, while he does his job as well as he does.'

'Oh, I see!' Jack stormed. 'You're saying I don't do mine well, are you?'

McKenna twiddled his pen, staring at the wall behind Jack. 'You're an inspector. Dewi's a constable.' He focused his eyes on Jack. 'You should know better than to behave like this, and you should have learnt not to let yourself be riled by a bit of mouthiness.'

'That's bloody unfair, and you know it!'

'You're not on the receiving end of the damned feuding between you and him, are you? I'm sick to death of it! And I blame you because you overreact most of the time.' McKenna paused, then held up his hand as Jack opened his mouth to speak. 'And don't tell me I have no interest in discipline. I was under the impression you at least were a mature adult, and that discipline as such should not be an issue. And certainly not an issue allowed to interfere with the course of any investigation.'

'Have you finished?' Jack snarled.

'No, I haven't. Not quite.' McKenna lit a cigarette. 'I think your domestic life may be affecting your judgement, and I think you ought to take stock of the situation as a whole. In fact, it might be useful for you to take some leave while Emma is away.'

'Is that an order?'

'Not at this moment. Whether or not it becomes so is entirely up to you.'

'And what's that supposed to mean?'

'Exactly what it appears to mean.'

Jack paled. 'You're trying to get rid of me, aren't you, because I don't fit in with your cosy little clique! Because I'm not pally-pally with the superintendent and I don't suck up to the bloody councillors, and I can't speak your horrible peasant gibberish! Have you any idea how I feel when you talk about things in Welsh and I haven't a sodding clue what's going on? You do it on purpose to make me feel left out, don't you? Well, I'm getting the message! You don't want me here, but you haven't got the guts to tell me to my face!' He wrenched open the door. 'You Welsh are all the bloody same! You smile in someone's face while you're sticking a knife between their shoulder blades.' He drew an angry rasping breath. 'I'm not surprised you never catch the arsonists and bombers! You're a bunch of sodding anarchists, and it wouldn't surprise me if you don't plant the bombs yourselves! Language of the hearth!' he sneered. 'We all know what that means in English, don't we? Terrorism and arson and bombing!'

McKenna heard him blunder off down the corridor, the soft thud as the fire door at the head of the staircase shut itself. He closed his own door, and stood at the window waiting for the search party to drive out of the police station. The ash tree growing outside his window, he noticed, was beginning to cut off rather too much light. Jack's car screeched suddenly from the driveway, narrowly avoiding collision with a Purple Motors bus and its cargo of early shoppers. McKenna stared at the wall of the telephone exchange, the cherry tree on the lawn in front dropping pink blossoms on to grass littered with drink cans and chip paper and crisp packets, and asked himself why he had deliberately set out to wound Jack, wondering what perverseness, what malice, put the words in his mouth. Words, he thought. Only words, without purpose or intent left to themselves, merely a collection of symbols. But once uttered, once given life, such innocent words could leap and fight, crash into each other, trip from innuendo to meaning to becoming powerful and purposeful, overpowering their creators and becoming an end in themselves. Perhaps he was trying to divest himself of all those people who intruded into his consciousness, bore significance in his life, and who, therefore, tethered him, tied him about with bonds of friendship and love and all the pain those bonds might cause if the flesh struggled against them. First Denise, now Jack, because Jack was tied to Emma, and Emma to Denise, and all of them weaving ropes and ties around McKenna's spirit, as if that spirit were a maypole, and he feared strangulation from its pretty dancing ribbons.

'Where's McKenna buggered off to?' Eifion Roberts asked.

'I don't know,' Dewi said. 'He'd left when I got back. D'you want me to call him?'

'It doesn't matter. Just tell him I'm doing the autopsy on Jamie. I'll get back to him.'

'Should somebody come down?'

'What for? Oh, you mean to sit in.' He laughed. 'There's a poor young copper sitting right beside me,

Dewi, getting ready to see his first cadaver sliced open!'

Dewi put down the receiver. The packets of drugs were on the way to the laboratory for analysis, with other trace samples taken from the caravan and its surroundings, and casts of some of the footprints found in the muddy earth under the dripping trees of the copse. Dewi took the cheque book from its plastic envelope, looking at the creased and stained cover. Told the book had not come from a local branch of the bank, Dewi asked the manager of Romy Cheney's bank in Leeds if it originated there, waited while the manager dithered and argued, finally conceded it would be no breach of precious confidentiality to answer the question, and promised to call back.

He was replacing the cheque book in its protective covering when he realized Jamie was probably the last to handle it: Jamie dead and cold and stiffening, supine under the pathologist's scalpel, his lungs and liver and kidneys and heart wrenched from the dark secret place occupied since the moment of conception, and exposed to cruel light and probing eyes, mauled by rough hands, cut into slices and slivers by knives honed to wicked sharpness. Dewi felt a lurch in his belly, a coldness slice through him as of sharp steel. He sat at his desk, oblivious to time, to traffic grinding down the road beyond the window, and wondered what colour his own heart would be, imagined it flopping out before him, pulsing and blue-veined, trailing slimy blood as it danced its death throes, before becoming still, withering before his eyes until it was nothing more than a shrivelled heap. Dead. If his heart was dead, he too would be dead. And how did it feel to die? He thought of Romy Cheney and the dread in her soul when her killer bound her hands and placed the noose around her neck and Romy knew there could be no escape, and he could not comprehend such thoughts, such terror without vestige of hope, no more than he could travel to the furthest star in the heavens. And when Romy's killer looked upon their handiwork, and knew the heart was stopped and the last breath from her lungs, and the last thought dead in her mind, and that person understood, in that instant, there was to be no going back, not then, not ever, from what their wickedness had brought about, had the killer, Dewi asked himself, understood the unimaginable enormity of what had come to pass? Had terror come to the killer then, with the knowledge that nothing could ever again be the same? How could a person go on living, he wondered, with such a burden in their heart and mind and soul, lying ponderous and crushing in every atom of their being? And what might a person do after killing another person, he thought? Go home, make a pot of tea or a cup of coffee, eat a meal, go shopping, go to work, watch television, read a book, go to the pub, make love, sleep, dream, wake up, take an aspirin for a headache, telephone friends, write a letter . . .? A sob caught his breath, and he prayed God had for once been merciful, and taken Jamie in his sleep.

Jack opened the office door to find Dewi slumped over the desk, head cradled on his folded arms.

'Where's McKenna?' he barked.

Dewi raised his head slowly. Under the mass of

curly black hair, his face was gaunt, and Jack thought he saw tears misting the blue eyes.

'What's the matter with you, Prys?'

'Nothing, sir,' Dewi mumbled.

Relieved of a tension he had not known existed by the concentrated effort expended in searching Stott's house, Jack felt calmed, almost light-hearted. 'McKenna been at you as well?' he asked. 'He's not in the best of tempers this morning.'

'I was thinking about Jamie, sir. That's all,' Dewi said. 'We used to be together all the time when we were kids until my nain butted in when he started thieving. We still got together. Used to sneak off to the swings by the river, and go home separately.'

'Why d'you always talk about your nain? Did she bring you up?'

'Mam and Dad brought us up, but Nain sort of decides about things, if you know what I mean. Decides what's right and what isn't. Because she's old.'

'How come your parents don't mind?'

'Mam couldn't say much, could she?' Dewi said. 'Nain's her mam. And Dad knew when to keep his mouth shut, because his mother was Nain's best mate.' He smiled. 'Those old women had terrible fights sometimes, over this and that . . . wouldn't speak to each other for weeks, maybe months, and every Sunday after Chapel they'd come to our house for dinner, still not talking, and we had to relay messages backwards and forwards over the table while they sat looking daggers at each other.' The smile faded. 'Nain cried for weeks after the old lady died. She still takes flowers to the cemetery every Saturday afternoon.'

'Everybody should have somebody to grieve for

them, I suppose. Even the Jamies of this world. Maybe he wouldn't be where he is now if his nain had looked out for him.'

'He never even knew who his real father was,' Dewi said bitterly. 'And nobody would tell him, not even his mam. She reckoned she'd fallen in the family way after a Saturday night out. She told him she'd been with this man up against a wall at the back of the Three Crowns, and he made Jamie on her, and they were drunk, his mam and this man . . . When he was little, he used to cry about not having a dad, went roaming the estate asking kids with fathers if he could go and live with them, so he'd have a dad. And people called him a little bastard and told him to bugger off back to his tart of a mother. And sometimes, the other kids were told to throw stones at him, like he was a mangy dog . . .' Dewi stared at Jack, his eyes glittering. 'And now they all reckon he got what he deserved. I heard an old witch in the shop this morning say whoever got rid of him should have a medal.'

'We don't know anybody got rid of him,' Jack said. 'And we all feel guilty when somebody dies, because we only remember the good things about them, and the bad things we did or said. You'll get over it. I want you to help me make an inventory of the stuff from Stott's place.'

'What did you find?'

'Just about everything, because Mrs Stott was only too happy to show us. Furniture, clothes, underclothes, diary, jewellery – expensive stuff by the looks of it – ornaments – no pictures; I take it Mrs Cheney wasn't overkeen on pictures – books, the books Allsopp told the chief inspector about, with Allsopp's name as bold as brass on the flyleaf, and they would've been returned because our Gwen isn't partial to Dickens, only she didn't know where to send them. You wouldn't credit such bloody cheek, would you? And we found a bottle of that perfume, almost empty. Absolutely reeks of carnations.'

'Were there any letters? Or bank books or credit cards?'

'No. Not in her name and not in Stott's. And no money to speak of, apart from what she said was the housekeeping in her purse.' Jack yawned. 'I don't know about you, but these early starts get to me. You must've been up half the night.'

Dewi shrugged. 'Can't we arrest her and do a body search? Unless she's thrown anything incriminating, like that buckle Allsopp told Mr McKenna about, she must be carrying the credit card at least.'

'What do we arrest her for? We can't do her for stealing by finding because we've no proof all these weren't given to her, just like she said, and the only person who could tell us is long dead.'

'We've arrested her husband. Why not her?'

'He hasn't been charged, and we'll have to let him go before long.' Jack stood up. 'I'm going for coffee. D'you want some?'

The bank manager from Leeds committed himself to the fewest words. 'Stupid bugger!' Jack slammed down the telephone, and gulped coffee. 'He can't tell us this and he can't tell us that. He can't tell us bloody anything because his client's business is confidential, and will we stop harassing him because he's said more than he should've done already, and if it ever gets out he'll be for the sack. Serve him bloody right!'

'It was her cheque book, then?' Dewi said.

'Didn't you hear me? He can't tell us.'

'If he can't say because his client's business is confidential, the cheque book must belong to one of his clients. And the only likely one is Romy Cheney.'

Jack grinned. 'Well, that takes us a mite further forward, doesn't it? Far enough to get an order to view the account. Anything from Dr Roberts yet?'

'He rang earlier. He said – he said he'll let us know.'

'The sooner the better. We need to know what killed Jamie.' Jack picked up the empty coffee mugs. 'If somebody did kill him, we know who didn't: Stott for one and Prosser for another, but knowing Jamie's lifestyle, any number of villains could've taken him out. He had friends in bad places.'

'I wonder where she was yesterday?'

'Who?'

'Mrs Stott.'

'No idea. Probably sitting on one of Romy's overstuffed sofas with her feet up, stuffing chocolates into her gob, watching telly and getting cramp in her fat bum . . . I noticed a satellite dish on the back wall.'

'Did you ask her about the suit Wil found at Gallows Cottage?'

'I wish you'd shut up about that bloody suit! More likely belongs to her husband than her.'

Chapter 31

In a quiet pub near Rhyl station, McKenna picked at a smoked chicken sandwich, then pushed it away half-eaten, lit a cigarette, and asked the waitress for a glass of whisky. Downing the liquid in one swallow, he paid his bill and left. A chill wind swirled in the street, spattering rain on his face and coat as he unlocked his car.

He drove left from the promenade, towards the town's sprawling suburbs: hundreds upon hundreds of red-roofed bungalows on curving streets behind sandy heathland crowning the sea defences. Wind whined and whistled past the open window, filling the car with salty scents and the smells of rain in the air.

Serena Kimberley inhabited a bungalow indistinguishable from all its neighbours: each detached, each set in a little plot of land, each with a patch of front lawn edged with borders, wrought-iron gates giving on to little driveways and a narrow view of back gardens with swings and rotary washing lines and glimpses of the railway line between London and Holyhead. No landmarks caught the eye, no points of orientation, no differences, except the occasional distinction of a red front door, or a blue one, each embellished with a cartwheel of stained and leaded glass, each bay window to the side of each front door dressed with curtain nets, frilled and patterned and looped and swathed, concealing life within from prying eyes without.

'You should've telephoned,' Serena said. A smile took any sting from the words. 'Come in. Jenny's in. Dreadful weather, isn't it?' He saw a pink plastic clothes basket on the kitchen floor. 'The washing hadn't been out ten minutes when it started to rain.' She smiled. 'With my son being away, I'd forgotten how much extra washing one teenager makes.'

'How is Jenny?' McKenna asked.

'All right, considering everything.' She led him into the room with the bay window, and lit the gas fire. 'These rooms get very cold very quickly. Too much window, I suppose, as well as the house being below sea-level. Sit down while I make a drink.'

Returning with a pot of coffee and china mugs on a tray, she pushed an ashtray towards McKenna. 'Jenny's upstairs at the moment. Just say when you're ready to see her. You know, people say,' she went on, 'that children are resilient, but I've never believed that. I think they hide a lot of their feelings, and the bigger the feelings, the more they get hidden. Especially the really painful ones they don't know how to deal with. They do it so their parents and family won't be hurt. I can still remember some of the agonies I went through, and not over anything more important than boys.' She grinned. 'You know, does he love me? Will he marry me? D'you know what girls do? They write names in exercise books instead of doing their homework.'

'What names?'

'Well,' she said, pulling on the cigarette McKenna

had offered, 'if I fancied a boy called Jimmy Martin, for instance, I'd write down "Serena Martin" and say it out loud a few times, to see if it sounds like somebody I'd want to be. And when I got the shivers and wobbly knees over another boy, I'd do the same with his name.'

'And did you ever fancy being Serena Martin?'

She laughed. 'I met my husband in junior school, but it never stopped me looking elsewhere, just in case!'

How could one family, McKenna wondered, produce this bold and rather joyous woman from the same stock as the brother; she full of energy, he bequeathed little or nothing?

'I wonder if Romy Cheney wrote names in books until she found one she was comfortable with,' McKenna said.

'Romy Cheney?' Serena repeated. 'It's a very silly name, don't you think? Quite unreal. As if she couldn't make up her mind what she was and what she wasn't . . . It sounds like an anagram, or even something made up at Scrabble if you had too many Ys and not enough vowels.'

'Your brother said he thought she was a fake.'

'Well, with a name like that, I'm not surprised. He had a fairly normal reaction for once.'

McKenna helped himself to more coffee, his throat still dry from whisky. 'Doesn't he have normal reactions very often?'

Serena sighed. 'He's always unsure about what to do. Always has been. Lack of confidence, I suppose, which is nothing unusual in itself, but if you live with the likes of Gwen for any length of time, and you aren't very sure and confident to start with, any hope you might have of reacting normally, of just seeing things in a straightforward fashion, will go right out of the window.' She took a biscuit, and bit into it. 'I have never in my life come across anybody so twisted, so able to twist anything and everything into something nasty. And for no reason except that she likes to cause trouble.'

'Did your brother or Jenny ever talk to you about Romy Cheney?'

'Not in any detail. She only seemed to matter to Gwen, and it was a long time ago anyway.'

'Why doesn't Mrs Stott have a job? I understand she often complained about being short of money.'

Serena laughed. 'Gwen wouldn't work! She isn't qualified for anything, and she'd never demean herself by doing an unskilled job. Anyway, if she went to work and admitted some responsibility towards family finances, she'd lose the biggest stick she has to bash Chris over the head with.' Serena offered him a cigarette, and asked, 'Didn't you come to see Jenny? Shall I call her down?'

'Not for a moment.' McKenna stood up to look through the window, gathering his thoughts, playing for time, feeling as if enmeshed in a seafog, blundering along a cliff-top path. One more false step and he would be lost. Virtually sure Gwen had killed Romy Cheney, and Jamie too, for greed or spite or jealousy or fear, or simply because they crossed her in a way only she could explain and understand, he knew he could prove none of it, and the investigation, its people, its dragging load of misery, weighed him down.

'Your brother told me Mrs Stott made a number of allegations about him.'

'What allegations?' Serena asked. 'Who to?'

'To Romy Cheney. Possibly to others.' McKenna answered her second question.

'What did she say?

'She said he sexually abused Jenny.' McKenna watched her face, her eyes. 'She also said he allowed a friend of his to abuse the child.'

Serena leaned back in her chair, staring at McKenna. 'You're not serious!'

'Unfortunately, I am. And I must discuss the allegations with Jenny. I have no choice.' Serena continued to stare, her face drained of colour, eyes wide. 'I would prefer,' McKenna went on, 'to talk to her with you present, although such a procedure is not strictly proper because you are arguably biased by your relationship to Mr Stott.' He broke off, hearing pomposity in the words, as always when he was pressured or disturbed.

'And what would be proper procedure?'

'An impartial adult, usually a social worker, present for Jenny. A policewoman, and possibly a solicitor.'

Serena lit a new cigarette from the stub of the old. 'Have you told Social Services?'

'I don't wish to involve other agencies unless it becomes unavoidable. And I don't think Jenny should be caught up in the victim industry.' He sat down. 'It's a growth industry in our recession-hit times, where any number of people home in on victims of alleged abuse, ostensibly offering support and counselling, and making sure history doesn't repeat itself.'

'What's so awful about that?'

'Nothing in theory,' McKenna admitted. 'Except

the victims must play their part in keeping the industry going and, in order to do so, they must remain, as it were, locked into the time period in which the abuse occurred. Hardly beneficial to any healing process, is it?' He watched Serena's face. 'I don't think it will do Jenny's emotional or psychological health any good if she's forced into a situation where she must constantly repeat what happened to her – that is, if anything did – must let others examine and re-examine, analyse and re-analyse, the misery and trauma and distress in the minutest detail. And I don't think Jenny should be forced, at this stage anyway, to consider the prospect of having to give evidence in court against her own father.'

Serena shook her head. 'I can't take this in. I really can't! You say Chris actually told you Gwen made these accusations?'

'We do come across false allegations, you know. And allegations of sexual assault are always the hardest to deal with, because unless there is clearly identifiable forensic evidence, as in a rape, we must rely on testimony from others. Allegations of unspecified sexual assault are very easy to make, but very, very hard to prove or disprove.'

She stubbed out the half-smoked cigarette, moving the crumpled butt round and round in the ashtray, making patterns in the grey ash. 'D'you know what I thought as soon as the words were out of your mouth? I thought: this is Chris's way of making sure Jenny never goes back to that house. Or to her mother!' McKenna saw tears brimming her eyes. 'Now d'you understand what I mean about twisted thinking?'

Raincloud, dark and ponderous, massed over the city,

diminishing daylight. 'Put the light on will you, Jack? Like a cave in here,' Owen Griffiths said. 'What can I do for you?'

'We need an order to inspect Mrs Cheney's bank account. The cheque book found on Jamie very likely belonged to her, but the bank manager's being obstructive.'

'When are you going to find out who topped the woman? And why couldn't Jamie've killed her and then himself? That would be nice and tidy.'

'I don't see why he should suddenly decide to do away with himself,' Jack said. 'Not after all this time.'

'It could've been accidental. Whatever it was, you're not getting very far, are you? It's all "might have" and "maybe" and "perhaps" and "if this" and "if that". Look at things from my point of view, Jack. You've got people accusing each other of just about every perversion known to man, and not a shred of hard evidence one way or another to prove any of it. Now you want a court order to go snooping in somebody's bank account.'

'What would you have us do, sir?' Jack asked. 'We can't make bricks without straw. We've got plenty of straw, but it's all the wrong sort . . . just blows about.'

'Don't ask me. You and McKenna and that lad Prys are supposed to be the detectives.'

'You're supposed to be in overall charge, aren't you? Keeping tabs on things, making sure we don't waste valuable police time, or upset our sensitive public, or make general arseholes of ourselves!'

Owen Griffiths stared. 'McKenna rattled your cage, has he? He's very good at that . . . Lifetime of practice,

I shouldn't wonder. You shouldn't let him get under your skin. A lot of people make that mistake. If you simply ignore some of his remarks, it's better for everybody. He's not a particularly happy man.'

'He's not happy? He makes bloody sure nobody else is, as well!'

'Yes, well that's as maybe. But I'm quite sure you can take care of yourself. You work well together most of the time, don't you? We don't want to let a tiff ruin a good partnership. It'll blow over, sure as a gale from the west blows itself out.'

With rare recourse to figurative speech, Jack said, 'And as soon as one gale blows itself out, there's another one out at sea ready to give you a battering.'

'Exactly! So you trim your sails, don't you? Other people's emotions can take us into stormy waters . . . very treacherous waters. If you want to spend your days tacking along inshore, nice and quiet and safe, you shouldn't set sail with them in the first place.'

Working systematically through the files on the death of Romy Cheney, Dewi discarded all but the strictly relevant, disposing of red herrings as a trawlerman might discard unmarketable fish from the night's catch, even jettisoning the sleek grey car which had driven in and out of the investigation, making holes in its fabric so the pattern became torn and impossible to decipher. Left only with money and greed to consider, he told the manager of the bank in Leeds that a court order to inspect the account would put the bank and the police to a great deal of inconvenience. 'And I don't know, sir,' he added, 'but what your head office might not get upset about it, and say why didn't you just tell us what we want to know without all the palaver.'

'And what do you want to know?'

'How much money is left in the account?'

'One pound thirty seven pence.'

'When was the last withdrawal?'

'Friday last week.'

'How much was taken out?'

'Six hundred pounds.'

'Cash or transfer to another account somewhere?'

'Cash. From a machine.'

'Any savings account in the same name? With you or any other bank?'

'Not that I know of.'

'Which machine was used?'

'Our branch in Bangor.'

Dewi grinned at his reflection in the computer screen. 'You've been most helpful, sir. I can't thank you enough. Just one last thing. We need cancelled cheques for handwriting analysis. You wouldn't want us making a blunder over thinking somebody got at one of your accounts when they shouldn't. People want to know the banks won't let any Tom, Dick or Harriet empty an account without checking the money's going to the rightful person, don't they? So we'll expect all the cancelled cheques from the last four years. And statement copies, and records of standing orders. You should be able to get them in the post today. Mark the envelope for Chief Inspector McKenna.'

'We don't keep cheques that far back. And accounts are databased.'

'Microfiche copies of the cheques will do nicely,

sir.' Dewi heard the man breathing fast and heavy, as if he had run a race. 'Before you ring off, sir.'

'Yes?' The man sounded as if he chewed glass.

'You keep individual data files on your customers, don't you? Personal details as well as account information? So, we'll have disk copies of everything to give us a nice full picture.'

Chapter 32

Jenny, apparently oblivious to her aunt's drawn and anxious face, the undertones of tension in the small front room of the bungalow, looked relaxed, even happy. Unless, McKenna thought, she was merely doing what Serena said children do, and hiding her feelings.

'Is my father all right?' she asked.

'Yes.' McKenna tried to summon a smile. 'Yes, he's quite well.'

'That's good.' She tucked her feet underneath her bottom.

McKenna willed her not to ask about her mother; at least, not for the time being. 'How are you?'

'I'm all right. I should be at school, really, but Aunt Serena arranged for me to stay off.'

Smiling back at the child, McKenna had coldness in the pit of his stomach, knowing he might destroy all she held dear, all that bound her world together. That she might want him to sever those bonds did not occur to him, for he saw himself as a corrosive personality, as destructive as her own mother, bitterness from his soul poisoning whatever it touched. Cloudy daylight filtered through the curtain nets at Serena's bay window, but the light McKenna saw upon himself was harsh and bright, divested of the holy love apportioned alike to saint and sinner. Sin must be cast out, but he thought one must first recognize the disguises sin wrapped about itself before it might be rejected, and wondered why his church only told of that sinful by any standard, but kept its peace about the other dark things, the gall of loneliness, the tragedy of lost hope, which spread tentacles and squirted acids and wreaked destruction more terrible and profound than any knife or bullet or noose.

Jenny stared, waiting for him to speak. Serena rose suddenly, saying, 'I'll make another drink,' before picking up the tray and hurrying from the room.

'Have you seen my mother?' Jenny queried.

'Not since the other day.'

'I wondered if she'd gone away, only I can't think where she'd go.'

'Why should you think that?'

'She wasn't there, was she?'

'Wasn't where?'

'At home, of course.' Her voice was a little sharp, as if he were stupid. 'I went there yesterday with Auntie Serena because I wanted to get more clothes and my diary and things. There was nobody in.'

McKenna watched her. 'Did you go into the house?'

'Of course we did. Daddy gave me a key ages ago.'

'Perhaps your mother was shopping at Safeways. They open on Sundays.'

'The house was very cold, so I don't think the heating had been on at all.' She uncurled her legs, stretching down to massage the cramped muscles. 'Anyway, it didn't matter because I had a key.'

'What time was this, Jenny?'

She frowned. 'I'm not sure. Before we saw Daddy. We went there straight from the station.'

Serena returned with a tray of drinks and sandwiches and cake. 'What time did we go home yesterday?' Jenny asked her. 'I was telling Mr McKenna how Mummy was out.'

'I don't know, dear.' Serena put the tray down. 'One o'clock? Half past? Some time around then.' Still leaning over the coffee table, she looked at McKenna. 'You don't want to talk about Gwen's to-ings and fro-ings, do you?' she said.

'No.' He turned to Jenny. Anxiety began to stretch over her features, distorting their youth and serenity. She turned her gaze to Serena, and saw there the same gravity. 'What is it?' she whimpered. 'What's happened? Has something happened to Mummy?'

'No,' McKenna repeated. 'Nor to your father.'

'Why are you both looking at me like that?'

Serena put her hand on McKenna's arm. He was aware of its strength and its softness. 'Leave this to me,' she said. Jenny kept her eyes on McKenna's face, knowing that although Serena might be the messenger, his was the message.

'Mr McKenna's been told something, Jenny, and he has to ask you about it.'

'Why?'

Why did children always ask 'why'? McKenna wondered.

'Because you're the only person who can tell him if it's true or not,' Serena said.

'Oh.' Jenny leaned back. 'I see,' she said. Then, looking at McKenna still, she corrected herself. 'No, I don't see.'

McKenna lit a cigarette, then offered one to Serena. She shook her head. 'Jenny –' he began. 'Jenny, I have been told you may have been a victim of abuse.'

'What d'you mean?' The frown returned, drawing two little lines between her eyebrows. 'What sort of abuse? Somebody cursing me?'

'No.' McKenna felt himself floundering, while at the back of his mind, a little voice nagged, asking if a girl of this age could be so naive, or was it not more likely she played for time? 'I was told you may have been subject to sexual abuse.'

She stared at him blankly. Serena intervened. 'To put it bluntly, dear, even though I don't particularly want to, Mr McKenna was told somebody might've interfered with you. Touched your private parts. Even tried to have sex with you.' She reached for a cigarette from McKenna's open packet. He noticed the long fingers trembling and fumbling. 'It grieves us both to have to ask you, Jenny, but there's no choice.'

Jenny began to shudder: her shoulders, her hands, her whole body shaking and rattling its teeth and bones. She wrapped her arms around herself. 'No!' Her voice, a whisper, sussurated around the room, echoing from the sculpted ceiling, down the walls, trembling in the air. '*NO*!' she screamed. 'It's not true!'

'Stop it!' Serena raised her voice. 'Stop it this minute!'

'It's not *true*!' Tears flowed down Jenny's cheeks, as if a river of grief had finally burst its banks. 'It's a wicked, wicked *lie*!'

McKenna let the cold in his heart have its way with his feelings, shrivelling and withering the tatters of humanity left there. 'Have you been abused in any way? In the way your aunt suggested, or in any other way? Beaten? Kept hungry or cold? Anything?'

'No!' The girl looked at him as if he were the most odious creature ever to draw breath. 'No! No! *No!*'

'Behave yourself, Jenny!' Serena warned. 'Mr McKenna's got a job to do, and it's no nicer for him than it is for you. Children are abused. They get raped and beaten and starved, and even killed, and the police have to deal with it. I expect you to help, not hinder.'

'I know,' Jenny said. 'I know what happens to kids. You read about it all the time . . . we had a girl in school who'd been put in a children's home because her father raped her.'

'Quite.' Serena lit the cigarette she had been holding. 'So you know perfectly well what we're talking about, and there's no need for all this performance. Or for being coy.' She turned to McKenna. 'There's no point treating Jenny like a wilting flower. You can only protect people from so much. I've always thought Chris was over-protected. Everybody was too nice to him, and look where it's got us all.'

'If you know what I'm talking about, Jenny,' McKenna asked, 'why react so violently? Why pretend you didn't know?'

The girl looked from him to her aunt, like a cornered animal. McKenna wondered how long it would be before Serena ate her own last words, and told him to stop the torture. Instead, she said, 'You may as well tell us, dear. I don't really think you'll be telling Mr McKenna anything he doesn't already know. It has to come from you, though. It's no good coming from anybody else.'

Jenny pulled a wad of snow-white tissues from her

sleeve, and wiped her face dry, slowly and carefully. 'Who told you?' she asked McKenna. 'Was it my mother?'

'No.'

'Then who told you?'

'Why does it matter who?' Serena asked. 'What matters is whether there's any truth in it.'

'I've a right to know!' The girl's face pinked. 'I've a right to know who's saying things like that about me. Have you any idea what people say about girls who get raped? They call them tarts and whores and slags, and I'm not!'

'Nobody's calling you anything.' Serena's voice was firm, even sharp. 'Will you stop prevaricating, and answer Mr McKenna.'

McKenna intervened. 'Your father told me yesterday. He said your mother made allegations about him to Mrs Cheney.'

'That's all right, then.' Relief smoothed her face, took the harsh edge from her voice.

'All right? How can it be all right? Don't be ridiculous, child!' Serena was astounded.

'Mummy told Romy Cheney all sorts of silly lies about Daddy and Mr Prosser.' She paused, gathering her thoughts. 'I didn't understand, but I knew Mummy was saying horrible things about Daddy. Except . . .'

'Except what?' McKenna prompted.

She drew a deep breath. 'These were sort of more horrible, if you see what I mean. And then . . .' Her voice faded away again. McKenna waited, watching Serena, who stared fixedly at the girl. Jenny drew another breath, and McKenna heard it catch in her throat like a sob. 'Mummy told these lies, then Mrs Cheney got me on my own at the cottage. That's why I went there. Mummy went upstairs, and Mrs Cheney started pumping me about Daddy and Mr Prosser, and I kept telling her "No" and saying I didn't understand.' Silence fell, punctuated by tense and laboured breathing. 'Mrs Cheney said if I didn't understand she had to make me. She said Daddy and Mr Prosser could go to prison for ever, and if I didn't tell her the truth, somebody would come and take me away and lock me up in a children's home until I did talk. She –' Jenny broke off, looking up at McKenna, with defiance glittering in her eyes. 'Mrs Cheney showed me exactly what she was talking about, Mr McKenna. She touched me, asked me if Daddy or Mr Prosser ever did the same. She explained about sex, very clearly. She even showed me a magazine with photographs in it so there couldn't be any mistake. And all the time, I could hear Mummy wandering about upstairs, walking from room to room and opening and shutting drawers and cupboards. Mrs Cheney told me abusing children was a dreadful thing, and how no man would ever fall in love with me if he couldn't be sure I hadn't been raped by Daddy or Mr Prosser. And I hated her because she made me feel so dirty. She had no right to do that, and I'm glad she's dead because she can't ever do it to anybody else. And my mother let her. My mother let Romy Cheney do that to me, and I'll never, ever, forgive her for it.'

McKenna walked into his office to find Owen Griffiths sitting behind the desk.

'I've been waiting for you, Michael. Where've you been?'

McKenna dropped his briefcase on the desk. 'In Rhyl.' His voice was curt.

'Yes, I know you went to Rhyl. What for?'

'To see Jenny Stott and her aunt.'

'I see.' The superintendent fiddled with a pencil. 'Am I permitted to know the outcome?'

'Nothing you need concern yourself with.'

Griffiths stood up, his face whitening. 'I've had it up to here with you and this bloody investigation! Jack Tuttle's on the point of asking for a transfer because you've been using him for a punchbag, and Dewi Prys is going off right, left and centre like a machine gun with its sodding trigger jammed!'

'What's Dewi done?'

'He's only gone and put the screws on some high-up bank manager in Leeds, hasn't he? There was no need. We were asking for a court order!'

'Perhaps he's as sick of waiting for things to happen as you are,' McKenna said. 'I'll tell him to curb his enthusiasm if I think it necessary.' He lit a cigarette. 'What else would you like me to do?'

'Jenny told her father what Romy Cheney and Gwen Stott had cooked up between them the weekend it happened. Stott had the best motive of all for killing the woman,' McKenna said. 'In fact, I'd say he's the only person who did have one.'

'That we know about, sir,' Dewi said. 'My money's on that wife of his, though I can't understand why nobody's bumped her off. She's poison.'

'At least we've got grounds for questioning her. You

never know what she might let slip. That leaves us with the problem of what to do with her husband. I think we'll keep him where he is for the time being. He's less likely to come to harm that way.'

'We've still only got people saying things about each other. And people tell lies.'

'Circumstantial evidence. But it's building up nicely, and I think we might have to rely on that in the end. Nobody's going to confess, and whoever's been covering up their tracks so far has made a bloody good job of it. When is Eifion Roberts going to know about Jamie?'

'Later today, he said.'

'And where's Inspector Tuttle?'

'I don't know, sir. I don't think he's in the building.'

'I want Gwen Stott in for questioning first thing in the morning. Under caution, with a policewoman and solicitor present.'

'What do we ask her?'

'Specifically, about the tale she told Romy Cheney about her husband and Trefor Prosser, about letting that woman molest Jenny, and about where she was yesterday afternoon. Otherwise, I'm sure you'll find your way to asking her about a few other things, won't you?'

Chapter 33

The smell of the hospital made McKenna feel ill, his memory responding to this most powerful of the senses. Dr Rankilor's office, where he waited for the psychiatrist and Trefor Prosser, was scented with aftershave, and the throat-drying odour of new carpet.

Prosser trailed behind his guardian like a bit of flotsam in the wake of a liner, looking ill, diminished, the once shiny, well-filled skin wrinkling and loose about his bones. Head still bandaged, he snuffled and sniffed, eyes rheumy and dulled.

'How are you, Mr Prosser?' McKenna asked. 'It's very good of you to see me.'

Prosser subsided into a chair, looking carefully to make sure it was in the right place, as if his bones were stiff and his body unreliable. McKenna realized he was probably heavily sedated. 'I knew you'd come,' Prosser whispered. 'I knew you'd get to me sooner or later.' He spoke as if Nemesis came clothed in McKenna's garb. 'I can't keep running away. I'm too tired.'

'Remember my warning,' Dr Rankilor said, as he left the room. 'My patient is not to be upset.'

Prosser smiled bleakly. 'They're convinced I tried to kill myself. I keep saying it was an accident, but nobody believes me.' He sighed. 'I suppose it suits their purpose, doesn't it? Makes sure they stay in business . . .'

McKenna sat down. 'Was it an accident?'

'It was, and all my own fault . . . my own stupid fault. I don't have the guts to do away with myself . . . I don't have the guts for a lot of things . . . no doubt why there's been so much trouble. I've had a lot of time to think in here – there's damn all else to do with your time . . .' He fell silent. McKenna waited for the rambling thoughts to be given their voice.

Prosser smiled. 'You'll really think I'm mad if I say I'm glad you've come, won't you?'

'Why should you be glad?'

'Because you can set me free . . . that's how I see it now. You've given me an escape route.'

'Free from what?'

The response was oblique. 'When psychiatrists decide you're suicidal, you have to think about it. So I did. As I said, there's been plenty of time.' His voice was growing stronger, more sure of itself. 'And God knows, the more I thought, the more I was surprised I hadn't tried, if you understand me.'

McKenna wanted to walk from the room, so that Trefor Prosser, reaching out, could not touch him where he hurt.

'You see,' Prosser continued, 'I'm one of those people who feel, deep down, if things are too awful, God or somebody will come along sooner or later and make a bit of breathing space. So you can build up your strength again for the next onslaught.'

'What onslaught?'

'Life, Mr McKenna. It's a battle for some of us, isn't it? Always got something up its sleeve to clout you with when you least expect it, something to fight if you want to survive . . . I'm a timid little soul afraid of the world, afraid of offering any challenges to life, trying to keep my head down below the parapets, as it were . . . not give people the chance to take potshots at me. That's why I love my job. I can hide in my little office behind the castle walls, pushing pieces of paper here and there, safe and cosy, and get into my car and drive home, and lock my front door against the huge dangerous outside.'

'And who invaded your safe little world? Who laid you to siege?' McKenna leaned forward, the antiseptic smell of Prosser's clothes sharp in his nostrils. 'Was it Christopher Stott?'

'Christopher Stott? Oh, no, Mr McKenna. Chris has been crouching down behind the parapet with me for a good long time. I suppose,' he said, almost laughing, 'you could even call us brothers-in-arms, except we had no ammunition. It wasn't Chris. Surely you know that?'

'I'm not sure I know anything.'

'Perhaps you don't. Perhaps you're just as much blundering around in the dark as me, not knowing which way to turn to get out . . . the door slammed in your face every time you see a chink of light . . .'

'We're mixing metaphors an awful lot.' McKenna watched the other man, wondering if it were merely fancy, or if Prosser were in reality growing before his eyes, filling up his skin and retrieving his self from wherever it went to hide in terror and in shame.

'Aren't we indeed. Are you fully recovered? I heard they brought you in here.'

'Yes, I am better. Thank you for asking. Do you know when you'll be discharged?'

'When I can convince them I'm no risk to myself, I suppose.' The little man rose to stand with his back to McKenna, looking from the window on to a paved quadrangle where an elderly man bent over a flower bed, scrabbling in the soil, looking for something he was unable to find, and crying to himself in his distress. 'Before I become like that poor old soul out there, I hope.' Prosser turned. 'I also heard you had Chris in custody. Have you charged him with anything?'

'No.'

'I won't ask you if you will, because I don't think you know. Anymore than you know if you'll charge me with anything except driving under the influence of drugs and not wearing a seat belt.'

'You won't be charged in connection with the accident.'

'No? Well, that's very civil of you, I must say.' He sat down. 'One load off my mind, at least.' He stared at McKenna, forcefully. 'If you want my opinion, for what it's worth, I think you should keep Chris locked up until such time as you've put his dear wife away where she can't do any more harm. God knows, she's already done more than the rest of the monstrous regiment put together!'

'I've spoken to Jenny at some length. She's staying with her aunt.'

'Have you?' Prosser smiled brilliantly. 'Then you've already opened the door wide for my escape, haven't you? And for Jenny and Chris.' The smile disappeared, as the sun behind a swift-blowing cloud. He spoke almost in a whisper. 'We can all get out now . . . after all this time . . .'

'Tell me, Mr Prosser. Just tell me.'

'There's little to tell that's of any use to you. Only a small tragedy . . . two weak men enfeebled by their own weakness, as you might say. But the child . . . now, there's the big tragedy, and I don't know what God or man can do to put it right.' His breath rasped a little in a lengthening silence. 'Gwen Stott blackmailed me, blackmailed Chris, and crucified her own child,' he said eventually. 'And we let her, make no mistake about that. We let her because we're as weak and as fearful as she is amoral and wicked. If you ever want to know about wickedness and evil, Mr McKenna, ask a woman. Women have the imagination for it. More importantly, they have the stomach.'

'What did you do for her?'

'I took the mail for that woman at Gallows Cottage and gave it to Gwen.'

'And what did her husband do?'

'Chris did nothing, Mr McKenna. He did nothing and said nothing. That was his sin.'

'Why didn't you come to us and say you were being blackmailed? Why didn't her husband take the child away?'

'Because Gwen would have branded us, not only as homosexuals, but as child abusers. And then what would happen?' Prosser asked. 'You know as well as I do, don't you? We would have been arrested, and Jenny would've been put into a children's home and left to rot . . . or worse: she might've been left alone with Gwen, utterly and completely at her mercy.' He stared, challenging McKenna. 'What would you have done, knowing the consequences for Jenny? I'm not making excuses for myself, because there aren't any, and I must live with that. But Chris and I thought if we let Gwen have her way about the post and the furniture and whatever, it was simply the least of a lot of evils.'

'Was Jamie blackmailing you as well?'

'Jamie Thief? Of course he wasn't. Why should you think he was?'

'The car?'

'All Chris ever did over the bloody car is cover up for Gwen. She let Jamie use it . . . I wonder why? Why don't you ask him? He might tell you. Whether he'll tell you the truth is another kettle of fish, isn't it? Jamie never tells the truth when a lie will do. Has it occurred to you, Mr McKenna, that he might've been blackmailing Gwen?'

About to tell Prosser of Jamie's death, McKenna changed his mind, suddenly exhausted, bankrupt of sleep, of any will to talk or think or feel, as if the energy returning to Trefor Prosser had been stolen from his own body. 'What about Romy Cheney?'

Prosser's face hardened. 'What about her?'

'Do you know anything about her death?' McKenna's voice betrayed his weariness.

'Only,' Prosser said, his eyes cold, 'that if somebody hadn't got to the evil bitch first, I would've killed her sooner or later, because if Gwen had never met her, none of this would have happened.'

'How do you know?'

'In my heart!' Prosser pushed his fist into his chest. 'That creature was a catalyst. She breathed life into Gwen's fantasies, gave her the strength to bring them to life. Gwen's as weak and inadequate as the rest of us, and until she met that woman, she lived her life second-hand, draining people of their experiences, then regurgitating what she'd taken in . . . Even then, she'd get it wrong one way or another. Whatever she said or did would be soured by her own bile, the poison in her soul.' He smiled bitterly. 'D'you know what I call Gwen Stott, Mr McKenna? The Queen of Night, after the character in Mozart's *Magic Flute*. A serpent lives upon her tongue as well.'

'How much sleep did you get last night?' Eifion Roberts asked.

'Couple of hours, I suppose,' McKenna said.

'It shows. You're a bloody fool.'

'So you keep telling me.'

'And I'm wasting my breath, aren't I? You've never heeded anybody in your whole life: parents, teachers, the parish priest . . . always gone your own sweet way.'

McKenna lit a cigarette, coughing as the smoke seeped into a throat already raw from too many others. Eifion Roberts noted with clinical interest the pointers of decay which wove around McKenna like a cloudy web, sucking the life from him. 'I can't sit by and watch a friend go from bad to worse in front of my nose. I think you should see your doctor.'

'Why? I doubt I've suddenly fallen foul of some mortal sickness.'

'Perhaps it won't be mortal sickness that takes you to your grave, Michael. Folk can die of a broken heart, you know.'

'I doubt I've a heart to break. I hear all this misery and despair from people, see their fears thrust up in front of me like monsters, and ask myself if I really care.' He leaned against the window ledge, his shadow on the blind. Ash dropped from the cigarette, drifted to the floor. 'I'm as empty as Jamie Thief. No conscience, no heart, no love, no understanding . . . I pretend compassion because I can afford to. There's no need for me to fight and scavenge for survival, is there?' He slumped into his chair. 'Look what I've done to Denise. And for why? Why should I need to do that?'

'D'you want to know why your marriage has gone to blazes?' Dr Roberts asked. 'Because you and Denise should never have got together in the first place. You're like chalk and cheese, and it's as simple as that. Still, you've got to have some excuse for all this selfish whingeing, haven't you? I suppose throwing out one bit of dead wood from your life is as good as any.'

McKenna turned his head away. Eifion Roberts slammed his fist on to the desk. 'I could kick your bloody arse from here to Chester and back again! You're so wrapped up in the misery you've made for yourself you can't see straight! D'you think Denise is sitting on her pretty backside wallowing in misery? She's not, is she? Our Denise is busy packing her sun cream and her bikini and her fancy clothes and her frilly undies to go swanning off enjoying herself in Greece. I might not think much of her, but she's got a bloody sight more sense than you'll ever have!'

McKenna took a cigarette from the almost empty packet, looked at it, then put it back. He raised his eyes, regarding the pathologist almost warily. 'Did you finish the autopsy on Jamie?'

'I finished cutting him up, if that's what you mean. I haven't found out what killed him. I'll know that when I know, and I'll tell you when I know.' Dr Roberts stood up, pushing back his chair. 'You shouldn't set yourself apart from the common herd, Michael. Arrogance is a sin in your church. We all know the world's a detestable place, and the likes of you thinking they've got the right to remind folk doesn't make it any less so. And I'll tell you something else. Jamie had a heart like the rest of us. I know because I cut it right out of him, held it in my hands, felt the weight of death in it . . . and for all we know, he could've had a conscience to go with it. Not his fault if he never knew where to look, was it?' He walked to the door. 'We all die of it in the end, you know. It's what we do while we're waiting for death that hurts or not, as the case may be.' He pulled the door open. Standing in the opening, he looked back at McKenna, and sighed. 'And I suppose you won't speak to me for weeks now, will you? Avoid me like the plague, because I've seen through you, and had the cheek to say I'm not smitten with what I've looked at. And when you can't avoid me any longer, you'll put on the snooty face and the icy voice and the snotty attitude you're so good at.' He walked into the corridor. McKenna heard him say, 'Well, you can please your bloody self!' before the fire door closed behind him, leaving McKenna to the night.

Chapter 34

Beyond the window of Owen Griffiths's office, early morning traffic moved down the road as sluggishly as the rubbish swilling against the pavement beside the bus stops, washed by remnants of the night's rain draining from the mountain and through the city streets. McKenna leaned against the window ledge, weariness dulling his eyes.

'When will Eifion Roberts know how Jamie died?' Owen Griffiths asked.

McKenna shrugged. 'I've no idea. Why don't you ask him?'

'Because that's your bloody job! You've got Stott locked up in one cell and his missis being questioned under caution in another. What d'you propose doing with them if you don't know they had anything to do with Jamie Thief?'

McKenna lit another cigarette, the third, Jack counted, since this meeting began. Jack watched him, noting the crêpey skin beneath his eyes, the hollowed cheeks.

'And why don't they have the same solicitor?' Griffiths added. 'Why has Stott got one and his wife another? It's all adding to the cost.'

'Conflict of interest. Stott will be expected to give evidence against her.'

'Will he? What's she being charged with?'

'I intend to charge Gwendolen Stott with extortion, perverting the course of justice, procuring a minor, and permitting the minor to be abused. And if Jamie and that Cheney woman weren't out of the way, I'd charge her with conspiracy, as well.'

'Don't you think it might be a good idea to make sure Prosser and the girl's father didn't molest her before you go committing us to a particular course of action?'

'I am sure.'

'How? I'm not. We're not equipped to deal fully with allegations of sexual abuse, let alone make decisions. Those are jobs for the social workers and Crown Prosecution.'

'Nobody's made such an allegation. Least of all Jenny Stott.'

'Yes, she has,' Griffiths argued. 'She said the Cheney woman touched her up. But only after you'd raised the issue. Can't you see how conveniently it's all been put together? Stott tells you first, to pre-empt anything his wife might say. Then the girl throws a wobbler when you ask her about it, and gives you a first-rate reason for not making the allegation herself. Fortunately for both of them, Romy Cheney's not around to say yea or nay to anything.'

'What reason did Jenny give?'

'What she said about how other people regard girls who get molested by their father. That's enough to keep any girl's mouth shut a damned sight tighter than her legs, isn't it?'

Distaste soured McKenna's face. 'Do you believe what you're saying? Or are you playing Devil's advocate?'

'Neither. I'm pointing out the way we need to look at this mess. You've got to consider every angle. Say for the sake of argument that Stott did molest her, and maybe Prosser as well. So what happens? Gwen Stott somehow finds out. She tells her mate Romy, asks her advice. Romy challenges Stott, tells him to leave the kid alone. And then Stott gets the wind up. He kills Romy, and sets up this great big smokescreen.'

'And what does Gwen Stott do?' McKenna asked. 'And Jenny?'

'They go along with it. You know how families cover up as well as I do, McKenna. They stick together, because they think there's less to lose that way.'

McKenna ground out his cigarette in the ashtray, and immediately lit another. 'If Stott hadn't told me, we would never have known.'

'You can't say that because you've no idea what his wife would've said.'

'She hasn't said anything so far,' Jack pointed out.

'That's not to say she won't. In any case, I get the impression Jenny Stott doesn't like her mother very much, so she's hardly likely to drop her father in the shit, even if he belongs there. And for all we know, she might be wanting revenge on her mother for something.'

'D'you really think either the girl or her aunt would protect Stott if he had abused the girl?'

'I'm saying,' Griffiths said with mounting impatience, 'that we don't know. And buggering around the way we are doing, leaping to conclusions just because they suit us, won't find out. We must adopt the proper procedures. Social Services must be told, because they've got the expertise to deal with child abuse, and Jenny Stott must be medically examined.'

'No,' McKenna said. 'If we do that, we'll set in motion exactly the train of events Stott and Prosser jumped through Gwen Stott's hoops to avoid.' He drew savagely on the cigarette. 'Don't you understand all this happened to protect the child in the first place?'

'You're letting your sensibilities interfere with your work, McKenna. Not to say cloud your judgement as well. A quick and simple medical examination is all that's needed to find out if Jenny Stott is still a virgin.'

'A quick and simple medical,' McKenna said. 'Is that how you see it? All over and done with in a few minutes, and no backlash? You wouldn't mind, then,' he went on, staring at the superintendent, 'if one of your girls had a "quick and simple medical" to see if she was *virgo intacta*?' He turned to Jack. 'Would you mind? Would you and Emma be happy for one of the twins to be subjected to that kind of interference in such circumstances? Medical examinations like these can be as much an abuse as the other, with equally dreadful consequences. Look at what happened in Cleveland and elsewhere. And you,' he added, turning to face the superintendent, 'don't seem to know very much about girls. If a doctor is looking for evidence of abuse which occurred several years ago, all he can hope to find is a broken hymen. And many girls of Jenny's age and younger will not have an intact hymen, simply because they take part in sports like gymnastics. And if she's ever sat on a horse, the result will be the same.'

'You like causing problems, don't you?' Griffiths asked.

'I am simply trying to point out the likely outcome. We could put Jenny through a most dreadful trauma, for no valid reason, and be no wiser in the end . . . we could ruin her life, in fact, or what's left to ruin after her mother's finished with her. Jenny Stott is a person with rights, not simply part of a detective puzzle, or a potential social-work case. She categorically denies that her father or Prosser ever touched her. She has a right to be taken seriously.'

'And where does that leave us?'

'Where we were. Gwen Stott will be charged, and she will have every opportunity to state her case.'

'I only hope you can make it stick,' Griffiths said. 'And I only hope it doesn't blow up in our faces.'

'If it does, it does. It's a risk I'd much rather take.'

'What about the furniture that went missing? The car? Maybe money, as well?'

'We can't prove theft, so there's no point in trying.'

'I see. Well, that just leaves us with the small matter of a murder, doesn't it? Or maybe two,' he said with some asperity. 'And who d'you intend to charge with that?'

'Who would you suggest?'

McKenna sat in his office, cloudy morning light spreading shadows around the room. Rain spattered against the window, the leaves of the overgrown ash tree gleamed bright and fresh, brushing against the glass as the wind moved through its branches.

Pernicious as a fatal sickness, Gwen Stott waited for him to unravel her mind, her vicious fantasies. Her daughter, he thought, would wait the rest of her life for forgiveness: not forgiveness for her mother, but for herself and the blood coursing through her own veins, carrying the same sickness. He wondered how Jenny would escape her inheritance, except in another world of fantasy as lethal as that her mother inhabited.

Romy Cheney's diary lay unopened on the desk. Bound in embossed blue leather, he sensed it soiled, by the woman's thin, probing fingers daubing vestiges of Jenny Stott's lost innocence like snail trails on the binding, the thick creamy paper within. He pushed it aside, and walked to the window, staring through the branches of the ash tree, watching raindrops slide down leaves and fall to the ground like tears. He knew Jack was avoiding him, that Eifion Roberts would be wary as an antelope in the presence of a lion for a long time to come. He knew Denise had tried to contact him three times last night, that there was no reason to withhold the courtesy of responding. Soon, he knew, there would be no one left to want his company, and the prospect suited him very well.

'I don't intend to discuss McKenna,' Owen Griffiths said. 'He's been ill, and he's bound to be despondent about Denise. That's not to say things can be allowed to go haywire indefinitely. I daresay he's getting on your nerves as much as anyone's, but people like him exact a price at the best of times. I expect you to heal the rift, not make it deeper, so just behave as if there's nothing amiss. Pretend if needs be. McKenna'll come round sooner or later. Now, how are you getting on with Mrs Stott? Dewi Prys calls her "gwenny Gwen". Says it's local argot for dowdy and dated and dull. Suits her down to the ground, wouldn't you say?'

'Not today, I wouldn't,' Jack said. 'You haven't seen her. She's got up to the nines in some posh new outfit, make-up plastered all over her face, perfume stinking out the interview room.'

'What's the perfume? Carnations?'

'No. Probably what they call power perfume . . . By the way, I interviewed Jamie's mother yesterday. She claims she knows nothing, says he's been doing his own thing without consulting anyone since he was so high, and she doesn't really want to know what he might've been up to because it will only lead to more grief for her one way or another.'

'Sound like she's relieved to have him off her hands. You wonder if some people have proper feelings, don't you? Then again, folk can only take so much . . . What's Mrs Stott got to say about Jamie?'

'Nothing much. Says she was sorry for him, enough to help him out now and then with the odd five quid or so . . . she reckons he was getting his leg over Romy.'

'What about him being suddenly dead?'

'She arranged her face into one of those horrified looks and said he must've fallen foul of a criminal gang from England, like it said on the TV news. Then she did a bit of muttering about the wages of sin until her solicitor told her to shut up.'

'What's she got to say about her ladyfriend?'

'She's still swearing blind she didn't know Romy was dead, but as she is, she reckons Christopher Stott and Trefor Prosser must be responsible.'

'Those two sound like very handy scapegoats. Not

that I'd want McKenna to hear me say that. Where was Gwen Stott yesterday afternoon?'

'I haven't asked her yet, though I daresay she'll tell me she went for a walk or took the bus to B&Q to look at new wallpaper for the bedroom or went to a car boot sale or sat on the pier watching the boats, and had her fortune told at one of the booths by Gipsy Jane.' Jack grinned. 'I don't think she's going to say she was up by Dorabella Quarry putting out Jamie's light. Do you?'

'You never know, Jack. You might strike lucky for once in a blue moon.' Griffiths paused, chewing at his pen. 'I'm still in a real quandary over this abuse allegation. I've a nasty feeling in my guts we're not handling it right . . . maybe even letting ourselves be led up somebody's garden path. The problem is, I've an even nastier feeling we could make things worse. McKenna's remarks about medical exams really hit home.'

'That's the harsh reality. It's a no-win situation. If we don't believe Jenny, and she's telling the truth, we really screw up her life. If we believe her and she isn't telling the truth, one child abuser at least gets off scot free.'

'And do we place her at further risk if we don't act? That's what worries me. Should we bring in the social workers?'

'She's away from both her parents and Prosser for now. I think we should leave the sleeping dogs be until we know a little more about Gwen Stott. She's the lynch pin to all this, one way or another.'

Christopher Stott went home at noon, coming from the cells into dismal daylight blinking and red-eyed, a timid animal released from its prison. He refused the offer of a lift, and walked slowly towards the city centre, weaving a little from side to side as if his leg muscles, deprived of light and oxygen, had atrophied in the dingy cell.

'You should be telling the chief inspector, Dr Roberts,' Jack said into the telephone.

Eifion Roberts sniffed. 'I'm telling you, aren't I? You can tell McKenna.'

Cast now in the role of go-between, Jack sighed. 'And what shall I tell him?'

'Got a pen handy?'

'Of course.' Jack drew a notepad towards him and picked a yellow ballpen from the holder on his desk.

'First of all, fingernail scrapings. Debris on clothing and skin, although not all the results are back yet. I found a deal of skin and blood and fibres under Jamie's nails . . . quite long, his nails were, far too long for a bloke. Anyway, the skin and blood don't belong to him.'

'He was in a fight, was he?'

'I suppose you could call it that . . .'

'What else?'

'Time of death as I told McKenna on Sunday night. Between noon and three in the afternoon of Sunday, probably nearer three.'

'D'you know how he died yet?'

Dr Roberts ignored the question. 'There's faint bruising on his throat and face, and more pronounced marks, like somebody thumped him, on his ribs and chest. And grazes on his shins . . . and a few marks on his wrists.'

'Maybe somebody kicked him.'

'Maybe.'

'Cause of death?' Jack waited, pen poised.

'There are all the signs of chronic alcohol abuse in his system, and the residue of some other substance, possibly crack.'

'And that killed him?'

'No,' Dr Roberts said. 'No, that didn't kill him. You might say he met his match. Somebody sat on his chest and suffocated him to death.'

'Are you sure?'

'There's considerable literature on it in our trade, Jack. Used to be called "Burking", because it was favoured by Burke and Hare so that corpses they sold to the medics weren't too battered.'

'I see.' Jack wrote down 'Burking' on his pad, and 'suffocation' in brackets alongside. 'What about the fight he had?'

'He fought with the Devil, didn't he?'

'Oh, come on! That's more McKenna's line of talk.'

'I'm not talking about Lucifer. I'm talking about the devil who killed him. Because, believe me, whoever killed Jamie Thief is a fiend, someone who really enjoys the job of killing.'

McKenna felt remote from the world, as devoid of the capacity to feel as Jamie Thief, who lay on a mortuary slab with a cloth over his face and genitals, a huge scar stitching its way from pelvis to throat and from sternum to shoulder, where Eifion Roberts had stuck in his scalpel and turned the boy inside out. He wondered idly what Eifion Roberts had used to stuff up the gap where Jamie's heart had pulsed and throbbed, the heart Roberts had weighed in his hands.

'The house to house in the quarry village hasn't come up with anything useful,' Jack said. 'We haven't heard from all the bus drivers on Sunday afternoon shift yet, or all the taxi people. And as far as we can make out, sir, it seems most of Bangor knew Jamie was in the caravan. Apart from us, of course.' His voice sounded bitter, McKenna thought. 'We seem to be the last to find out anything in this Godforsaken place.'

'Jamie's caravan was a rat hole.'

'Suited him then, didn't it?'

'How big would this person need to be? The person who sat on him and crushed the life out? How heavy? How strong? Were his hands tied?'

'Dr Roberts didn't say there were any marks. He reckons whoever killed him really enjoyed it. I find that very hard to believe, actually. Nobody can walk away from a killing without knowing they've broken the last taboo.'

'Not necessarily. Jamie's killer probably didn't feel anything at all except an overwhelming need to shut his mouth, and a gigantic sense of relief after the job was done. Anyway, you wouldn't know. You're not a killer.' He turned to take a new pack of cigarettes from his coat pocket. 'Gwen Stott won't be killing anyone else for a while. That's one consolation.'

'Sure it was her, are you? What about the villains from over the border? The drug pushers, the suppliers?'

'What about them? He was out of their league. He was just the tip of the big rat's tail.'

'I still think you should be careful not to twist the facts to suit your theory.'

'Do you? I don't think there's any danger of that. I don't have any bloody facts to twist.'

McKenna went home to feed the cat, who waited for him behind the front door, wrapping her body around his ankles as he crossed the threshold, clawing his trouser leg to be picked up. He sat in the kitchen while she ate, then in front of the parlour fire, a mug of tea at his side, the cat draped across his knees, and fell asleep, waking to darkness dancing with fireglow, and the shrill bleep of the telephone. Listening to the voice of the custody officer, he thought of Jamie, who had walked in his dream.

'I think we should get a doctor to see your remand prisoner, sir.'

'Why? Is Mrs Stott ill?'

'No, sir. She's got some marks on her, and the lass on duty is getting worried in case one of us gets accused of knocking Mrs Stott about.'

'Mr Tuttle said nothing about marks.'

'He wouldn't've seen them. She was covered in make-up until she had a shower a while ago. Took a fair bit of scrubbing off, I'm told.'

Waiting in his office for Gwen Stott to be returned from the hospital where she had gone for examination, McKenna looked through the documentation derived by Dewi Prys from the floppy disks which arrived in the morning post from Leeds: sheet upon sheet of paper, covered in figures and notations, too jumbled, too arcane for him to decipher.

Eifion Roberts walked into the room at a quarter to ten, nodded to McKenna, and sat down. 'Went up to your house first. Thought you'd be at home by now.'

'Why?'

'Why what?'

'Why do you want to see me?'

'Not to look at your pretty face! Or listen to any more of your soul-searching drivel. I want to give you some information, McKenna,' Dr Roberts said, his tone measured. 'In my capacity as pathologist.'

'Couldn't it wait until tomorrow? I'd hate to put you to any trouble.'

'I was thinking about you last night when I couldn't get to sleep, and I came to the conclusion you should buy a hair shirt and a scourge. I expect the parish priest has a mail-order catalogue of suchlike for flagellating the erring Papist spirit. Your church teaches masochism along with the catechism, doesn't it?'

'Why don't you say what you came for, then bugger off back to the mortuary? You can't do much harm there.'

'Shunning me because I've seen too many of your unguarded moments won't make the slightest difference. You need to take yourself in hand, change your ways of looking at the world. Nobody can do it for you, which is why social workers farting around with the likes of Jamie Thief never do an ounce of good. You won't survive if you don't, Michael. Not in this world, anyway, and none of us know if there's another one, do we?'

'Jamie will, by now.'

'He will, won't he?' the pathologist agreed. 'I came to tell you who sent him there.'

'I know.'

'She's covered in scratches: face, arms, the side of

her neck . . . and several bruises. All around two days old.'

'She was plastered with make-up when we brought her in.'

'Jamie fought hard for his life, however awful it was.'

'And he lost, didn't he?'

The pathologist stood up, stretching his arms. 'Our Gwendolen refused to give tissue and blood samples, and that dickhead of a police surgeon nearly wet himself when I told him to take some blood anyway.'

'You know we'd never get away with that. We'll get court orders in the morning.'

'Bear in mind, Michael, that Gwen Stott's no fool, for all she's a moral imbecile.'

'You think she'll try to plead diminished responsibility?'

Eifion Roberts shrugged. 'Mad or bad, she gets locked up for a good long time. Young Jenny's got to live with the fact her mother killed, and it might go easier on her to believe Gwen wasn't entirely in her right mind.' He sighed. 'If the lassie can believe that . . . She knows what Gwen's capable of better than any of us ever will.'

Chapter 35

Dewi Prys put his coffee mug on the edge of McKenna's desk. 'That just leaves us with our Romy, then.'

'What does?' Jack asked.

'We know who killed Jamie,' Dewi said. 'So it's just a case of finding out who killed the other one.'

'We don't know, Prys!' Jack snapped. 'We haven't proved it in a court of law.'

'Only a matter of time,' Dewi concluded. 'Isn't it, sir?' he asked McKenna.

'Not necessarily,' McKenna said. 'Far be it from me to twist a few scratches and bruises into evidence to fit a theory. Mrs Stott is telling us she had yet another fight with Mr Stott, who every so often, she claims, throws the sort of screaming tantrum highly inappropriate for an adult man, and slaps her around when he can't get his own way. She was merely defending herself.'

'Stott was in custody long before she got scratched and bruised,' Jack said, holding his temper against McKenna's jibes and Dewi Prys's arrogance.

'We don't know that,' McKenna said. 'We only have an opinion about the age of the injuries, and it's an inexpert opinion. Gwen Stott must be properly examined today by two independent doctors for an expert opinion which will stand up as evidence.'

'Well, she can't tell us where she was Sunday afternoon,' Dewi pointed out. 'Who's going to believe she can't remember?'

'And can you remember exactly what you did on Sunday and when you did it?' McKenna asked. 'Of course you can't, because it's perfectly normal not to remember. She says she went for a walk round town. We can't prove she didn't.'

'We're questioning everyone within a two-mile radius of the caravan again,' Jack said. 'Someone must've seen her. She's hardly invisible.'

'If she was there,' McKenna said.

'There can't've been many people around of a Sunday,' Dewi added. 'I mean, she had to get to the caravan in the first place, and I can't see her walking. It's all of five miles from here.'

'Rather than snatch hypotheses from the air to fit your theories,' McKenna said, 'it would be more to the point to garner whatever facts are to be had.' He pushed the documents and floppy disks towards Dewi. 'Perhaps you could finish this job while Inspector Tuttle arranges a medical examination for Mrs Stott. Superintendent Griffiths should have the court orders by now.'

Dewi rubbed his eyes. 'These computers send you cross-eyed, sir.' He grinned. 'I'd better be careful I don't end up looking like Beti Gloff. I wouldn't want the female likes of John Beti to be all I could get to share my bed!'

'You've got a cruel tongue on you, Dewi Prys,' McKenna said. Leafing through the printout stacked beside the computer, he asked, 'What does this tell us?'

'Dunno, sir. I haven't finished yet. Are you going to see Mrs Stott? She needs talking to, doesn't she? She needs asking properly about Jamie.'

'I'd rather wait until I have a few facts to drop in her lap.' McKenna lit a cigarette. 'I'm not too taken with the idea of letting her make a monkey out of me.'

'I suppose not. If I were you, I don't think I'd want to be talking to her anyway. I don't think I'd be wanting to breathe the same air after what she did to Jamie.' Squinting at McKenna, he added, 'If headquarters even hear you've been smoking by the machines, sir, they'll put you back in uniform. Back on the beat. As a constable. At the very least.'

'You're getting like Jack Tuttle.'

'You've often said I could do worse, haven't you? I mean, I'm not nagging, but why d'you think they stuck that big "No Smoking" sign on the wall over there?'

'I don't know, do I? Because smoking's suddenly become politically incorrect? Because they're miserable sods?'

'Could be, sir. Then again, it could be because smoking's bad for computers.'

McKenna grabbed his cigarette packet and slapped it on the desk under Dewi's nose. 'And where does it say so?'

Dewi picked up the pack, carefully reading warnings spelled out in large gold lettering. 'It says "Smoking seriously damages health" and,' he added, turning the packed over, ' "Smoking when pregnant harms your baby".'

McKenna snatched the packet out of his hands. 'I'd better ring headquarters, hadn't I, Prys?' he raged. 'Tell them we've got a pregnant bloody computer with lung cancer and emphysema at the very least, and it's all my bloody fault!'

'Where's the chief inspector?' Jack asked, looking over Dewi's shoulder at the columns of figures and notations on the computer screen.

'Having a tantrum.'

'What's that? What did you say?'

'Having a tantrum,' Dewi repeated. 'Because I said he shouldn't be smoking near the computer.'

'Oh, I see.' Dewi awaited the harangue about impudence and insolence and insubordination. Jack sat in McKenna's recently vacated chair. 'I've said the same myself, but he never takes a blind bit of notice. He's addicted to the things. That's the problem. In my opinion, for what it's worth, smokers are addicts just as much as the morons shoving heroin in their veins.' He flicked the edge of the printout with a pen tip. 'Any of this any use to us?'

McKenna was getting back into his car when Christopher Stott inched open the front door of his mean little house, rubbing sleep and misery from his eyes.

'I thought you must be out,' McKenna said. 'I've been ringing the bell for the past five minutes.'

Stott held the door open. 'Come in, Mr McKenna.' He shuffled into the room with the huge sofas and the ugly carpet. 'I've been trying to catch up on my sleep.' He smiled a little. 'Your cells don't exactly invite sound and restful slumber. Sit down. Can I get you a drink?'

Even in the midst of what must be the most significant crisis of his life, Stott had it in him to observe normal civilities. And even, McKenna thought, after being married to Gwen Stott for so long. 'Some tea would be welcome.'

'Smoke if you want,' Stott invited, going to the kitchen. Clad in pyjamas and bedroom slippers, he resembled a frail elderly soul scouring the rooms and corridors of an old people's home, with nothing left to do but wait for Death to come calling at the door.

'Where did you think I might be?' He leaned down to place a mug of tea on the carpet at McKenna's feet, the sourness of sleep in his hair and on his breath.

'I don't know.'

'No, I don't either.' A wan smile took any sting from the words. 'I can't think of anywhere I might be wanted at the moment.'

'With your sister?'

'I don't think so. Jenny's better off without me for the time being.'

'What d'you call the time being?'

'I suppose,' came the reply, 'until we know what's happening.'

'Yes, I see,' McKenna said. He sipped the tea, hot in a solid earthenware beaker. 'Do you know when Mr Prosser will be discharged from hospital?'

'I spoke to him last night. He seems very much better, I'm glad to say, although he didn't have much good to say for the hospital, which struck me as a bit ungracious, considering they no doubt saved his life.'

'I don't think it's so much the hospital as some of the staff.'

'You mean the psychiatrist? Trefor thinks he's on the wrong side of the bars.'

'Well, let's hope he's able to go home soon.'

'Yes, let's . . .'

'Will you be able to go back to work?' McKenna said eventually.

'You mean, have I got the sack? No, I haven't, although I can't think why not.'

'They don't have any call to sack you. You haven't done anything.'

Stott winced, as if the words were needles piercing his body. 'Don't you think I should've done something? Long before that Cheney woman came on the scene. If I had,' he added, his voice harsh, 'Jenny wouldn't've had her innocence destroyed, and Jamie might still be alive.'

'With the best will in the world, you can't stop others from doing what they want.'

'I didn't have any will.' The words were bitter. 'I really find it quite odd for you to be trying to convince me I should let myself off the hook.'

'What's done is done, isn't it? You won't be of much use to Jenny if you spend the rest of your days wallowing in misery and might-have-beens and should-have-dones and whatever.' He thought he might do well to heed his own words. 'You and Jenny should simply discuss what happened, talk about why and how, shut it away and get on with living . . . leave it shut away, until it stops hurting, until it's lost its power. It will, given time. You can be sure of that at least.'

'I'm going to see Jenny later. What should I tell her about her mother?'

Stott no longer referred to Gwen as his wife, as if

she were already divorced, in spirit if not in fact. McKenna wondered how Jenny now regarded her mother, if she had begun to weave from the cruel reality a romance to cover its ugly face.

'Mrs Stott will be charged with the murder of Jamie Wright.'

'Is that all? What about the other one?'

'We have no evidence. None at all.'

'Neither do I, unfortunately,' Stott replied. 'And, believe me, if I had, you'd know.'

'Mrs Stott has a number of scratches and bruises on her face and upper body. She claims they resulted from a fight she had with you late last week.'

'Does she? I had no fight with her, Mr McKenna. I can't prove it, of course.' He smiled. 'But then, neither can she disprove it . . . Marriages, eh? I'll give you a statement, for what it's worth to you.'

'I shall need to take a statement from Jenny. She is, regrettably, a material witness. She knows her mother wasn't in the house at the time Jamie Wright died. And, of course, the other matters . . .'

'Yes,' Stott nodded. 'I know you've told me to shut it away, but while Jenny was visiting me on Sunday, and I was talking to you, and you were talking to Jenny and Serena, and I was sitting in that cell thinking the worst had to be over for all of us, Gwen was out there killing that young man, and the worst he'd ever done was nothing compared to what she'd set in motion. How do you shut that sort of thing away, Mr McKenna? How many years and years will go by before that kind of thing loses its power?'

'I don't know,' McKenna said. 'I don't know what I should say to you, or what I should not say. I don't know if I should tell you that we've been forced to consider whether Jenny should be regarded as a possible victim of sexual abuse by you and Mr Prosser, and dealt with accordingly. I don't know if I should tell you I believe her, believe that neither you nor Prosser laid a finger on her, because I might be mistaken. I don't know what I believe any longer, because there are so many untruths, so many improbables, so much deception, that no one can know, and I'm left with nothing to guide me except my instincts.'

'I believe,' Stott began, 'that Gwen intended to tear our family apart.' He stared at the carpet, traced the toe of his slippers round and around a bright orange whorl in the design. 'She's got her way. I don't expect she's where she intended to be at the moment. I think she had a dream of living with Romy Cheney, having the dust of the woman's glamour drift on to her, being able to scuff her feet in it like you or I scuff through fallen leaves in the autumn . . . Maybe she killed her because Romy didn't want her. I don't know. I don't know where Gwen will be this time next year. But I do know Jenny and I will not live together again.' He took hold of his mug of tea, held it to his mouth with jittery hands. 'Mud sticks, you see, Mr McKenna. It'll stick on me and it'll stick on Jenny. And even though I would do nothing to harm my child, she might begin to wonder, mightn't she? She might begin to think, in the way that women do – this tortuous, frightening way – that Gwen did what she did because she saw, with her woman's instincts, her mothering instinct, what lay at the heart of me; saw what I really wanted, even though I didn't know it myself.'

★

'You really shouldn't've bitten Dewi Prys's head nearly off because he told you not to smoke by the computers,' Jack said. 'I don't know how you'll cope when the whole building's a non-smoking area. Why don't you try to give up?'

'Why don't you try to give up being an old woman?' McKenna snarled. 'You could try minding your own sodding business at the same time!'

'It is my business. What about passive smoking, then? I probably get through twenty a day just being in the same room with you.'

'You know how to deal with that particular health risk, don't you? By taking yourself and your delicate little lungs and your nanny bloody mentality somewhere else!' McKenna bared his teeth. 'By God, you're sure to get a medal for political correctness, aren't you? Did the chief constable take you aside at the last Lodge meeting and promise you one?'

'I do not belong to any lodge!' Jack shouted. 'I don't belong to bloody anything!' He flung from the room, almost flooring Dewi Prys, who sidled through the door carrying sheaves of paper from the computer. He placed them on the desk, and dropped the bundle of floppy disks on top. 'I've finished the first trawl, sir,' he said. 'I'm happy to say the computer didn't keel over coughing its guts up, and it didn't give birth, although it was labouring a bit by the time I finished.'

McKenna looked at the smooth innocent face and guileless eyes. 'People can cut themselves if they get too sharp, Dewi Prys,' he said. 'And what did the computer produce for you? Was it worth the trouble?'

Dewi smiled. 'It was well worth the trouble, sir.' He

pulled up a chair. 'I've made notes to save going through every little detail.'

Stifling a yawn, McKenna felt the weariness of age within him, an age come before its time. He thought briefly of a holiday, of days spent in the company of Denise on an Aegean island, both of them alone with each other and the tedium of long acquaintance, then thought of being alone with Emma Tuttle in the hot dark nights of an island a million miles away.

'What it all amounts to,' Dewi was saying, 'is that on the twelfth of December four years ago December coming, Margaret Bailey's current account started to pay out regular sums of money by standing order into a deposit account at the same bank. There's a tidy balance, and it's earned a decent interest. Another current account was opened on the same day. There's been money in and out of that: cash in, corresponding with cash out of Bailey's current account, then cash out, mostly from machines in Bangor and Chester.' He flipped through his notes. 'The last deposit to the new current account was £500 in cash last week. The account in Margaret Bailey's name is all but empty because the money's gone to these others.'

'What name are the accounts in? Stott?'

'Oh, no, sir.' Dewi smiled. 'Both of them belong to Romy Cheney, according to the records. I reckon our Gwen'll keep the shrinks busy for years explaining why she pinched a name not only off a dead woman, but off a woman she's probably killed in the first place. Especially as it wasn't Romy Cheney's real name, and Gwen must've known that.' He paused. 'The bank manager's been very obstructive. Quite deliberately bloody awkward from start to finish, making a gigantic fuss about confidentiality when we asked a few legitimate questions. I don't think I'd want to be in his shoes when his bosses find out just how careless he's been with Margaret Bailey's money. And come to think of it, Jamie might not've been killed if we'd known about the money earlier. The cheque book, by the way, is an old one belonging to Margaret Bailey. Issued before she died.'

'I wonder how Jamie got hold of it?'

'Dunno, sir. He might've pinched it off Gwen Stott, for insurance, as you might say. It doesn't really matter, because the cheque book ties him up nicely with Gwen Stott.'

'It ties him to Romy Cheney,' McKenna said. 'And all we can say is that she didn't kill him. Gwen Stott is out of that particular sequence, so we may as well ditch the cheque book as evidence.'

'What sequence, sir?'

'The dance we're doing to Gwen Stott's music. A minuet: two steps forward and one back.'

Chapter 36

McKenna stood at the wide bay window on the middle floor of his house, the cat in his arms, watching an exquisite dawn break in the east to bring in the first day of May. At the stroke of midnight from the cathedral clock, he had said 'white hare' for luck, laughing at himself as he did so.

Beyond the wooded crest of Bangor Mountain, a sky so brilliant it seared the eye spread pink and gold ripples across the waters of the Menai Straits. Gulls wheeled over the city, their wings tipped with light, settled on roof ridges and began calling and screeching, disturbing the still sleepy cat. High in the sky, the tailstream of an aeroplane turned to ragged pink streamers, dragged by the wind.

Summer would come soon, dulling the sparkle of spring green upon the trees, fresh new grasses in the parks and on the great sweep of hillside below the old university building. Under the trees there, bluebells cast a purply mist upon the ground, and on the mountain opposite, heads of bright yellow gorse shone from the bracken. McKenna loved the early months of the year, even February, when bitter winds shrieked in from the east, snow riding their back and the scent and sense of distant lands upon their breath. The sap rose in his spirit as it rose in the earth, and fell prey as quickly to the decay of autumn and the barren spirit of winter, when sickness and weariness reconnoitred for the Grim Reaper, marking out souls for harvest.

He hoped to die on a fine spring morning such as this, his soul with the strength to rise to heaven, and knew that without understanding of mortality, there could be no joy in life. His time seemed to pass more swiftly with each week or month laid to rest, whole days disappearing in the blink of an eye, the sigh of a breath. Today was Thursday, yet like no time at all since he stood, Dewi Prys at his shoulder, in the sadness of Jamie's caravan, and looked upon Death yet again. Craving for immortality grew apace with his years, even in those fleeting moments when the weariness of life became leaden and the beauty of final peace seduced the mind of man, but there was no child to carry his legacy into the future, no wife to mourn him, few friends to grieve. Bored, hungry for her breakfast and the sweet fresh air of morning, the cat struggled to be let free. He put her on the floor, and followed her tittupping tail downstairs, thinking it would be enough that he had lived and died.

'Bloody paper!' Jack complained. 'Look at it. I'm surprised we don't disappear under a paper mountain.'

'Computers were supposed to stop the world being smothered with paper,' McKenna said. 'And save some of the trees.'

'So why haven't they? Why is there more bloody paper than ever before?'

Dewi sifted and sorted, glancing at Jack and McKenna. 'Computers actually generate paper. Folk learned the hard way.'

'Learned what?' Jack asked.

'Information gets lost in computers, sir. Data gets buggered up by power cuts and electronic memory blips and microchip faults. And if you haven't printed it all off, you may as well kiss it goodbye. What shall I do with these court orders?'

'How many are there?'

'Blood and tissue samples from Mrs Stott.' Dewi placed one sheet on McKenna's desk. 'Handwriting samples.' Another sheet drifted down on top of the first. 'And the bank in Leeds.'

'Mr Tuttle will see to Mrs Stott,' McKenna said. 'You can take a statement from the taxi-driver who dropped her off near the caravan on Sunday afternoon.'

'Which taxi-driver?' Jack asked.

'The one who came in last night after his boss told him we were wanting information about women taking trips out on Sunday,' McKenna said. 'He's already identified her.'

'Nobody told me about that,' Jack grumbled.

'Probably because you weren't here.'

'Some of us do have homes to go to. Even though mine's like a bomb site at the moment. Still, they go on holiday tomorrow, so things should settle down.'

'Do we know how Gwen Stott got back?' Dewi asked.

'Oh a broomstick, probably,' Jack said. 'When do we interview her again? There's a lot of questions need asking.'

'And no guarantee we'll get any answers,' Dewi said.

'There never is,' Jack pointed out. 'Par for the course in this job. Shouldn't stop us asking, though.'

'Speaking for myself,' Dewi added, 'I can't say I even want to set eyes on that woman ever again, never mind talk to her.'

'That's all very well, Prys,' Jack said. 'We're entitled to our feelings, but we can't let them interfere with the work.' He stood up, pulling in his stomach, and McKenna wondered if he would lose any weight while Emma holidayed in the sun, denying her husband the comforts of bed and food. 'I'll make a start,' Jack added, taking the court orders. 'Get the samples we want.'

'Suppose she won't co-operate?' Dewi asked.

'Don't be stupid, Prys. She'll be done for contempt of court if she doesn't.'

'I can't see that bothering her. She's locked up already and likely to stay that way, so a few more months for contempt won't be any hardship.'

The newly painted walls of Gallows Cottage glittered in the sunshine, vestiges of an early morning mist drifting against its footings and sidling around McKenna's ankles. On ground still sodden from the rains, and squelching underfoot, he stood where the track gave out to the cottage garden, listening to a silence unbroken save for the muffled distant clank of machinery on Port Penrhyn, a whispering in the trees behind him. Fresh grass already sprouted along the ridge of the trench where Rebekah's remains languished for so long, wove a carpet of bright green over the top of the septic tank. Within a few weeks, there would be no trace of Wil's passage, and summer visitors would search in vain for Rebekah's sad resting place.

'Did you come to look at the view, or was it something else you wanted?' Wil stood in the shadow of the door, head slightly to one side.

McKenna walked down the little slope towards him, feeling cold damp from the ground wrap itself around his feet, for all the warmth in the sky above. 'Just thought I'd call in to say hello.'

'Hello, then,' Wil grinned. His eyes darkened. 'Thought for a minute you might be the other one, until I saw you wasn't.'

'What other one?'

'The other one some folk say is a gippo, and I know is nothing of the sort.'

'How d'you know?' McKenna recalled the night on the path beside the village graveyard, the cold on the back of his neck and the fear crushing on his heart.

Wil regarded him searchingly, unsure, reluctant to make of himself a fool or worse. McKenna touched the carving above the doorway, new paint smooth and thick on the three heads of the dog.

'I see you've painted this. Odd thing to have over the door to your house, don't you think? Can't think why anyone should want it there.'

'Why? What's it supposed to be? Apart from bloody ugly, that is.'

McKenna followed him inside. 'The only three-headed dog I've heard tell of is Cerberus. Legend has it he guards the entrance to the Underworld.'

Wil shifted an upturned crate for McKenna to sit down, then put the kettle to boil on the Primus. 'That figures, doesn't it? Just the thing for this benighted place.' He leaned against newly fitted kitchen units, stuffing tobacco into his pipe. 'Must be where the gippo who isn't a gippo comes from then,' he said, squinting at McKenna. Despite its new paint and sparkling windows, the bright yellow sunshine outside, the cottage was shadowy and chilly, its sad history imprisoned inside thick stone walls, crowding out the living.

'Does he come often?'

From behind puffs of sweet-scented smoke, Wil said, 'Once would be too bloody often with the likes of him, wouldn't it?' He turned away, placing his hand against the side of the kettle to test the heat. 'Know who I'm talking about, do you?'

'Yes.'

Wil turned back, his face grave. 'Fair makes your scalp crawl, doesn't he?'

'Yes,' McKenna repeated.

'Ah, well.' Wil put three mugs in a row, and a handful of teabags in a stained metal pot. 'It's a comfort to hear you say I'm not going out of my mind with it.' The kettle whined to the boil. Wil made tea, put the pot back on a low flame to brew for a while. 'Not the sort of thing you want to talk about with most folk.' He disappeared up the staircase to return with Dave.

'The bloody English and all the other bloody foreigners are welcome to the place. And everything in it.' He poured tea and handed round the mugs. 'See you've solved one of your murders, then. Found out who strung up her in the woods yet?'

'What happens if I refuse?'

Jack looked from Gwen Stott to her solicitor, the three of them crowding the fusty dismal interview room where the tape recorder blinked and whined.

Beyond the open door, a young policewoman leaned against the wall, staring down at her scuffed shoes.

'You can't refuse, Mrs Stott,' the solicitor said. 'The police have court orders.'

'I can!' Gwen Stott insisted.

'If you do, you will be charged with contempt.'

'Then what happens?'

'Then you can be sent to prison.'

'Are you sure?' Doubt, a small uncertainty, drew a frown on her face.

'Absolutely positive. Usually for quite a while. Contempt is regarded with the seriousness it merits.'

'And you always go to prison?'

'Of course you do! Where else d'you think you're likely to go? Butlin's Holiday Camp?'

'Well, there's a lot in the papers about juveniles getting fancy holidays when they've been robbing and mugging, isn't there?' She leaned back in her chair, her weight forcing creaks from the plastic shell. Curdles of fat around her thighs overflowed the edges, the dingy fabric of her skirt creased under her buttocks. In his mind's eye, Jack tried to clothe her in the suit from Gallows Cottage, and failed to put the picture together. He stared unashamedly, seeking visible signs of the person who dwelt inside the unlovely body, behind the plain and pudding face; searching for the one who went with murderous intent to Jamie Thief, fought with him, felt his nails draw blood, and crushed the breath and the life from his body. Now her face was scrubbed of make-up, Jack saw the scratches clearly, fading jagged brownish lines on her pasty skin, a little bruised about their edges, as if drawn by a child with a smudgy crayon in its hand.

And he sought the will and determination which manipulated money and people and time, the cleverness which covered her faint tracks through the paths and thickets of Snidey Castle woods, the wickedness which probably tied a noose about the neck of Romy Cheney and hung her body from a creaking branch, but found nothing of what he sought, could imagine nothing of what had happened. She was ordinary, a person one would pass in the street without thought or glance, a person without true dimension or substance or presence, as if merely cut from paper. So very ordinary, he thought; almost banal. He saw her only in the shadow of his own prejudices, unaware that evil, like every other human condition, wore the same ordinary face.

'Yes,' McKenna said. 'I know I must interview her.'

'When are you going to do it?'

'When we have a match for the blood and tissue samples.'

'Well it's a near miracle we got them. I've never come across such a rigmarole.'

'Eifion Roberts said she's nobody's fool.'

'You also said he said she's a moral imbecile,' Jack said. 'What d'you think he meant by that?'

'She's a bloody psychopath! What d'you think he meant?'

'I don't know, do I? I do know she's spread one almighty pile of shit on people.'

'And it rubs off on us.' McKenna lit a cigarette. 'Like all the other shit off all the others rubs off on us. And God knows what effect it has in the long run.' He stared at Jack, smoke pluming towards the ceiling. 'It probably all adds up like a huge supermarket bill you can't afford to pay, or a debt from a loan shark . . . I'd like to throttle the bitch. But I won't. I'll talk to her nicely and take a statement from her, and do my job properly, and talk to her daughter again, and turn the knife in the child's guts to get her used to the feeling.'

'D'you have pictures in your head? Is that why you talk the way you do?'

'How do I talk?'

'I'm not sure.' Jack shivered while fresh warm air breezed through the open window. 'I just don't like the pictures you make in my head.'

Chapter 37

Slouched in his chair, McKenna watched tobacco smoke drift towards the office ceiling, its discoloration remarkable where heat from the light attracted the most smoke. Undecorated for too many years to remember, the seedy air of degeneration about the police station symbolized the erosion of will so typical of human behaviour in hard times, daubing places and people indiscriminately with despondency, the dingy grey colours of poverty. The ash tree outside dragged its branches against the window, smearing the dirt from dust and rain and traffic fumes. A Woolworth's plastic carrier bag caught in its branches hung full to bursting with rainwater.

Watching the curls and whorls of smoke, casting about for something to do, he acknowledged the lack of professional detachment keeping him away from Gwen Stott, and decided it was neither irrational nor unreasonable, but merely a normal human response to abnormal circumstance. Castigating its police when humanity deserted, society understood neither the causes of desertion nor its implications, knew nothing of the marauding images which first sickened and disturbed, before exciting and enthralling the mind of a man. He wondered about the pictures waiting to be found in Gwen Stott's mind by psychiatrists and counsellors, by professional victim-seekers, and the portrait to be painted of her for display to the people she had wronged. Perhaps a trauma from her own childhood lay in wait, to be hauled into the light of day for examination and magnification, for extrapolation and rationalization, to become a peg upon which to hang all her culpability. He imagined her cocooned within a chrysalis fashioned from reasons and justifications, emerging blameless as a fragile insect, guilty of being only the victim of another's victimization. To strip people of the dignity of individual responsibility was folly, he thought, for responsibility was a form of human currency, and inequitably distributed, Peter would be robbed to pay Paul, until Peter stood firm against having the last crust of innocence snatched from his lips. Then the whole edifice of social order might collapse like a row of dominoes, felled by the momentum of pass-the-parcel blame.

Somewhere in the building, Jack was shuffling papers, organizing people, preparing documents for the crown prosecutors. McKenna let his thoughts drift again to Greek islands and sunshine hot enough to stir the blood, warm nights fragrant with exotic flowers and the remains of day, and to passion and Denise, her pale elegant body and gilded hair. Again he thought of Emma Tuttle, and stood up suddenly, restless and touched by an indefinable sense of loss, of mourning for something as much beyond reach as if it had never been, or were already dead.

Gwen Stott looked at her solicitor, then at McKenna, face and eyes betraying nothing beyond boredom and the stirrings of irritation. The tape-recorder light gleamed like a Cyclops eye in the dismal room, waiting to record whatever she might say, or simply, her silence. Silence might be her best defence, McKenna thought, leaving no opening for prying minds to gain access to her fears and weaknesses, her petty vices and shameful secrets, or the cherished self-image for which she had killed rather than allow its destruction. Then he asked himself if this woman were capable of fear or shame, if she had not killed simply because it was expedient to do so, the life she took of no more import than the life of an insect upon which she might tread as she plodded the streets.

'I wish to discuss with your client her relationship with Mrs Margaret Bailey,' McKenna said to the solicitor. 'And Mrs Bailey's death.'

'I don't know anybody called Margaret Bailey.' Gwen Stott's voice was calm, without inflexion.

'Then we will refer to Mrs Bailey as Romy Cheney,' McKenna said. 'As you know, Romy Cheney's body was found some weeks ago in Castle Woods, and has since been positively identified from medical and dental records as that of Margaret Bailey.'

Gwen Stott watched McKenna fixedly as he talked of Gallows Cottage, its erstwhile tenant and her furniture and effects, of her car and bank account, of computerized transactions unravelled painstakingly by Dewi Prys, of Christopher Stott and Trefor Prosser and Jenny, of Jamie Thief and a tell-tale taxi-driver.

'What can you tell me about Romy Cheney?' he said finally.

The woman smirked. 'I can tell you plenty about her. And none of it good.'

'Then please do so.'

'Well,' Gwen Stott began, eyes flicking from McKenna to her solicitor, 'she drank a lot, and smoked a lot, and encouraged me to drink and smoke even though she knew I didn't like to. And she took pills.'

'What sort of pills?'

'Pills for being depressed. Pills to go to sleep. Pills to keep her awake. She was always moaning about being miserable and depressed and saying nobody wanted her.' Gwen Stott smirked again. 'I'm not surprised she killed herself in the end. She talked about it often enough.'

'Romy Cheney did not commit suicide, as I'm sure you know. There has been considerable publicity about the fact that her hands were bound behind her back. That is not consistent with suicide.'

Gwen Stott shrugged. 'I wouldn't know about that.'

'Where did you meet her?'

'At some do at the Castle. I went to stop my husband making a fool of himself in public, but he did anyway.' Anger distorted her face for an instant. 'Somebody introduced us to Romy, and instead of saying "Hello" like normal people, he had to show off, didn't he?' Her eyes took on a distant look, as if she no longer saw McKenna and her solicitor and the colourless walls of the interview room, but viewed instead a film of her life. She began a monologue, showing McKenna the same film, its people moving jerkily through a time long gone in grainy monochrome images. He tried to interrupt, to ask questions. She ignored him, until the solicitor finally dammed the avalanche of words.

'Mrs Stott!' he exclaimed.

'What?' Her eyes turned slowly, dreamily.

'My job, Mrs Stott, is to protect your interests while the police question you. We have been here –' he stopped to look at the expensive watch on his wrist – 'for over an hour, and seem to be no further forward than we were at the outset.'

'He asked me about Romy Cheney.' She jerked her head towards McKenna. 'So I've been telling him.' The counter on the tape machine clicked down to twenty-nine minutes. 'And she was the one who said Jenny was acting funny.'

'I beg your pardon?' McKenna said.

'Romy Cheney said Jenny was behaving funny, and did I know what that Trefor Prosser was like. She said he wasn't safe around kids.'

'And?'

The woman shrugged again. 'That's all. She reckoned Jenny should be kept away from him.'

'Is that why you took your daughter to Gallows Cottage, Mrs Stott?'

'Why what?'

'Why you permitted Romy Cheney to interrogate your daughter about Mr Prosser and your husband?' McKenna said. 'Why you colluded with her in her sexual assault upon your daughter?'

'What're you talking about?' Gwen Stott's face betrayed only a seething impatience.

'We have a statement from your daughter. Romy Cheney sexually assaulted her, whilst claiming to demonstrate to the child, who was then only ten years old, the actual nature of such an assault.'

'Did she? I don't know anything about that.'

'Don't you?' McKenna demanded. 'Your husband

and daughter both say otherwise. Your daughter says you were in the cottage when the assault took place. She says she heard you walking around upstairs.'

'Well, I didn't know what was going on, then. Did I?' She looked to the solicitor for support. 'If that child's saying I knew about it when I was upstairs at the time, you've only got her word for it, haven't you? You should know what girls are like.'

'We are talking about your own child, Mrs Stott.'

'So?'

'Why did you take Romy Cheney's furniture and personal effects from the cottage? Why did you take her car?'

'She'd gone. She wasn't using them anymore. Everything was going to waste. I've told you how much she paid for the furniture and carpets.'

'Where had she gone?'

'How should I know? She was always going off. A real fly-by-night, Romy Cheney was.'

'Did she say you could take her things? Did it never occur to you that she might want them?'

'Oh, really!' She fidgeted in the chair, crossing and uncrossing unshaven legs, the dark hairs tangled beneath pale stockings. 'What a stupid question! If she wanted them back, she only had to ask, didn't she? And,' she went on, glaring at McKenna, 'she never did.'

'That is hardly surprising. The woman was dead.'

'If you say so.'

'What do you know about Robert Allsopp?'

'Who's he?'

'When did you last see Romy Cheney? When did you last speak to her?'

Gwen Stott turned to her solicitor. 'Do I have to answer that?'

'It would be better if you do.'

'Well, I can't, can I?'

'Why not?' McKenna asked.

'Because I can't remember!' she said scathingly. 'Most people can't remember dates and times off the top of their heads, especially from years back.'

'Did you expect to see her again? Had you made any arrangements with her?'

'We never made plans like that. I've already told you. You don't listen, do you? She used to ring up when she was coming.'

'I see.'

'Have you finished, Chief Inspector?' the solicitor asked.

McKenna ignored him. 'Did you like Romy Cheney?' he asked Gwen Stott.

'I did at first. She was very glamorous. Different and sort of exciting . . . a lot more interesting than most people.'

'And later?'

'Well, my husband said she was a bad influence, making me discontented, which wasn't hard with the sort of life I have to lead with him . . . I couldn't make up my mind if he was right, or just being spiteful and mean-spirited, afraid she'd show me what I was missing.'

'Your husband thought she was a fake.'

She chewed her bottom lip with small mean teeth. 'He might've been right about her being a bad influence. She put into practice what other people only dare dream about . . . things a lot of people would be too scared to think about, let alone do . . . Romy Cheney took people for a ride,' she said. From the corner of his eye, McKenna watched the tape counter snapping towards zero. 'People got carried away by her, did what she suggested, believed what she said . . . then she dumped you like a bag of rubbish. She dumped a man like that before she moved here. She latched on to people, played with them, used them up, then dumped them.' Memory tore at her features, set her eyes alight. 'She picked you up, like you were a hitch-hiker, and along she comes in her big posh car to take you for a ride . . . fast and exciting and dangerous. Then she opens the door and pushes you out on to the road, and you've got nowhere to go except further down the road where she left you, because you don't know the way back, and you're desperate to catch up with her again to hitch another ride . . .'

'Did you kill Romy Cheney?' McKenna asked.

'You'll never prove I did.' Her face lost all its animation. 'Nobody'll ever tell you.'

'And you cannot prove you didn't. What were these things she did that others dare not even dream about?'

Gwen Stott laughed. 'You wouldn't understand if I told you. You *couldn't* understand. I'd have to show you, and you won't let me, will you?'

'No, I won't. I won't hitch a ride with you anywhere.' He watched her fidget with the hem of her skirt, pulling it over her knees, while knowledge muddied the eyes watching him. He saw himself like Alypius at the Gladiators' Fight, more vicious and brutal, debased and greedy for simply having been in her company, in danger of being intoxicated by the same heady lusts.

She rounded suddenly on the solicitor. 'You shouldn't let him say I can't prove I didn't kill her,' she accused. 'It's his job to prove I did.' The tape clicked to a halt, the machine whining in a breathy silence.

Chapter 38

'That,' Dewi Prys observed, 'is the biggest load of eyewash I have ever heard.' He turned to McKenna. 'How you could sit through it is beyond me, sir.'

'Didn't notice the solicitor complaining,' Jack said. 'All money in his pocket, isn't it?'

'You didn't ask her about the money, sir,' Dewi added.

'He didn't ask her about the car, either. Or Jamie Thief,' Jack said.

'It's amazing how a person can say so much and tell you nothing,' Dewi commented.

'Well, she said her husband's a dead loss,' Jack said. 'Not that we hadn't figured it out for ourselves, without her help. And she said her marriage is a disaster, so we know how she feels about that, but none of it's any use where Romy Cheney's concerned.'

'It could be,' Dewi said. 'Knowing how Mrs Stott looks at life might explain why she kills people.'

'We don't need psychological claptrap like that, Prys.'

'You don't know it is claptrap,' Dewi countered. 'You don't know why Mrs Stott did whatever she did.'

Jack smiled, rather patronizingly. 'Take my word for it. When we get to the bottom of this, if we ever do, we'll find the same reason we always find.'

'And what might that be?' Dewi asked.

'Greed,' Jack said. 'Pure simple greed. You can dress it up in the finest words you can think of, but that'll be what it amounts to.'

'We can't say she killed Jamie out of greed,' Dewi said.

'She didn't,' Jack agreed. 'She killed him to shut his mouth. Of course, if she's not going to be asked about it, we'll never know, will we?'

McKenna lit another cigarette. Jack glanced disapprovingly at him. Dewi said, 'Didn't you get the impression she was too pat, sir? Like she'd almost rehearsed every word?'

Jack nodded. 'Like her husband. A great long yarn about nothing you can get your hands on. Then again, she's had plenty of time to think up a story if anyone ever asked, hasn't she? Nearly four years.'

'Mind you,' Dewi said, 'she did a fair bit of badmouthing people. Her husband, Trefor Prosser, Romy . . . even her own kid, if you can credit that. If you believe the woman, Christopher Stott's a pervert, like his friend Prosser.'

'Takes the attention off her, doesn't it?' Jack said. 'And gives her an excuse if by any remote chance we ever make anything stick.'

Dewi chuckled. 'Teflon Woman!'

'Gwen Stott could teach most of the villains I've ever come across a thing or two about giving the police the runaround,' Jack said. 'What we need now is a big fat clue falling out of the sky, tying everything up nice and tight, like they used to have in those Greek plays.'

'The only thing likely to fall on us is another load of

shit,' Dewi said. 'Seems to be all we ever get out of life, doesn't it?'

McKenna stubbed out his half-smoked cigarette. 'Have you two quite finished? If so, perhaps you wouldn't mind doing some work.' He picked up the tape recording, put it in an envelope, and placed the envelope in the safe, slamming the door.

'What shall we do, sir?' Dewi asked.

'Whatever you were doing before.'

'I've finished that.'

Jack stood up, stretching. 'I'm off home unless there's something urgent. You haven't forgotten I'm off tomorrow, have you?'

'Are you?' McKenna focused his eyes. 'Why?'

'I'm taking Emma and Mrs McKenna to the airport.'

'Oh,' McKenna said.

'Well, then . . .' Jack walked to the door. 'I'll say goodnight.' Dewi made to follow him.

'Stay where you are, Dewi Prys,' McKenna ordered.

'Sir?' Dewi stood obediently to attention before McKenna's desk.

McKenna fidgeted with his lighter, flicking the flame on and off. 'Gwen Stott is no fool.'

'No, sir.'

'That being so, we must not let her make fools of us.'

'No, sir,' Dewi conceded.

'Therefore, we do not spend too much of our valuable time asking her this and that. And getting whatever answer suits her.'

'No, sir.'

'We make sure we have the answers we want without having to ask her.'

'Yes, sir.'

'So we firstly decide what those answers must be. Which means deciding what the questions are.'

'Yes, sir.'

'The questions to which we require answers concern two things: the death of Romy Cheney and the death of Jamie Thief.' McKenna put his lighter down. 'Everything else is incidental. And,' he added, an edge of anger to his voice, 'if we'd spent a bit less time footling around chasing shadows and bloody cars, we might not be sitting here now still asking the same bloody questions we were asking weeks ago. And Jamie might still be alive.'

Dewi sat down. 'We can get her for killing Jamie. There's forensic evidence, the taxi-driver, Jenny saying she wasn't at home when it happened . . . I don't see how we'll ever be able to prove she killed the other one. I mean, even with all the circumstantial evidence in the world, all we can say is she pinched the woman's furniture and car and money.'

'You don't listen, do you?'

'To what, sir?'

'To what Gwen Stott actually said.' McKenna looked at a sheet of paper on the desk. 'When I asked her if she had killed the woman, she said, and I quote: "You'll never prove I did. Nobody'll tell you." Tell me what you infer from that statement.'

'She killed Romy Cheney and somebody else knows about it.'

'Precisely. I think the crucial bit is her use of the word "tell". There's no implication that the person or persons in the know can't tell us, so she couldn't mean Jamie, because he'll never tell anything to anybody ever again.'

'She might just be careless about the way she speaks.'

'Yes, she might.' McKenna eyed Dewi, an expression of near despair in his eyes. 'But as we're right out of other options, we might as well see if this person exists.'

'And where do we start looking?'

'You can talk to Mary Ann, and I'll talk to Stott again. And Prosser, because she hates him. She almost spits vitriol when his name crops up.'

'She hates her husband, too.'

'No, Dewi. She merely despises him.'

Envy. Hatred. Contempt. Dewi drove from the yard behind the police station, thinking of feelings powerful enough to kill, of which he had no personal experience and the hope he never would. Gwen Stott, on the evidence of her recorded statement, sheltered only the cruelty of despair and inadequacy in her heart, sour bile where a drop at least of the milk of human kindness should trickle. She resented her daughter, despised her husband, and had been deranged by envy of Romy Cheney and her expensive trappings. Or had she simply found in Romy Cheney something worthy of the love denied her husband and daughter, Dewi wondered, and killed when that most precious gift was derided and spurned?

Relationships made costly demands upon people. Some could not afford to pay, others merely forgot to read the small print to the contract: Jack Tuttle in debt to anxiety because his wife planned an innocent holiday; McKenna in arrears to unpaid instalments of the emotions forcing him out of marriage and away from a wife who neglected to pay her own debts to her origins; comradeship between Jack Tuttle and McKenna near bankrupted by friendship between the women. Dewi sighed over the carelessness, the sheer negligence with which people ran their life, a moment's thoughtlessness or stupidity creating havoc for years to come, much as Jamie's mother gambled, when she could ill-afford the wager, up against the wall of a public house with her boyfriend. Wages of sin, he thought, and all of it down to sex in the end: nothing more, and nothing less.

Turning on to Beach Road, almost blinded by sunshine glittering off a sea mirror-smooth, cracked and cracking around its edges where the waters lapped against the shore and underbelly of the pier, he told himself it was wrong to judge with hindsight, but knew he might never forgive if McKenna, short-changed by his wife, had been too preoccupied with his own losses to make sure no one cheated Jamie. Would Jamie still be alive if Denise McKenna were a more loving wife, who knew her place in the scheme of things and was content with the place? Too much to expect of the high and mighty Mrs McKenna, he reflected bitterly, who started life in a council house in the valley, but wanted to climb to the mansion in the mountains without the surplus baggage of children and responsibility, and devoted all her time and most of her husband's money to the equipment for her grand ascent.

Pulling down the sun visor, he took his Rayban

sunglasses from the glove compartment. To his left, the sea glinted, ripples upon the water smashed to a dazzle of diamond-bright light. Jamie's life-blood ebbed and flowed with the tides of that sea, hosed off the autopsy table, into the sewers, spuming into the waters of the Menai Straits with the rest of the city's effluence: a scandal in this day and age to find human turds running atop the tides, used condoms and streamers of lavatory paper eddying against the shore and washed up on the embankment below Britannia Bridge by a heavy swell. On those days when Eurus blew spitefully in Bangor's face, the stench burnt off the waters was enough to sicken the strongest gut. The city's rats scavenged rubbish tips and newly sown crops, but fed also at the shores of the Straits before dropping back into the waters and up sewer outlets, their leavings taken by the fish. Dewi thought of Jamie's life-blood drifting on the tides, a drop here, a drop there snatched by a hungry sea creature and gulped into the food chain, Jamie's genes reborn without end in the bodies of fish and rat and man and woman; and knew he would never again eat of the sea's bounty.

Accelerating along the new road out of Bangor, car windows down, sunshine glinting off the bonnet, he gazed at the distant mountains, their blue haziness a promise of fine weather. He would, with luck, have the weekend off duty, and thought he might ask the very pretty girl on the supermarket checkout to drive out with him on Sunday. Watching the speedometer creep over the limit, he vowed to himself not to make a mess of his own relationships, to make only selective dalliances, and dreamed of a sunny spring afternoon in those hazy mountains and an evening in the deep blue dusk and singing mountain silence, a sweet blonde girl by his side and the scent of her skin on his hands.

Turning into Salem village, he parked beyond the school gates and strolled towards Mary Ann's cottage, sniffing the air. Beneath the scent of sun-warmed flowers in cottage gardens, a fresh tang off the sea, still there curled that smell of decay, of something rotten in the heart of the village. He rapped on Mary Ann's front door, and waited, rapping again before peering through her parlour window at vague static shapes in the dimness behind her curtain nets. Waiting a little longer, in case she had to come in from the privy in the back yard, he rapped once more before wandering off down the lane.

Wrought-iron gates under the lych closed and fastened with a chain and padlock, Dewi thought it a sorry commentary on social order when sanctuary was denied to the needy. He leaned against the gates for a while, holding on like a child, peering up the walk of close-ranked yew trees, their branches locking overhead to form a dark tunnel towards the west porch. He had no recollection of recent marriage or christening in this church, a place seemingly fit only for the burial of the dead, of cold dark sorrow with no room at its heart for human joy or hope. Letting go of the pitted iron bars, he walked slowly down the path beside the graveyard, quietness growing with every step he took, even the cawing of rooks silenced. The air lay heavy in his lungs, almost like dank water, sweetish and decayed. Each footstep echoed loud in his head, a snapping twig underfoot a gunshot in the stillness. He saw not a living soul and heard only his own breath and tread.

John Jones stood amid the weeds and overgrown meadowgrass on his patch of land, nettles standing almost as tall. 'What the fuck do you want?' he demanded.

'Not to get downwind of you, John Beti. That's for sure.'

'Does your Paddy boss know you're out without the grown-ups, then?' John Jones painted a sneer on his face.

'Oh, shut up! You get on my bloody nerves.'

'Is that a fact?' John Jones stuck his thumbs into his belt, legs straddled.

'Where's Beti?'

'Out.'

'Where's Mary Ann, then?'

'How the fuck should I know? I'm not her fucking keeper.'

'You've got a dirty mouth, John Jones.'

'What you going to do about it? Fist me in the gob like you tried before?'

Dewi looked up and down the path, hoping for Beti's twisted shadow to precede her, to hear her peasant feet hopping from clod to clod, but the world remained empty of all but himself and John Jones and the silent rooks hooked to high branches above them.

'What d'you want with Beti Gloff?' John Jones demanded.

'Nothing I'd tell you about.'

'Well, then, Mr Policeman, you'd better fuck off back where you come from, hadn't you?'

Dewi regarded the weasel figure among the nettles, fronds of hemlock brushing against John Beti's dirty breeches. Late afternoon sun broke through trees here and there, a shaft of gold light picking out the sharp end of John Beti's nose, glinting on the buckle of a dark leather belt strapped around his middle. Thumbs stuck in the belt, fingers gnarled and dirty like the rest of him splayed each side, he stared back. About to walk away, something rooted Dewi to the muddy ground, some little thing shifting in memory. John Jones began to fidget under his scrutiny.

'Didn't your mam learn you it's rude to stare, Dewi Prys?'

Dewi wrestled with the wisp of a thought playing hide and seek like a mouse beneath the wainscoting. John Jones stuck his sharp fingers into Dewi's chest. 'Bugger off, Prys. You get on my fucking nerves.'

'I'll be back.'

'Oh, yes? You and whose army?'

'Tell Beti I want to see her,' Dewi said, walking past a rotted gate askew on its hinges, away from John Jones and temptation. He turned, looking once again. 'D'you know what I wish on you?'

'More of the fucking horrible life I've already got, most probably.'

Dewi laughed. 'A rat's dick, John Beti. That's what I wish on you!' Still laughing, he walked up the path, the voice of John Jones and its foul imprecations slithering through the trees behind him.

Chapter 39

'I called to tell you to enjoy your holiday, not to be interrogated. And if you have questions like that to ask me, I suggest you ask them when you can't be overheard by Jack and Emma Tuttle and probably their daughters as well!' McKenna's angry words, muffled behind the office door, reached Dewi as he stood in the corridor. He waited until the telephone rattled into its cradle, then knocked at the door.

'I didn't see Mary Ann, sir. She was out.'

'Then you'd better sit on her doorstep until she comes back. I want her interviewed tonight.'

'I saw John Beti.'

'So what d'you want? A medal?'

'No sir. I thought you might want to know.'

'I'm not interested in John Jones. I'm interested in what Mary Ann's got to say. So go back to the village and find out.'

Dewi reached the supermarket as the minute hand on the town clock raced towards 5.30. Pushing past the fat youth in a blue overall about to lock the plate-glass doors, he rushed to the checkout, where the blonde girl sat behind her till, cashing up the day's takings. When she smiled his heart leapt to his throat, cutting off the words, because she was suddenly very beautiful.

Like her name, he thought, walking on clouds back to the yard behind the police station, keys and coins jangling in his pocket. Her name was Arianwen: it meant pure silver, and she wanted to spend all day Sunday with him.

No light glowed behind the windows of Mary Ann's cottage, no smoke curled from her chimney into the deepening blue of a May dusk. A little worried that she might have had an accident, Dewi made his way round to the back yards of the row, shining his torch through the windows of lean-to kitchen and back parlour before meandering along the lane and down the path towards Beti's cottage, torchlight dancing before him, midges rising and whirling under the trees. Branches creaked and cracked under the weight of rooks and crows settling to their roost; he heard an owl call softly in the distance. Beyond the wall, mist billowed through crooked gravestones and twisted trees, drifting upwards to wrap itself into foliage and branches, making more ghosts to haunt the village night.

Standing by the broken gate at the bottom of Beti Gloff's garden, Dewi thought her dwelling like a fairy-tale cottage, hidden in the woods, hiding all manner of nightmare and terrifying magic. Light burnt dim behind ragged curtains, smoke rose mean from the chimney, and through the stillness and the whispering trees, he heard a whimpering, the stifled yelp of an animal in pain. Tangles of thorn and nettle snatching at his trouser legs, he stole up the path and sidled to the front door, leaning so close the smell of hot sun lingering in old wood burnt his throat. He listened to gasping breath and rhythmic squeals and the rasping undertones of a woman's voice mouthing ugly words, and took hold of the door knob, stumbling into the room as the door swung inwards under his weight.

Dirty dishes, the detritus of feeding, lay upon the kitchen table, newspapers spotted with grease stains and jam folded carelessly amidst crumbs and crusts of old bread tipped from its wrapping. A knife stabbed a lump of runny butter in a cracked dish, a fly crawled up and down a wedge of yellow cheese and hopped on to the butter. A spider hung upside down from the lamp above the table, its legs curled about its body, casting a huge shadow over table and floor and the two figures moving like animals in the lee of the table. Beti Gloff knelt on rough stone flags, her hands splayed before her, fingers scrabbling in the dirt, tethered by the neck to a table leg, clothes slung over her humped back and grotesque face, mounted like a bitch in heat by her husband, whose urgent whimperings had brought Dewi to their door. The tether jerked and slackened with each convulsion of the old woman's body: dark greasy leather writhing and leaping, the buckle tinkling and scratching on the flagstones. Dewi stared at the buckle, mesmerized and horrified, unable to shut eyes or ears to the beastly coupling, while each time the buckle hit the floor, a little more dirt and tarnish was scoured from the two faces of the Roman god.

'Has Beti made a complaint?' McKenna asked.

'No, sir,' Dewi mumbled.

'What did she say?'

'She didn't say anything.' Dewi fidgeted with his

notebook. 'She waited until that dirty little bugger finished with her, pulled her drawers up and her skirt down, untied herself and went to sit by the fire.' He shuddered. 'She didn't even look at me. You'd've thought I wasn't there.'

'What else could the poor bitch do?' McKenna said. 'I can understand why you were worried, but you shouldn't have gone in.'

'The curtains were shut, sir. I honestly thought an animal was hurt . . . the last time I heard that noise was when a dog got run over outside our house, and it lay in the gutter crying while it died.'

'People call it a little death,' McKenna said. 'I suppose it is for a man . . .' He poked a pen at the wreath of silver laurel leaves around the finely wrought head of Janus. 'And I suppose you must report how you found this belt.'

'Everybody'll know about Beti and that bastard if I do, sir. Can't I say I recognized it earlier?'

'Everybody except us probably knows already,' McKenna said. 'And you can't afford to suppress the facts to spare either her sensibilities or your own.' He again nudged the buckle with his pen. 'I don't know how John Jones got his hands on this, but it certainly wasn't a present from Robert Allsopp, and we're likely in for a long session trying to find out, because I don't think he's suddenly going to give us chapter and verse.'

'No!' Jack shouted into the telephone. 'You are not interrupting my dinner. I'm not getting any dinner, am I? Unless I cook it myself.'

'Is – er – my wife still there?' McKenna asked.

'No, she isn't. And neither is my wife,' Jack seethed. 'They've gone out for a drink. What are things coming to? You wouldn't credit the way your life can just fall apart in front of your eyes. House like a bloody bomb-site with all the stuff your Denise brought for this garage sale they're going in for after the holiday; suit-cases, books, underclothes, swimming costumes all over the place. You name it, it'll be here somewhere, and the only thing I can't find is something to eat.'

'It'll sort itself out, Jack. I daresay Emma's rather overexcited. Come and share a canteen dinner with me,' McKenna offered. 'We might be able to provide a little after-dinner cabaret.'

'How's that, then?'

'Oh, no!' John Jones stumbled from his chair in the interview room, trouser waist bunched in his hand. 'I'm not speaking to no fucking machine! Devil's business, they are! Pinch your voice like photos steal your face.' He sat down again, nowhere else to go in the room overcrowded by police officers and the solicitor on night call. He spat on the floor. 'You coppers don't know nothing about fucking nothing!'

'Superstition, isn't it?' Dewi lounged against the wall, hands in pockets. 'I shouldn't think the Devil'd want even a smell of you, John Beti, let alone your voice. He's not that hard up.'

John Jones sneered, 'You'll learn, you bastard! Learn the hard way what some folks know already. And serve you fucking right!' He turned on the solicitor, snarling, 'And you can fuck off back where you came from. You're not getting your greedy hands on my money!'

'Oh, give it a rest!' Dewi said. 'This isn't the first time you've been here for some evil-doing, and you know bloody well the brief comes for free.'

'Does my client have a record?' the solicitor asked.

'For poaching salmon out of the river, pheasants off Vaynol Estate, and robbing half a ton of coal from the railway yard. That we know about,' Dewi said.

'Didn't have no fucking money for food and coal, did I? What's a body to do, then, Mr Clever Dickhead? Starve? Let his crippled wife go cold and hungry?'

'My heart is bleeding,' Dewi said. 'You sold the salmon and pheasants and coal and spent most of the money down the Three Crowns and on the dogs.' He stared at John Jones. 'Pity you don't think about your crippled wife and her welfare more often, isn't it?'

'Fucking bastard sticking your nose in where you've no right!' John Jones raged. He rounded on McKenna. 'Why're you letting him bully me? Think I'm nothing but shit, don't you?'

'What else are you, then?' Dewi demanded. 'I reckon you're the biggest lump of shit outside the biggest cesspit in Wales.'

McKenna slammed his fist on the table. 'Enough! Keep your mouth shut, Dewi Prys, unless you've something worth saying. And you, John Jones, can stop acting the fool!' He switched on the tape recorder, holding the belt with its buckle for John Jones and his solicitor to see. 'This unusual buckle matches the description of the buckle probably missing from the belt which bound Margaret Bailey's hands. Perhaps Mr Jones would care to say how it came into his possession.'

'None of your fucking business!'

'May I remind you,' McKenna said, 'that this tape recording can be used in evidence. May I therefore suggest, Mr Jones, that you moderate your language.'

'Mr McKenna's telling you to stop swearing, John Beti,' Dewi added.

'And I heard him tell you to shut your fucking trap, Dewi Prys! So why don't you?'

'Mr Jones, will you please answer the questions put to you,' the solicitor intervened. 'In your own interests.' He picked up the belt and scrutinized the buckle. 'I wouldn't imagine there's another buckle like this in the whole of Wales, so without pre-empting any investigation or compromising the interview, if you refuse to answer, I can't see the police have any choice but to charge you with the murder of Margaret Bailey.'

John Jones's face became a sickly grey mask. 'I didn't kill her! I found her body.'

'We know that,' McKenna said. 'You came to tell us, didn't you? Tell me, when did you first find her body? When did you first know she was dead in the woods?'

Chapter 40

'Her hands were tied up with the belt. I cut the buckle off. And that's all I did.' John Jones stared at the floor. 'No use to her, was it?'

'When did you cut it off?' McKenna asked.

'When I found her, didn't I?'

'And when did you find her?'

'If I tell you, what'll you do to me?'

'Why don't you tell us first, and we'll see about that later,' McKenna persuaded.

Voice piteous, John Jones said, 'Can I have a fag? I'm gasping.'

McKenna gave one of his own cigarettes to the captive.

'It was that fucking bitch, wasn't it?' He drew in a chestful of smoke.

'Who?'

'Her you've got banged up in the cells.'

'What did she do?'

'Killed her from Gallows Cottage, didn't she?'

'How do you know?'

''Cos I fucking saw her, didn't I?' he snapped, spittle flying on to the table. 'How the fuck else?'

'I don't know,' McKenna said. 'You tell me.'

'They was having a row. All three of them.'

'Which three was that, then?'

'Her from the cottage, that bitch Stott, and Jamie Thief.'

'And what were they rowing about?'

'Dunno, do I?'

'Oh, I think you do, Mr Jones,' McKenna said. 'I think you were probably listening.'

'So what if I was? No fucking law against listening to folk rowing, is there?'

'Not that I know of.' McKenna almost smiled. 'So what was the row about?'

'Money, wasn't it?'

'And who was rowing about money?'

'Bitch Stott was creating hell because the other one wouldn't give her money for something or other. They'd been at it long before I got there.'

'And Jamie?'

'What about him?'

'What was he doing there?'

John Jones took another cigarette from McKenna's packet on the table. 'What d'you think he was doing there? Picking fucking daisies?'

McKenna took the cigarette out of his mouth. 'Listen to me, John Jones. Answer my questions. When I ask them. Why was Jamie there? What time of day was this row? What was the row about?'

'They was rowing about money. I said.' John Jones eyed the cigarette, still in McKenna's fingers. 'It was in the morning, earlyish.'

'How early?'

'About nine o'clock . . . bit later, maybe. I went past the cottage to the woods because my boss told me to clear some dead trees.' John Jones spat.

'Fucking English slave-driver making me cart wood like I'm some sodding peasant!'

'There's nothing demeaning about carrying wood,' McKenna said. 'After all, our Redeemer had to drag His own cross to Golgotha, didn't He? Why was Jamie there?'

'Jesus wept! D'you want a fucking diagram? He was at the cottage most nights she was there. He was screwing her, wasn't he?'

'And Mrs Stott?'

'Suppose she got the early bus, or walked. I don't know, do I? I never stopped to ask.' He sniggered. 'Maybe they was having a threesome.'

McKenna put the cigarette down. 'When was this? How long ago?'

'Years, wasn't it? Nearly four . . . November . . . Fucking cold and pissing down like usual.'

'Early November? Mid? Late?'

'Before Bonfire Night. The Rugby Club was having the dead trees for the bonfire.'

'Good.' McKenna offered a light. 'See how much you can remember when you try? What happened next?'

'They had a fight.'

'Who did?'

'Bitch Stott and the Englishwoman.' John Jones paused, savouring the taste of tobacco. 'Jamie was screeching for them to stop, and they didn't take a blind bit of notice . . . went at it hammer and fucking tongs. I heard the other one call bitch Stott bad names, saying she'd made that poncy husband queerer than he already was and turned her kid into a slag with all her goings on . . .' He paused again. 'Couldn't make no fucking sense out of it, except the English one said she wouldn't give Stott the dirt from under her fingernails after what she'd said and done. She told Stott to get off her fat ugly arse and get a job, because she wasn't getting any more money off her.'

'And?'

'And there was a horrible shriek and it all went quiet . . .' He looked into McKenna's eyes, his own dark with some pain. 'Jamie comes rushing out, white like a fucking ghost, and throws up on the garden path.'

The tape recorder began to whine. McKenna waited for Jack to replace the tape, listening to John Jones's breath rattle in his scrawny chest. 'You should give up the cigarettes.'

John Jones ignored him. 'Stott comes waddling after Jamie and gets him round the neck like she's going to choke the life out of him, and he's screaming and trying to fight her off . . . she said if he didn't help her, she'd tell you lot he'd killed the other one.'

'Did they know you were there?'

'Eh? Dunno . . . I was in the trees . . . Jamie goes back inside, comes out again, falling around like he's drunk . . . into that lean-to and out wheeling a barrow, and Stott's watching from the door . . .'

'Then what?'

'They disappear inside the cottage . . . and come out again, and Jamie's pushing the barrow, and bitch Stott's pushing him down the path, like a fucking dog worrying sheep.'

'What was in the barrow?' McKenna asked quietly.

'The English one . . . bundled in like a bag of old rubbish, her hand dragging on the stones and her head bumping and thumping on the path, hair getting all dirty . . .' He shivered violently. 'Can hear it now, I can!' he whispered. 'Fucking dream about it! Thump! Thump! You wouldn't believe the noise on it.'

'Was she dead?'

John Jones stared at McKenna. He licked his lips and swallowed the taste on them, and stared again. 'No,' he said after a long silence.

'How d'you know?'

'She woke up, didn't she?' he mumbled.

'Would you repeat that, please?' McKenna asked. 'Louder, so the tape recorder picks it up properly.'

'I said,' John Jones snapped, 'she woke up!'

'When?'

'When Jamie Thief was pushing her into the woods . . . struggling and yelling and screaming, she was,' John Jones said, his voice stricken with awe. 'Knew what was happening, didn't she?'

'And?'

'Bitch Stott pushes Jamie out of the way, and starts fighting with her . . .' His voice sank away. 'I couldn't've done anything. I couldn't've stopped them.'

'Stopped what?'

'The fighting . . . and the rest of it . . .' The old man gulped on his cigarette. 'Stott was a-pushing and a-shoving, screeching for the other one to shut her fucking gob, slapping her around . . . slip-slap over and again at her face, knocking her head this way and that . . . bodies all over the fucking shop, and the screaming and scriking and the fucking crows in the trees watching it all . . .'

'What else did you see, John Jones?' McKenna asked.

'I dunno . . .' He stared pleadingly at McKenna. 'I dunno . . .'

'I think you do. What did Mrs Stott do?'

He sighed a weary breath. 'Leaned on the other one, pushed her back in the barrow. She's got arms like fucking shanks of ham, and she goes red in the face with the effort of it. The other one went quiet, and Jamie screamed and Stott fisted him in the face so hard he fell over . . .'

'What about the belt?'

'She made Jamie Thief do it, didn't she? She pulled the belt off the Englishwoman, and held her down while Jamie strapped her hands up . . .' He paused, tapping ash slowly from the end of his cigarette. 'Then she grabbed a fistful of dirt and dead leaves off the ground, and stuffed them in the other one's gob to shut her up from any more screaming . . . I didn't see no more, and that's the truth.'

'When did you find the body?'

'Two, three days after,' John Jones muttered. The ashtray overflowed with cigarette stubs, its smell pungent in the stuffy room, seeping into clothing, weaving itself into hair, laying a greasy patina on to the skin.

'Had you been looking?'

'Dunno, really. I reckoned they'd tip her in the river or bury her . . . I found her on the Sunday morning when I were out. Beti goes to chapel of a Sunday morning.'

'Tell me why you were out,' McKenna said. 'To get the record straight.'

'I were setting rabbit traps, if you've got to know. And I didn't fucking catch any, so you can't do me for it.'

'Where was she?'

'Hanging off the fucking tree where you found her! Where d'you think she was?'

'And when did you take the buckle?'

'Some time after.'

'Why?'

'Why? I've said! No use to her, was it?'

'And what state was the body in?'

'Jesus! Don't you know anything?'

'I'm asking you to tell me.'

'She was crawling, 'cos she was hung like a fucking pheasant, and the bloody maggots dropped off on me when I took the buckle. Her eyes were gone by then . . . crows or magpies, I suppose. Dunno which.'

'Did you take anything else?' McKenna asked. 'Did you go into Gallows Cottage at any time, and take anything?'

'Maybe.' John Jones stared at the table. 'Maybe not.'

'Yes or no?'

'I went round the place after that bitch cleared it out. Christ! You should've seen her heaving stuff into the back of a van like fucking Tarzan, and Jamie Thief standing gawping.'

'What did you take?'

'Some fancy jacket and skirt she'd left on the floor. I reckoned they were good enough for somebody, so I took them to Beti.'

'And what did she do with them?'

'Gave them to that witch Mary Ann, on account she's fatter.'

'And?' McKenna prodded.

'And that Mary Ann throws a fucking wobbler, doesn't she?' John Jones announced. 'Says you get evil luck for stealing off the dead, and chucks them back at Beti.' He took another cigarette. 'Beti makes me take them back to that cottage, so I stuffed them under a floorboard upstairs . . . stank they did, like the body in the woods.'

'Are you telling me,' McKenna asked, 'that Mary Ann and Beti knew about the body all the time?'

John Jones sniggered. 'The whole fucking village knew, except for his holiness.'

'Then why did no one tell us?'

'Tell you? What for? She was dead, wasn't she? Telling folk wouldn't make no difference. Anyway, she were a fucking foreigner, and I reckon things happened on account of it. Folk don't want to get mixed in with nothing like that 'cos they never know where it'll end. Look at all the trouble now, just 'cos I told you.' He paused, then snapped up his head. 'Should've kept my stupid fucking mouth shut, shouldn't I? The body wasn't doing no harm.'

'Why did you tell us then, John Jones?'

The old man shivered. 'Her! I reckon she must've seen me in the trees, or that Jamie Thief did and grassed me up. She set that gippo after me, everywhere I bloody go, day and fucking night! And I don't know what she's told him to do. Look what happened to Jamie Thief.' He stubbed out the cigarette. 'Didn't fancy swinging off some fucking tree like the other one, did I?'

'If you'd told us sooner,' McKenna said quietly, 'Jamie might still be alive.'

'So what if he might be?'

'You could've saved him, couldn't you?'

'What for? When've the likes of Jamie Thief been worth saving for anything?'

'Well, Jack,' McKenna said, 'your *deus ex machina* turned up right on cue. Not quite in the shape you imagined, I daresay.'

'Didn't it?' He yawned. 'Emma will have my hide. Have you seen the time?' Grinning, he said, 'Young Dewi really got more of an eyeful than he bargained for in that cottage, didn't he? Should make him the star attraction in the canteen for months to come.'

'I don't think he'll want to discuss it,' McKenna said. 'He wanted to keep it out of the report, as much to save his own face as the old woman's . . . Can't somehow imagine her and John Beti having it off, can you?'

'You can't imagine a lot of people having sex,' Jack said. 'And not just because they're as bloody ugly as those two. Oh, well, it takes all sorts . . . at least we've sorted out who did what to who, although convincing a jury's another matter.'

'It usually is. What time are you taking Emma and Denise to the airport tomorrow?'

'Their flight leaves at midday, and they reckon to be in Rhodes in time to go out on the town.' Jack fidgeted. 'I can't stop worrying about them, you know. You hear about dreadful things going on abroad, don't you?'

'Dreadful things happen everywhere. We should know that better than anyone.'

'You're a great comfort, aren't you?'

'Your wife is a big girl now. So is mine. I'm sure

they're more than capable of taking very good care of themselves.'

'I know that,' Jack fretted. 'But suppose Em doesn't want to? Everybody knows what hot sun and a drop of drink can do to the best intentions.'

'If Emma knew what you thought, she'd be deeply insulted,' McKenna said. 'With every justification.'

'I thought you'd've gone home by now, sir,' Dewi said. 'I saw Inspector Tuttle leave a while back.' He sat down beside McKenna's desk. 'Those two in the cells are fed and watered and locked up for the night.'

'Has Beti Gloff been told we're keeping her husband?'

'Yes, sir. Are we going to do anything about her and Mary Ann? Led us a bit of a dance, didn't they?'

'I'm more than tempted to drop a conspiracy charge on them,' McKenna said. 'And tomorrow, I shall tell Beti Gloff, with her lame legs and cross eyes and croaking voice, and Mary Ann, with her cups of tea and packets of biscuits and tales of yesteryear, exactly how lucky they are not to be joining John Beti and the other one in the cells.'

'Bit of luck finding the buckle, I suppose. I could've done with finding it some way else, though.'

'No, Dewi, it was a bit of very good detection. And there are much nastier sights waiting for you behind closed doors than two old people having sex,' McKenna said. 'What's Gwen Stott had to say? Owt or nowt?'

Dewi ran his fingers through his hair, a gesture reminiscent of McKenna's own. 'I dunno if it's a good idea to have her and John Beti in the same building, never mind next door to each other.'

'Why's that?'

'We all heard John Beti tell about her heaving furniture into the van. Like Tarzan, he said, didn't he? It wouldn't surprise me if she doesn't tear the wall apart to get at him.'

'What did you say to her?'

'I just sort of mentioned this and that. I went to ask what she wanted for tea, and she started rabbiting on about how Romy changed all of a sudden, stopped being her friend and so forth,' Dewi said. 'Then she comes out with this spiel about Romy making a web round her of all her deepest and darkest secrets, then attacking her like a spider goes for a fly trapped in the web. And she reckons Romy made her feel even more worthless than her husband does, and that's saying something, apparently.' He frowned. 'She claims she took Romy's name to get shut of the inadequacies other people say she's got.'

'Interesting,' McKenna observed.

'You think so, sir? I think it's what Inspector Tuttle calls "psychological claptrap". Anyway, I happened to mention we'd talked to John Beti, and she starts spitting words at me. John Beti, she says, is a filthy pervert Peeping Tom, snooping around the cottage and sniffing after Romy, who was too busy having it off with Jamie to notice overmuch.'

'So?' McKenna prompted.

Dewi shrugged. 'So I mentioned what John Beti's been telling us, and she goes ape-shit. Sat staring at me with those awful cold dead eyes she's got on her, and said, "Do you know something, constable?" So I said, "What?" And she says, "Jamie Thief kept wanting more and more money to keep his mouth shut, so I sat on his chest and listened until he stopped breathing. And I'll do the same to John Jones." She fair made my skin crawl. She means it, you know.'

'I've no doubt she does,' McKenna said. 'John Jones would be well advised to arrange to be dead of natural causes by the time Gwen Stott gets out.'

'D'you reckon she's mad, sir?'

'No, I don't, but she wants us to thinks she is, and I daresay some psychiatrist will be only too happy to oblige her way of thinking before the trial.'

'D'you think she'll get off with diminished responsibility, then?'

'As Dr Roberts pointed out, mad or bad, she gets locked up,' McKenna said. 'To my mind, she lacks a conscience far more than Jamie Thief ever did. Let's call it a day, now, shall we, Dewi? There'll be a lot of sorting out to do tomorrow.'

'I'm not on duty this weekend, sir.'

'I know that. Anything special planned?'

'Oh, you know . . . the usual . . .'

'You'll no doubt enjoy yourself more than Jack Tuttle, whatever it is,' McKenna grinned. 'He was right about why that woman was killed. Plain greed, whatever fancy notions Gwen Stott would like us to believe.'

'It usually is,' Dewi said. 'Folk always want something they think other folk've got: love, money . . . If it's not one, it's the other. Both, some times.' He made a neat pile of the loose papers on McKenna's desk. 'Folk never learn not to be greedy, do they, sir? Never learn you can't take and get away with it.'

Walking up the hill to his home, McKenna hoped Dewi's bright spirit would never be stifled by a web of greed spun by some golden-haired princess, that the boy's wisdom would not desert him when most needed. A vain hope, he told himself, turning into his own street, for Dewi would fall into the same traps as other men, even the wariest: traps baited by life with the promise of all manner of magic.

The cat kept her vigil behind the front door, wrapping herself around his ankles as soon as he stepped over the threshold, purring and talking. He carried her downstairs, and stood by the open back door while she quartered the little garden, checking her territory, beneath a sky alight with the hues of rare gems. Below the terrace on which the house so precariously balanced, dense thickets of trees and wild shrubs clothed the hillside, dark leaves tipped gold by a setting sun. McKenna looked over the city, at the slope of a roof, the angle of a gable, visible here and there in the secret gardens behind the shops and offices on the High Street, at flowers luminous in the near dark, smoke rising in a thin pencil line from some tall old chimney. A flurry of bats erupted from the trees, fluttering black against the sky, watched by the cat, who raised her head and stood alert, ready to spring. Over the mountain ridge to the east, a new moon hung dazzling in a deep blue sky, like the Grim Reaper's sickle hammered from gold.

Epilogue

Afternoon sunshine blazed outside McKenna's office window, swathes of shadow dappling walls and floors as a breeze stirred the branches of the ash tree. He placed Beti Gloff's statement in a folder with statements from the other residents of Salem village, her evidence, like the rest, barely worth the paper upon which written. She knew nothing, suspected nothing: anyone saying otherwise, her husband included, simply allowing imagination to run riot. Mary Ann, equally ignorant and unsuspecting, was pungent in her condemnation of John Jones's deceptions, his excesses of imagination, his innate stupidity, taking pains to deride his claims of persecution at the hands of a gipsy.

Lighting a cigarette, he turned to Dr Rankilor's report on Gwen Stott, noting from the covering letter that the report was not a definitive statement upon her competence or otherwise to stand trial, but merely a psychiatric assessment of her presenting problems. Before he completed reading the first paragraph, McKenna knew Dr Rankilor tilled the wholly familiar field seeded by Freud, gleaning a bumper crop. Gwen Stott was no heartless killer, no ruthless manipulator of people and money, but joined Romy Cheney and Jamie Thief in the ranks of that ever-growing army of victims, enlisted by unmet needs and the failure of all those to whom she entrusted her naive and trusting self.

Her life one of impoverishment, both materially and emotionally, she escaped the cold fire of her family home into the empty frying pan of marriage to Christopher Stott, a man emotionally immature, inadequate and fearful, unable to provide in any way what his wife could rightfully expect, his uncertain sexual proclivities an insupportable insult and betrayal.

Romy Cheney entered the equation at a critical time, to become catalyst and instigator of the chain of tragic events which followed, its first link forged the day she met Gwen, and found in her a strength, honed by adversity, she herself lacked. Romy, her own impoverishment cloaked with the trappings of material wealth, pursued Gwen with gifts and weekend breaks at the luxurious cottage, tales of riches and excitement, tantalizing and inevitably harrowing glimpses of a world where Gwen could book no reservation and must content herself with crumbs from the rich woman's table. Quoting Freud, the report stated: *unsatisfied wishes are the driving power behind fantasies; every separate fantasy contains the fulfilment of a wish, and improves on unsatisfactory reality*. Allowed to inhabit Romy's fantasy, Gwen's own began to suffer erosion at the teeth of envy, an envy such as the homeless derelict might feel for one who dwelt in a mansion.

McKenna stubbed out the cigarette burned to a broken column of ash, and stared through the window, eyes dazzled by sunlight bouncing off the wall of the telephone exchange. Dr Rankilor had style to his writing, he thought: too much perhaps, for it enticed him away from facts into the realms of speculation, of imagination, and ultimately, of romance.

Friendship with Romy the bright lantern light in the narrow corridor of greyness down which her real life meandered, Gwen saw a turning here, a diversion there, hers for the taking if she heeded Romy's advice, and travelled the remainder of her journey without the encumbrance of a husband. Romy presented the enormity of marital schism as of no consequence, for she had abandoned her own husband, and then her lover. Cajoled and persuaded to believe that people should be used only while useful, then discarded like worn-out garments, Gwen failed to see the warning signals, failed to understand, until too late, that Romy would sooner or later apply that same philosophy to their friendship. Realization dawned when the die was long cast and Gwen Stott thoroughly enmeshed in Romy's silken, sticky web.

On that cold November morning Romy turned on her, for no reason, with no warning, the purring cat unleashing claws and striking out to kill. She said terrible things to Gwen; taunted her, diminished her, sneered at her, tore her fragile dreams to bloody tatters and flung them like soiled rags at her feet, as if suddenly crazed, her mind perhaps turned by drink and drugs. Gwen panicked, driven mad in her own way by the knowledge of hope dead, of choice snatched away, of nothing left but return to the bitter raw bleakness of her marriage. *Mrs Stott was distraught*, Dr Rankilor wrote. *She temporarily lost all control, all understanding of consequence*. Romy struck out at Gwen, pulled her hair and tore at her face with long sharp nails, while Jamie, there because Romy had taken him for her lover, tried to pull her away. She fell, striking her head against a corner of the hearth, and Gwen remembered only the terrible crunching sound of the impact, Romy sprawled stunned at her feet, and Jamie's hysterical screaming.

Jamie decided to kill; Jamie went for the barrow; Jamie picked up the limp form of the woman whose bed and body he so recently enjoyed, and bundled her into the barrow. Jamie pushed the barrow deep into the woods; Jamie bound her hands; Jamie tied the rope around her neck and around the branch, and braced himself against the trunk of the tree while he pulled and hauled the rope and its load off the ground. Jamie stayed up the tree, legs astride the gallows branch, smoking one cigarette after another, long after the body of Romy Cheney stopped jerking and dancing at the end of its rope. Gwen only watched, dazed and stupefied and terrified beyond all comprehension, and Jamie went to his own grave three summers later with a worse name given to him by Gwen Stott's malicious mouth than the bad one he gave himself.

Jamie died by accident. Crazed himself with drink and drugs, greedy for more and more of the booty, he threatened to brand Gwen a killer if she refused his demands. When she found the courage to do so, he attacked her like a rabid dog. Dr Rankilor drew attention to the photographs taken of Gwen's injuries: *more than ample proof of her words*, if proof were needed.

For Gwen, the days and weeks following Romy's death passed in that seamless stuporous fashion coming in the wake of any bereavement, when time is suspended, senses numbed, awareness obscured. Jamie insisted on taking Romy's furniture and effects to the

Stott house, saying the cottage must be empty, nothing left to raise curiosity about the tenant's sudden disappearance. Finding the cheque book and credit cards when she packed away the detritus of Romy's existence, Gwen realized she might still salvage some good from all the bad, not for herself, but for her child. A braggart as well as treacherous, Romy made no secret of her wealth or its origins, and Gwen convinced herself that Romy's money was like all money, owned by whoever possessed it. Taking it into her own possession, salting it away for the rainy days of Jenny's future, she spent only a few pounds on herself in the years since that terrible event, too fearful of discovery, of making holes in the only safety net available to her child. She watched helpless as Jamie's never-ending avarice made the holes for her, until the time came when she could watch no longer.

McKenna stubbed out yet another cigarette burned away, and turned to Dr Rankilor's concluding paragraphs, an ending providing no conclusion, but raising further questions, opening up more ways to travel into the mind of Gwen Stott, pathways twisting and looping and overlapping and ending up where they began. Tortured by her memories of that dreadful day, ambushed at every corner since, she took Romy's name perhaps through some bizarre logic, resurrecting the woman to avoid confronting the fact of her death. Or perhaps she stole the name and all its connotations to make a dustbin into which she tossed those things about herself she so loathed and despised. Romy had to die because Gwen Stott, like anybody else, must be rid of the person who evoked their shame; *for nobody*, Dr Rankilor wrote, *would ever be able to say of Romy*

Cheney that her life was like the snowdrift, leaving only a mark but never a stain. Indeed not, McKenna thought, seeing Jenny and her father and Trefor Prosser stained indelibly with Romy Cheney's dirt. *And thus,* Dr Rankilor continued, *Mrs Stott simply rid the world of some rubbish, some poisonous waste, and what the world regarded as her scavenging of the body and death of Romy Cheney was but a form of atonement, of taking on the sins and badness of the woman, as the sin-eater takes of the feast laid out on the corpse, and atones once more for being an outcast.*

Speculation and imagination exhausted, Dr Rankilor turned to romance, suggesting that Gwen Stott unconsciously wished for Romy's death, and thus failed to save her from Jamie's depredations. For Romy exposed the canker within Gwen's own family, the terrifying bogey of incest, all the more terrifying once Gwen understood that her daughter played the dual role of victim and seductress, slipping eel-like from one to the other. *A classic scenario,* the psychiatrist wrote, *where only the mother could effect rescue.* That such rescue was merely another fantasy, Gwen could not know until the tragic repercussions began reverberating about her head.

Lighting his third cigarette, McKenna let words and pictures run through his mind, underscored by Gwen Stott's words telling him that Romy picked her up, took her for a ride, then abandoned her on the road. Which road, he wondered? And what excoriating injury did Romy inflict upon her friend when she pushed her from the speeding car, left her bouncing and tumbling on the hard surface of that unknown road? He put Dr Rankilor's report away before its tentative siren call evoked compassion, and scrawled notes on a large sheet of paper to remind himself that nowhere did Dr Rankilor make any mention of John Jones, because John Jones was the fly in the psychiatrist's soothing balm, the nasty little Nigger poking up his head from the great woodpile of rationalizations and justifications and defences for the indefensible.

The cigarette burned away between his fingers while he thought of the notions fashioned by Dr Rankilor, who seemed, like himself, unable to bring Gwen Stott into focus. Like a person seen in the mirror, she was a visual fallacy, and each person who looked saw only another reflection of the original untruth, as if the image and its untruthfulness were reflected infinitely in two parallel mirrors. Only Gwen Stott could find the reality, because she knew where it festered behind the image, and McKenna knew she never would, because there was nothing she needed or wanted to see.

Pulling down shirtsleeves and fastening cuff buttons, he stacked the huge pile of papers on his desk, took his jacket from its hanger, and left the office for a city quiet with the emptiness of a Sunday afternoon, only a few bored youths and their gaudy girls lounging on the pavement outside Woolworth's. Saturday's litter skipped down the street, harried by a rising westerly wind, sunlight glittered on rooftops, highlighting dirt on the pavements, weather-worn paintwork on old window frames. The sharp tang of gorse blew from the mountain, lemony and fresh, as McKenna, jacket unbuttoned, strolled to the end of High Street, on to Beach Road, and down to the pier; one third of a mile of ornate ironwork and timber striking out into the

Menai Straits. Standing at the pier-end, the sea running fast beneath his feet, he took off his glasses, afraid of losing them to the snatching wind. Across the water, the shores of Anglesey looked near enough to touch, the mountains behind him sharp and clear against a pale-blue sky. Westwards, Menai Bridge spanned the Straits, graceful and precise, a mathematical formula proved in stone and iron.

On the terrace of the pier restaurant, he ate chicken sandwiches and strawberry gâteau, drank two cups of coffee and took Denise's letter from his inside pocket. He put his glasses on to read, pausing here and there at some word or phrase among the many scrawled in her rather untidy hand on crinkly blue airmail paper. Cigarette burnt down in the ashtray, he stubbed it out and lit another, gazing out to sea at dark swathes of shoals under the running tide, gulls wheeling and diving, early tourists taking their turn on the pier. Off Beaumaris, a small flotilla of yachts tacked into the wind, sails full, like ice-cream cones bobbing on the sea, and in the far distance, the grey whaleback shape of Great Orme lay in the water against a cold eastern sky. He stared, some wisp of a recollection flickering along the edge of memory like a sputtering flame. Trying to catch the tail, hold it still long enough to look, he was left thinking only of a dreamscape on the edge of the world, glimpsed and gone.

Bill paid, letter folded safely in his pocket, he walked back up Beach Road and onwards to the council cemetery, through its high wrought-iron gates, crunching along gravel pathways to wander among the graves. Beyond rows of headstones, trees tossed on the wind, leaves full out and bright as new paint, their scent on the air. Seated on the hard slats of a bench, he looked at another aspect of the mountains seen from the pier, this view a backdrop for the smoke-stained chimney of the crematorium. Wispy smoke and a mirage of white-hot heat from Romy Cheney's remains singed the air above the chimney three days before, her funeral graced by the village rector, himself and Dewi, and Eifion Roberts, gossipy with a man from the council. Robert Allsopp offered to pay for the funeral, receiving in return the little carton of ground wood and bone ash to scatter on a patch of Derbyshire moorland, there for it to swirl on the winds, be trodden under the hooves of a thousand sheep, washed into gullies by torrents of rain, and buried deep under the snows of winter. Romy Cheney needed no memorial, McKenna thought, for she lived too vividly in the memory of Jenny Stott ever to be decently forgotten, as the dead should be with time. He thought of her hanging among the trees of Castle Woods, feeding nature as carrion nourishes, her worldly wealth scavenged by human vultures, and felt not the smallest twist of grief.

Allsopp identified the buckle without hesitation, anonymous technicians and scientists identified the scrapings from under Jamie's nails as the flesh of Gwen Stott, the six fingerprints from Jamie's squalid caravan as her own, and matched the many signings of Romy Cheney's name with Gwen Stott's script, wrapping around the woman a neat and tidy parcel of guilt. John Jones remained incarcerated, insistent on the protection of thick walls and locked doors, enjoying notoriety, expecting only a slap on his scrawny wrist for the little theft.

McKenna ground out his cigarette end, scuffing it

over with gravel, and walked towards a grove of trees beside the river, hearing the rush of water below the fall of land. He might meet Beti Gloff, he thought, out on her interminable perambulations, or Mary Ann escorted by her son to view her husband's grave. Running them to earth the day Denise flew to Rhodes, he confronted the two women in Mary Ann's sour kitchen, where they cackled amid the teacups like the witches John Jones said they were. Neither cared very much about what he had to say: Beti Gloff shrugging her humped back in silence, Mary Ann favouring him with the observation that God's Will was God's Will, and who was he or she to argue with that?'

Legs aching a little, he found another seat on a low marble bench in the shadow of the trees, the river behind him fast and full with rain from the mountains, unmown grass damp underfoot, sprinkled with daisy heads open to the sun. He thought of Christopher Stott, Jenny and Trefor Prosser, sure there was yet more bad to come, despite Prosser's newfound optimism, Stott's belief that rust ate into his own chains at last. Jenny remained the hostage, her future bleak, the mother who should embrace and protect her locked away with fantasies for comfort.

He pulled Denise's letter from his pocket, wind crackling through the pages, one small gust threatening to carry them whirling high into the trees and out of his grasp for ever. No salutation, no 'Dearest', as she would have once written, not even his name, but merely a date scrawled under 'Athens', and over a long, gossipy woman's letter, interrogations between the lines, cattiness sharpening words as vacant of sensibility as her heart was devoid of that yearning which filled the gulf between reality and the ideal. He refolded the pages, realized she would return in two days' time, knowing she had become a figment of her own imagination, and the wife he desired a figment of his own. He thought of all the women in his world, these soldiers of Trefor Prosser's 'monstrous regiment', and thought there were no words more true than those of the Russian woman who said: 'What is women's life about if not legends, gossip and rumours?'

Gravel turned underfoot as he walked slowly towards the cemetery gate, cramp dragging at his legs, evening chill pinching his neck and finger ends. He wondered where Rebekah's murdered baby might rest, little bones crumbled to nothing, and saw the raw black earth of a new grave still making a mound over its coffin, flowers withering yellowy-brown and sour-smelling around its edges, and felt a jolt in his belly, for Jamie lay below the black earth, his place marked by a lopsided wooden cross painted untidily with a number. Standing at the foot of the grave, McKenna recalled the dismal hurried service in the cemetery chapel, a hasty interment while he and Dewi waited apart from the tiny group of mourners, watching Jamie's mother, thin in dusty black, her face faded by misery, clutch the arm of the man people said begat her son, but who married her sister. Losing Jamie was almost like losing a friend, he thought, for if nothing else, Jamie was the known devil, and no one could know who might come to take his place in the scheme of things, fill the hole left by his passing. Would the family give him a headstone as soon as the earth stifling him hardened and flattened itself? And what might be inscribed upon it? He turned to follow the progress of a grey squirrel suddenly bounding from behind a marble cherub, watched it scuttle towards the trees, hoping no twisted sense of humour had 'Jamie Thief' engraved on marble or black granite or purple slate. The squirrel disappeared from view in the long grasses, and turning back, McKenna looked straight into the eyes of the man who stood at the head of Jamie's grave, sunlight striking brilliant lights in long black hair hung about an ashen face, wind lifting ruffles about the throat. Breath frozen in his lungs, McKenna tore his eyes away from those steeped in the darkness and despair of centuries, and stumbled blindly up the path, straining to hear the footsteps behind him, knowing there would be not the slightest whisper of sound as the man came close enough to lay his dead cold hands around McKenna's neck and breathe the grave-smell in his face.

READ MORE IN PENGUIN

READ MORE IN PENGUIN

A SELECTION OF CRIME AND MYSTERY

Devices and Desires P. D. James

When Commander Adam Dalgliesh becomes involved in the hunt for the killer in a remote area of the Norfolk coast, he finds himself caught up in the dangerous secrets of the headland community. And then one moonlit night it becomes chillingly apparent that there is more than one killer at work in Larsoken . . .

Gallowglass Barbara Vine

When Sandor saves little Joe from the path of a London tube train he claims his life for himself. In adoration and gratitude, Joe willingly offers himself to him, becoming Sandor's *gallowglass*, servant to the chief. 'Of all living writers, she can enter most convincingly into the criminal, or even pathological, mind' – *Sunday Times*

Death among the Dons Janet Neel

'*Death among the Dons* is probably the best crime novel set in a women's college since Dorothy Sayers's *Gaudy Night*' – T. J. Binyon. 'Janet Neel sets her nerve-tingling plot in a wonderfully alive and intelligent collegiate milieu' – *Sunday Times*

Pleading Guilty Scott Turow

Gage and Griswell is a large law firm with an even larger problem: $5.6 million has suddenly vanished from the coffers of its largest client. 'Extravagant with danger, sex and especially money – and full of surprises to the end' – *Independent on Sunday*

The Big Sleep Raymond Chandler

Millionaire General Sternwood, a paralysed old man, is already two-thirds dead. He has two beautiful daughters – one a gambler, the other a degenerate – and an elusive adventurer as a son-in-law. The General is being blackmailed, and Marlowe's assignment is to get the blackmailer off his back. As it turns out, there's a lot more at stake . . .

READ MORE IN PENGUIN

A SELECTION OF CRIME AND MYSTERY

Paper Doll Robert B. Parker

Olivia Nelson had almost been a candidate for sainthood – perfect wife, perfect mother with a perfect home in the best part of Boston. Too perfect, perhaps. Because someone murdered her. But when Spenser sets out to solve the case, nothing – least of all the life and death of the victim – is what it seems . . .

This Way Out Sheila Radley

The thought of doing away with his mother-in-law would never have entered Derek Cartwright's head, if he had not begun to suffer from bad dreams – and if he had not met Hugh Packer. Sheila Radley's spine-chilling story traces the descent of an upright husband and citizen into blunder, nightmare and murder. 'Here is an author who can be bracketed with the best' – *Observer*

Fatlands Sarah Dunant

'Make way for Hannah Wolfe, one of the best private eyes, either sex, either side of the Atlantic' – *Daily Telegraph*. Hannah's latest brief is to mind teenage rebel Mattie Shepherd. But what began as a Knightsbridge shopping trip ends in an act of explosive violence.

Guardian Angel Sara Paretsky

When a friend of Mr Contreras, Vic Warshawski's loyal neighbour, claims that he has some information that will make him a rich man – and then turns up dead in the canal, Vic knows it's no coincidence. 'The richest and most engaging yet of Ms Paretsky's thrillers' – *The New York Times*

Berlin Noir Philip Kerr

Ex-policeman Bernie Gunther thought he'd seen everything on the streets of 1930s Berlin. But then he went freelance and with each case he tackled he became sucked further into the grisly excesses of Nazi sub-culture. And even after the war, amidst the decayed, imperial splendour of Vienna, Bernie uncovered a legacy that made the wartime atrocities look lily-white by comparison . . .

READ MORE IN PENGUIN

A SELECTION OF CRIME AND MYSTERY

Ripley Under Water Patricia Highsmith

Tom Ripley's past would not bear too much close scrutiny. But he has carefully covered his tracks as far as murder and forgery are concerned. Or so he thinks. 'Ripley is back, as polite and lethal as ever . . . he does what he wants and gets away with it. That's why we like him' – *Time Out*

Death of a Partner Janet Neel

His relationship with wilful girlfriend Francesca on the rocks, a harassed Detective Chief Inspector John McLeish is assigned to the case of missing Angela Morgan. An attractive, wealthy lobbyist, and fiancée to a high-ranking government minister, Angela courted success – and the envy of her detractors. When her badly decomposed body is found a week later, the shock waves ripple through Whitehall, and only the murderer knows why.

The Patience of Maigret Georges Simenon

They called it Maigret's longest investigation. For twenty years there have been a series of daring raids on Paris jewellers. The Superintendent has his suspicions about the organizer – but no proof. Then there is a murder that begins to provide the missing threads.

The Complete Richard Hannay John Buchan

From Scotland to Constantinople, rural England and the bloody battlefields of France, Richard Hannay's adventures in the pursuit of justice are classic, compelling reading. Collected here are: *The Thirty-Nine Steps*, *Greenmantle*, *Mr Standfast*, *The Three Hostages* and *The Island of Sheep*.

Pronto Elmore Leonard

'The American crime master moves to Italy and stays on top of his form in a cracking tale of small-time criminals' – *Independent*. 'Book by book . . . Elmore Leonard is painting an intimate, precise, funny, frightening and irresistible mural of the American underworld' – *New Yorker*